Contents

*To the memory of
Roberto Bolaño,
Vladimir Nadal,
Isabel Quiroga,
and Jorge Mosconi,
fictivos o reales,
los aguardo en el misterio.
—A.B.*

El Misterio Nadal

A Lost and Rescued Book
Purportedly Compiled and
with Introduction in 2001
by Roberto Bolaño

Edited by Isabel Quiroga and Jorge Mosconi

Translated by A.B.

SPUYTEN DUYVIL
New York City

Cover Photo taken on the Alameda Central of Mexico D.F., ca. 1977, shortly before Bolaño's permanent departure from Mexico. From left to right: Roberto Bolaño, Victoria Soto, unidentified male, María Salomé (Roberto's sister), and (possibly) Vladimir Nadal. (Photographer Unknown.)

Library of Congress Cataloging-in-Publication Data

Names: Bolano, Roberto, 1953-2003, compiler, writer of introduction. | Nadal, Vladimir, author. | Quiroga, Isabel, editor. | Mosconi, Jorge, editor.
Title: El misterio Nadal : a book lost and rescued out of Uruguay / purportedly compiled and with introduction in 2001 by Roberto Bolano ; edited by Isabel Quiroga and Jorge Mosconi ; translated by A.B.
Description: New York City : Spuyten Duyvil, [2018] | Includes bibliographical references. | Translated from alleged Spanish translation of French and Portuguese original texts.
Identifiers: LCCN 2017055052 | ISBN 9781947980204
Subjects: LCSH: Bolaäno, Roberto, 1953-2003--Correspondence. | Pâeret, Benjamin, 1899-1959--Criticism and interpretation.
Classification: LCC PQ8098.12.O38 Z48 2018 | DDC 863/.64--dc23
LC record available at https://lccn.loc.gov/2017055052

Translator's Presentation of the Edition, by A.B.

I never met Roberto Bolaño, or Isabel Quiroga, or Vladimir Nadal. The entire manuscript that follows, which I have largely translated from the Spanish (a good portion of which had, supposedly, been originally rendered from the French and Portuguese), has come to me by way of a torturous route. As I write this, even now, I still harbor a sense of the marvelous about it all.

The mystery of this book's provenance is as yet unsolved. While I have been able, through interviews in Mexico, to discount two of the six or seven possible authorial involvements this eccentric novel dangles, mobile-like, before us, the other possibilities most definitely remain. Not least the possible central involvement of Roberto Bolaño—either as the original compiler and editor of the papers linked to Vladimir Nadal, or else as their concealed forger, whether in part or in whole.

As the translator of this work, I feel a measure of my responsibility has been to transmit the full spectrum of authorial indeterminacy that seems originally intended by whoever the author(s) might be, so I will not reveal the particular two authorships that certain facts allow me to now discount. This is a work where the reader appears meant to play detective, as it were. Some of you may well be able to discount other suspects, or to even discover the actual source of this book. May you have better luck than I.

Let me now proceed with an overview of the strange background facts to what you hold in your hands, so as to provide some bigger context for what the faithful reader will encounter and soon puzzle over—for there are more than a few peculiar riddles to be found herein.

❄

In the fall of 2010, at a small conference on translation in Bilbao, Spain, I had met Jorge Mosconi, a Uruguayan scholar of Lusophone literature, who was, at the time, teaching as a visiting instructor at a small college in California. A group of about a dozen attendees had gathered in the evening at the hotel bar, and he and I were the last ones to leave, staying until 2 or 3 AM, in intense but pleasant talk, topics ranging from the Tupamaros during the 1970s, to Fernando Pessoa, to problems and theories of translation, to the books of Spanish novelists Enrique Vila-Matas and Javier Marías, to the great Brazilian poet and critic Mario de Andrade, and to other odds and ends.[1]

It was that night, the connection lit by the topic of Vila-Matas, that I learned of "Isabel Quiroga," the pseudonym (according to Mosconi) of a Chilean translator of Russian poetry and friend of Mosconi's, whom Mosconi had met when both were exiled in Paris, in the late 70s. Later, they'd encountered each other a couple of times, in the early 2000s, at conferences in Latin America, and they'd stayed in touch, sporadically, over email. Mosconi shared with me an unusual detail about Quiroga, which the latter reveals in her Preface to these materials. The moving revelation might show us something, as well, about Roberto Bolaño's spirit.

It was in early 2009 that Quiroga, out of the blue, and about two months before her death from pancreatic cancer, had mailed Mosconi a large package containing the materials that follow, including the Preface by herself and the Introduction by Bolaño. The accompanying letter from her requested that Mosconi finalize the editing of materials and find a way of arranging for the manuscript's publication. Mosconi described the archive to me that night at the bar, and I was, to say the least, transfixed by the strangeness of it all, not least, of course, because of the close relation of the manuscript's mystery to Roberto Bolaño, one of my literary heroes. Mosconi promised to share the "lost" work with me.

In our emails over the next year, I expressed to Mosconi my eagerness to see portions of the document, a bit impatient and annoyed that he was taking so long; he promised, in reply to repeated queries, to send it to me, as soon as he had it properly collated and Xeroxed. I, in turn, promised to consider it for possible translation into English as soon as I received it. Mosconi indicated that this meant I would be charged with the final editing of it all, as he was simply too bewildered by its labyrinthine nature to tackle a full editorial task. "It seems to me maybe a bit too baroque, too unlikely in all its layers, fascinating though it is on a number of levels," he wrote. "I'm not sure I want to dive in, when there are no evident ways out. And I've got pressing stuff with my own work and family to think about right now. Not that you don't, too. I'm just passing it on to you, a bit shamefully, though confident you can make the best of it. But if you don't wish to deal with it and prepare it for some kind of publication, just let me know."

Mosconi was killed in an automobile accident outside Piriapolis, Uruguay, in December of 2011. Around a month after learning of his death, I was able to make contact, by phone, with his widow, in Montevideo, in April, 2012. I told her of my friendship with Mosconi, of my discussions with him, about the purported Bolaño documents, and of Mosconi's wish that I translate them into English. She was aware of the material—yes, her husband had often spoken of it—and agreed to track it down in his, as she put it, "still intact disaster of an office." I sensed a distance or coolness in her references to him, but phones, of course, can mislead. I promised to forward some of the email correspondence between Mosconi and me for verification of our prior discussions. I meticulously listed for her the materials that Mosconi claimed were present:

1) Bolaño's introduction and solicited email reminiscences from acquaintances of a "Vladimir Nadal," 2) a xeroxed biographical sketch of the great Surrealist poet Benjamin Péret by

the American anarchist and poet-scholar Franklin Rosemont, appended to a briefer commentary by Bolaño, 3) two typescripts partially recording police transcripts from the interrogation of Péret during his detention in Rio de Janeiro, Brazil, in late 1931, 4) a satirical "Soviet Infrarrealista" text by Nadal, 5) "translations" by Nadal from Péret's poetry collection *Le Gran Jeu*, 6) an essay by Péret in Xeroxed form (in published English translation), 7) A handwritten letter, dated January 4th, 1954, by Sylvia Beach, proprietor of Shakespeare and Co. in Paris, and the first publisher of James Joyce's *Ulysses*, 8) a sketch of Vladimir Nadal, date and artist unknown, though likely done after his return to Chile near the end of his life, 9) an original snapshot print of Bolaño and four other young people, in Mexico City, ca. 1976, in which Nadal may be present, and 10) Quiroga's Editorial Preface.

I followed up with an email, detailing the list, and around six weeks later I received a box containing a Xerox copy of the manuscript. All the components discussed by Mosconi were there, save the poetry selections from *Le Grand Jeu*, which Ms. Mosconi, as she indicated in accompanying note, had not yet located. But two weeks later I did receive these— a Xerox, again, from old selectric text, and same font as most of the manuscript.

Shortly thereafter, Mosconi's widow informed me over email that she had come upon a "five-page prose typescript, including notes," titled, in handwriting, as "Péret—O Almirante negro," and which I recognized as a document referred to by Quiroga in her Preface. I wrote to request that this be sent along, though at the time I had no clear idea to what it pertained. Research would reveal that these pages were no doubt a translation into Spanish from a holograph manuscript, in Portuguese and French, of the only four extant pages (the originals are apparently held in the Mario Pedrosa archives in Rio de Janeiro; it is unclear how Nadal would have accessed the surviving text) of Péret's extensive study—otherwise destroyed by the Brazilian police in December, 1931—of La revolta da Chivata (the Revolt of the Lash), a heroic and spectacular Potemkin-like 1910 uprising within the Brazilian Navy, led by João Cândido Felisberto, an Afro-Brazilian sailor. Tragically, this excerpt was either never sent, or else lost in the mail. I re-inquired with Ms. Mosconi two or three times, but received no response. I learned some months later from her daughter that she had taken her life not long after my last communication with her.

I do not know if the "O Almirante negro" typescript had been originally part of the Nadal manuscript, or if the lost translation was done by Bolaño as a "side project," where he somehow came into possession of the original Péret document (Bolaño in his introduction does not mention the text as present in the Nadal papers, though he does show knowledge of it in a footnote to the Péret interrogation document). It seems possible, as well, that Mosconi was prompted by this mention to track it down and translate it himself. Already, the reader may sense why Mosconi refers to this case as "labyrinthine," while Quiroga, in her Preface, calls it "a maze, with a trap set at the end."

In any event, to partially compensate for the major loss, I have added a later essay by Péret, translated into English by none other than Samuel Beckett, and originally published in 1934 in Nancy Cunard's legendary *Negro: An Anthology*. Péret (writing years after his original manuscript had been destroyed) briefly summarizes the Revolta event in this essay, which also deals more generally with topics pertaining to his serious ethnographic studies in Brazil. In addition, the two other previously published essays included in the package I received are reprinted verbatim here. These appeared in the furtive and now defunct journal *Radical America*, in 1970. One is the previously mentioned introduction to the life and person of Péret, written by the great American anarchist and labor scholar Franklin Rosemont, with whom Bolaño reveals he had been in contact; the other is a translation of Péret's polemical and (at least in France) infamous 1945 essay "The Dishonor of the Poets," which he wrote in Mexico, and wherein he suggests that Stalinist-championed "Resistance" poetry in France bears affective affinities to ads for pharmaceutical companies.

Because the *Radical America* pieces are, to my knowledge, unavailable elsewhere in English, and because the journal issue in which they appear is extremely obscure [*Radical America*, ed. Paul Buhle, Vol. IV, No. 6, August, 1970], I have decided to include them. Someone, either Bolaño, Quiroga, or Mosconi, felt these pieces had some suggestive correspondence to this manuscript and chose to interleave them; and I agree, for the themes of cultural critique, poetic resistance, and anarcho-communist militancy that inform them certainly echo long-abiding concerns in the life and work of the French poet. And of Bolaño, too, for that matter, who loved not only the Surrealists, but was, like many of them, a close sympathizer of Trotskyist and anarchist tendencies. These three reproduced pieces, then, are the only documents in this book whose absolute authenticity is verified. Everything else remains under question.

❋❋❋

Isabel Quiroga speculates in her "Editor's Preface" on the authorial uncertainties that suffuse this text. She asks: Is Vladimir Nadal an actual figure, an old Infrarrealista acquaintance of Bolaño's? Or is he, rather, a fictional character out of Bolaño's imagination, in an unfinished work intriguingly tethered—in its topics and multi-voiced form—to the first two sections of his great novel the *Savage Detectives,* published less than three years before Bolaño purportedly found most of what follows? More specifically, she asks if Nadal's possibly fictional persona may be linked in quasi-sequel fashion to the Chilean—and also classical-prosody-obsessed—"Juan García Madero" of the *Savage Detectives.*

We must add three other questions, it seems to me—ones that are just as reasonable to ask as the prior ones, given the apocryphal mists enveloping this book: 1) Might the pseudonymous Isabel Quiroga herself have actually invented Bolaño's presence in all of this, so as to tether, in the spirit of homage, an enigmatic, apocryphal work to the metafictional-loving author's massive (and still not exhausted) archive? The second question naturally follows, even if such a maze-like fictional architecture would be nothing but "baroque," to use Mosconi's own term, and almost insane if true: 2) Might all of this (with exception of the previously published Péret essays, which we know to be authentic) be the work of *Mosconi*, who—erasing any claim of his own authority—has invented not only Bolaño and Nadal, but the figure of Quiroga, as well? Or 3) Could there be yet another author, perhaps one hiding in plain sight within this book—one to whom Mosconi, indeed, was providing cover?

It is all quite beyond me, as Mosconi claimed it to be beyond him. And humbled by the singularity of it all, I know I really have no choice but to hide my own name, in deference to the mystery of these pages and to their power—and in deference to he, she, or they who brought them into being with no apparent wish for recompense save the noble pleasure of adding a measure of enchantment to the world. There is a very loud traveling carnival from Tarragona right outside my window. And the pseudonym I take as the translator of this apocryphal book is (could there be, truly, any other?) Arturo Belano.

Dear reader: I urge you to continue.

A.B.

March, 2018

1. *All names and groups mentioned above are identified and discussed in Notes sections elsewhere in this book.*

A Note Regarding The Annotations Of This Text And The Troubled History Of Certain Materials

The annotations to this text (with the exception of the notes to the republished materials relating to the great Surrealist poet Benjamin Péret) have been made by "Roberto Bolaño," "Isabel Quiroga," and me. One set of notes (to the Octanovich Pazinsky speech, at end of this book) is possibly made by Jorge Mosconi. I place the names of Bolaño and Quiroga in quotes in this first instance, for the nature and extent of their involvement with this manuscript, handed down to me by Mosconi, is still open to question (see my Translator's Presentation, preceding).

The annotations to the police interrogations of Péret in Rio de Janeiro were present when I received the manuscript and are supposedly made by Bolaño, following his purported discovery of the documents as transcribed by Nadal. The somewhat eccentric annotations to the Preface signed by Quiroga were also present and are apparently by herself. I have lightly edited both these sets of notes for spelling, punctuation, and clarity when needed. The annotations to the Introduction attributed to Bolaño, along with those to the "In Search of Nadal" section of epistles, are by me. I have at times entered bracketed expansions or clarifications into Bolaño's and Quiroga's notes. A small number of bracketed additions are entered into other parts of the text by both Bolaño and myself. The annotations in the reprinted Franklin Rosemont essay are by Rosemont proper. I am unsure who composed the notes to the Soviet Infrarrealista speech: Nadal himself, Bolaño, Quiroga, or—as indicated above—Mosconi. They were printed out in ink-jet, on separate sheets from the speech proper. I have also lightly edited these for style and typographical matters.

The manuscript in its earliest stage, after I received it from Mosconi, was shared by me, much to my present regret, with someone whom at the time I trusted as a friend: An American poet and translator, who shamelessly appropriated and then published under his name (having reframed and partially re-written them) the Cáceres and de Amat sections, and later Na-dal's Soviet Infrarrealista speech, in an actual book of his "own" poetry. I will not stoop to name him. He will be unmasked by the future. And his reputation, or what is left of it, will be forev-er darkened by his actions.

But this is secondary, ultimately, to the abiding mystery at hand. The book begins.

—A.B.

EDITOR'S PREFACE
ISABEL QUIROGA

I'll be brief. The readers of this book will make up their own minds. Maybe among them will be one or a few who can unravel it all, find clues that have escaped me, and follow them to some closer determination than I have been able to achieve. To become, that is, "the Sherlock Holmes's of the future" that Volodia Teitleboim[1] hopes for, in a letter contained within another letter in this text, concerning a different, though also Chilean, poetic mystery…

I want to believe that what you have in your hands is a lost work of Roberto Bolaño— one that, if not written wholesale by the great author, is at least authentically introduced and partly annotated by him. Readers familiar with *The Savage Detectives*[2] will not be able to miss that key structural devices—most notably the extended epistolary section that follows his introduction—are reminiscent of that book, published three years before Bolaño claims to have "found" the manuscript "by" a furtive figure called "Nadal."

To be sure, a compound question remains open: Are these *actual* letters about an *actual* Nadal sent by correspondents Bolaño queried, with the names of their writers changed by the latter,[3] or are the letters really written by Bolaño *himself*, in his making of a *Savage Detectives*-like fiction (or is *Nazi Literature in the Americas* a better analogy?)[4], albeit one where a final Authorial disappearing act is tacked on for ironic end-of-life measure? Not to mention most of the other "documents" found herein.

Which is to say: Writing this, I'm already losing my sense. Though I have my hunches, I cannot speak with final authority about the status of this text, and I have now, quite sick, run out of living time to find the answers. It's too late for me to travel to Mexico and attempt to hunt down those who remain from Bolaño's—and Vladimir Nadal's—time there. Assuming they would wish to speak with me, that is. I have tried to inquire with the only living contributors to the manuscript whose names are (for whatever reason) *not* altered in the manuscript. But neither the Spanish novelist Enrique Vila-Matas, nor Rubén Medina[5], a founding Infrarrealista activist and close friend of Bolaño's, responded to my various queries. Nor the literary agents of either. I do not know why. It seems strange they wouldn't, given what I believe are the obvious stakes in this case. Or are they, perhaps, trying to hide something here? Future investigators may wish to query the archives of these two writers in years to come.

Let me now try to set some further context.

I first met Bolaño in Barcelona, in 1989, some years after he'd settled in nearby Blanes. He was periodically coming to Barcelona in those days, usually on the weekends, to hang out. I'd been living in the city for over a year, in the Raval,[6] between a seller of antiquarian maps and the oldest whorehouse in the city, to be exact. It was a party at the home of A.G. Porta, in Sant Pere, by the Palau de la Musica Catalana. I remember Bruno Montané and Raul Escarí[7]were also there. Back then, Bolaño still had a drink from rare time to time, and he was somewhat tipsy, it seemed to me, though to be fair, everyone else, including me, was in a much more inebriated state.

So I don't remember much about that night with any real clarity or dignity, though I recall Bolaño and I ended up talking, on a couple bean bag chairs in the reddish glow of a lava lamp, about Borges, Parra, Cortázar, and Pizarnik,[8] I think. I talked about the venerable ruin of my town Cartagena, which is also the town of Vicente Huidobro,[9] and he talked about Valparaíso and (Chilean) Los Ángeles, where he spent his childhood. So our pasts shared the Chilean sea. I'd told him about the small press collections I'd translated of the semi-samizdat Russian poets Vsevolod Nekrasov and Gennady Aigi,[10] and he seemed impressed by this. And I listened to this guy in his mid-thirties (I was, too) with dirty long hair and bad teeth go on and on, about so many obscure writers and works I'd never heard about—including, for example, medieval authors from four or five languages, who and which, he insisted with great emotion, deserved more recognition—that I started to feel self-conscious about my ignorance (who the hell *was* this learned, home-less-looking dude), and so I moved away, as soon as he turned his focus on a couple young women who had come over with a joint the size of a small cigar. I remember looking back from where I'd set my drink, jealous, feeling attraction to him, even with his ridiculously big glasses, noticing that he only took a couple drags, apparently not inhaling, blowing perfect, thick smoke rings.

We saw each other a few times over the years, maybe half a dozen, actually. I'd like to say we were close, and be able to offer lots of memorable anecdotes, poignant vignettes, but there's really nothing much like that. Nearly all our encounters after that party were brief, conventionally courteous, pleas-ant, somewhat awkward, in the way of sober encounters after the drunken one (we'd both foresworn drinking), all of them in Barcelona when he was visiting, and when other people were present, in cafés or at parties, one at Jorge Herralde's,[11] it comes back (in a neighborhood where there are no obvious whorehouses), where everyone seemed to be sucking up to the great editor, including, I have to say, Roberto—Herralde having no idea at the time that the unkempt guy discoursing seduc-tively about the street bum Villon[12] would make him millions). But these meetings never quite approached the quasi-intimacy of our buzzed moment back in '89.

Well, with two partial exceptions, I suppose: Once, in late 1997, when I came across him by "chance" at the Bar Marsella,[13] where it was known he liked to write when he was in town on weekends, so I suppose I might have wandered over there, purposely hoping to run into him. Actually, I'm quite sure that's what I did: I'd read his recent books and I was starstruck. It was mid-afternoon, so the place wasn't crowded. I found him writing at the back Merzbau-like corner,[14] a stack of papers and books on his table, though a combination of shyness and reluctance to interrupt him caused me to dissimulate obliviousness, I'm not sure how to better put it, and I went over to a table on the other side of the room, by the front window. But soon Bolaño looked my way. I looked away and then looked back and awkwardly waved, and so he came over to get a better look, because he couldn't see from that distance,[15] even in good light. And he came close, serious, and stared at me for a few seconds and said, I know you, I think. Where have we met? And I said, I doubt you'll recall it, but we first met at a party in 1989, at Antonio Porta's. We sat by a lava lamp on some bean bag chairs, and you talked about a bunch of writers and I talked to you about the Samizdat avant-gardists I was translating. Back then, my name was Clemente. Now it's Isabel. I've gone through lots of changes since we last met almost three years ago, as you can see.

I wasn't sure what to expect, of course. But then, a big, warm smile came over his face (I noticed he now had perfect teeth, so I wasn't the only one who'd had work done), and he said, Wow, yes, of course I remember, and he leaned in and gave me a real kiss on the cheek, as if I'd always been a close friend named Isabel. That moment, to me, pretty special in those days, when being trans was still a perfectly dangerous thing, said a lot about him, I think. Sometimes, you can tell when a person is a good person, through little gestures of their kindness, and even if the goodness has had a struggle with the bad. I mean we all have that struggle, obviously, it never ends. I don't mean to romanticize him, because of course he had all sorts of crap in his closet, like me and you. But he was, at the core, a decent man, in the simple and true ethics of things.

He went back to grab his papers and books and tea and brought them over to my table, and we sat and chatted about this or that, me praising him for his recent successes, the prizes and reviews that were starting to gather, and the appearance of *Distant Star*,[16] which had come out a few months back. It was a pleasant ten minutes or so: small talk, really, which included some chuckles about that first party eight years earlier, and how things had changed so much. He made a couple of casual, gentle jokes about the understatement of our topic—Change—jokes that were perfectly natural, and the easy way he did it made me feel good. But soon I said I had to leave, because I knew he wanted to get back to his work, and it would have been awkward, to say the least, for me to keep sitting there, with him back at his original table. Plus, I wanted to end the encounter on the upswing, as it were.

You look great, Isabel, he said, as I got up to leave. He kissed me on both cheeks. I remember I felt happy the whole way home. And truly comfortable in my own skin, for maybe the second time in my life. Men smiled at me and I smiled back. Those were the days when I was in my prime. It was a lovely early evening. Only now do I realize this was a few weeks after Nadal had been with him, and right there, in fact, in the same bar.

The second episode that involved some quality personal time was July 27, 2002. I don't know why I remember the date, about one year before his death, when he crashed at my flat after a reading at Libreria 22[17] by his good friend Enrique Vila-Matas, on the occasion of the latter winning the Fernando Aguirre-Libralire prize,[18] I think it was. Roberto was too beat to go out afterwards or to take the train back to Blanes, which is always a pain for anyone, regardless, because it's an hour and a half slog. When we got back to my place, I made some manzanilla tea (his favorite) and spaghetti, and we chatted in the kitchen, just the two of us, for close to two hours. I knew of his illness,[19] and I'd told him not to feel bad if he just wanted to go sleep, but he insisted on talking for a while. Even in the low light, I could see his jaundice. He asked me if I had ever married, had children, or if I'd always known I desired to be a woman, and there wasn't the slightest hint of strain on his part in asking, even if the formulation was a bit clumsy and stilted. But you don't have to tell me, he said, That's probably too presumptuous of me to ask. I said that No, I'd felt I was female inside for a very long time, since I'd been fourteen or fifteen, maybe. He asked what writing I had done of my own besides my translation, some of which he had read, the small collection of Nekrasov and Aygi, especially, and his references to particular poems in that book—his memory was astonishing—proved it.

I told him I was incapable of writing my own poetry or fiction, that I'd stopped trying some time ago, when I'd stopped even translating, that translating poetry deepened my frustration about my failure as a poet. I told him this was a double shame, that it made me feel my translation might be, at bottom, not prompted by generosity, but by a drive to compensate a sublimated, mean ambition. He said he hated the word "sublimated." He said, Sorry to be blunt, but it sounds so stilted and academic. And he wondered, blowing smoke rings again, if maybe the activity of translation itself, the degree of my absorption in it, might have had something to do with the blockage, that perhaps the love and admiration I felt for work to which I was plugging myself in at such voltage (his figure of speech) short-circuited a current of creativity that was, really, still there in potential, waiting for the wires to get uncrossed and re-plugged through a twinned outlet. And in that sense, and I'm no electrician, he said, so forgive my metaphors: Since when is poetry, say, one thing and translation another? Where is, really, the boundary between the two? What if translation were conceived as the gateway into forms of poetry waiting to be imagined? If we can have the works of, say, both Brahms and John Cage understood as Music, the art of both Watteau and Duchamp understood as Painting, the writing of both Tennyson and Nekrasov understood as Poetry,[20] why can't we imagine that the task of Translation might extend, for the sake of certain purposes, beyond the relatively delimited protocols and horizons that currently frame the practice? One never knows what might happen: Once upon a time, for example, a very unfaithful translation by a Scot named James Macpherson[21] was translated into German, and German Romanticism was born!

Well, so he said something close to that, anyway. Then he started talking, brilliantly, about Schleiermacher, Benjamin,[22] and an obscure American poet named Piercer, who had done false translations of Lorca, and a furtive Canadian, named Bepe Nicola, I think it was (though I've never found a reference to either on the internet), who had invented one hundred different modes of translation, about how, in fact, When you think about it, he said, the Western novel begins with a fake "translation," into Spanish, from the Arabic, you know, the Quijote.[23] So maybe, he said, there is still work for you to do of your own, and encounter, there, unsuspected accretions that will build and gather as you go, something new and strange you'll find not outside of translation, but deep down inside its subterranean canals and sewers, and what's just waiting is for you to get down there into the muck and to begin. Maybe the muck is where the sublime is, you know?

I winked at him and said: I hate the word sublime. Sorry to be blunt, but it sounds so stilted and romantic.

We both laughed, though I don't think he'd been joking about what he'd said.

Sometime during the chat he mentioned a "weird manuscript" he'd come across, something an old, recently dead friend had left at his home back in 1997, and that he was working on editing it, which he felt he had to do—was obligated to do—in whatever time was left, among so many other things. He referred to the task as a kind of "sympathetic translation," but we must have turned to talking of something else…

He slept on the couch and left at dawn, before I was up, leaving a sweet note of thanks, which I still have and cherish. Like in a Mexican soap opera, I guess. Or a ranchera. That night was the last time I talked to him.

His death stunned me, as it did everyone else. He'd left on the fly, like he'd left Mexico D.F., back in '76, his friends scratching their heads, both sorrowed and a bit affronted by the abruptness of the exit.

❄❄❄

Nine months later, I received in the mail the contents of this unfinished book you hold. The package contained no return address nor any explanatory letter clarifying its source or purpose. The address label was typed. It was postmarked from Barcelona. All of which sounds absurd, of course, barely believable, a discovery version of Shakespeare's Cardenio, or Plato's Hermocrates, or Rimbaud's "La Chasse spirituell," or Hemingway's earliest stories, or Benjamin's suitcase, or the actual Quijote of Cide Hamete Benengeli falling into the unsuspecting hands of an unknown academic.[24] Someone who found my name in his address book and maybe connected it to a note Roberto might have left about me somewhere, perhaps remembering our talk that night in 2002? I really have no idea. But there you have it, and now it is in your hands. I wash my own.

Isabel Quiroga

December, 2008, Barcelona

Postscript (by Isabel Quiroga)

But I need to add this:

Bolaño is either being straight up about Nadal, or he is playing a kind of trick from beyond, maybe one he wished would never be resolved. If the latter, he must have imagined me (or maybe someone else he'd shared the secret with) writing this someday, as his "editor," an Archimboldi-like note[25] to his final, apocryphal, posthumous tale, the editorial presence plotted by his extraordinary imagination. His greatness, of course, is beyond me. (I am but a simple translator of Russian avant-garde literature.)

The medications are killing me. I'm doing my best, but sometimes I feel like I'm outside my self.

❊❊❊

OK, better now. So as I was saying:

The bibliographic outline is as follows: The typed manuscript, mostly double-spaced, consisting of 292 pages (though approximately fifty of these are only partially filled, with large blank spaces seemingly denoting areas to be developed), is composed on both selectric typewriter and computer.[26] It consists of Bolaño's introduction (including the appended email communications from others concerning Nadal); the 1931 transcript of the interrogation of Benjamin Péret in Rio de Janeiro by military police officers of the Vargas regime; an accompanying transcript recording a detention interview conducted concurrently by an apparent secret service operative from the French Embassy in Brazil (these last two items annotated extensively by, apparently, Bolaño); an attached selection of (mostly) very free "translations" by Nadal of poems from Péret's collection *The Big Game* (*Le Grand Jeu*); a bizarre, satirical text in the guise of a speech by a Stalinist official in Moscow, praising the new "Soviet-Infrarrealista Poetry"; a handwritten letter by Sylvia Beach, by all indications genuine, which Bolaño refers to herein; a drawing from Bolivia of Nadal, referred to by one of Nadal's acquaintances in a letter herein; three photocopied texts from previously published sources that are authored by Péret *[Only one photocopy of prose by Péret was contained in the manuscript handed down to me from Mosconi. A.B.]*; and a first-ever translation into Spanish from the French and Portuguese of the only remaining part of a manuscript by Péret (its extant four pages), which was confiscated and otherwise destroyed by his Brazilian interrogators in 1931.

The aforementioned introduction by Bolaño is a typescript composed on selectric; the "translations" from Péret's *Le Grand*

Jeu are likewise in such form, these perhaps retyped by Bolaño from handwritten copies by Nadal (assuming, of course, the latter is not merely an invention of Bolano's). The interrogation documents and the satirical "Soviet-Infrarrealista" speech, along with the transcribed *O Almirante negro* fragment, are in computer ink-jet printout. Save occasional penciled brackets around certain words, phrases, or passages on the introduction document (apparently marks for possible revision), along with occasional checkmarks, question marks, and underlines, no handwritten notes are present in the texts.

—Isabel Quiroga

❄❄❄

[note: The below appended section, partly repetitious of remarks made earlier, is in a different font and paper (a rose-colored paper) clipped to the text of Quiroga's Preface, apparently for possible use in a revision. AB]

The status of this book is distressed, to say the least. It is like a maze, with a trap set at the end.

What are its true origins? To whom does it belong? It seems it must be the "queer manuscript" Bolaño had mentioned to me in 2002. But who, really, sent it to me? And how would whoever did so have known of my half-remembered connection to it from that night? Had Bolaño left instructions to someone that it be sent? Apparently so. And I confess it moves me, deeply, if so, that he would have remembered our talk that evening and entrusted it to me.

The questions, though, go beyond the mystery of the identity of the "sender." Though we know that the dates and details referenced in the document concerning Péret's arrest and incarceration in Brazil are factual, do the interrogation documents here really come from forgotten, perhaps deep-sixed police files, translated by Nadal, however he managed to get hold of them?

Or were they fabricated by Nadal, bearing thus a forged status that is analogous to his (albeit transparently) invented "Soviet" speech and purported poem "translations" from Peret's *Le Grand Jeu*? All attempts by me to verify their authenticity have been frustrated, not least the numerous unanswered queries I made to the Archives Division of the Brazilian Ministry of Justice, who referred me back to the Archives Division of the Federal Police Department, who in turn referred me to the Ministry of Justice, and so on and so forth. My attempts to contact the Mario Pedrosa Archives Foundation ended in frustration.

But the major question haunting me is this: Could it be that the entire book is, his death having been in sight, a species of "Big Game" conducted by Bolaño himself? Who is inventor, even, of the ghostly Nadal, who seems, in turn, like an older Juan García Madero, bearing many of his traits, the whole work a novel in extremis—unfinished or *intended to seem unfinished*—whose fiction expands like an ether or infection, suffusing—and in the end consuming—authorial reference proper? Who has created it? Is it *all* by him?

My days are numbered now, as Bolaño's were. In all likelihood, someone else will need to finish this, too, for me. Sherlock Holmes poets of the future, please help me.

—Isabel Quiroga

[undated]

NOTES [BY ISABEL QUIROGA]

1.   Volodia Teitleboim (1916-2008), a prominent Chilean literary critic and Communist Party leader. He edited, with Eduardo Anguita (1914-1992), the influential 1935 *Antología de Poesía Chilena Nueva* (Anthology of New Chilean Poetry). *[The Teitleboim quote that Quiroga refers to appears in a 1996 critical edition of* Defense of the Idol, *by Omar Cáceres, a book originally published in 1934. The entire edition, save two copies (one held by the National Library of Chile and the other by an anonymous book collector in California), was supposedly incinerated by the poet immediately after its publication. See the letter by José Requena in the* "Some Memories of Nadal" *section of this book. A.B.]*

2.   The novel that brought international fame to Bolaño, *Los Detectives Salvajes*, was published by Anagrama in 1998. *[The English translation appeared as* The Savage Detectives, *from Farrar, Straus & Giroux in 2007. A.B.]*

3.   It is interesting that most of the surnames for the correspondents in the "Some Memories of Nadal" section are *also* used as pseudonyms in *The Savage Detectives*. However, it is clear that the pseudonymous surnames applied in the letters herein do *not* denote the same historical persons to whom the surnames are applied in the *Savage Detectives*. Is this nominal recycling and scrambling just a convenience, or is it a kind of joke by Roberto?

4.   *La Literatura Nazi en America* was published by Seix Barral in 1996. *[The English translation appeared as* Nazi Literature in the Americas, *published by New Directions in 2008. A.B.]*

5.   Enrique Vila-Matas (b.1948), a lifelong resident of Barcelona, was a good friend of Bolaño and has written about their friendship on different occasions. The poet Rubén Medina (b.1955) was one of the core members of the original Infrarrealista group. He edited the only issue of *Correspondencia Infra*

(October, 1977), in which both the Infrarrealista Manifesto by Roberto Bolaño and the legendary long poem by Mario Santiago Papasquiaro, "Consejos de 1 discípulo de Marx a un fanático de Heidegger," first appeared. He has taught at the University of Wisconsin, in Madison, since 1991. *[Medina edited* Perros habitados por las voces del desierto: Poesía infrarrealista entre dos siglos *(Aldvs, México, 2014), a key critical anthology of the Infrarrealista movement. A.B.]*

6. The Raval is one of the most historic neighborhoods of Barcelona. Long a working class and bohemian area, it has in recent years, along with many other urban spaces in the city, suffered significant gentrification. *[Unfortunately, the process Quiroga describes has only gained momentum in recent years. A.B.]*

7. A.G. Porta (Chile, b.1954), coauthor with Bolaño of *Consejos de 1 discípulo de Morrison a un fanático de Joyce* (1984), whose title is adapted from Mario Santiago's poem, mentioned above; Bruno Montané (Chile, b.1957), one of the key members of the Infrarrealista group who continued to collaborate with Bolaño in Barcelona; Raul Escarí (Argentina, b.1944), author, artist, editor, and close friend in Paris, during the 1970s, of Enrique Vila-Matas, as the latter recounts in *Never Any End to Paris* (2003), the author's most beautiful book, in my humble opinion.

8. Jorge Luis Borges (Argentina, 1899-1986); Nicanor Parra (Chile, b.1914); Julio Cortázar (Argentina, 1914-1984); Alejandra Pizarnik (Argentina, 1936-1972). The four are giants of Latin American avant-garde writing. I once spent an unforgettable afternoon at Isla Negra with Parra, and had a somewhat awkward lunch with Pizarnik, in Paris, two months before she killed herself.

9. Vicente Huidobro (Chile, 1993-1948), central figure of the Latin American vanguardia and author of *Altazor* (1931), widely considered one of the great works of the international avant-garde. Cartagena is an old coastal resort town between

Santiago and Valparaíso, long past its heyday, but still beautiful in its venerably ruined way. If you come, I will show you around; it is full of ghosts. Huidobro is buried there, at the city's tallest point, overlooking the sea.

10. Vsevolod Nekrasov (Russia, 1934-2009) and Gennadiy Aygi (Russia, 1934-2006) were two of the leading experimental poets of the Soviet Union during the second half of the 20th century. Their work circulated almost entirely in furtive Samizdat editions.

11. Jorge Herralde (Spain, 1935), the legendary founder and editor of Anagrama editions, one of Spain's great publishing houses, and the publisher of most of Bolaño's original works as well as those of Vila-Matas. *[Though Vila-Matas was soon and controversially to jump from Anagrama to Seix Barral in July, 2009. A.B.]*

12. François Villon (France, 1431-disappeared 1463), poet and ruffian, arguably the medieval period's great "Infrarrealista" poet.

13. An old bar in the Raval.

14. The reference is to the residence of the Dada artist Kurt Schwitters in Hanover, Germany, whose reconstruction I visited, in fact, with Enrique Vila-Matas and other writers, on a tour during a conference on "Lost Literature" there. The original inside and outside of the building was, beginning in 1923, subjected to a radical transformation via continuous accretion of architectural and design elements—a species of tridimensional assemblage, halfway between architecture and sculpture, constructed with sundry discarded materials, which he continued to add until the basement and three floors were consumed by the project, making the living space of the house smaller and smaller, until the building was hit by a bomb in the Second World War. *[I have been unable to find any record of a conference by such name. AB]*

15. Bolaño was very near-sighted.

16. *Estrella Distante* was published by Anagrama in 1996. *[The English translation appeared as* Distant Star, *published by New Directions in 2004. A.B.]*

17. A Barcelona bookstore.

18. Premio Fernando Aguirre-Libralire, which Vila-Matas received for his book *Bartleby and Company* (2000).

19. Bolaño was on a waiting list for a liver transplant at the time.

20. Johannes Brahms (1833-1897) and John Cage (1912-1992), both composers; Antoine Watteau (1684-1721) and Marcel Duchamp (1887-1968), both visual artists; Alfred, Lord Tennyson (1809-1892) and Vsevolod Nekrasov (Op. cit), both poets.

21. James Macpherson (1736-1796), Scottish poet and forger of the Ossian epic, a major controversy of the 18th century, which had significant influence on late 18th and early 19th century Romantic poets. Author-glorifying Romanticism and Author-scrambling Forgery joined at the hip. Imagine!

22. Friederich Schleiermacher (Germany, 1768-1834) and Walter Benjamin (Germany, 1892-1940), who each wrote major, revolutionary works on the subject of translation. *[The "obscure American poet named Piercer" is clearly referencing Jack Spicer (United States, 1925-1965). Quiroga obviously misheard, ignorant of Bolaño's reference. Likewise, she poignantly and humorously misnames the Canadian experimental poet bpNichol (1944-1988) A.B.]*

23. The word "translation" is in quotes because Miguel de Cervantes first presented *El ingenioso hidalgo don Quijote de la Mancha* as a translation into Spanish by "Cid Hamet Ben Engeli" of a found manuscript written in Arabic. It is interesting, to say the least, that the first great novel of the West was, in fact, a species of "Orientalist forgery." Ah, forgery. It seems to whisper everywhere in this book.

24. The titles are all cases of famous lost works.

25. A reference to (Benito) Archimboldi, the mysterious German author at the heart of Bolaño's posthumously published *2666* (2004). And I, now, in search of Bolaño. A supporting character come into the real. Life imitates fiction, indeed! *[Quiroga, touchingly, seems to compare herself to one of Archimboldi's four devoted scholars, who in Bolaño's novel, set out to track down the German writer. AB]*

26. Bolaño used a selectric typewriter between 1993 and 1995, when he switched to a word processor. If the manuscript is authored by Bolaño, the detail would suggest it was begun before the end of 1995, meaning its composition would have likely run parallel to *Nazi Literature in the Americas* and the *Savage Detectives* *[Nota bene: Some of the names mentioned by Quiroga, such as those of Juan Garcia Madero and Mario Pedrosa, are introduced in later sections. A.B.]*

INTRODUCTION
ROBERTO BOLAÑO

PHOTO OF ROBERTO BOLAÑO, CA. 2001

Vladimir Nadal called me out of nowhere, in October, 1997. I hadn't seen him since 1977, in Mexico, DF. I know it was October—October 18th, to be exact—because I remember when the phone rang I was reading an article in *El País* about the grand interment of Che Guevara's remains in a mausoleum in Santa Clara, Cuba. They'd been repatriated the week before from Bolivia.

It took me a while to place him. I remembered the name, but memories were sparse: A friend of Harrington's, a Chilean, a drinker of impressive capacities, though nothing unusual about the last bit, as far as our old group was concerned. Quiet, on the margins of things, semi-indigenous, hanging back, looking out from under a pulled-down Guerreros of Oaxaca cap. That was the hazy recall.

I took a cab to the Blanes station to bring him back to the flat. We greeted each other diffidently and made the usual small talk. At his request, we stopped at the Bar Stadium, a few blocks from the apartment. He drank three grappas, fairly fast; in that respect he fit my faint memory, though if I'd seen him on the street, I wouldn't have recognized him. He was a skinny kid back then, from the half-image I was calling up; now he was taller than I remembered, somewhat stockier, too, tinted glasses and a moustache in the broom-mode of García Márquez, a writer that, at least back in '76, he and the rest of us would have held in a bit of fuck-you regard. But I couldn't remember him any clearer than I'd been able to remember Roberto Arriagada and Renato Czischke back in '73 (they had García Márquez moustaches, too), who'd assured me we'd all been classmates in our first year of high school at Liceo de Hombres in Los Ángeles, and who snuck me out of a torture den, in Concepción, at risk to their own lives.

Nice that Che got back to Cuba, eh? I said. The bartender filled Nadal's grappa glass, leaving the bottle.

I don't know, he laughed. I wonder if he wouldn't have rather stayed put as he was, as San Ernesto de la Higuera... That Mausoleum they stuck him in looks kind of monolithic. Fidel shouldn't have embalmed him; that was over the top.

Huh? How could Fidel have embalmed him? I said. He's been dead for almost thirty years.

I see your point, he said, refilling his little glass. Just kidding. But no doubt the Soviets left the latest formulas behind, even for advanced stages of decay. By the way, since when did you start smoking Kent cigarettes? You used to be a Delicados man to the death, you sell out to the yanquis, you.

We got jabbering about politics and things in relation; he asked me to tell him about my return to Chile in '73, and my transit through El Salvador, on the way back to Mexico. We talked about Roque Dalton, whom I'd met in San Salvador, briefly, a year before he was doused in gasoline and set on fire by his own comrades in the ERP. He wanted to know every detail of the meeting, what Dalton said, what he was like. I told him most of it was all quite old and fuzzy.

It turned out that Nadal himself had been in El Salvador much longer than I had, and more substantially, for sure, fighting with the FPL forces of the FMLN for ten months, in Chalatenango, in the early 80s, where he commanded a ragtag internationalist squadron made up mostly of Mexicans and Hondurans, the latter training for an armed front in process of formation, doomed to be crushed a couple years later, in a dirty war coordinated by the U.S. Embassy in Tegulcigalpa. The Mélida Anaya Montes assassination, in '83, convinced him it was time to get out. He crossed into Honduras in early '84 and made his way to the Mosquito coast, catching boats, malaria-ridden, back to Mexico. I pressed him on all those details, too, especially his personal contact with Comandante Marcial, who'd ordered Ana Maria's *[Anaya Montes's nom de guerre. A.B.]* murder. In '86, after driving a taxi for two years in Juárez, he secured a visa with the help of Ricardo Pascoe and ended up working odd jobs in Texas and

Colorado, then as a dishwasher for seven years at the University of Arizona, in Tucson, until his long-expired papers got flagged. So here he was now, lost in Europe, like me, twenty years before.

Listen, I love *Nazi Literature in the Americas*. So much better than *Elephant Path*, qualitatively so, to be honest. But what's this book I hear you're writing about our Infra days? *That's* intriguing. Am I in it? Nadal asked.

Well, thanks for that compliment, I think. Truth is, mano, you were new to the group and showed up right before Santiago and I took off, and we barely spoke, from what I can recall. But where the fuck did you hear about my next book?

What do you mean we barely spoke, huevón? You don't remember the time Chuautémoc, Luscious Skin, Harrington, and I were advocating for kidnapping Octavio Paz? We argued with you for two hours in Café El Popular about it. That the ransom would be that *Plural* and *La Cultura en México* would each publish a special issue of Infra poets? Releasing him unharmed, of course, even if they didn't do it… Or the time we proposed going in with pistols to a reading by Monsiváis and David Huerta and firing them up in the air? I recall you at first went for that one, but chickened out.

You were involved in that kidnapping idea? I mean really, I assumed Chuautémoc's proposal was a joke. That would have been suicide, huevón. We'd have gotten shot. And anyway, I don't remember having any argument about it in El Popular.

Well, it sure would have changed the course of Latin American poetic history, you have to admit, if we'd had the guts to do it. At least I can say I was the one who poured a drink on Paz's shirt at Huerta's. You weren't there, as usual. Not that it upset him that much, which was deflating. He smiled at me like I was a child, like he understood my adolescent need to be impudent, you know?

Actually, he continued, some months later I found out that Benjamin Péret threw a drink on Paz, in Mexico City, at Leonora Carrington's house, back in 1943, and that Paz totally lost it and had to be restrained. Apparently, they were arguing about Neruda's role in the Siqueiros raid on Trotsky's house—Paz was denying Neruda had anything to do with it. He and Pablo were pals at the time, I guess. You ever hear about that?

Really? Who told you that? That's wild, I said. I love Benjamin Péret.

Efraín told me. He was there. Of course, Efraín would have been defending Neruda, too. Apparently, Péret started yelling about Neruda's betrayal of the POUM and anarchist fighters in Spain, and they had to carry him out because he said he was "ready to kill some fucking Stalinist poetasters," and there were of course quite a few of them there.

I looked at him and thought back. I tried to match him to my memory, when he would have been twenty or twenty-one. He looked so different it crossed my mind that maybe I was remembering a different person and putting a wrong name, in memory, to the face. But it couldn't be that: there were definitely only four of us Chileans in the group, not counting Barbara. He would have been the one among the four of us who was on the margins of things, the one we more or less ignored, not out of disregard, but because he came late, and he only half seemed to be there, passing through, more than anything. I forgot to follow up on how he'd heard about the *Savage Detectives*, which wasn't even yet out.

We went back to my place and I heated up the leftovers of a very good paella I'd made two days before, with baby octopus to boot, for Jorge Herralde and Juan Villoro, who'd come to visit. I went to bed early. Nadal went back out to the bars.

❄❄❄

He stayed five nights, not just two, as he'd promised. He was on his way to Paris and then to Vienna, where his brother lived, a car mechanic, who had a job for him at his shop and a room above it. I gave him a few contacts there, suggested a couple good cafés in the area, which I knew quite well. He seemed to forget about the *Savage Detectives* hearsay and didn't bring it up again, until the day he left, that is, so I was off the hook with that, not having wanted to discuss the thing in the first place. We did talk about Santiago, both of us agreeing that one day his name, in Latin America, at least, would have an importance for the young equal to Ginsberg, Kerouac, or Rimbaud. Not just for his poetry, but for his inimitable life, which is to say for his poetry… I remember thinking, as we were talking, that I needed to call Mario, invite him back to Barcelona, pay his way over. I never made the call, and a few weeks before writing this, I learned he was hit by a truck and killed.

On the night before Nadal left, around 2 AM, on the way back from the Bar Novo, as we headed down an unlighted stretch of Lluís Companys, a group of four kids stepped out from an alley and blocked our way, front and back. Blanes, with heroin and crack on the rise, was enjoying a crime spike, big time, and it was obvious we were about to get mugged. Nadal straightaway saw it, too.

Stay with me, he said.

One of the punks flicked open a knife by his thigh, and demanded our cash. All your cash, motherfuckers, he said, specifically. Nadal said, Sure, took out his wallet, offered it to him, and when the kid reached, Nadal, like in a Kung-Fu flick, grabbed his wrist, yanked him in, kneed him in the balls, screwed his arm behind his back, grabbed the knife, and karate-chopped his neck, and hard. One fluid motion. I took a swing at the one nearest me, connected with his nose, somehow, knocking him down; the other two ran. The kid whose arm Nadal might well have broken was on the ground, screaming, and Nadal gave him a swift kick in the jaw. I heard it break. The kid I'd punched got up, blood coming (to my pride and surprise) from his nose, backed away, and then ran, yelling over his shoulder that next time they'd shoot us. You goddamn bourgeois pricks, he yelped, his voice breaking. Nadal closed the knife and put it in his pocket.

Fuck, I said. What the fuck. Where'd you learn *that*? Fuck!

The FPL, he said, tucking in his shirt. From Sandinista advisors, who learned, in turn, from the sons of Che. Though you didn't hear it from me. But you were damn good, Bolaño. Nice left hook…

He seemed absurdly composed, under the circumstances, like in some B-level noir flick from the 50s.

Is the little creep alive, I asked, still shaking.

Oh, he's fine. Just dozing. He'll likely still become a banker or politician, or something, said Nadal. I heard the young thug moan.

We hadn't walked twenty feet, when someone leaned out from the shadows. Nadal stopped, ready to tangle again, but right away I knew it was Estela, an addict I'd been helping out for a while, with food and such. She'd studied at the Sorbonne back in the late 70s, and was a regular visitor to my mom's shop, though she never bought anything.

I know Roberto doesn't play, so I don't ask him, but for a man like you, sir, I have a discount, she cooed, stepping towards Nadal.

Roberto doesn't cheat, my love, Nadal said. Because he's my boyfriend.

Estela made a deep hooting sound, like she was half-owl.

Roberto! she cried. I'm telling your mom.

He's lying, Estela, I called back, shaking even more now, the shock of the fight setting in.

Don't worry, Roberto. I know who you are, she laughed, as we turned onto s'Abanell street. But do you really know who your boyfriend is?

Moon on the surf; the sound of waves and the laughter of a

whore, who'd hung out at the Café de Flore, and once chatted, intimately, with members of Tel-Quel.

You should put all that in a story, Nadal said from the dark.

It would seem too fake, I said, lighting a smoke, looking around, expecting something else.

Well, but that's one of the charms of your fiction, Roberto. That you make the most unlikely and uncanny things seem perfectly plausible. A literary school of Nazis? Who could have thought that up and made it work, but you?

(REVISE PREVIOUS TWO PAGES. TOO AFFECTED AND MACHO.) *[The note—by Bolaño, Quiroga, or Mosconi, impossible to tell—is typed in CAPS directly into the text. A.B.]*

❄❄❄

Other than the knife fight, it was a pleasant visit, really, though I was probably a bit too much on the distant side, over-all, because I was working hard at the time to finish *Savage De-tectives*, in the last stretch of revisions. But Nadal left me pretty much alone during the daytime, with no problem, it seemed, while he toured the bars of Blanes. He was good company, all in all—very complimentary to my mother, and she was taken enough with his courtesies and charms that she took us out to a grand paella dinner at the Hotel Horitzó, on his last night there. My mother didn't really have that kind of money to spend, and I was pissed off at her for the splurge, not to mention my sus-picion she'd been flirting a bit with Nadal. I'd just gotten a little bit of prize money for my story "Sensini," and said I'd pay the bill, but she told me to order some tapas and shut up. We ate like PSOE officials at a Royal State Dinner in London.

Over dessert, the best flán any one of us had tasted, and with no way of knowing I was a big fan of the movie *Repo Man*, Nadal started telling us he'd met Alex Cox, an auteur I loved, on a train to Denver, sometime in 1986 or '87.

Mano, are you kidding. You're messing with my head. I love Alex Cox. Seriously? What was he like?

Alex Cox

He was wearing a baseball cap that said "Repo Man," custom-made, I guess, said Nadal. And I was sitting behind him and listening to his conversation with an ancient Black woman he was next to, and I noticed how polite and attentive he was, even though she clearly had dementia. I could see he had a book of poetry by Bukowski, published by Black Sparrow. So when he went up to the café car, I followed him, mainly to chat about Bukowski, and pointed at his cap, and told him I loved the movie *Repo Man*, and then he tells me that he directed it. So I said, Oh, yeah, right. But quickly it became clear he really was Alex Cox and I couldn't believe it. So then, tongue tied, I said something about how in Mexico a number of poets I knew could probably drink Bukowski under the table, and I started telling him about our days back then, and it turns out he's a big fan of Paz, in a naïve sort of way, so he was asking me all these questions. Anyway, we hit it off, and we ended up circling the spotlit Mormon Tabernacle Temple in Salt Lake City, because we had a three-hour layover for a mechanical problem, Amtrak is an embarrassment to train culture, truly sad, and there I was, telling him about Efraín Huerta and Mario Santiago and Manuel Maples Arce and the Estridentistas and the Hora Zero, and he was really interested, even said, later, on the train, that he thought Santiago should have a movie made about him, and he gave me his card and asked that I contact him, but then I lost the card.

Shit, I said, That's amazing. You're making that up about him saying he wanted to make a film about Santiago, right? I mean, it would be a film about all of us, right?

No, I swear, it's true. I even gave him my precious copy of *Pájaro de calor*, which one day will probably be worth a couple hundred dollars in the book trade.

What movie was he working on when you talked to him?

Well, he'd just finished *Sid and Nancy* and said he was going to Nicaragua to make a movie on William Walker.

Huevón, I saw that Walker film! I said. But it's really a letdown, nothing like *Repo Man*…

Well, said Nadal, *Pierre: or, the Ambiguities* isn't as good as *Moby Dick*, either. The analogy's a bit overdone, maybe, but it's not false. Something like that might happen to you, too. You know how it goes. And Doña Victoria, I can't thank you enough for this wonderful meal, sitting here next to the ocean, in such wonderful company. It truly has been a pleasure getting to know you, and I shall not forget you soon. This is without doubt the best paella I have ever had.

You mean better than mine? I said, a bit hurt.

And neither shall I forget you, my sweet dear, said my mom,

taking his hand across the table. You make sure to come back soon. Don't you ever forget to call on us when you are anywhere in the area. Nadal was pretty suave and charming for someone who'd once wanted to kidnap Octavio Paz. Frankly, it was all starting to make me feel a bit weird. Somehow, I forgot to ask him if he told Cox about his bad-movie experience in El Salvador. Probably he didn't.

The next morning, he and I stopped by Joan Planell's shop for sweet rolls and coffee before taking the train into Barcelona, from where he was flying to Vienna that night. I was staying in town for a few days myself, to get my checkup tests, stop by Anagrama to talk about the revisions, and to spend time with Carmen. But I promised Nadal I'd hang out with him that first day. He wanted to see the Bar Marsella, one of my hangouts—a tavern in the Raval where the furniture hasn't changed and nothing's been dusted since Hemingway drank absinthe there, in the twenties. As I suspected he would be, Vila-Matas was having his noon-hour café con leche in the Merzbau-like corner where he always sat at that hour, alone, enjoying his time before the famous daily depression that would descend upon him around six or seven in the evening. Not wanting to interrupt him, I waved and so did he, nonchalant, returning to his coffee and reading. That's Vila-Matas, I said. Oh, really, he said. I dig *A Brief History of Portable Literature*, and I just read *Sons without Sons*, fantastic, he's good. Shouldn't we go over to say hello?

I explained the situation, that his solitary mornings in the corner were a kind of Shandyist eccentricity, that it would be an indiscretion to interrupt him, that he'd come by the table later to say hello, on his way out. I started to tell Nadal of the recent occasion—only a few weeks after Vila-Matas and I had first met in the Bar Novo in Blanes, in November of '96—that we'd run into each other at a retrospective of Joseph Beuys at the MACBA, and how we wandered into a room where there were, spread around the rotunda, a series of vitrines on tall legs, containing strange and sundry objects, including, notably, pieces of dark felt and bars of cooking fat. And under one of these vitrines were a number of toiletries and cosmetic items that Beuys claimed (according to the informational card) to have stolen from the bathroom of Leni Riefenstahl, during a party at her home: a brush with hair still in it, a tube of lipstick, a case of eye shadow, a pill cutter, a rouge pad, tweezers, a toothbrush, a half roll of toilet paper, a bottle of Bayer aspirin, nail polish, mouthwash, and other things I can't recall. And interspersed among them were stills from the horrible film *Storm over Mont Blanc*, which she had starred in. And Vila-Matas was looking at these things, solemnly, with his hands behind his back, slightly bent over, and he said, though more to himself than to me, Wow, you know, I wonder what fascism might have to do, deep down, with the Avant-Garde?

I've been turning that question over in my head, I said to Nadal, ever since then. Because I can't tell if he meant the question in earnest, or if he meant it ironically, vis-a-vis the obvious fact that the avant-garde has fascism, via Italian Futurism, in its first genes. And I keep forgetting, for some reason, to bring it up with him, on the occasions we cross paths. So, when he comes over, I said, why don't you tell him I told you he said that, and then ask him what he meant by it? He'll like that. It will be a way for the two of you to connect and for me to stop forgetting to ask him.

Sure, he said. Anything to help you out with your flagging memory, Bolaño. But you just published a prize-winning book about avant-garde fascist writers, so I'm not sure why you wouldn't have the answer already, you know? And by the way, regarding Beuys, it's interesting, because the question would more specifically be: I wonder what fascism might have to do with the *neo*-avant-garde? Because Beuys is really a key figure in the whole post-war spectacularization of art and its capture by Capital—seminal in that regard, with Klein and Warhol. I mean, aside from the fact that he was a Luftwaffe Stuka gunner shot down over the USSR and saved by Tatars, or so he claims, his work is totally entwined with the emerging culture of the spectacle, which for the historical avant-garde was not an issue, but which for the neo-avant-garde becomes the be-all and end-all, the invasion and colonization by the Culture Industry of the realm of "vanguard" art. And in the 60s it's sort of like a blitz-krieg, actually, even as Adorno went on thinking avant-garde gestures provided a refuge of negative critique against the com-modifications of the Culture Industry, and so on. I was reading Benjamin Buchloh a while back, a great art critic, do you know his work?

Joseph Beuys

Um, no, I said. Who's he?

Sort of a radically modified Adornoist—turning Adorno on his head like Marx did to Hegel, very smart. He talks about how when artists and writers in the late teens and twenties shocked and scandalized their audiences, it was perceived by everyone—not least the bourgeoisie—as political and social provocation, an attack on the very foundations of cultural and rational order. Like the Cabaret Voltaire in 1916, or Schwitters's readings of his Merz sound poems, or the various outbursts against received sense and decorum by Breton, Péret, Éluard, those guys, though Péret turns out to be different from most of the originals and never backslides. They're not just giving the easy finger to hegemonic rituals and conventions of sense-production; they're offering models of culture and community that are alternate forms, however utopian they may be, of social, communitarian, revolutionary praxis. But when artists of the neo-avant-garde engaged in scandal and shock, on the other hand, the most evident effect of their actions would be—in accordance with the rituals of the culture industry—the spectacularization of the artist as "star" and the social role ensuing from that. Beuys and Klein and Warhol were the first to fully incorporate the principles of spectacle culture and strategies of cultic visibility in their personas as much as into their work. Once cultural practice had been severed from all utopian and political aspirations, the neo-avant-garde inevitably consummated the shift into an exclusive register of spectacular visuality. Which is analogous, of course, with the operational logic of fascist culture. So maybe that's what Vila-Matas sort of had in the back of his mind when he said that. It's interesting to think, isn't it? That Documenta, in Kassel, is genealogically leafed to a fascist branch, from which it falls, each fall, to return, in the spring.

That's superb, I said, amazed at the eloquence of his ramble. I wondered if he'd memorized it from some art text, though it didn't sound like he had. He said it naturally, with lots of pauses and "ehs."

Ah, mano, I love this place, he said, gazing around. I love dark bars, you know? Where else but in old bars does social class and pretense most authentically take back seat?

A soccer stadium? I said.

No, no. The workers sit in the worst seats, the bourgeoisie in the best ones. Plus, some teams are proletarian, others are bourgeois.

Churches? I said.

Come on, Bolaño. Churches, beneath the show, are all about class, you know that. Vatican II regardless. Plus, half the clerics are pedophiles. It's *taverns* where things are levelled. Where else is self-pity so ancient and communal?

OK, I said. *Buses?*

The waiter finally came over, old enough to have served the young Hemingway himself.

So Nadal ordered a late morning half-liter of grappa and I ordered some manzanilla tea, and we turned to talking about the old scene in D. F., and he filled me in on things from when after Santiago and I had left, some of which I'd heard about, some of which I hadn't. Gossip about people like Orlando Guillén, Carla Rippey, and Enrique Krauze. And talk about Santiago's last wandering in the desert, Nadal's own militancy with the PRT in Juárez, following El Salvador, incidents with Efraín Huerta, the resentments of those getting left out of *Naked Guys under the Rainbow of Fire*, most of that involving the collapse of the old affinities, the final triumph of the Pazistas... The usual story of the avant-garde, etc. How it loses in the end, coopted, in various submissive poses of defeat. Or else dehisces into eternal nothing, at its outermost factions. How the cycle keeps repeating. Most of it depressing, in other words.

So much for "Abandon everything, once again," eh? He said, with a smile.

Vila-Matas had finished his coffee and was on his way out. He stopped by, somewhat red-eyed, and I introduced him to Nadal. I asked Vila-Matas what he was reading these days, by which I meant something like "this week." He replied that he was reading four things, and that he allowed himself to read only from one of these four things each day, in an exact sequence, and with a limit of no less and no more than fifty-four daily pages, even if in some cases this meant going back and rereading: The Pessoa biography by Simões, the collected poems of J.V. Foix, *Murder in the Central Committee*, by the crime writer and gastronomist Vàzquez Montalbàn (our mutual friend), and *El Quijote*, for the fourth time. I have never felt stronger or better in my reading, he said. It is making me taller, day by day. I was going to ask Vila-Matas how he was getting "taller" from reading, when Nadal asked him what he was "*writing* these days."

I am writing a book composed entirely of footnotes, about many diverse writers who are unable to write due to some paralysis of will beyond their control, or who have resolutely willed themselves not to write, or who have, in a few cases, vanished mysteriously from public view. Writers of the *No*, you might say…And there's not a single Nazi among them, said Vila Matas, faking a gentle cough.

Ah, my tribe! said Nadal. But apparently not yours, Vila-Matas, since you are quite occupied, as they say, *writing away*?

This struck me as a bit impertinent, considering I had only introduced Nadal to Vila-Matas a moment ago. But Vila-Matas laughed, amiably. He invited us to join him that evening at Casa Leopoldo with Ignacio Echevarría and Miquel Bauçà, apologizing for not being able to stay, as he was meeting Javier Marías for lunch at Pinoxto.

Miquel Bauçà? I said. You're joking. No one's seen him for years.

I know, said Vila-Matas. But he's agreed to see us and that's why you should come. It will be dinner with the Pynchon of Cataluña.

Nadal explained that he would love to, but was leaving town around eleven at night, for (he said it in English, unaware it might as well have been Eritrean to Vila-Matas) "the shadowy land of the Freud," as he put it, by which I think he intended a pun on "fraud." I made up some excuse, not wanting to meet up with Echevarría, who I'd heard was preparing a negative review about me.

So Vila-Matas said OK and goodbye, wishing us to always be accompanied by the "sickness of literature," or something loopy of the sort, and ambled out. After a minute or so, Nadal said, Shit, I forgot to ask him about avant-garde art and Riefenstahl's lipstick. Maybe I should run after him?

No, forget it, I said. I'll ask him later myself.

And what's with no more than fifty-four pages of reading a day? he asked. *That's* weird.

I reminded him of Vila-Matas's obsession in *A Brief History of Portable Literature* with the number twenty-seven, an obsession that haunts other of his books. It's a real thing, I said. And multiples of it are important to him, too. Fifty-four is twice twenty-seven, obviously.

I'll take another grappa, please, but doubled, said Nadal to Hemingway's waiter, who returned, anciently, with carafe and two glasses.

Nadal downed a shot, and proceeded to pull out, one by one, the books in his bag, stacking them carefully in a tower on the table. Thirteen of them, plus a crumbling copy of Adrienne Monnier's *Les Gazettes*, which he slapped down at the top of the pile, the spine split clean in half. It seemed like some sort of magic trick: his pulling that many books out of his rucksack, which contained all his clothes and toiletries, to boot. Would you believe I found this copy of the Monnier last month, in Paris, at the Puces de Montreuil flea market, and as I'm leafing through, not all that interested, I see that there's this handwritten letter folded in there, and it's by Sylvia Beach, on her personal stationary, written to an American student in the Columbia University Paris program in 1954, who's inquiring about Proust, and Beach says here that she and Mlle. Monnier are "totally ignorant about Proust," so she refers the kid to the editor of Gallimard. Isn't that odd?

I agreed it was. He took out the letter, still folded in the book, and carefully opened it up. I read it, and it was exactly as he said. Holy shit, what a find! I said. The hand of the first publisher of *Ulysses*... And she was still ignorant about Proust when she was in her sixties!? That's amazing. What are you going to do with it? He paper-clipped it to a thick stack of papers he had. I was going to ask him about those, because they looked like a manuscript, but I got distracted by his pile of volumes.

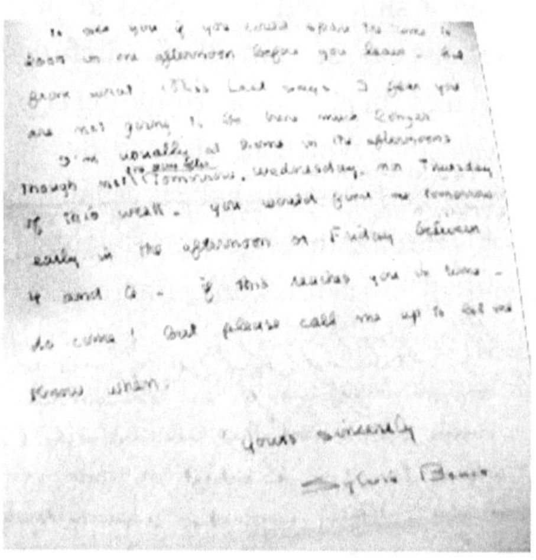

PHOTO OF HANDWRITTEN LETTER BY SYLVIA BEACH

The other ones were nearly as tattered—dog-eared stuff by people we were onto, even back in D.F.: Parra, Borges, Jaime Gil de Biedma, Rimbaud, Vallejo, Sor Juana, José Agustín (though that one a bit of a surprise), Queneau, Ungaretti, Pizarnik, Cortázar, an old anthology of Chilean poetry, and a few U.S. poets in original editions (Nadal had good English): Frank O'Hara, Ted Berrigan, and a Lynette Hejinum, whom I'd never heard of.

Who's she?

Part of an experimental group called Language, they put equal signs between the letters.

What, between every letter of their poems?

No, I mean the letters of the name of the group, L=A=N=G=U=A=G=E…

Maybe they're named after Jack Spicer's book, except for the equals signs? I asked.

I don't know... I don't know who Spercer is... But these dudes are sort of Marxist, Tel Quel-like, maybe; they're against the Academy and official kinds of verse, like we were, only they're a lot more theoretical, French-aroused, you could say. I don't mean Rimbaud and Baudelaire, but Derrida, Kristeva, Lacan, Deleuze, that sort of thing. Sort of chaste and Apollonian, to the Dyonisian that grabbed *us*... Enemies of the Self and the authorial "I." There's a guy called Bernstein who is sort of like the Breton of the group, it seems.

Well, I hope they're triumphant, I said. Here's a toast to their not ever capitulating to the Academy. May they fight to the last breath. I raised my cup of tea. Hejinum's title, *My Life*, suggests they will, like Trotsky, no? Unless Bernstein turns out to be a kind of *Eduard* Bernstein. You know how the avant-garde goes!

Actually, said Nadal, and as I was saying, mano, we weren't exactly separate from the way "the avant-garde goes," were we?

No, we weren't, I said. Correct. We were pieces in the big game they set up after Tlatelolco. We were right to reject the most obvious temptations, but you could say we really didn't. Didn't reject it, I mean. And not just because we ended up publishing in *Plural* or *Punto de Partida*, I mean. That first resistance and disruption was our way of trying to get what we really wanted, which was at bottom pretty similar to what our enemies wanted, you know. I'm not totally sure about that, but I wonder sometimes.

Yeah, he said. Though there were other groups that got more quickly eaten up than us: The Acá cell, *El taco de la perra brava* collective..."

The Suma and the Peyote gangs, I added. Yeah, we were the tightest, the smartest, and the bravest, really. The others did a few manifestoes and that was pretty much it.

So here we are, Bolaño. You're getting famous and I'm on my way to work in my brother's car shop. Have just one with me, Bolaño, like in the good days. He finished off his fourth or sixth grappa.

Well, at least I still smoke, I said. You, on the other hand, have become a healthy boy, I guess.

Salud, he laughed. Oh, wait, I see I need another. Sorry, I have a terrible fear of flying.

And I see you have a copy of the Teitelboim and Anguita. Nice. Haven't looked at this in years. Poor Teitelboim, such a good anthologist and such a terrible writer. I picked it up and flipped to the table of contents in the back.

Omar Cáceres, he said. A true writer of the No.

Yeah, really strange about Cáceres, I said. Funny how our most famous surrealist poet is *Jorge* Cáceres, but that the phantom Omar was really our *first* surrealist.

Yes, spot on. You know, I've been thinking a lot about Cáceres.

Yeah, which one?

The one in the book here—mysterious, apocryphal Omar. I have a literary-crime theory I'm working on, and I think there's circumstantial evidence that makes it plausible. You want to hear it?

Sure. I'm always up for detective tales about poets, mano, I said. I've always said that if I hadn't been condemned to be a writer, I would have been a detective. My ears are yours. Take them.

He raised his hand to the waiter for another round, after pretending he was going to hold my ears. OK, so bear with me. And afterwards, remind me to show you something else I have.

And so he talked for almost an hour about his Cáceres hypothesis (about which more, further ahead). I was riveted. When he was done, I told him he needed to write a story or novella about it. He seemed to think that was an interesting idea. I told him about my fascination with the mysteriously vanished Surrealist Gui Rosey and that I had a half-finished story that involved him. He went on, then—at length and as if he'd had it all planned out—to describe a possible plot where Rosey makes it out of France on a boat to Chile in 1939, changes his identity, and meets up with Cáceres. It was amazing how he could do things off the cuff like that. I even started to jot some of it down.

But I've talked too much, as usual, he said. Like I'm back at La Habana, in the months after you left. You tell me now about this crazy idea—the novel you're writing on the Infras. And by the way, I do expect to be in it, because I *know* you really have to remember…I was *there*, mano. Don't yank my chain about not remembering me. It hurts my feelings, huevón.

I was going to ask him what he meant about talking too much at the Habana, since I had almost no memory of his ever having opened his mouth back then, but I was distracted by this or that. The tourists starting to come in… Young Barcelona artists and writers coming in to play at bohemia. And we both apparently forgot about the other thing he was going to show me. So, I sort of walked him through the novel. Somehow, he'd convinced me to have a drink. I remember getting somewhat carried away in my synopsis. He seemed impressed. And bummed that he wasn't in it. I actually had three drinks. My first drinks in I don't know how many years.

We walked to Calle Mallorca in the Eixample, stopped by the Bar Belvedere at Nadal's insistence (so he could have a drink in Gil de Biedma's old chair; I didn't have any more and haven't since), and then made our way to La Central bookstore, where we poked around for half an hour and talked with Ricardo Cano Gaviria for a spell, who came in, eerily, right after I'd pulled his book about Walter Benjamin's last day on earth from the shelf. I have not made that up.

I had the clerk call a taxi for the airport, and the taxi came. Nadal and I hugged and promised to keep in touch. "Don't forget to start the novella about Cáceres!" I called after him.

Don't you forget to start the novella about Gui Rosey and Cáceres, he laughed, stumbling more than a bit, and got into the cab, and that was the last time I saw him. And then, fortified by the liquor, having changed my mind and ready for a duel, I went over to Casa Leopoldo to wait for Vila-Matas and Echevarría to show up. Which they never did.

I remember that the next morning I drafted, in a straight rush, thirty pages about four scholars at a conference on German literature, each of them obsessed with the work of a mysterious novelist named Benno von Altenhofen. And when I had this, I saw the key to a book I'd been hitting my head against for years, with no clear direction or exit in sight. But that morning it all came together for me, as a book, a mystery, and a battle map, suddenly, like that.

A few months later, he called. He was doing OK, set up with his brother in Vienna, working in the shop, making decent money, feeling grounded in the labor of doing stuff with cars, going to the library to research and write. This and that. He asked if I'd found his "papers" after he'd left, the ones, he said, he had

wanted to show me, but didn't get around to, for whatever reason, he said.

What papers, huevón, I said.

The interrogation of Péret, he said. And some translations I
did from his poetry in *Grand Jeu*. There was another document
there, too. And some photocopies of other stuff, plus the Infra
manifestos and some ethnographic things Péret did in Brazil.

You mean *Benjamin* Péret?

That one, he said.

Oh. Well, no. No Péret around here, at least not in the sense of
his being interrogated, or whatever. You know I love him. Didn't
we mention him when you were here? I've got some books by
him, in French… What do you mean "interrogation"? The cops
interrogating Péret? I know he was arrested a few times. In the
army for communist agitation in World War II, and before that
in Spain, I think. In Brazil, too, in the early Thirties, I'm pretty
sure? Which interrogation?

Yeah. Could you maybe poke around a bit more? I had to
have left the stuff there. I know it was in my bag at your place,
so the stuff *has* to be there.

But why didn't you tell me about this when you were here?

I was going to show it to you at the Bar Marsella, I remember,
after we'd talked with Vila-Matas—I told you there was something else I wanted to talk to you about. And because it involved
the Surrealists, I knew you'd be interested. I suppose I was leading to it, but there didn't seem to be time, and I only saw it was
gone when I was in the air.

No, huevón, I said. I remember you had your bag with you
at the bar, the day before you left, when you showed me the
Poesia Chilena Nueva copy, and you told me all about Cáceres.
You went out a lot without me to the bars in town, you know.
Maybe you left the papers at one of them? At the Cartago Bar?
Or maybe at the Marsella, even? I can ask around, though I
doubt it, after all this time. But don't you have it on file? What

were they, handwritten?

Yes, mostly handwritten, except for the Xeroxes and one other thing. There was another translation there I had more or less finished, handwritten, too—a speech given by a demented Stalinist hack on Socialist Realism, in Moscow, in the thirties.

That sounds like fun, I said. Is it connected to the Péret thing?

Connected. What do you mean?

Well, you know, Aragon, with Vallejo, could have been a delegate in the hall, cheering on the Stalinists, no?

I don't know, he said. Lost like Aragon. And I'm surprised you would say that about Vallejo. Though it's true... And if it's all lost, then none of it is part of anything, you know.

I asked him to tell me more about the total plan of the Péret novella, said I was intrigued, that I loved Péret, I repeated, remembering more clearly now that the poet had come up in conversation when we'd been in Barcelona.

There was a silence. He told me he'd rather not give a synopsis—that the grand idea, almost all of it still waiting to be written, was too layered, "too elaborate," he said, "over-determined," and that he'd actually begun to lose the thread of the project, too labyrinthine for its own good, too much of a maze. He'd put a lot of thought into it, had all sorts of plans for working up "strata," whatever he meant by that, around the interrogation documents, which he explained he'd had to copy by hand from Xeroxes a friend had made, who'd stumbled upon the file in Brazil, doing research on the history of the Prestes Column, at the National Police Legal Archives, in Rio de Janeiro. His friend, planning to publish facsimiles of the unknown transcripts, would only let him copy them by hand, and Nadal was able to write out little more than half the contents. But he was ready to let it go, in any case, he said. He'd lost the thread, he said again, or something like that.

Say again? I said.

I don't know how you do it, Bolaño, it all seems so easy for you. I probably never would have gone anywhere with it, anyway. It was maybe fifty or sixty pages total, in any case, that I had so far. Not much really. But the Péret files have some historical worth and curiosity, for sure… Those need to be found and published, somehow.

I'm really sorry, mano. But tell me something about it, anyway. Maybe I can give you some thoughts on how to reconstruct and proceed. Tell me how I can help. I feel bad for you about this…

No, forget it. I can't remember very well, to tell the truth. But there are two interrogations, one with the cops, whom Péret has grand fun with in this waking-dream tirade about the nature of Surrealism; the other's an interrogation by the "Cultural Attaché" from the French Embassy, an agent of the Secret Services, quite fascinating, even if half of it is missing. Though I tell you what, Roberto, and please. If you do come across it—and I know it has to be there, somewhere, have you looked under all your papers—will you promise me that you'll find a way of slipping it into one of your books or a story sometime? I'm serious. Listen to me. This is what I ask and want. Anything you would want to do with it. Make me your second Porta, except don't put me on the cover, you know? I don't want it to be mine.

Mano, as I said, if I were to find it, I'd send it back to you— you're the one who needs to finish it, of course. Maybe you could find a way of mixing it up with the Cáceres mystery, don't you think?

Come on man, you know I couldn't. I'd just procrastinate, that's my way, and the days and months would go, and so on, blah blah, you know. Can you believe how the time goes? Our parents used to say it, and we'd smirk. You know how to use it, I don't. Time, I mean. I'd be happy, overjoyed, if *you* did it. Maybe you could even bring me into the story, as a character, under a different name?

That's crazy, huevón. Get hold of yourself, I said. I'll call you right away if I find it, obviously.

I'm not doing well, Bolaño. Not much time. You find it and do something with it, OK?

What do you mean? Are you ill?

We're in leaking boats, the two of us. Though mine's more fucked up than yours, it seems. But I don't want to talk about it. Things happen. How's your mom and Carolina and Lautaro? And how's the book about the Infra days coming along?

How long have you been sick? What is it?

The good old prostate, it's cooked. I've known about it a few years.

You never told me, mano.

Well, you never brought up your shit with me, either, Bolaño. I guess we weren't tight enough, or whatever. At least *I'm* telling you; I heard about *you* from your mom.

That put me off a bit, for whatever irrational reason. I said something that he didn't like, and then he said something I didn't like. I tried to say something to get the conversation on track, to half apologize in the "manly" way, but that was misunderstood, too. I think he tried to say something that didn't work, as well. So one of us hung up.

❄❄❄

It would have been almost a year later later that he called from Valparaíso. Things with his brother hadn't worked out. Nor in Slovenia, he added, oddly. But he was living now on Cerro Los Placeres, where he'd recently moved into "a little hovel of a house, but with a Nerudian view," as he put it. No more travels, he said. I'm home.

No, I said, I'm sorry, the Péret thing isn't here. I'm sure I would've come across it by now. You lost it somewhere else… I told him I clearly remembered his story about Cáceres and that he should turn that into a novella, once and for all, dammit.

That's the book you should write, I said. It's already half way there. It will be spectacular.

I doubt it. We'll see. I spend my time thinking about all the real things I'll write and never do. One reason or another. And when I finally do start something, I fucking leave it at someone's house on my way to Austria… I seem to be cut out for feuilletons, more than anything with substance. So, screw it, you know? I mean, I could have had a footnote from Vila-Matas in that book about writers of the No, ey? I hear it's a hit.

There was a pause.

What are you doing now for money? I said.

Not much, he said. But I did quit drinking, for whatever that's worth.

That's great, my friend. I'm happy for you. But how are you, Nadal? The prostate thing?

The connection dropped. Nadal? Nadal? That was it.

❋❋❋

In February of this year, clearing stuff out, and half remembering what he'd said about "under your papers," I found Nadal's stuff—the Péret fragment and numerous other things, all of them in an old transparent plastic folder with a string clasp—beneath a pile of drafts for *Nazi Literature in the Americas*. Dates I'd penciled on some of those drafts showed I'd composed them in November and December of '93. So how the folder could have gotten hidden under that old stuff, I don't know. Maybe I moved the Nazi matter at some point to the bottom shelf of the bookcase and somehow gathered up Nadal's papers in doing so. Though I have no memory of the drafts being anywhere, anytime, other than where they were. And these had a nice layer of dust on top that seemed the sediment of a good five years. It was almost as if someone—maybe Carolina sometime—had slid them under there by accident or on purpose, after a fight?

My mom, on some occasion when she was over to help with
Lautaro? No, they told me, they never would have moved anything like that. Carmen hadn't yet been over to my place at that
time… I'd had some friends over in the intervening months—
maybe one of them had shifted things around? I do remember
Vila-Matas poking around my bookcase one night, taking things
out and putting them back. But it's silly to think he would have
moved my papers in that way.

But anyway. And actually: Could it have been Nadal, after all,
who'd put them there on purpose? Could this have been his precarious way of placing the work into my hands after the death
he knew was near, and thus prompting me, through a sense of
responsibility to posthumous spirit, to put the work into some
kind of form he could not? On the chance I'd find it, that is…

Though in doing so, he'd have wagered he would be gone
before I was—a 50/50 bet. It's strange, and I don't here, in what
is probably my own small remaining time, have any good answer. Maybe it was a Mario/Rimbaud-like gesture of farewell,
one meant as a kind of reminder to me, of ideals I'd left behind,
for all I know: That writing is one thing and the mind's auction
another. That in the face of death, an author may choose to sev-
er his ties, and leave his writing to find its own fate, outside his
or her name. Something which I most definitely have not done,
in the end, where I am.

❄❄❄

In the dream I was in a room of manuscripts that Nadal never wrote (they lined the walls) and I took one down and began
to copy it, and kept going, furiously, through manuscript after
manuscript, until I had copied them all, while Nadal sat there,
drinking, repeating, Hurry Bolaño, hurry! And then Santiago
climbed through the window, his hair was a dark lion's mane,
five feet wide, and on the desk and the floor he put down stacks

of manuscripts—his own and those of all the Infras, written in notebooks and on scraps and envelopes and receipts, they were like fragments from codices pulled out of caves in the desert, covered in sand and dust —and he said Hurry, Bolaño, hurry, copy these now for us, copy, mano, copy... And I did, and it took years and years, but I kept going, while Santiago was whispering in my ear that there are caves in the desert full of manuscripts, torn and faded and covered in dust, this is just the start, and I wept at the thought of it, as I kept copying, and when I was done, after thousands of years, I think, I collapsed into Santiago's arms, and he told me I'd done well, and Nadal came over and stroked my long hair from back then, though now it was white, and I was crying, and so were they, and we were all wiping each other's eyes, and then everything I'd copied started to burn, as was foreordained, and the flames enveloped us, and we just let them, we didn't try to get out of the room, and we didn't scream, because there was no pain, or feeling at all, and that pleasure together was the end of the ridiculously melodramatic dream.

I hadn't been able to ask Nadal for his number or address in Valparaíso. I tried to track him down through friends in D.F. and Chileans in Barcelona who might have had some inkling. Nothing. No one in D.F., it seemed, even knew he'd left for Europe in the first place, and the last they'd seen him was in late 1980, before he'd disappeared to who knows where.

And so, his recovered manuscript in hand, weighing what I should do with it, I decided to try to get some information about him—memories from whoever had come to know him better than I had, before and after I left, back in '76. I wrote Rubén Medina, Carmen Boullosa, and a few others to track down some email addresses of people who might have known him; they sent me around a couple dozen contacts, and, in some cases, faded remembrances of him. I sent out a general query, explaining my reencounter with Nadal, indicating I had something important he'd left behind, and that I needed contact information to urgently return it to him. I also asked people to provide me with any anecdotes or accounts about him, that this would help shed light on the fascinating materials I had in hand. Some never responded. Others had no idea who I was talking about. And a few, not happy about my most recent book, told me more or less to go shove something up my ass.

And yet, over the course of the next couple months, interesting and sometimes strange responses began to arrive—half over email, half in the regular post. Not that many, around nineteen or twenty, eleven of them of substance and curiosity. I have decided to include those here.

❆❆❆

Only yesterday, a friend passed on a week-old copy of *La Tercera*. He thought I'd want to see an article there on Raúl Zurita. Accompanying the piece was a somewhat grainy photo, from 1981, the caption said, of a clandestine CADA meeting somewhere in Santiago: A group of eight, in semicircle, including Zurita, Diamela Eltit, Lotty Rosenfeld, Fernando Balcells, and Juan Castillo. Two of the others I couldn't recognize, but there, sitting on the floor, back against the wall, looking at Zurita, who with a map on the ground in front of him points to some secret spot in the city (which looks like it might be the Parque Forestal, actually) is Nadal. Hair down to the shoulders, thinner, but no less him for that—the scar on his chin, gaunt-faced, the glasses slightly dark. I was stunned. I knew he'd gone to El Salvador sometime in '82, and then back to Mexico and then to the U.S. only a couple years later, but he'd not said a word to me about having gone to Chile ca. 1981 and working with the CADA. It all made sense, of course, ideologically speaking. And why he would have left for El Salvador from there—fled, that is—something confirmed in one of the letters sent to me, which I include here.

But it struck me as strange—and still does—that he wouldn't have said anything when he was over here with me, especially since he'd read *Distant Star*, and would have known the poetry sky-writing motif was drawn from Zurita. Maybe he didn't want to sour the visit with disagreements? It pains me when I think that two years after we'd been together—and only a few months before he returned there to die—I'd have an infamous dinner at the home of Jorge Arrate and Diamela Eltit back in Chile, when things went south and the crap started flying, and I regret it now.

Some of the materials that follow are signed, here and there, as "Vladimir Nadal," and I take this as the pseudonym the author wished to attach to these works. His actual name does not appear in the pages left behind, so I have decided to speak of him using the pseudonym he appears to have desired. I have also changed all mentions of his actual name in the epistles section back to the "Nadal" pseudonym. Future detectives of poetry may uncover his identity, if they look hard enough.

That's all.

Roberto Bolaño
Barcelona, November, 2001

SEARCHING FOR NADAL:
ELEVEN LETTERS BY VARIOUS WRITERS

Group photo of young Infrarrealistas in Mexico, D.F.

Damn, Bolaño, what a strange thing to hear from you. And even stranger, yet, because you are writing to ask after Vladimir Nadal. How are you? I am not so well. But I'll leave it at that. If you want to know more, you'll write me to ask before twenty more years go by. No, just kidding, more or less.

Did you get the manuscript of my novella I sent you years ago? The one based on our little Infrarrealista adventures from the mid-seventies? It was about one hundred pages. Maybe not; the Mexican post was unreliable back in 1983, before there was email and attachments, not that it's any more reliable today. It was never published, and I don't even know where my copy is now. Maybe you still have it somewhere in your office? Not that it matters. Now that you're famous (congratulations on making it with the literary establishment; enclosed is a precious mimeo copy, maybe one of three left, of the Infrarrealista manifesto you read standing on a table at Bruno's, in 1976). As I said, I don't even have a copy of my novella left, since my wife lost my original typescript on a train to Paris. Maybe you should be the one to write the story about us, in a very elegiac sort of tone. If so, at least I will have given you the idea by sending you mine. To thank me, you can include me in any future editions of *Pájaro de Calor*, since you left me out of the first one. Or else you could include me in a new edition of *Muchachos desnudos bajo el arcoiris de fuego*, which you left me out of, too.

But, no, seriously, it's good to hear from you after eighteen years. Beatriz and I divorced ten years ago. I'd written you seventeen years back to tell you we were getting married, don't know if you remember or even got the letter, the way the Mexican post is, as I was saying. She was sleeping around with the Peruvian guy Ribeyro had introduced us to, a really bad painter who at the time was enjoying a burst of attention. Ribeyro was back here for a show by this same painter, in a gallery on Bucareli, a remodeling of the great Bar Dolly, where you might recall we spent a few nights, talking about shit that came to nothing. Everything's changed, you'd not recognize it. The Habana is still here, but it's a place for yuppies. And most of the reporters drink somewhere else. The painter came and went back to Lima and then he came back a year later and stayed, and no one paid any attention to his painting anymore, except for Beatriz, and they went on fucking each other right under my nose for years. Then she wrote me a letter, from Lima, where she'd supposedly gone for a meeting for Aero Mexico, for which she still works, except in Lima, now, where she moved in with the painter, who then left her a year ago, or maybe she left him, I heard this all through the grapevine in a drunken haze, you know how it goes. Once, in 1987, only some months before she wrote me from Lima, we'd gone to the U.S. on a little vacation because she could get two free flights a year through her job, and we rented a car and drove from Chicago up to Spring Green, Wisconsin, to tour Taliesin, the home of Frank Lloyd Wright, outside the town of Spring Green, an incredible place, though alarming how much neglect and disrepair there is. The gringos can build Embassy fortresses and military bases around the world, but they can't even bring themselves to preserve one of the great masterpieces of world architecture—there are even these huge Chinese and Japanese landscapes Wright bought, from the 1600s and 1700s, hanging there on the walls, totally unprotected, and the snow drifts in under the doors and the bats fly around the place at night, shitting all over the furniture and the carpets. I came back and told Luis Barragán about it (you might recall, though probably not, assuming you got the letter, that is, that I started working as a draftsman in his office in 1984), and he was horrified by what I told him, of course, and he immediately contacted the Governor of Wisconsin, who apparently had just been sworn in, and expressed his outrage, asking how it was possible a Mexican could care more about Frank Lloyd Wright's home than the people of Wisconsin themselves. And then Barragán got on the phone to Richard Meier in the States and got him riled up, and Meier organized U.S. architects to write and call the Governor, and apparently the Governor was very much impressed, because it turns out he soon got the wheels rolling on some State-sponsored Preservation Society to protect and rehabilitate the Taliesin buildings. A few months later, and the day after I received Beatriz's letter from Lima, Barragán died, and I lost my job. Did you know that in 1914, at Taliesin, one of Wright's cooks went mad and took a pickaxe to Mamah Borthwick, Wright's live-in lover, and also to her children, along with four other people, including a couple of Wright's draftsmen, people like me, killing seven in total and then burning down half the main house? Reading about this, I was put in mind of what we used to claim we wanted to do to the Mexican literary establishment, not that we'd ever have gone beyond pouring a drink on Octavio Paz's tie at Huerta's house, you might remember that was me, though now that I think of it, you weren't there that night; it was when you and Beatriz were having a little fling, so maybe she was sucking your dick in the shitter of some pulquería in Guadalupe Tepeyac, on 27 Calle Samuel, or something. Anyway, Taliesin is fine for now, at least enough for tourists to come and go, genius Modernism crumbling, foundations sinking, ceilings leaking, everything decaying, crows cawing in the trees and on the roof and in the sky. Like all vanguard dreams, by and by.

And you know, speaking of pickaxes and the arts, it only occurs to me now, as I write this about Frank Lloyd Wright's home, that Stalin's only daughter, Svetlana Alliluyeva, ended up in Spring Green, Wisconsin, in the late 1960s, unofficially adopted by Wright's wife after Mamah, the mad, Theosophical zealot Olgivanna, and there Svetlana still is, in Spring Green, the daughter of Stalin himself, in this quaint U.S. small town, pretty much forgotten, growing old and unhappy. And to think that the daughter of Stalin has that intimate relationship with a placid, rural U.S. place where the first companion and lover of the father of architectural modernism was murdered by pick-axe, while we, the messengers of revolutionary, anti-Stalinist culture in crazy-urban Mexico D.F. had an intimate relationship with Verónica Volkow, the great-granddaughter of Leon Trotsky himself, who was pickaxed in Mexico by Svetlana's daddy, Josef. I mean, it's an odd crossing of historical happenstance, don't you think? Or maybe I'm just creating my own coincidences, like this Spanish writer, Enrique Vila-Matas does, whom maybe you've met, since he's from Barcelona. Or like Paul Auster does. Or W.G. Sebald. Or you. All writers obsessed by hidden ghosts of chance, a kind of contemporary neo-Theosophical school, you could say, or a neo-Jungian Synchronicity school, not that you're the only ones. I'd include myself, except no one wants to publish me. But I know where you're coming from. Spookiness is a way of giving sense to the absurdity of life: We're on the watch for coincidences and we grab and frame them when they visit us, like they're these special messages from another realm that might promise something above ours, when this one, we know deep down, is the only one there is, with Littlewood's Law attached.

But no, forgive my sense of humor, really. Here we are in 1999, and we're all grown up, and you're the toast of the Latin American Literary World, published by Anagrama, winner of the Herralde Prize, no doubt soon to be translated into English and published by the leading houses of the Imperium. Could you please look for my manuscript, Bolaño? It's both a fiction and a real history of the days in D.F. when we were young and poor and happy, and you and Mario and Bruno are in it, and everyone else, too, and everyone is crazy and full of life, just as life was once so full of us. It's like six-hundred pages long, so if it ever got to you (I mailed it in three separate packages, again, ca. 1987, after I recovered from my suicide attempt), you should be able to spot it. I know you read it.

Alright, but seriously, and sorry for my Phillip K. Dick dark streak, but now to Nadal, about whom you ask, and from the matter of whom I seem to have taken a little digression. I was with him some, yes, back in '78, I guess it was, and '79. He was becoming popular with a faction of the group, which expanded after you and Santiago and Montané took off (thanks for all the goodbyes!), though most of these new kids were more of the fellow-traveling type, UNAM-types, mommy and daddy bourgeois runaways, pretend drug addicts, a few poets who couldn't make it in the Anábasis circle, etc. A couple dozen or so, added to the twenty-some originals, and these kids would come and go, split and coagulate amoeba-like, and a lot of these kids started to hang around and follow Nadal, who would sit there at La Habana, pontificating like he was Desnos channeling Sor Juana, or something. And these kids, plus a few from the old gang even, like Ramón and Mara and Jorge would attend to him, ply him with grappa, and he'd go off with a monologue on whatever. Carlos Pilsen and his friends from the Architecture Department were also among his fans. Nadal and Harrington were the main figures of this faction, though it wasn't programmatic or announced as such.

But most of the old gang were close to Mario, who'd come back, unlike you, and that would have been the other tendency, not that people weren't still mingling as always. Harrington and Nadal were promoting a neo-Surrealist revival of Desnos-like dream-state writing (or drunken-stoned-state automatism might be more accurate) and for Mario and some of the old guard this represented a kind of recycled, exhausted aestheticism, not least because Desnos was deemed a traitor to Surrealism and socialist-revolutionary ideals, as upheld by Breton and Péret and Éluard, all of whom Santiago revered, though I guess Éluard ended up with the Stalinists. Nadal and Carla and Pascoe organized a reading and talk series at Librería Sótano, and that was quite popular for a while, and everyone attended those, regardless of existing or incipient divergences, though I remember that once Santiago got into Nadal's face, a sort of hazy memory, admittedly.

Anyway, I hung out a bit with Nadal, and the funny thing was, when I was with him, he wasn't at all the same sort of guy as he was in his oracle mode, even when he was drunk. He was pretty quiet, self-effacing, melancholic, socially anxious even, in more intimate settings. It was almost schizophrenic, really. We'd talked about starting a new magazine, but it never got any-where, and when I moved to Jalisco we kept in touch, sending each other poems every once in a while, and we hooked up in the early days of email in Mexico, somewhere in '95, it would have been, when he was in Arizona. He'd write these long, weird things, essays more than letters. But I haven't heard from him in three years now—the last few emails I sent went unanswered and I asked a couple people in D.F if they knew where he was, but they'd been out of touch with him longer than I had, so I just accepted the mystery. The ones here are the last I had from him, in September and October '99, when he was writing from Austria, or Slovenia, I've lost track.

So I thought I'd send you these two, which I still have after I lost most of my files about a year ago. The one on your com-patriot Cáceres you'll probably find especially interesting, you surely know of him. I think Nadal was planning to write a book about him, or so I think he'd said in a later mail. Maybe you can do it (it would make for a great poetry detective story), given that Nadal seems to have fallen off the world. Of course, it's entirely possible he's dead, too. His health habits were not the greatest. Unlike the rest of us, ahem.

OK, Bolaño, here you go—two long letters from Nadal. Thanks for getting back in touch with a Nobody like me, which was so thoughtful of you, now that you have made it big by using the rest of us as background fodder for your picaresque epic. I hope your chest is swelled with it, comrade. Swelled with pride, I mean.

Solidarity,

Pepe

❆

e-mail from Vladimir Nadal to José Requena
Dear Pepe:
According to Volodia Teitleboim's faintly remembered telling, a thin, tallish man, seeming to be in his late twenties, had suddenly appeared at the café where the editors and a few other notables had sat down to begin planning the *Poesía nueva chilena* anthology. This would have been in early 1934. The unannounced visitor quickly handed Teitleboim a single handwritten poem, bowed in adieu, and disappeared without a word. Stunned by the originality of the text he had left them, Anguita and Teitleboim somehow contacted the ghostly figure, via an intermediary, to request more poems. The whole thing is a complex of sentiments, with its association of politeness and mischief, of humility and action. At the prearranged and secret time, as they waited on a busy Santiago corner, the same gaunt, pale man walked up to them "with utmost elegance of gait," passed off a large envelope, and without breaking stride, vanished into the crowd of passersby.

They were blown away by his work. And it seems that when his poems were published in the anthology, the editors had no idea they had appeared a year earlier in Cáceres's only book, the fifteen-poem *Defensa del Idolo* (*Defense of the Idol*), the entire edition of which an enraged Cáceres (this is known) stacked in a pyramid on his patio, doused with kerosene, and burned to ashes the day it was delivered to him. Margaret is orange; William a fresh pale blue. Three copies are believed to have survived.

Save that he hailed from the northern desert town of Arica,

virtually nothing at all is known of his biography; only one image, a pencil sketch, had been known to exist, drawn from an obscure artist's memory, perhaps dream, of a glimpse he'd had of the poet.

There was rumor (though most had discounted the picturesque story as apocryphal) that he earned his living as a violinist in an itinerant band of blind musicians, he being its only sighted member. Other gossip had it that he was a member of the Rosicrucian Order, and that he traveled to Peru, now and then, to receive instruction at its Latin American headquarters in Cuzco.

Rumors also began to circulate that Neruda, de Rokha, and Huidobro had been seen on two occasions, as a group, visiting his cinder-block house. There is a sign of violence in all these figures, in which an over-excited creature emerges from a lifeless shell. And it was said (later verified) that de Rokha had been engaged to his sister in the year before *Defense of the Idol* was published, the engagement broken off, in unexplained Kierkegaardian fashion, shortly after the book's publication and mass immolation. Here is one of Cáceres's poems.

MANSION OF FOAM

With my heart, beating you, oh unbounded shadow,
I graze the total zest of these eternal-images;
escaping his life, I think, he who flees cleans the world,
and thus is allowed to reflect his sweetly earthly likeness.
    A village (Blue), laboriously flooded.
The hard season will come balancing its landscapes.
Time fallen from the trees, whatever sky could be my sky.
The white road crosses its motionless storm.
    Speechless voice that lives under my dreams,
my friend instructs me in the naked accent of her arms,
beside the balcony of disciplined light tumultuous,
from where one is warned of still-undreamed misfortune.
    Dressed again in distance, between man and meager-man,

everything is wrecked 'under the banner of the final adieu';
I gave up existing, I soon fell abandoned by myself,
for a man loves only his own, obscure life.
   Unknown idol. What must I do to give it a kiss?
Legislator of urban time, unfolded, rushing, copious,
I confess my crime against myself because I want to understand it,
and on the reefs of its rock alcohol I spread out my words.

Now, a truly remarkable piece of Cáceres's story is that a brief essay, signed by Vicente Huidobro, appears as introduction to *Defense of the Idol*. The preface for the unknown poet stands as the *only* introduction Huidobro ever penned for another author—despite the fact that writers of international repute often approached the famous man to request his endorsement. This would be odd enough… But in June, 1935, shortly following the appearance of *Anthology of New Chilean Poetry*, a rhetorically violent exchange broke out in the pages of the national daily *La Opinión* between de Rokha and Huidobro, over matters pertaining to the anthology (de Rokha claiming, for one, that Huidobro had influenced the editors to keep the former's young bride, Winétt de Rokha, out of the book), which quickly devolved into a venomous outpouring of insults and threats on both sides, ostensibly over who had really been the first to be asked by the unknown Cáceres to introduce *Defense of the Idol*, a book only *they* seemed to have known about at the time. (de Rokha claimed Huidobro had forced the suppression of his already-written preface in favor of Huidobro's own; Huidobro suggested de Rokha stick his envy up his arse and go back to raising chickens.) North, South, East, or West, does the dream of the avant-garde always end in a nocturne, pounded out on a grand piano?
   Then, as suddenly as the vicious fight had erupted, it stopped. Cáceres never said a word, which is unsurprising, to be sure, since no one apparently ever spoke with him, save for half-recalled anecdotes of fugitive encounters. In any case, Huidobro

and de Rokha were soon seen, and often, drinking and chatting amiably with each other at bohemian cafes, as if nothing had ever happened…

And so everyone forgot about Cáceres, until some seven years later, when in September, 1943, a small, out of focus photograph, resembling nothing of the person in the putative sketch, appeared over a brief obituary in *El Mercurio*, two weeks, or so, after the deceased's body had been found. It had taken some time for the authorities to identify the bloated cadaver. Logicians draw circles that overlap or exclude, and all their rules immediately become clear. Cáceres had been murdered and dumped into the Mapocho, the great sewer river that traverses the city—murdered, as someone else put it, on a date that is unknown, by assailants unknown, for reasons unknown…

And then everyone more or less forgot about him again, until Pedro Lastra, the fine Chilean scholar, working from the single copy held by the National Library in Santiago, published a scholarly edition of *Defense of the Idol* (Ediciones LOM) in 1996, almost immediately establishing Cáceres as one of Chile's greatest poets of the century, which is saying a lot, given my country's magnificent literary history.

In September, 1997, right before I went to Europe, I wrote to Lastra, and asked, in part, the following:

Dear Mr. Lastra:

[…]

First of all, it's fascinating that Cáceres was such a furtive, spectral figure during his life, and we *[it is not clear why Nadal would have used the plural here. R.B.]* wanted to ask you something that we realize may seem a bit silly to you, but we ask you directly, in any case. And we ask in spirit of Volodia Teitleboim's words in your edition of *Defense of the Idol*: "It is up to the Sherlock Holmes's of today, or of the third millennium, to unravel the case of Omar Cáceres."

And though we are hardly Holmeses, we have been wondering: Is the authorial existence of Cáceres a sure thing, or do you believe there may be at least *some* possibility that Cáceres "the poet" was the invention of another? That is, we ask if it's possible that a man named "Omar Cáceres" did exist (this seems to have been the case), whose name and identity were appropriated by another Chilean poet (or poets) in a species of heteronymity. Is this possible, in your view? For instance, it seems very curious to us that Pablo de Rokha apparently almost married Cáceres's sister in the year before *Defense of the Idol* was published, and that he and Huidobro should have had such a ferocious public debate over the introduction to Cáceres's book before anyone had really heard of it, or its "author." Is it possible (and forgive us if our hypothesis is at this moment causing you to chuckle) that the poems of Cáceres were in fact authored by the often-pseudonymous de Rokha (possibly in a collaboration with Huidobro)? Is it possible that the man-ghost who so timidly and momentarily appeared here and there was a man named Omar Cáceres, who (under instructions of another) played the role of Poet for a time, but who regretted having done so in the end, even perhaps felt deep shame for having done so, destroying in an act of rage and humiliation the book that (possibly without his knowledge) had been falsely published under his name?

Of course these questions are likely products of our over-active imaginations. However, the extravagant hypothesis seems to have at least a measure of merit in face of what seems to us something no less fantastical: Cáceres's "biography," such as it is— sophisticated vanguardist poet seemingly emerged from the void, bizarrely evanescent and known by virtually no one, reputed Rosicrucian, violinist in a band of blind musicians, etc.

[...]

Two years went by without reply. On August 29, the intact remains of the magician and alpinist Leticio Machado, missing since summer 1914, had been released by the Santa Concepción glacier, ninety years later. On September 27, the same date as that of my initial letter (and the same date, I later discovered, as the appearance of Cáceres's obituary in *El Mercurio*!), I received a long e-mail from Lastra, in which he stated his strong belief that Cáceres did in fact exist, that there were scant but legal documents that confirmed his existence, that there were those who did remember seeing him, had memory of exchanging words with him, however fleeting… and pledging to assist us in any further research or translation we might undertake of the poet's work.

I wrote back, reiterating that I did not doubt that an "Omar Cáceres" once existed. But, I asked, once more, Is it possible that he was a stand-in for de Rokha, who would have known him through his courtship of Cáceres's sister? After all, I said, it is well-known that de Rokha wrote a good portion of his work under various assumed identities, a kind of Chilean Pessoa. Would it not be possible that he adopted Cáceres as another one, possibly in collaborative consort with Huidobro (their theatrical public debate having been, in that case, a clever smoke-screen)? Who, for instance, can distinguish between the russet and the blond cuckoo?

I did not hear back from Mr. Lastra after this letter… I *did* hear from the great poet Cecilia Vicuña, whom I'd also queried, and who told me that her very elderly father, a member of Neruda's circle in the 30s and 40s, seemed to recall seeing Cáceres here and there, that he'd struck him then as a bit of a "maricón" (a queer).

And then, lo and behold, some several months back, I received, from the prominent Chilean poet and fiction writer Antonio Gil (who at a conference in Berlin not long before had regaled me with much gossip concerning the Cáceres affair, including the scandalous and no doubt false story that Communist Party goons at behest of de Rokha—a CP leader—had murdered Cáceres to keep him quiet) an astonishing email. And this email, a forwarded announcement from one of Chile's best-known antiquarian book dealers, César Soto Gómez, states that a box with thirteen folders had miraculously come to light, containing materials belonging to... yes, the poet Omar Cáceres. Among the materials therein, according to Gómez, were the following:

1) The original typescript of *Defense of the Idol*

2) Various unknown poems in draft form, holograph and typescript, including a notebook of juvenilia

3) A complete typed manuscript of poems, dated 1943, titled *Allegations before the Unknown*

4) Various carbon copies of letters addressed to the Supreme Temple of the Rosicrucian Order (AMORC) for North and South America in San Jose, California

5) Around a dozen visual pieces, mostly sketch drawings, but including a stunning, if faded, photograph of the poet in his late twenties, or so

6) Two notebooks of musical annotation, within which are mentioned composers like Aretino, Beethoven, Bellini, Glück, Handel, Haydn, Mozart, Mendelssohn, and Villa-Lobos.

7) The typewritten copy (with many emphatic erasures and corrections in pencil) of the suppressed Introduction for *Defense of the Idol*, written by Pablo de Rokha

8) Various musical scores of traditional tunes played by traveling folk orchestras in Chile

9) An empty violin case, receipt of 1928 purchase enclosed

10) A complete translation into Spanish, in holograph, of Jules Supervielle's 1925 novella *El hombre de las pampas*, into which Cáceres has inserted sentences to follow every one of Supervielle's, thus creating both a translation of the book as well as a brand new para-novella

11) Two carbon copies of letters to T.S. Eliot, written in 1941

I have contacted a number of Chilean poets, and I am satisfied that these discovered materials are genuine—that a man-ghost poet named Omar Cáceres really did exist, spectacular-ly unlikely as his existence may have been. Chests, especially small caskets, over which we have mastery, are objects that may be opened. Whether he was killed for his simple violin, or for esoteric motives by agents of the Rosicrucian Order is still to be determined. But that his dark, shimmering figure stands as one of the great enigmas of Western poetry, of any era, is unarguable.

Now, I had said I had something "unbelievable" to share with you. And it is this, the first of Cáceres's letters to T.S. Eliot, a Xerox of the carbon which was sent to me through the kindness of the book dealer in Santiago. The letter is dated August 1, 1943, about a month before the poet's body was found, washed up among garbage, in the Mapocho. *[The copy, regrettably, is not contained in the manuscript handed down from Mosconi. A.B.]*

Esteemed Brother, Mr. Thomas Strearns *[sic]* Eliot,

Our mutual friend and Brother of our High Order, Vicente Huidobro, has encouraged me to write to you. He has told me you are generous enough to not mind if I direct myself to you in my language; it is my failing to have never learned English.

It is a very special occasion for me to write this letter, since I have admired your poetry deeply, in various and widely discussed translations done by Mr. Huidobro, Mr. Rosamel del Valle (also our fellow Brother), and Mr. Pablo Neruda. For me, poems such as Prufrock, The Waste Land, and Ash-Wednesday are unquestionably among the greatest accomplishments of our century and shall remain so.

My work is decidedly modest in comparison. And I do understand that your many obligations will perhaps not permit a response to someone like me. I offer these enclosed poems, then, with a serene humility; should it happen that you would find time to remark on them with only a few words, I will be always grateful.

Some of these poems were published in *Anthology of New Chilean Poetry*, 1935, edited by Eduardo Anguita and Volodia Teitleboim. A few others were printed in my book, *Defense of the Idol*, which was published in 1934. Unfortunately, I was compelled to immediately destroy the edition, given the surfeit of embarrassing errata made by the printer.

The long dramatic poem here, *Conversation with the Chevalier* [the poem is apparently lost, VN], is unpublished. It is my latest poem, and it is one I know is influenced profoundly by your own work. Perhaps you will sense this.

Brother Eliot, I do not write, as I said to Brother Huidobro one day, "driven by ambition to make Literature," which is what almost all poets in my country are driven by, but rather as servant of impulses I feel come from beyond my station and control; I aim to obey, that is, a need to express the truths of my "I" in time and space as these are defined for me, beyond my Self. A new ethical and aesthetic modality must achieve, necessarily, something rooted in a TRUTH that has nothing to do with mere self-expression. Or with the "truth" of a "biographical" self we are told defines our horizons… As Hölderlin says: "For when I heard that one of the near islands was Patmos, I greatly desired there to be lodged, and there to approach the dark grotto." *[sic]*

I do not claim, in any way, to have achieved such a sovereign goal. But my hope is fully consonant, I humbly feel, with your profound thoughts on the poetics of Impersonality. (The avant-garde poets in my country, Brother Eliot, have way too much personality, even as they try to hide and deny it. They all want (I except the great poet

Vicente Huidobro) to be heroes and screen stars, frankly. They all want to be the next Rubén Darío, festooned with institutional honors. They are in service not to Poetry, but to a foul carapace of this world, accreted around it.)

But I will not take any more of your time.

Please accept my most sincere respect and gratitude for your work. I enclose my humble poems.

With warmest wishes, and in Everlasting Holy Fraternity,

[signed] Omar Cáceres

Discovered photograph of Omar Cáceres

(Hi Bolaño, me again, Pepe the pop-up. So here's the second email, which came about two months later. In between, I recall, there were two others, both very long, one about the mad Nicaraguan poet Alfonso Cortés, and the other on the Uruguayan Marosa Di Giorgio, lost with most else in my file accident. As with Nadal's other emails on writers (collected, they could have been a great book on Latin American *raros*) it begins in media res, without the expected introductions.)

Dear Pepe:

Coincidentally or portentously enough, Carlos Oquendo de Amat went down to the sea in ship, for in his mid-twenties, young Secretary of the Communist Party in Arequipa, he fled his country to Spain, where he died under unknown circumstances, in 1936, aged 29, in the first month of the civil war there. His single book was published in Lima, in 1927, when he was 21. *5 metros de poemas* (*5 Meters of Poems*) has long been a classic of Latin American avant-garde poetry: It isn't bound at the spine, but pulls out, accordion like, stretching to a little under five meters, revealing texts laid out in decidedly quirky typography, whose clear inspiration is Mallarmé and Apollinaire. Of course, only the dreamer who curls up in contemplation of loops understands these simple joys of delineated repose. The few surviving original copies sell for several thousands, now, in the book trade.

Here is one of its poems:

G   a   r   d   e   n

Trees tincture

                     the shade of gowns

Roses will flee
Their stems
Child spilling water from his eyes

And, far corner

THE MOON SHALL SWELL LIKE A PLANT

What is known of de Amat is extremely sparse and largely anecdotal. He is a spectre: His well-off and bohemia-connected parents provided him with a fine homeschooled education, during which time he met leading figures and fellow travelers of the Creacionista and Ultraísta movements, like Vicente Huidobro, Jorge Luis Borges, César Vallejo, the great Marxist leader José Carlos Mariátegui, and (if the story is not apocryphal) a poet even more enigmatic than he, "Omar Cáceres"—avant-garde writers who had set out to confront the played-out *Modernismo* of Rubén Darío and company, in much the same way, and at roughly the same time, as the Anglo-American Modernists were confronting the staid literature of a burned-out Romanticism. Now, a vaporous ether overspreads a broad dormant sheet of melody.

In any case, apart from a few pieces in Peruvian journals, later gathered in *5 Meters of Poems*, his only other published work is an essay entitled "New Literary Criticism," published in 1926, in the magazine *Rascacielos (Skyscraper)*, which in its entirety reads: "Carlos Oquendo de Amat is a fucking loser. (signed) Carlos Oquendo de Amat."

Today, the ghostly de Amat is revered by large numbers of younger Peruvian poets and artists as something of a saint (there was a short-lived Lima journal, published by an Hora Zero split-off, titled *Santo Amat*), and every year, on the date of his birth, verses of his poems are written out on 50 or (on one spectacular occasion) 500-meter banners, and unfolded across the hills of Lima, Cuzco, and Arequipa, to much declamation, drinking, marijuana smoking, and indigenous music, the human reminded of its animal ancestry, the body. The blurred image of his handsome visage is pasted up on walls and utility poles, as if he were a candidate for high office.

Photo of Carlos Oquendo de Amat

Amazingly, his only extant unpublished writings (with exception of his notational entries into the Arequipa Communist Party branch finance ledger) are four holograph letters in English, recently found in the archives of the poet E.E. Cummings. There appear to be earlier, now lost, letters, and no letters from Cummings to de Amat have been found, so the originating circumstances of their correspondence remain a mystery. A passage from one, dated August 30, 1935, Madrid, reads as follows—your English is sterling, so de Amat's ungrammatical elements are left largely unnoted, save in a couple instances where clarification seems necessary:

[Dear Mr. Cummings:]
[following polite greetings; questions after Cum-

mings's health and recent travels; description of de Amat's current lodgings in Spain (not very good); national communist politics having to do with the Trotskyist *Izquierda Comunista de España*, to which, he tells Cummings, he feels increasingly drawn; gossip about scandalous doings between Federico García Lorca and Salvador Dalí; and commentary on recent writings contra Aragon by André Breton]

...And in this measure, Mr. Cummings, I am in the most full agreements with Breton, for Poetry can never, never be contained by any ideological system, it does not import if that system is of political or poetical. To the marrow of the case: Poetry exists to leap over the contingent fencings of ideology—not to leave ideology as inferior to it or to laugh at it or to menospreciate it [de Amat means something like "hold it in contempt"]. Ideology is as real as rocks or sky; we walk in it, even touch it, can also make useful objects out of it, in its critical reflection, like democratic centralist revolutionary organizations. But poetry exists, as I said, to leap over all fencings—to so then stand there, regally, for a long time, even as it perishes in utter injustice and slow surprise: What manner of theatre is it, in which we are at once playwright, actor, stage manager, scene painter, and audience? Astonished ibis on fire, in the barren field...

[...]

Of course, this is what Marx says in the *Economic and Philosophic Manuscripts of 1844*. He, also, is at his loss concerning Art and Poetry. Where does it come from? And in a manner it is a question of Being. It is a social practicum, yes, and elements of the superstructure, but yet it escapes in deep ways the historical conditionings of the usual social practicums. Not even for his [him] can their sphere be reduced to historical system: Art, Poetry,

are strange, precisely because they can not be systemat-
icized. Which of course is what I sometimes fear is the
fate of the Vanguard of my continent (in least, [at least in
the] Andean region!), already turning the principles of
Ultraísmo, for an example, into dogma (and you are right,
Mr. Cummings, that these principles, in their first declaration by Borges, were very, very similar to Pound's Imagism, nevertheless dissimilar in applications)—too much
certitude, theoretizationing, exclusionness, suppression
of the past, and more than these. It is a turning of Poetry
into systematicization (is this a correct word? I mean as
is made into an ideology, a dogma that clenches up the
imagination like a fist, etc.)).

Ah! Pretty soon we shall have technical workshops in
the how to write proper poems! Vanguard poems, their
proprieties taught at Universities of Higher Learning! All
younger poets to render homages in their fashionable
clothings!

Well, forgive my enthusiastic and fantastical futur-
isms. It is likely a result of my boredoms and lassitudes,
here in the heated summer of Madrid. Which is presently
most oppressive.

[letter closes with a restatement of thanks for Cummings's
previous reply; a polite request that he send new poems in
his next; a question about recent activities of Ezra Pound, T.S.
Eliot, and Archibald MacLeish; and a fervent wish that a personal meeting might one day be possible between de Amat
and Cummings.]

❋❋

Letter from Luis Barrios
Hi Roberto,
Yes, I certainly do remember Nadal. He'd been hanging

around the Infra margins, you'll recall, more tagging along back in the heroic years—I think it was Harrington who'd first brought him around. After you and Santiago and Montané took off in '77, he was much more present for a period, and even became a kind of organizing figure around whom some of the younger kids started to gravitate. After Harrington left in October of '77 to hunt down you and Bruno in Spain, his prominence on the scene grew. He'd be at Café Habana almost every day, and often at the Bar Nivel, by the Zócalo, at night, or else the Pizzeria del Gringo, or the Cantina, holding court, giving spontaneous mini-lectures on various things, or reciting texts from memory, and he had a frightening one, photographic, for sure. Maybe the ones that seemed spontaneous weren't so spontaneous, some people thought it was all canned. He'd spout off after he'd had a few, and people would try to get him juiced up and prod him into letting loose. It could be very impressive when he was on, and sometimes he'd take off on riffs about Greek prosody or the New American poetry or the Russian Formalists with this oracular tone, at the top of his voice, his eyes rolled back into his head, and there might be thirty people around his table, cheering him on, in the way they imagined Kerouac cheering on Ginsberg at the Six Gallery. You could say he was starting to sort of assume your mantle for the Infra second generation, and after you left, for around a year, there was this burst of activity and fresh faces at the bars and at a reading series at Librería Sótano and Librería Ghandi that Nadal and Carla Rippey organized shortly after Nadal moved in with her and Ricardo Pascoe, which led to us jokingly calling them "Vladimir and the Gringo Briks." And the series at the Sótano lasted for maybe three events, because then the owner realized people were stealing books right and left, and so it moved to Librería Ghandi, where it was harder to steal books, and went for maybe nine more readings. Veronica Volkow, José Luis Rivas, Francisco Segovia, Carmen Boullosa, and Rubén Medina all read in the series, I think, though my memory is fuzzy, even Mara Larrosa read there once, totally terror-stricken, as cool as she was otherwise, and she started sobbing in the middle of her reading, and Darío Galicia had to come up and finish reading for her, it was quite something. Juan Pascoe would MC, usually, and there would be music at intermission—once Chavela Vargas actually showed up, and she was totally tanked and she just kept going, and so someone never got to read, which was OK— it might have been Jaime Sabines, because I remember she got him up there to sing with her, though why Jaime Sabines would have been invited, I have no idea. Considering this would have been late 1977, that might have been Chavela's last performance before she went into rehab and vanished for fifteen years. But the series was a big hit—it was called *Martín el Pescado*, which was pretty clever, and the place was always jammed, every reading. And then everyone would go out, of course, somewhere on Bucareli or around the Zócalo, and invariably Nadal would be the center of attention, and off he'd go, plastered, on one of his automatic talking sprees, his eyes rolled back, and everyone would start clapping and chanting NA-DAL, NA-DAL, NA-DAL, and GO! GO! GO! like Kerouac waving his wine bottle in 1955.

One day Nadal and Carla had a big fight at a party at Efraín's place, though no one could figure out what about, and of course the rumors started flying, and so that was the end of the reading series, because both Pascoes broke things off with Nadal, too, I'm pretty sure, and people started to sort of choose sides, even though there was no reason to, because there were, apparently, no reasons of any substance involved, save the rumors about an affair, which I doubt, because I'm pretty sure Nadal was gay, though then again, I suppose that wouldn't have meant much anyway, in our circle, except to maybe Luscious Skin or Galicia.

And right around that time, in '78, was when Mario came back from Europe, and he threw himself into the movement again, trying to get people connected, fired up, reminding them of the original manifesto, by which he meant *his*, I'm afraid, not *yours*. And Nadal must have seen that his little moment as the second-generation Breton was over, or at least seen that nothing was to be gained by being in competition with Mario, especially since Mario made it clear one day at some bar in Guadalupe Tepeyac that he was going to beat the living shit out of Nadal if he ever saw his poetaster face again, or so Verónica Morelos told me, who'd heard it from Vera Larrosa, so that maybe makes it apocryphal. And then shortly after that, around early 1980, I guess, Nadal was gone, and no one really knew where to or why, sort of like you in '77.

But here's the main thing: It turns out that Clara Lustero started taping Nadal's soliloquies back in the day, though I don't know if he was aware he was being taped or not. And in 1981 she and I lived together in Veracruz for a few months, which was hell, and when she left I found a couple of the tapes, and so getting your letter, and because I don't have a social life, I went ahead and transcribed a few of them at random. They're not the best stuff he did, from what I can recall, though the "Leyenda del Sol" piece is pretty cool—I think Nadal was studying Meso-american literature with Miguel León-Portilla at UNAM at the time, so that's from where that one more or less comes. Anyway, they'll give you an idea. I've been faithful; there's almost no ed-iting. There are no dates nor indications of place, but in the one on poetry and sculpture you can hear Efraín and Damián laugh-ing in the background, singing a ranchera. Unmistakably them, though it would have been rare to have Damián around back in those days, pissed off as he was, and who could have blamed him, that was pretty cold of you and Mario... For the one on American poets, I only transcribed the first five stanzas and ran out of steam—it's about three times as long, a true tour de force of spontaneous recitation. Or else a true feat of mnemonics.

Take care. The transcribed performances by Nadal follow.

Luis

[Performance I]

Here, on the night of 16th July, 1979, I, Vladimir Nadal, at Café La Habana, in Mexico City, surrounded by friends, enemies, and indifferent ones, wish to present my thought about the differences between poetry and prose, though these differences must remain speculative, even if it sounds like we—by which I mean you, my friends and enemies, and indifferent ones—are certain of what we propose. I speak, as my comrades can attest, with no notes or aid of books or anything of the sort to prompt my memory. It is only mescal that aids me tonight, as it does, these days, on most nights, when I am with my friends, enemies, or indifferent ones... Do I repeat myself?

Therefore, when considering the difference between poetry and prose, the following thought will occur to us: Whereas in prose it often does happen that writers come from the blue, presenting from their heads without warning remarkable works of prose that make their authors suddenly successful artists, as if they'd been dropped from the sky like packages of accomplishment, express delivered by some callous god who is heedless of the feelings of all those who have labored away at writing for years without recompense of any kind, thus inciting acute shocks of resentment and despair among these—they who have never known any success except the pathetic frisson of journal [inaudible], or the nomination for some ridiculous prize, but whose very identity and reasons for living depend, like ours, on a Literary Self-Identification—well, as opposed to that, as I was saying, it is, as we'll see, a very different case with poetry. For such upstart, unsuspected irruptions of unknown poets emerging with precipitous glory (as is so often the case with prose) rarely, very rarely happen in the poetry field. And this of course leads us to ask why the difference should be so; it leads us to wonder if perhaps fiction may be a lesser, simpler art than the art of poetry, requiring a lesser degree of predisposition or gift; it leads us to wonder if it is a more pedestrian pursuit, that is, something that anyone with a modicum of intelligence and a pencil or typewriter [inaudible]. As opposed to accomplished poetry, that is, which no Roberto Bolaño or Juana Ramírez can come along and just toss off by any stretch of the imagination, though all that's required there, as well, is a pencil or typewriter, to be sure, but it's not guns that kill people, people kill people, as they say, if that makes any sense.

So as we consider this, perhaps [inaudible] with the notion that the poetic path we have chosen makes us elect and of a special breed, another thought, an obvious one, should dawn upon us. And it is, in all its simplicity, that the art of prose has manifold more readers than does poetry, and so thus it is natural that among those vastly greater numbers the predisposition to turn from reader to author should be fulfilled many more times in prose than it is in the art of poetry, whose readers are, in any case, its writers, nearly exclusively, who write for the pleasure and admiration of their fellow poets, and who, of course, are no strangers to the darkness of envy, but who very rarely are made to suffer it by sudden, untrained upstarts who appear, full-blown out of nowhere, as in prose. And so it is that poets will rarely have to suffer the afflictions of resentment and shame that so often oppress the mid to lower levels of the field of fiction and non-fiction. The vast numbers of mediocre or bad poets are spared the humiliating, killing pain and shame which writers of fiction must so often bear. For the hierarchy is almost never broken in sudden ways in poetry. Its caste system is relatively impervious to major eruptions and disruptions. And it may teach [inaudible] that our curse of neglect, the isolation and disregard we suffer from those who are not like us, which is to say from normal human beings, is a blessing with which the fantasies of our self-esteem should not tamper.

[Performance II]

Here, on the night of 2 August, 1979, a brief statement, by me, Vladimir Nadal, at Café La Habana, in Mexico City. I will speak about poetry and sculpture, as it occurs to me. I ask the gods for inspiration now, surrounded by friends, enemies, and indifferent ones. I speak, as they can attest, with no notes or aid of books or anything of the sort to prompt my memory. It is only mescal that aids me tonight, as it does, these days, on most nights, when I am with my friends, enemies, or indifferent ones…

We all know the great saying of Michelangelo, about the nature of sculpture in its original, classical impulse: that its praxis simply frees the yearning form that is trapped inside the imprisoning stone. How strange that this insight—and that is the word, no?—should not just as naturally apply to writing, or at least to that writing which partakes of writing's most original, classical impulse! For it is perhaps writing's purest path to take the stone of another text and release the form that is hidden within it! And just as in sculpture, this must be done by subtraction, not construction; for construction creates something in addition, which is banal, false, and of the mimetic, secondary order of representation, whether the form constructed be realist or abstract. That which is True goes by subtraction and, defying logic, by means of Deceit—though it is a higher, purer variety— [extended inaudible section] to create a falsehood (be this, again, mimetic or abstract in form) that brings us nearer the Truth. Fuck Plato. Only second-hand composition that chisels away at the eternal stone of Writing can truly be called Literature! The rest is interior decorating, or perhaps gardening. That is all I have to say tonight. Where's Mayra?

✳

[Performance III]

Here, on the night of 12th August 1979, a poem from my head, by way of our great Nahuatl ancestors, who were spoken through, in turn, by their gods. It is from me, Vladimir Nadal, at Café La Habana, in Mexico City, surrounded by friends, enemies, and indifferent ones. I speak, as they can attest, with no notes or aid of books or anything of the sort to prompt my memory. It is only mescal that aids me tonight, as it does, these days, on most nights, when I am with my friends, enemies, or indifferent ones…

Here, from the old codices, is what is known of how, long ago, the earth was brought into being. One by one, here the various foundations. How it began, and in what form each sun was manifested 2513 years ago, from this date today, 22 of May, 1558. This sun, of calendar sign 4-Jaguar, lasted 676 years. Those who inhabited the earth beneath this first sun were consumed by jaguars in the time of the 4-Jaguar. And what they ate before they were eaten was the sustenance we ourselves know, named by its calendar sign 7-Grass. They lived 676 years. And the time in which they were consumed lasted 13 years. Thus they perished and everything vanished and then the sun imploded to a dark seed. And the year of this was 1-Cane. They began to be consumed on a day during 4-Jaguar and with this everything vanished and all perished.

This sun has the calendar name 4-Wind. These, who followed in the world, were carried away by the wind at the time of the sun 4-Wind and perished. They were battered by the wind; they became monkeys. Their houses, their trees, everything was battered by the wind and this sun was also carried away by the wind. And what they ate was the sustenance we ourselves know, what is named by the calendar sign 12-Serpent. The time in which they lived lasted 364 years. In this way they perished in only one day, carried off by the wind, in the sign 4-Wind they perished.

Their year was the calendar sign 1-Flint. This sun named 4-Rain was the third. Those who lived in that third age of the sun 4-Rain also perished, fire rained down on them. They became geese. And the sun also boiled, all their houses burned and they lived in this way for 312 years. They perished, for a whole day it rained fire. What they ate was the sustenance we know, what is known by its calendar sign 7-Flint. Their year was 1-Flint and their day 4-Rain. Those who perished were the ones who had become geese. Thus, their descendants are now called *pilpil-pilpil*.

This sun has the calendar 4-Water. The time of the water lasted 52 years. Those who lived in this fourth age were in the time of sun 4-Water. It lasted 676 years. That is how they perished. They were swallowed by the water and they became fish. The sky imploded in one day and they perished. What they ate was the sustenance we ourselves know, what is named by its calendar sign 4-Flower. Its year was 1-House and its sign 4-Water. They perished. Every mountain crumbled to seed-pebbles. The water was spread over the land 52 years and thus ended their years.

This sun has the calendar name 4-Movement. This is our sun, the one in which we now live. Here is its sign, how it fell into the furnace of the sun, into the sacred fire, over there in Teotihuacán. It is also the sun of our prince in Tula, of our father Quetzalcóatl. It is the fifth sun. 4-Movement is its calendar sign. It is named sun of *[inaudible]* because it moves, follows its way. And the old teachers say, in it there will be the movement of the earth, there will be hunger and heat and great drought and the land and the sea will bake and with this we shall perish.

❇

[Performance IV]
Here, on the night of 7th of September, 1979, a short histo-

ry of Gringo Poetry of the 20th century, by me, Vladimir Nadal, at Café La Habana, in Mexico City, surrounded by friends, enemies, and indifferent ones. I speak, as they can attest, with no notes or aid of books or anything of the sort to prompt my memory. It is only mescal that aids me tonight, as it does, these days, on most nights, when I am with my friends, enemies, or indifferent ones…

John Ashbery was born in 1924. The Thames at night in gold and blue changed to a harmony in gray, the color of the face of Monsiváis; a barge with hay of gold dropped from the wharf. But how could a barge have dropped from the wharf? And how is hay spun to gold? I want to win the Salvador Novo Prize. He is *teonanácatl* and in his verses is concealed the antipast, which is breve, longum, longum, breve. It hides like a hedgehog in a golden hay. It is Amado Nervo who speaks through me. He says: Poetry in general is like playing tennis with the net down.

Elizabeth Bishop was born in 1911. Down from the ceiling, by the picture-windowed edge, that in our modern villa, Savoy style, designed by Félix Candela in these hills, with vista to the darkened sea, with huge and black projection over-browed, large space beneath, our maid so dark did hang a lamp, designed by Niemeyer, bought in France, and all the peasants in delight did dance their dance, far out of sight. At Los Manantiales, in Xochimilco, I broke a bottle over a poet's head. I want to win the Cervantes Prize. But why were peasants in delight? And what is the sea doing in sight of our table at Los Manantiales? She is *ololiuhqui*, and in her verse is concealed the ionic a minore, which is breve, breve, longum, longum. It hides like a maid huddled under the black of a wharf. It is Ramón López Velarde who speaks through me. He says: To have great poets of the avant-garde, there must be great audiences of the bourgeoisie.

Robert Creeley was born in 1928. His hair was once black and glossy as the raven's and fell in strands across his brow. This was in the day of the workshop of Juan Bañuelos, at the UNAM.

This long pendulous hair is peculiar to those whose minds tend heavenward, that sea which is hidden from us by the darkened luster of our minds. As a student of William Carlos Williams, I whittled my stick to a walking cane, with a chicken head on the handle, and a trigger beneath and a barrel inside. I want to win the national Poesía Jóven Prize. But why should heaven be projected as a sea? He is *amoxcalli*, and in his verse is concealed the choriambus, which is longum, breve, breve, longum. It hides like a skull-lamp with a candle behind the eyes, which a maid hangs for our delight. She will stand in judgment of we. It is Manuel Carpio who speaks through me. He says: It is like ladling soup and a horse comes out.

Hilda Doolittle was born in 1889. I am not for criticizing electric fences and famished cattle. I flee the Zona Rosa in order to forget the Zona Rosa and all its apparatuses and whirligigs. There are those who for this purpose go to piss-scented saloons in La Peralvillo, to drink pulque and bear the weight of Empire on their backs. As the most famous woman Imagist, I like more elbowroom, a place without pinball machines and cars. I want to win the Punto de Partida Prize. But what are these cars doing inside the saloons? She is *chalchíuitl*, and in her verses is hidden the dochmiac, which is breve, breve, longum, breve, longum. It hides like a pinball machine behind a car in heaven. It is Manuel Acuña who speaks through me. He says: I could no more define poetry than Ezra Pound could define the consciousness of a bat.

T.S. Eliot was born in 1876. Nothing is so beautiful as the Casa del Lago in spring. Sometimes a marionette from Wiesbaden came out and smoked its cigarette on the steps that descended to the garden. There is a column of rippled jade on the Thames; the dim lines of a passing barge kindle into oily curls. The moon, worn like a shell, makes a sea-sound rasp in the ear, and dulls to Wiesbaden all we are. I wish I were a woman. And I want to win the Casa de las Américas Prize. But how does the moon make a sea-sound, and what are we doing, suddenly, in

England? He is *xochicalli*, and in his verses is hidden the paeon, which is longum, breve, breve, breve. It hides like a car on the moon. It is Efrén Rebolledo who speaks through me. He says: Poetry is an imaginary garden with real dead poets croaking in it.

❄❄

Letter from Sonia Rosas

Roberto, I just opened your email. I can't believe it's you! It was nice of Mara to give you my email address. She's such a sweetie, always thinking about others. I want to write a longer, proper letter to you soon. It has been ages, and I've often thought of you. Your name is on everyone's lips these days. I am happy for you! We all sort of dispersed after you and Mario left, but I hear that some people still stay in touch, like Juan Esteban, José, María Guadalupe, Ramón. Most of us gave up on our poetry. Or at least on the crazy dream of bringing down the literature institution, whatever that was or is. I think that's true, anyway. I was sort of on the outside (I'm surprised you remember me!) and never stayed much in touch with the others. Anyway, I should only speak for myself. I haven't written anything in ages, and the only poem I ever published (in *Anábasis*—when I was sleeping with one of that group, whom I will not name) will be seen by no one, because I doubt there's a single copy in existence anymore. I guess I'm one of the few people left in the country who read poetry and don't write it! But as I say, let me tell you more when I have time. I actually had a small stroke (at 33!) about ten years ago, but I have done well and am now quite active in my Pilates class, though people say my personality has changed in certain ways. I work as an assistant paralegal for a firm representing Pemex, and I've got this case report I have to type up for tomorrow (after my stroke, I type faster than anyone in D.F.). You can see how different my life is from those Infra days! I should probably apologize.

But to answer your question right away, however, so I don't keep you waiting. I didn't really know Nadal. From what I recall, he was Chilean (Peruvian?), a friend of Harrington's, or maybe of Catana's, so I suppose that's how he started to hang around La Habana. A quiet guy, from my faint memories. I think he was doing graduate work in indigenous literatures at UNAM. Did he write you? Why do you need to know about him? For a new novel, maybe? I'm curious, though you don't have to tell me!

As I say, I really pretty much dropped away in the year after you left and didn't stay in close touch with the gang. And anyway, Edgar Altamirano and Cuauhtémoc had more or less started a blacklisting campaign against me because I'd committed the sin of publishing that poem in *Anábasis*, which only happened because I happened to innocently give a copy to Carmen Boullosa, whom I was friendly with, and who was close to the guy I was sleeping with, and I didn't even know it was coming out, for goodness sake, I was as surprised as everyone, though I don't deny I was very proud of it. Plus, I wasn't the only one who was friendly with people in the *Anábasis* group (we all frequented the same spots and dressed the same! We wore huarachas, they wore huarachas; we carried backpacks; they carried backpacks), so it was really kind of unjust that I was singled out like that, don't you think?

I heard that Harrington sort of took charge for a while and that he was advocating a return to dream-state writing, like the Surrealists would do, in the twenties, Breton, Desnos, Duchamp, and so on. Apparently, he gathered a little following for a while, and Nadal, someone told me, was his righthand man. I heard, though, that things changed after Mario came back from Palestine, or wherever he was, and that some tensions developed, with a Santiago faction on the one hand, and a smaller Harrington/ Nadal faction (meeting mainly at the Bar Nivel, I think) on the other, with each of them claiming to be the true Infras. Mario was saying that unless we all went back and studied Revueltas and Hora Zero that we'd be lost. He called the Harrington/Nadal faction petit-bourgeois and "neo-Zanguanists," even. The Harringtonistas were starting to say that the Santiaguistas were cultists waiting for UFOs to beam them up to the great pulquería in the sky. In the meantime, Rubén Medina, who had edited *Correspondencia Infra*, was trying to mediate and bring about some kind of rapprochement, I believe. Then things sort of fizzled out in general, and even more people took off, including Medina and Anaya and the Méndez brothers, who went to Morelia and started a bakery! Luscious Skin, too, who split for Paris and became a painter. And then Mario got killed by the truck, and I didn't have contact with anyone anymore, and I started law school and then had my stroke. I saw Efraín once, when I was walking by Café La Habana, it would have been in 1981, and he was sitting there all alone, in the middle of the afternoon, this zombie of an old man, maybe hoping someone would show up, just staring at the Reloj Chino, he was, like he was in shock of the time it was chiming, it was very sad, and he died maybe five months later. The kids who put their lot in with Paz were the smart ones. A bunch of them made it, like Carmen, José María Espinasa, or Juan Villoro. But I guess you know all that. From our little suicidal group, you're the only one who went on to write anything that will be remembered! But here I'm going on too long. Let me write more in a few days, over the weekend. I'd love to be back in touch, and maybe I could visit you sometime in Spain, even with my cane. Are you still in Blanes? That's what I heard. I think of you, looking at the sea. I mean *you* looking at the sea, not me. I actually go to Europe a couple times a year with my boss (a total bitch) when there is business over there, usually Paris, but I've also been to Vienna and Frankfurt. Don't get me wrong; I'm more like her wardrobe attendant. We all become what we become. Though even so, who are we and where are we going?

Sorry I can't help more with the mysterious Nadal. Funny, if you take the last letter of his name and put the sound of it in front, it's like El Nada! Only someone who's had a stroke would think of that, ha ha.

Kisses, and talk to you soon,

Sonia

❋❋

Letter from César Oster Madero

Roberto,

I don't want to talk about Nadal. I could, but I won't. Let him have the fate he sought. We all only talked about it—that we were willing to vanish into oblivion for poetry—we put that claim into manifestoes, even. (Remember your "ocean of the void"? Blah, blah.) When what we really wanted was to be known by the world, to be on every lip and tongue, as even Chatterton confessed. Did you ever confess it, Bolaño? Only Mario and Nadal (by choice, that is!) seem to have taken the charge seriously and gone, like Rimbaud, all the way. It pisses me off that you are writing with a query for your own purposes, after all this time. Did it ever occur to you to ask what has happened to us?

César

❋❋

Letter from Laura Puig

Hello Roberto, I am so happy to be able to write to you. I know all your books. I like your work very much, indeed. I have some things I remember about Nadal, as you will see. I knew him intimately. So let me give you some of my memories. I will call this letter "One time I remember," somewhat following the U.S. writer Joe Brainard, a friend of Frank O'Hara's, have you read him? I know you like Ted Berrigan (Nadal told me), so maybe so.

One time I remember we were walking on Avenida Reforma and Vladimir said, Oh, look, it's Alcira. And so Guadalupe Ochoa and I looked over into the big window of the café, and sure enough, there was Alcira Soust Scaffo, sitting there at the back, reading, drinking and smoking, all by herself, with her lion's mane of gray hair and her Bolivian or Peruvian poncho, and she was blowing smoke rings, one after another, these perfect, thick, white smoke rings, like her puckered mouth was some kind of mechanical smoke-ring machine set into the face of this elegant ruin of a late middle-aged woman's head. And Guadalupe said, Let's go in and say hello. Sure, I said, she looks lonely. And Vladimir said, No, let's not, it's too late. What do you mean, It's too late, I said, as we started to walk after Vladimir, who had already started walking, fast, down Reforma, with all its businessmen and beggars and sleeping dogs and peddlers, and I looked back and I caught a glimpse of Alcira, smiling her bad– toothed smile through the window, waving excitedly, because she'd looked up from her Benedetti and recognized us, and now she was coming to the window, I could still see at an angle, even though we'd all only met her once at a party at Roberto Vallarino's, where you and Francisco Segovia got into a Buster Keaton slapping match, and we walked into all the businessmen and the beggars and the dogs and the peddlers, and they closed around us, and Vladimir said, Run! for no reason at all, we were all high. And so we ran, and I felt sad for Alcira, your mother's old friend, very sad and also ashamed.

One time I remember he and I made love one afternoon in mom's apartment and watched soap operas in her bed, and my mom, who was supposed to be away for two days in Morelos, for her real estate company, came back and found us there. And Vladimir was very smooth about it all, totally unruffled, even as I was mortified, and so we got dressed and went out, and she was sitting there smoking, in her short dress and high heels, her legs crossed, looking like Catherine Deneuve, whom she did resemble, except with black hair, and he somehow managed to charm my mom, and she ended up inviting him to stay for dinner, even though he was twenty-two at the time and I was seventeen, so technically he was committing a statutory crime, not that it would matter in Mexico, and not that it should matter anywhere, because if I'd been three months older and eighteen, would that have made it perfectly fine, while our relationship, three months before, as it was, constituted a crime? Isn't that interesting? And later when we went out to the Cantina Bar, on Bucareli, and before Vladimir started to pronounce on whatever, with all the Infra kids gathered around him, he shouted at me above all the noise, and I'll never forget how it hurt me, though I liked him so much, and I was so young, I didn't let the hurt show: "I think your mom wants to fuck me." He was drunk, but still.

※

One time I remember we smoked pot in the car out in the trees by Los Manantiales, in Xochimil, just the two of us, and then we went in and sat down, and Octavio Paz was there, the very man, a few tables away, with José Joaquín Blanco and Monsiváis, and there were maybe five young poets with them, and Vladimir said they were from *El Zaguán* and *Anábasis*, acolytes of Paz, there were probably more than five of them, now that I think about it, maybe seven or eight, one of them was Francisco Segovia, and another Coral Bracho, whom I liked, and Vladimir was getting tense and tenser the drunker he got, because there they were, the people he despised, the "asshole suckers"

as he called the young Pazistas, and they were laughing away
and the Pazista kids were stealing glances at us and smiling,
all smug, because they knew who we were, or who we wanted
to be, and we were already feeling maybe a bit out of place,
the way we were dressed, and other people had already been
looking at us, the bourgeois patrons, all smug, too, and then
one of the kids, I can't remember his name, the review editor
of *El Zaguán*, I later found out, who was facing us with Paz to
one side and Monsiváis to the other, I can't remember his name,
squatted down under the table, put his hand between his legs,
grabbed his balls, and then gave us a downward middle finger,
while Paz and Monsiváis and Blanco, oblivious to it all (I'm sure
they had no idea who we were) kept jabbering like three kings,
in the glow of their obsequious retinue, and actually Paz really
did look like a king of some sort, he was a beautiful man, with
his Greek helmet hairdo, and Vladimir stood up, grabbed an
empty liter bottle of Modelo from the table of two guys in suits
next to us, walked over to the Pazista table, very calm and cool
and feline, like John Travolta in *Saturday Night Fever*, when I
think back on it, and raises the bottle and brings it down, crack,
onto the crotch-grabbing, finger-flipping young Pazista's head,
and glass goes flying, and he just falls down, the Pazista does,
crumples like a sack of beans after the beans have been poured
out, or whatever, and goes down under the table, and Paz and
Monsiváis and Blanco and the young bootlickers jump up and
start scattering in panic and a few other people at other tables,
too, and Vladmir picks up the copy of *Cuadernos de Literatura*
that one of them had and starts tearing out the pages and tossing
them up in the air, and he saunters back just like before, in no
hurry, and he takes my hand, and he says, Let's go, and everyone
is yelling, and a couple of beehived ladies are screaming, calling
for the cops, and we start running, we run like crazy out the
door and down the stairs to the car, an old Simca, sky blue, my
mother's, and Vladimir puts it into gear and we screech out of

the lot and take off, and I looked back through the rear window and saw the wave-roof of Los Manantiales, like a melting UFO, and the pond in front of it with all the ducks and scum, and a commotion of figures on the terrace, who grew smaller and smaller as we went, now in fourth, down the long drive, laughing and laughing, and the little motor straining at a high pitch, not so much like a real car as like a toy car, and it did all seem like it was just pretend, like in a Tin-Tin book, I felt, and I think that was one of the most happy moments of my life, bad as it was, and I looked at Nadal and saw him smiling, like Jean-Paul Belmondo, and I remember the thought crossed my mind of him and my mother in bed, but then he said, Let's go to El Popular, and then we'll go to La Habana, see who we can find, and I said, OK, and we did, and most everyone was there, at La Habana, and I forgot about the image of my mother on top of him, moving up and down like a beautiful forty-nine year-old Catherine Daneuve jackhammer.

One time I remember we went to La Soriana, in Guadalupe, and we were just walking the aisles, looking at stuff, and making up lists of things we'd buy if we had the money, what we'd cook up with what we'd get, mole recipes, for example, Nadal loved mole. We walked through the store, pushing our cart, we were just pushing along, happy, and we'd stop at the things we'd like to have and couldn't, and we'd pretend we were putting it in the cart or we'd really put it in, knowing we couldn't buy it, but just to push it around, you know, and we were laughing, high as we were, all these things we wanted, this fancy stuff, the steaks and shellfish and all these fancy things in jars and cans here and there, all piled about three feet high in our cart. And we pushed it up to the checkout, and they rang us up, giving us looks, and Nadal patted his pockets, and says, O, my, I seem to have left my wallet at the office, which of course he made up, and so they had to unpack everything, and all we could buy in the end was some bread and tomatoes and beans and tortillas and a couple pads of nopal, it was perfectly romantic, the bourgeoisie in line, cooling their heels behind us, mumbling and whatnot. And I felt so happy, and he did too, I could feel his happiness, we'd just come from a reading by José Emilio Pacheco, at Casa del Lago, which was terrible, though of course he got a standing ovation and then his picture taken with dignitaries, including the U.S. Ambassador and his Jackie Kennedy-looking wife, and as we were walking out, Nadal turned and shouted, *Long Live Lucio Cabañas!* And everyone spun towards us, wide-eyed, the place went quiet, and away we went. And so anyway, we paid at the checkout, and they had these fancy cash registers that looked like they were from a spaceship to us, where the numbers came on in a box in lights, we'd never seen anything like it, back then in 1979, and we made our modest dinner of bread, tomatoes, tortillas, beans, and nopales, and ate it by candlelight, with two six-packs of Tecate he'd stolen the day before, while we watched the big wrestling match between Dr. Wagner and Dos Caras on the little TV set, which Dos Caras won, much to Nadal's delight, since he was a big fan of him and El Canek. Which I here note for you and for all time.

One time I remember we went to Librería Baudelaire, on Calle General Martínez, near Calle Horacio, in Polanco. Horacio was the name of my first boyfriend, my neighbor, whose brother was Claudio, and this Roman-Empire loving family lived next door, on Isabelino Bosch, where I grew up, in Montevideo, next to the Sanatorio Americano and around the corner from the U.S. Embassy, where my second boyfriend, Bobby, lived, the son of the Ambassador, Robert Sayre, and there I once met the sister of Hubert Humphrey and another time Duke Ellington himself, who signed a program for me, which I still have. The father was the owner of Possogia Motors y Cia., on 18 de Julio, which sold British cars back in the 50s and 60s, Sunbeams I think they were called, and I would go flying in their little airplane on the weekends, this tiny thing with a V-shaped tail, the family of four and me crammed into the cockpit, and we'd go sailing out over the Río de la Plata and circle back and bank and climb and buzz over Montevideo, the toy plane bouncing all over the place, until we broke up after about a year, Horacio and I, which was probably a good thing, because about two years after that the plane went nose-first into the field of the brand-new stadium of Cerro Fútbol Club, in the last minute of a game between Cerro F.C. and Peñarol, killing the whole Possogia family, including their obnoxious, nippy dachshund, though miraculously not a single soccer player was seriously harmed, because Peñarol was somehow losing to lowly Cerro by one goal, and it was a corner kick in the 90th minute, and so Peñarol had sent everyone downfield in desperation, including the great goalkeeper Ladislao Mazurkiewicz (who had played so valiantly in England, in 1966, against West Germany, when the English referee, who'd been paid by the Germans, robbed us in the quarterfinals, expelling three of Uruguay's players in the first half) to head the ball in, and Rocha and Spencer and Abadie and Joya and Forlán and Goncalvez and all those legendary players in Peñarol's glory days were down there in the area at the last minute of the game, and I know you won't believe this, and I don't quite believe it myself, still, but *I was there*, with my third boyfriend, Pablo Palacios, who was a fan of Cerro, and I saw it all happen, the blur of the falling thing, the fireball and the mini-mushroom cloud, and it was only later that evening I found out it was the Possogias, when the cars and cops started to pull up to their house and go inside, which as I said was next to mine, though I clearly recall the plane fall and seeing the split tail and thinking, my God, that's just like the family plane of my first boyfriend, Horacio. So the great ball of fire exploded harmlessly (except for the Possogias, of course) in the middle of the field, while everyone was packed at one end around the Cerro goal, but the accident of course forced the cancellation of the game, and with less than one minute to go, and by rule, the whole game had to be replayed, though this time at the Centenario, because there was a big hole in the middle of Cerro's field, and Peñarol won this time, I still remember, though I wasn't there, 4-0, and without unusual incident. And so Nadal and I went into the Librería Baudelaire and started poking around, and Vladimir put books by Ungaretti, and Borges, and Piglia, and Sor Juana, and Bioy Casares into his bag, and the owner, who looked very much like Possogia pater familias, actually, not making that up, had spied him doing so, and he came running at Vladimir with what looked like Wittgenstein's fire poker, and Nadal dodged him, and called out, Let's go! to me, and out we went, and the adrenaline was pouring through my veins, or my brain, not sure how adrenaline works, and the evening crowd of 6 o'clock closed in around us, oblivious, everyone lost in themselves, and we were gone, like when we ran away from Alcira, and we laughed and laughed, like that time, too, but now I feel as guilty about it as I felt about her, too, because wasn't this poor bookseller our comrade, our friend? I mean, he was a bookseller of great titles, he loved books, they were his life, like they were life for us. Who were we and where were we going?

❄

One time I remember we were just wandering around, taking peseras here and there, walking, taking more peseras, we were on Dexedrine, we were on Niños Heroes, then we sat down to smoke in Plaza Pacheco, then we went to Colonia Navarte for some reason, and next I remember we're in Plinio El Jóven,

112

on Venustiano Carranza, and then next we're in the Lizardi, on Donceles, and then at Rebeca Nodier, on Mesones and Pino Suárez (don't ask me, it was an amphetamine blur), and the thing is, at Plinio de Jóven, Nadal steals *Diary of an Unknown Writer*, by a Japanese writer of the Second World War, supposedly, and he sticks it down the back of his pants, covered by his parka, which is four sizes too long, and along with this he steals a copy of Marco Manilio's *Astronómica*, with a Prologue by Alfonso Reyes, and this book is so thick that not even his X-Large parka can hide it, so it's like Nadal has this huge square ass, and he's waddling along, these volumes in his pants, and he says to me, calm as can be, like nothing's amiss, "I'm going to write a book about this unknown Japanese guy," and somehow the owner doesn't catch us and so we merge with the crowd, and then we get a chicha at a stand, and then we keep going, and Nadal is reading the Japanese book as he's walking, and he keeps bumping into people and people are saying, For crissakes, watch out where you're going, and he's so high he doesn't even know it, he just keeps reading, even when it starts to rain, which makes the pedestrians thin out a bit, it's pouring so hard, but he just keeps on reading about his Japanese writer, oblivious, the book getting all wet, and somehow we end up on Calle Aranda, I can't remember when we walked or when we took a pesera, and we went into Librería Mexicana, and I think he stole something there, too, though maybe it was at Librería Pacifíco, on Bolívar and 16 de Septiembre, where the mimes always are and the lepers, too, outside the church, holding bowls between their suppurating stumps, and then the Viejo Horacio, on Correo Mayor, we didn't spend much time there, the name made me think of my old boyfriend in the little plane, and we're walking and walking and dripping sweat, though maybe I'm mixing that up with the rain, and then we go into the Librería Orozco and we see Marco Antonio Montes de Oca and Ali Chumacero poking around the poetry section though we don't say anything to them, except Nadal burps really loud, and he says, Tastes like chicha from 1968, and Montes de Oca and Chumacero, who I think were together, look at him like he's some leper and move away to another aisle, and Nadal steals a book by Frank O'Hara, in English, *Sonnets about Lunch*, you have to read it, if you haven't, it's great, and that one was easy because it was small, I put it in the cup of my bra, over my heart, and we left, casually, though the owner was looking at us funny, and when he said, "STOP!" we ran and ran and merged into the crowd, and we're laughing, and the cowboy on Reforma is smoking overhead, and we go into Libreria Orozco, though we don't steal anything there, we just look at early 20th century reprints of Coleridge and Keats and Wordsworth, and Nadal says, I should do an experimental translation of one of these guys, and then we go to Librería Milton, on Milton and Darwin, and we talk to Don Fonso, the owner, who we like a lot, and he's kind to us, even though he knows we've stolen from him before, but maybe he's kind because he's a little senile, though only at moments, usually he's sharp as a nail, and as we're talking to him, who do you think walks in? Yes, it's Octavio Paz himself, with his regal coiffure, followed by three *Anábasis* kids from UNAM, though I can't now remember their names, and Paz is perfectly comfortable, natural in his skin, of course, but these kids are all full of themselves, you could tell, puffed-up like they're decked out and walking into a disco, they want everyone to notice they're with Paz, they're totally uptight, even as they're acting like this is just another regular evening out with Don Octavio, and they go back into the stacks, and Don Octavio is showing them the same books by the Romantics we'd just been nosing, and Nadal yells out, "Octavio Paz, why do you waste your time with such fake poetaster vermin? You know they'll grow up to be bankers and lawyers and accountants!" And they all just stood there looking at him, open mouthed, except Paz, who sort of smiled, eyebrows raised, with this gentle look of amusement mixed with bemusement, it was obvious he wasn't connecting us with Los Manantiales, funny how that look is still clear in my mind, and then Nadal grabs my hand and we run out, laughing, and merge with the crowd and we're so happy, still high before the shit-kicker hangover of the dex sets in. And then we went to Librería Mundo, on Rio Nazas, though I can't remember what happened there, but later we took a pesera to Calle Palma, and had a taco at La Palma de la Vida, and Nadal told me then of his idea to kidnap Octavio Paz and that the ransom demand would have been that *Excelsior* print a manifesto and supplement of our work, the Infra's work, and he said it really would be easy, that he could be lured and put in a car and taken to Santiago's place, maybe, or to Ramón Méndez's, or Luscious Skin's, even, to see how the other poetry half, the authentic kind, lives, and that we could take a photo of him in his underwear, with a sign around his neck that said "Labyrinth of Sonambulism," and that we would treat him real nice, so he'd get Stockholm Syndrome when we released him after two weeks, even if *Excelsior* didn't give in to our demands, and he said, smoking there in La Palma de la Vida, like Alain Delon, he said, it will be remembered forever, in all the history books of poetry.

Octavio Paz

And I said, with that picture in my head of Don Octavio gently smiling at Nadal only an hour before, I said, "You're crazy. You'd be arrested and thrown down some hole in the Sonora." And he said, lighting another Delicado, "No I'm not, I'm totally sane." And then Alejandro Aura and Juan Villoro walked in, and they came over, even though we didn't know them all that well, and we started talking about something else. Though then I remember thinking back about the lepers, and how I didn't dare touch them and I started thinking about Che Guevara, and how he took care of lepers in Venezuela, and he surely touched them, and I felt ashamed, and that led me to thinking about my dog, Hora Zero, I named him, after the Peruvian avant-garde poet group, and how he was incontinent in the end, and shitting and pissing in the house, because he couldn't help it, and once, when I was drunk, he shit in my bedroom, he'd shit while he was sleeping, and I was drunk and angry about something else, and I hit him over and over again, and I could see, in his yelping and wailing, that he didn't understand one bit why I was hitting him, because he'd done it in his sleep, for one, so how could he even know, and I hit him again, and he howled and went to lay down behind the couch, he didn't understand, and three days later he died, he died curled up behind the couch, and to this day I know now who I really am, the violence I have, and I cry and pull my hair and call the name of Hora Zero, and I don't know how to make myself feel better, because there is no way, I've proved myself to be bad in my soul by doing what I did, and no movie or novel or music or poem will cure it. You know what I mean?

✻

One time I remember Nadal said to me, after a reading by I don't remember who at Librería Ghandi, that the kind of writer

he wanted to be was the kind who leaves his work for someone else to finish. Something close to that is what he said. That
every writer, he said, seemed to assume he or she must finish
the work that he or she had begun, bring it to a close. I want
to be a writer, he said, who doesn't finish a work, who leaves it
to vanish, unread, or else to be found and restarted and then
finished by someone else. By one or two or three or more, it
wouldn't matter. A writer who disappears into other writers, and
thus becomes more real, more lasting, more elemental than the
kind of writer who puts his dumb name on the cover of another
book among a billion books. And then this university student
prize-winner kid who was sucking up all the time to the Paz
circle, I can't remember his name, came in, and as he passed
our table, minding his own business, I have to say, Nadal said,
Is your asshole nice and sore today from all the Poetry Orgy
Fucking you've been doing this week in Don Octavio's harem?
And so this guy spun around, and he said, What did you say,
you litte, worthless piece of shit, and Nadal stood up, though
not as tall as he, and stood on his tiptoes, his face right close up
to his, and repeated the question, word for word, as if there were
periods after every word in it, saying, in this voice that sound-
ed like it was four-hundred years old, Is. Your. Asshole. Nice.
And. Sore. Today. From. All. The. Poetry. Orgy. Fucking. You've.
Been. Doing. This. Week. In. Don. Octavio's. Harem. And the
guy's mouth sort of fell open and he backed off and hurried out
the door, and then we ordered a couple beers and laughed and
laughed, and then we went out and merged with the crowd.

❋

Once I remember I thought: My whole life I've thought to
myself that I didn't have anything to say, much less that I had
the ability with which to convey it. But what if I did, I said to
myself one day, what if I could write something that people like

you would like, admire, maybe praise? What if I reached down into myself and said, Please give me the power to say something, gods, grant me the right to write something out of the blue, what no one could have expected from me, me who is no one, the girl who was the girl of Nadal, me who is good for little but filing the nails of fingers and toes (I am in demand), painting them, listening to the people of these fingers and toes, talking to them, about the most abject, crazy shit, painting their toes, as I said, putting stenciled designs on their nails, etc. What if I could reach down into myself, granted the graces of the gods, to say something, Bolaño, that even you would say was worthy, at least a little bit? A tiny bit? Oh, gods, grant me the power to say what I want to say, to speak of his kindness, his shyness, his impotence, his way of rising above that, to be, when he was drunk, a kind of minor god, or a vessel of the gods speaking through him, how he could speak to the woman with no legs, her children beside her outside the church, and kiss her hands, and give her every peso he had, and cry into me, in the Chino Café, like a child, and compose himself, and then start talking to Darío Galicia, like nothing had happened, and then ask me to tell José Ribeyro and Mara Larrosa and Rubén Medina about the Carrasco Bowling Club, outside Montevideo, where I used to go as a teenager, where I'd bowl with my friends, because I was the daughter of a Congressman, believe it or not, and this is where we used to go, back in those days, the Carrasco Bowling Club, I'm Uruguayan like Alcira Soust Scaffo, and those were the days, there were four lanes, in the only bowling alley in Uruguay, and one night the Tupamaros blew it up, it was 1970, and our friend, though he really wasn't our friend, he was more like this old guy we condescended to, because we were smarter, more cultured, or thought we were, and with a bit of money, and he was poor, an old guy who was the nightwatchman of the club, a former gaucho from Tacuarembó, actually, who still wore the bombachas and the big silver belt buckle, and cleaned and swept at night, and after he was done cleaning, when everything was closed, after midnight, or whenever, he'd sit around smoking his rolled cigarettes, and then he'd push his broom around, probably, clean the toilets, smoke, think about things, wonder about this or that, maybe the meaning of life, or the unmeaning of it, I don't know. And so he was smoking a cigarette, on that same night we'd bowled, and I almost had a 200 score, my best score ever (I was one of the best female bowlers in Uruguay, actually, not that there were that many), and around 3 AM, because the Tupas only blew things up in the middle of the night, when there was (supposedly) no one there, because they were the most humanistic urban terrorist group in the history of terrorism, their huge bomb went off, and the whole Bowling Club collapsed onto its four lanes, and that was that, and good Don Mario Lavista (who had the same name as the great experimental composer from Mexico, whom you knew) was found, though they had to scoop up his remains, which were hard to scoop up, because he was mixed in with the concrete and the mahogany remains of the lanes, and the fiberglass of the pins and the balls, and Nadal said to me, Don't cry, that I had nothing to do with it. I was just a kid, just bowling and ready to suck the cocks of bourgeois kids, I did it, I admit it, it made me feel like I belonged, because my dad worked as a waiter at the Sorocabana Café, on Plaza Independencia (I lied about his being a Congressman, I'm sorry, I don't know why I did that, but the lie stays), where he used to serve Marosa Di Giorgio, have you ever heard of her, the great, strange poet of Uruguay, the equal and more of Lautréamont and Jules Supervielle and Julio Herrera y Reissig, she used to go there and sit by herself, poor woman, no one knew who she was, no one paid any attention, and there she was, in the great room of two-hundred tables, and everyone smoking and drinking coffee in the little cups, and Artigas in the Plaza on his steed with the pigeons on his head, and the Ciudadela behind, and the Palacio Salvo, the weirdest work of tall architecture still standing in the Western Hemisphere, after Gaudí, anyway, throwing its shadow over everything, and all the secrets and dangers of the Ciudad Vieja beyond, the Port and the Old Market, with its parrilladas and the Medio-Medios, and Marosa Di Giorgio just drinking her coffee with her bucked teeth, and everyone around her and no one knowing she was South America's Emily Dickinson, only stranger than even Dickinson, and my father bringing her coffee after coffee, and always wondering what she was writing but never asking, and always wondering because he was a poet, too, but never talking to her, because he was shy, and then he fled to Mexico with the coup, because he was in the 26 de Marzo, the political front of the Tupamaros, and he was one of the real people, in fact, on the bus in Costa Gavras's movie, *State of Siege*, the people who vote on the bus route, giving their vote to the comrade who sits down next to them in series and then gets off, voting on whether Daniel Mitrione, the CIA torturer the MLN had kidnapped should be executed or not, Mitrione was played in the movie by Yves Montand, did you see it. And my father was on the bus, and the comrade sat down next to him and gave him the hand signal or said some kind of code word, I'm not sure which, and my father had to say simply Yes or No, he was on a CUTSCA bus, the kind where the ticket collector had his little stall in the back, and he took your money and tore your ticket in half, which I used to ride to school when I went to the Instituto Crandon, in my blue dress and white blouse and big blue bow, where I had my first kiss in the tunnel under the street that connected the elementary and middle school to the high school, and the boy was a yanqui, with stilted Spanish, and he kissed me and asked me to go steady, we were twelve, and I remember the next day Mitrione was shot, though I know my dad voted against it on the bus, I mean I found this out years later, I had no idea he was a Tupa then. He stayed faithful to the movement's rules and never told me, during the dictatorship, anything about his militancy, even though he knew, as time went on, that I knew he had some involvement with the MLN, and knew I wanted him to tell me, but he never did, because those were the rules of the MLN, though he gave me hints, and then my father took his life, I'm not making this up, on August 10, the very 7th anniversary day that Daniel Mitrione was shot by the Tupas, which had led to the great repression under Bordaberry, and then to the military coup and the terror, which we barely got away from, he shot himself in the garden of the Museo de Bellas Artes, imagine that, and I came home, from school, and my mother opened the door, and she had make-up on to kill, which she put on every day, though for some reason this day she looked especially made-up, and she said, My daughter, your father is dead, forgive me for all these commas, I should write in regular sentences, I suppose, but it helps me this way. And sometime that week my mother told me everything about my dad the Tupamaro, and it was not a surprise to me at all, and I remember feeling proud of him, and knowing that he voted No on that bus, I know he did, as if I can hear him say it. And we were in the Centro Histórico, by the Antiguo Colegio de San Ildefonso, and Nadal said, Don't cry my love, don't cry, and he ran his thumb under my eyes, making my make-up smudge, and he tried to fix that with a napkin, but it only made it worse, so I looked like a woman coal miner, or a zombie, or my mother in the shower with him, and the next day he was gone. I later learned he had joined the urban guerrilla group Liga Comunista 23 de Septiembre and gone underground, and I never heard from him again. This was shortly after the New Year, in 1980.

Years ago, I learned he was in the U.S., in Arizona, they said, and I tried to track him down, but couldn't. I heard from a friend that he'd been in El Salvador, too, fighting with the FMLN for a while, but I don't know if that's true or not, though of course it would make sense. But I have no idea where he is now. And I have to admit I hadn't thought much about him for a couple years now, maybe subconsciously, you know, until Vera forwarded me your email. Maybe I've thought about him more than I realize, now that I think about it, our minds are unpredictable, aren't they?

I know I've gone on too long, Roberto Bolaño. I hope you won't mind, if you've read this far, and I hope some of these things that have popped into my head might be of use to you, for whatever reason it is that you asked about him. It's been fun for me to remember. Though sad, too, and it's brought up emotions, as they say. I send you good wishes, and admiring feelings for your amazing work.

Yours,

Laura

❄❄

Letter from Ricardo Ramírez Camarga

Halo Roberto,

When I began spending the afternoons in the bathroom reading Toussaint, I wasn't planning to set up my lodgings there. But time moved on, and before I knew, as if no time had passed at all, I began to see I had everything I needed: water; books stacked in piles to the ceiling, enough to last me a lifetime (the Collected Works of Marx and Engels, the Collected Works of Lenin, the Collected Works of Trotsky, the Collected Works of Mariátegui, all of Kafka, most of Montaigne, Stein, Cervantes, Di Giorgio, Hernández (Felisberto), Joyce, Walser, Shakespeare (de Vere?), Góngora, Beckett, most of Maigret, etc.); a sleeping bag and pillow stuffed in the corner, which at night I place in the tub; an outlet in the wall for my electric razor and laptop; a toothbrush, nail clipper, scissors, a plastic cup (toothpaste and shampoo are expendable; hot water and soap are sufficient); a box of Bic pens and packs of laser-printer paper that are also stacked to the ceiling; one change of clothes (the dirty one rinsed in the tub after fortnight on the first day of each month); a fan for hot days (the outlet has two plugs) and a space heater for the cold; a microwave, a bowl and a spoon (these stored in the cabinet beneath the sink); a trash basket, fifty LED bulbs, numerous cans of Lysol, all stored in the same place as the microwave; a towel. You might wonder about food: I have hired the mute woman in the apartment next door to bring me sixty packages of ramen and two rolls of toilet paper on the first of each month; she brings two bars of soap every other. She has the key to my front door, and she leaves the box of sustenance and mop-ups outside the bathroom with a knock (I pay her over Pay Pal).

I've been living in the bathroom for seventeen years now. And when I finish reading my books for the fourth time, now, I'll start over.

So no, I have neither any information about, nor any interest in, this person called Nadal.

Don't write me again, you fucking sell out.

Letter from Mateo Darrieux

Dear Roberto Bolaño,

I am a friend of Diamela Eltit and Raúl Zurita, whom I came to know back in the eighties, when I was active in the cultural resistance here in Chile. I'm aware, of course, that there are some tensions between you and Damiela and Raúl, and I trust you won't mind that this response to your query turns out to be somewhat connected to them.

I heard from Lotty Rosenfeld that you were making inquiries about Vladimir Nadal, and so I thought I would write you. I came to know Nadal briefly in 1981. He was a friend of Juan Castillo, though I'm not certain of the history of their acquaintance. They were both quite addicted to alcohol, so that may have had something to do with the fellowship. Though I should say both were able to be perfectly sober when the time demand-ed it. Nadal had recently returned to Chile, and he attended a few cell meetings of the CADA in Santiago, notably the planning sessions for the first National Art Museum action.

from left to right, Juan Castillo, Lotty Rosenfeld, Raul Zurita, Diamela Eltit, Fernando Balcells, Santiago, Chile, 1979.

Nadal didn't say very much, and rarely did, at least in my encounters with him (with the notable exception of one night, around Christmas, where Zurita, Balcells, Rosenfeld, Nadal and I were drinking on the terrace of the Brighton Hotel, in Valparaíso, and Nadal launched into this long, incredibly learned harangue about classical Greek and Latin prosody, stunning us all). But at that meeting (the Santiago one) he quietly volunteered to be the getaway driver of the pickup truck, to meet the commandoes after the bags of shit got dumped in the rotunda by Zurita, Castillo, and Eltit. He also volunteered, like everyone, to donate a week's worth of his excrement for the action's materiel. With one important exception, he performed his appointed job admirably (the driving, that is). He was an expert, deft driver, like in a noir film, with pilot shades and skin-tight gloves, and he dropped everyone off at the various designated locations after the event, losing three patrol cars along the way, and then successfully hiding the truck, which he repainted and altered that night.

But for some inexplicable reason, maybe in a kind of dare to fate, who knows, Nadal took off his fake beard while he was waiting in the truck for the others to dump the shit, and so he was recognized by who knows who or how, and so the cops started to look for him the day after the action. Multiple doors in Bella Vista and around UNC got kicked in. So, it was only a few days after the action that Nadal split for Peru, and from there to El Salvador, where he ended up, you might have heard, fighting with the FMLN for quite a while. In any case, in the email you sent out, which I saw second hand, you mentioned that you were with Nadal in 1997 in Spain, so it's likely you know some of this.

CADA ACTION

The main information I wanted to share is the following, in the event you have not yet learned of it through someone else: I found out early this year that Nadal, ill with cancer, had left Ljubljana, Slovenia in 1999, where he'd moved after he'd been working with his brother in Austria (I don't know what he was doing in Slovenia), and moved to Cerro Placeres, in Valparaíso. Mariela told me he was a regular, despite his illness, at the Bar Dominó and also the Bar Cinzano, which you will know, I'm sure, where he'd go to listen to tango. I'm not sure if you're aware he had prostate cancer and then on top of that leukemia—a low grade CLL he'd had even in 1981—which apparently had gone bad and was in fairly advanced stage when he got back to Chile, so it seems pretty clear he'd returned to die in his country. I am not certain of the date of his death, but it was just a few months back, sometime in October of last year, I think.

I hadn't spoken to Nadal since he went to Europe in the mid-90s (he called me on the phone a couple times when he was still living in the U.S. I don't remember anything of relevance to share about those conversations, except he told me before leaving that he hoped to connect with you). I didn't even know he was back in Chile until a couple months before he died (I'm way down south in Puerto Montt now), and not knowing how sick he was, I didn't make contact with him before he was gone. I only heard about his death second-hand, from someone who was in contact with family of his in Valparaíso. But this person is a very reliable source. I'm sorry to have to convey the news, assuming I'm the first to share it.

I am an admirer of your work, and I send you greetings of solidarity. If there is anything else I can do to help, please don't hesitate to let me know.

Mateo Darrieux

❆❆

Handwritten letter from Mariana Jiménez

Roberto,

Andrés Ajens in Santiago told me you were making inquiries on the poet Vladimir Nadal, and he gave me your postal address.

I don't have much for you, except the enclosed sketch, which is part of a portfolio of about forty sketches of writers and artists, most of them from the southern cone, that I purchased from a dealer in La Paz, done by a down-and-out Bolivian artist named Mauricio (I can't remember his surname; he didn't sign his works), who died around four years ago, a friend told me. I don't know where or when it was done, though I suspect Bolivia, given that the artist was apparently too poor to travel. It only says "Vladimir Nadal" on the back. Nadal had published in a couple Bolivian journals under pseudonym—a few times in *Global Lepidoptera*—so maybe that's how he ended up traveling to La Paz, if he did, to meet people and such.

I didn't know Nadal, but I have a memory of running across the poets Juan Luis Martínez and Juan Cameron here in Valparaíso, at the Bar Inglés, sometime in 1981, I think it was, and I'm pretty sure Nadal was the other guy there, though it was a quick chat with JLM and Cameron, and I don't remember Nadal saying anything, after we were introduced. I remember he was smoking Delicados, like you, if that helps (though not sure why it would—I seem to be fishing for details, and how he got Mexican cigs in Chile in 1981, I don't know). I think he was involved with the CADA in some capacity and then had to flee abroad. He only came back in '99, I think. And I do have a memory from last year, of Victor Hugo Bustamante, at Librería Ivens, on Plaza Aníbal Pinto, talking to someone who might well have been him. You might write VHB to ask; it's possible he'd have something, if Nadal was a regular patron, which wouldn't be surprising. I'm living in Puerto Natales now, and I don't have any contact with Victor or Cameron, so I can't pass on info directly from them. I wonder if maybe Eliana Martínez, JLM's widow, might know anything of Nadal? I don't have an address for her, but you could get it through VHB, who I'm pretty sure is close to her. I'm pretty certain she is still in Valparaíso. Another person you might ask, if you can track him down in Santiago, is Raúl Zurita, of course, who you might know hung out in his teen years with Cameron and JLM in Valparaíso, where I know you used to live as a kid, too, and so maybe he would have some information, even if indirect?

I'll certainly write you if by chance I hear anything else, but I doubt I'll be able to help further, from down here, in the sticks. But this is, I guess, a rough likeness of him, in his last years or months, which in the most unlikely manner, I happen to have.

Sincerely,
Mariana

**Tragically, this excellent drawing was lost, shortly
after I received the manuscript materials. A.B.**

Drawing of Vladimir Nadal, ca. 1999-2000

Letter from Enrique Vila-Matas

How's it going, Roberto,

I'm here in Lyon, supposedly to give a paper at a conference, and the organizers seem to have forgotten about me. Here I've been, in my hotel room for two days, and no one has even called. Which is fine by me; I'm certainly not going to call them, as I didn't really feel like coming in the first place, and all I have are some anecdotes about my various failed efforts in Ernest Hemingway look-alike contests, from Pamplona, to Paris, to Key West. A depressing topic. Not even an Honorable Mention… Besides, I gave the same talk in Nantes last year, and it didn't seem to go over so well.

Nice to hear from you. Sorry I was out last time you were in the city; Fresán mentioned you tried getting hold of me. I was in Lisbon when you were in town. I paid for coffee at the Café A Brasileira with a $100 Escudo bill from which Pessoa stared back at me in melancholy gaze, and (I recall it distinctly) I thought of you at that moment. The Café A Brasileira, I'm sure you know, was one of Pessoa's regular haunts. There is a statue of him in front of the establishment, in fact. Do you know the name of the business the Café replaced, when it was opened in 1905? The Hotel Borges. I shit you not.

Let's get together soon, brother. Make sure you call me in advance next time you're coming. I'll try to make a run to Blanes, too. How are you feeling? Steady as she goes? And. And. The book about the crimes. Tell me about the book about the crimes. Where it is and where you are. Everyone talks about you these days, you know. I see kids on the bus reading *The Savage Detectives*. I do not deny my envy. Paula says hi, too.

Photo of Enrique Vila-Matas with Roberto Bolano, ca. late 1990s.

OK, yes, Vladimir Nadal. It turned out he knew one of the group that had me to Chile in December of '99. He and I connected in Valparaíso, at the Brighton Hotel, where I was staying. He'd called saying he wanted to interview me for *El Mercurio*, though I don't think, looking back, that he had any relation to the paper whatsoever. So, we met on the late afternoon of New Year's Day (bar open for hotel guests), because I was leaving the next, and I was still in pretty bad shape when he showed up. He was pretty bloodshot himself, very thin. I thought he looked familiar, and he reminded me we'd briefly met in Barcelona, when he was with you at the Marsella, two years before. OK, I said, not knowing if he was making it up. So we sat on the terrace, overlooking the city and the bay (surely you knew the spot as a boy—it is, to my mind, one of the spectacular urban vistas of the world). The night before, one could barely move, it was so packed; now, with the exception of two old men at the far end, we were the only ones on it.

We talked and drank (he more than I) with a cassette recorder between us: He wanted to know about my invented interviews with Brando, Nureyev, Highsmith, and Burgess, etc.—asking if such "radical fabrication" might be legitimately enfolded into the writing of fiction or poetry, turned into something more complex and layered than mere fraud or forgery. He seemed a bit nervous and not all that well, but drink away he did, and he went on to ask me about some of my books, which he'd clearly read, and they were very good questions, really. We talked about Walser, Sebald, Kafka, others, you included, of course. And as we talked about *Savage Detectives* (he claimed the García Madero character is partly modeled on him?), he told me that some of you in the gang went through a phase where you were submitting false translations of imaginary English, American, and French Beat-like poets to the mainline journals and that they gobbled them up, never suspecting. He called it the "Quijote Operation." You will need to tell me more about this sometime. Sounds like promising material.

And he said you told him you and I had been together at some exhibit of Joseph Beuys at MACBA, and that I'd asked you out loud if there wasn't perhaps a deep relation between fascism and the avant-garde, and that you'd been wondering ever since what I'd meant by that and that he was curious what I thought that relation might be, if I could please elaborate on the question. And so I had to tell him that of course I'd never been to the MACBA with you, nor to any showing of the work of Joseph Beuys, nor, even, to any art exhibit with you of any kind that I could remember. I told him you had clearly made this up, and that you were quite well-known for making things up, such as your "encounter" with Roque Dalton, in San Salvador, which I never believed myself, and this seemed to upset him, and so the interview pretty much came to an end, and he said good-bye, telling me that before I left Valparaíso, I should check out a place a few streets over, called Café Turri, where the view was just as good, and it almost was, and who do I run into there but Carmen Balcells, who was in Chile to meet with a young, unpublished writer, who had sent her the rough draft of a novel.

I asked her who, and she said that of course she would not tell me, what a question to ask an agent on a secret mission, etc. I asked her when she had cancelled her retirement, and she said, "No, I haven't cancelled it, but when there's someone who seems especially intriguing, I can't help myself. But don't tell anyone you saw me here, or I will completely fuck you over." So I sat there with her, filling up with Valparaíso, and we talked about you most of the time. What a woman.

Anyway, I liked Nadal, I have to say. He was very smart, down to earth, self-effacing, funny. He got up and said goodbye very abruptly, very much like Aira likes to do, and left me sitting there, and I never heard from him again. I had to pick up his bill, which was five pisco sours. Apparently, he never bothered to transcribe the tape. At least I haven't heard that he did. Too bad, because it might have been pretty good. Not as good as my Brando interview, but still pretty good.

I'll call you in a couple weeks, after I get back from Istanbul, where I'm reading with Orhan Pamuk, up and coming writer, who has a new good book by the title of *My Name is Red*. You know of him, I take it?

Abrazo,

E.

❆❆

Letter from Oton Jarc

Dear Roberto,

It is an enjoyable surprise to have communication from you once more yet. I've been chasing your recent successes in the fiction. So far I've read *Nazi Writers in the Americas* and *Faraway Star*, in Spanish. Some of the stories, too. They are very magnificent. I want to pause for the *Detective Savages* to come out in German, nevertheless, because my Spanish is not tip-top, as you can tell from this letter. Little better than four years ago, as you should see. You must invite me to Spain. (smiley face) Sorry, I blurt out my desire. Then my friend I was with in Bosnia starts yelling at me. Then he never talked to me again. But I hear from my other friend Heinrich von Berenberg that translation is almost done and that Deutscher Taschenbuch will publish. Heinrich has given me some good description and I am pregnant with anticipating.

What I can tell you to the occurrences of Nadal is such, but not much, I'm afraid. As I have written you previous in answer to your former request (did you get letter?), I did visit him in Christmas time, three years past in Berlin, and we passed some nights in the giant beer halls, which he enjoyed in frequency to attend. I presented him to some of my friends, including Anton Osojnik, an old good chap of mine from Ljubljana, a philosopher and playwright who was in close contact with the artists of the NSK movement, which I have told you therefore when we met here in the year of '94. Some of NSK people, in addition, I know from Sovenia days. (Did I ever tell you I had long ago real tightness with Slavoj Zizek in Ljubljana, who was around NSK, when he was just creating his fame in writing articles for the publishers, in fake names of famous living Slovene intellectuals? In two of these I was the co-author, which no one knows this. Those were rosy and fast days of great weather, for sure. Now Slavoj is such a hot air balloon, doing implosion, though in West they love this implosion, with all the cartoon fire. All Slavoj, all the time.)

Anton and Nadal became friends and then Anton arranged for the Scipion Nasice Sisters Theater (this is the theater wing of the NSK) to do a performance in Vienna, in summer of '98. Nadal helped organize and the group stayed about a week. But Nadal fell in love with one of the Sisters, madly, and so he pursued her back to Ljubljana around summer of the 1998, though I do not have certainty.

I am not sure how he lived there or made work, but Anton heard he became involved in activities of the NSK, and he was commissioned to write an internal Discussion Bulletin for Citizens of NSK of the experiences of the CADA front of Chile, which he previously was of a member, so he said. It is said that in this internal Bulletin, he criticized NSK for being in a surfeit of Fine-Art-orientation, with not enough direct militant action of disruption, in the fashion that CADA was militant and disrupting. Nadal wrote, Anton said, that NSK would end up being like Marcel Broodthaers and the Musée d'Art Moderne, Département des Aigles, etc: A momentary critique that is very interesting and full of promise, yes, but soon cadavering in Museums and valued at millions of dollars. The NSK people were very incommoded by this and some were quite a bit with bees in the bonnet about it. The woman of the Sisters who he loved did not return it, and so he left Ljubljana, dejected, near spring of the '99. I do not know to where he went. If you would please tell me what you find or when you find him. I liked Nadal, he was very brilliant, though this was hidden beneath a commonness, like no one special, and this was a refreshment. Of course, he did drink much more than is good for the health.

When next you are in Vienna, Roberto, I request that you let me know. However small I am (smiley face) I cannot wait to read the *Detective Savages*. Good luck with your investigation. It is like you really are a detective now!

Greetings,
Oton Jarc

Letter from Rubén Medina

Hi Roberto,

Long time, brother. I'll write more later, but I'm under the gun with stuff here for my classes. I was thinking, incidentally, that maybe I could have you here (next year?) to do a talk and a reading. It shouldn't be too difficult to arrange. You have fans in our department and beyond. They can't believe we hung out together. So yeah, here I am, an academic. I can't apologize, shit happens.

What can you tell me about plans for English translation of *Savage Detectives* and some of the previous novels? No doubt Herralde is on that, but if I can help in any way by making queries and contacts, be sure to let me know. And I'm serious about having you here for a visit. I think you would like Madison. A chill town. Tell me and I'll start the arrangements. What would you need for a fee beyond the travel?

So quickly, mano, to answer your query: I met Nadal around the same time as you, I guess, which would have been in mid-76, six months before you left, when Harrington first brought him around. I know you and he were togethter at the Habana a couple times, at least. After you and Mario left (and Harrington, too, who took off to find you and Bruno and Mario in October of '77), Nadal started to draw some people around him—some new, second-generation folks—including some serious dudes like Edgar Altamirano, Pedro Damián Bautista, Mario Raúl Guzmán, and Rafael Catana, but a bunch of newbies, too, fellow-travelers from the UNAM and bourgeois kids who started to come around, though these last were in it for the scene, and poetry had little to do with it. He would go into these automatic composition reveries at La Habana or El Nivel after drinking a bunch, and some of the stuff was really quite good, I have to say. I wish someone had recorded it or written it down. He was kind of like the Mexican Desnos, or something. But I only caught a few of his performances. You'll remember I left myself for California in summer of '78. After Mario came back to D.F. in late '79, there were some tensions, I've heard, between the two. Mario saw himself, and rightly, as the core, and he resented, no doubt, that Nadal was attracting his own little faction. The original group (Peguero, Ochoa, Larrosa, the Méndez brothers, Monjarás, etc.) stayed loyal to Mario, of course. And by the end

of 1980, Mario had also won back most of the second-generation kids who joined after your departure. Nadal went underground, I'd heard, sometime in 1980, with the Liga Comunista
23 de Septiembre, and somehow got out alive and took off for
the States. I have no idea what happened to him in the end.

But I'd had some exchanges with him as I was preparing *Correspondencia Infra*, and I'd asked him to send me something. He
and I had a little falling out, because Nadal wanted Santiago's
and Ayala's manifestos in there too. He claimed just printing
yours played into your "mania of wanting to be the main guy,"
as I recall him putting it. Plus, I remember he argued that your
section in the beginning about women's clitorises was machista
in the extreme and would give the group a bad name in the
long run. I had to agree with Nadal on that particular line being somewhat weird and gratuitous, to tell the truth. You likely
think so now, too, I'd imagine. You were only 24, I think, when
you wrote that.

Anyway, by the time he sent me something, it was too late
because we'd already sent the galleys to the print shop. But I still
have what he sent. It's pretty strange and has that head-on-rush
automatism of his talk pieces, though always, as in those, from
what I recall, working off a narrative and structural backdrop,
of some kind. Obviously, the whole thing is made-up (it takes
place in the year 2066!), but the Fidel Estrada Blanco character
is quite charming and smacks a bit of the real.

So now I've gone on for way too long, and I probably won't
get these papers corrected by class time. I have to go. I'll be in
touch on my visit idea, though let me know what you think,
OK?

Un abrazo,
R.

*

[Poem by Nadal sent by Medina]

I also know what the greatest trial and struggle was for the esteemed poet and critic Fidel Estrada Blanco, Director of an MFA program in New Hampshire, and winner of numerous grants and awards, including the National Endowment for the Arts Fellowship, the Maurice English Poetry Award, the PEN/Voelcker Award for Poetry, and UNAM's National Poet Abroad Award:

Stroke.

Specifically, the massive embolism that rushed up his thigh and struck his cerebrum in September, 2001, near Maddampegama, Sri Lanka, while he was spending the money from an Amy Lowell Poetry Travelling Scholarship at a sleazy, two-star beach resort, on alcohol, drugs, sex with minors, and guided scuba tours of WWII wrecks a couple miles off the beach. In fact, it was while he was finning around down there, staring into the coral-encrusted cockpit of a Japanese Zero, that he was struck by the Stroke.

With great effort did the guide and three other divers kick his considerable bulk back to the surface. He was medevaced to Colombo, and then, the next morning, the day the great tsunami hit the resort, wiping it away and drowning nearly all the guests and child concubines there, he was on a medical plane back to the expert care of Dartmouth-Hitchcock Medical Center, in Lebanon, New Hampshire.

One could not be blamed for wondering at, as CNN was reporting, a few days later, the strange, ironic timing of poor Estrada's event. Was he, in short, a fortunate man, or an unfortunate man?

He made, by all prognoses, a rapid and miraculous recovery: intact in all his motor functions except for a noticeable droop on the left side of his face, a slight limp in his gait, and a perfect upper class English accent (his Spanish rang the same as it had before), accompanied by a mild stutter, which was, in the event, not so much a handicap or annoyance, as a charming and endearing Oxbridge-like trait.

This is not to say, however, that his changes were superficial. For he was, indeed, a profoundly changed man. Whereas once he had been driven by darker, atavistic desires, he now rejected the pursuit of these impermanent pleasures; whereas he had once been ambitious and mean in his attitudes, he now eschewed the backstabbing and gossip at which he had excelled. He was generous, even selfless, people said. He conducted himself with grace, humility, kindness, and a casually worn self-deprecation that provided to others moods of calm and common pleasure in his presence.

But above all, Fidel Estrada Blanco was utterly changed as a poet. For whereas before he had devoted himself, like all other poets, ancient and modern, to placing pleasing or disturbing writing onto the flatness of a page or screen (declaiming it with pride when he was prompted, of course, on arranged occasions), he now began to poetically write in a totally new form and semiology. Phonemes and morphemes were not now his medium; the medium was now Earth and Light. These in their infinite gradations and types and shades became his alphabet. And to these signs he gave himself in the second stage of his life, and with a tsunami of selfless ambition and labor that stunned the world and altered forever, for poets everywhere, the age-old assumptions about the very nature of poetry. Or of Poetry, in caps, let's put it, as History would have it.

In the Sonora, the Atacama, and the Sahara, in Patagonia and in the Canadian tundra, he constructed massive hills of earth, sand, and peat, tunneled through and honeycombed with secret rooms and vaults, and these were fashioned in such precise ways, with such varied apertures and at such meticulously planned angles to the passing sun and moon and stars and

clouds, that oscillating qualities of light—combinatory sublim-
ities of impermanence, as a critic would say—were experienced
by all those who traveled to these reaches and entered the new
and ever stranger hills. Dignitaries, Prime Ministers, Pentagon
Generals, Venture Capitalists, Football Stars, Drug Lords, and
Dukes and Duchesses came to be transformed by Estrada's poetry, and, having been, they showered money upon him, which
he spent, every cent of it, on the construction of more Earth-
Light-Poem-Hills, each grander and more intricate than the
last, so that soon, by June 6, 2066, the day of his passing into
the higher realms at 99 years of age, there were no fewer than
one hundred and twenty-seven Earth-Light-Poem-Hills, either
finished or under construction, spread across the deserts and
savannahs and pampas of the world, each with many chambers
and corridors, through which people walked, or lied down,
amazed, enveloped in washes and choirs of light that they could
virtually feel—literally *palpate*—on their skins (remote-sensor
experiments pinged to quasar 17-B, in 2060, were conducted to
confirm the many claims) as a shroud or skin that transmitted
an unexplainable sort of knowledge, which some would strain
to articulate, in stuttering, foreign-like accents, and with an absolute certainty, that the concept of Death, no less than that of
Life, is nothing less than light refracted through an infinitely
miniscule aperture of our making, and that there is nothing to
fear in the end, because beyond this aperture there is no End,
only Beginning and its infinite oceans of choral light.

And on June 6, 2066 the thought crossed many minds that
it was indeed strange that Fidel Estrada Blanco, a poet who had
once been petty and self-centered and vindictive like nearly all
poets, and whose material brain had been washed out in various
regions by a great cascading hemorrhage that struck in a place
of decadence and dissolution, would be the One to inspire a
new Faith of Poetry, a poetry transcending the mere signs of
alphabetic language, and which is now followed by millions

and of all races and preferences, whose churches are great light-pierced mounds of dirt and sand and peat, and whose symbol is an archetypal rhomboid form of Yves Klein blue.

Benjamin Péret

Two Interrogations of a Communist Surrealist in Brazil

(Preceded with a Commentary by Roberto Bolaño and an essay on Péret by Franklin Rosemont)

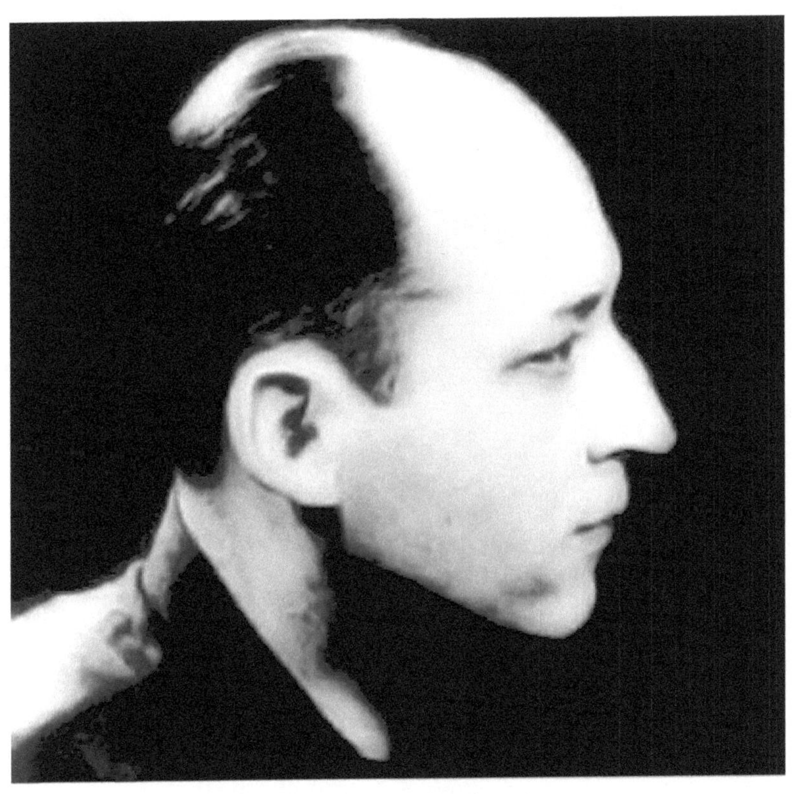

Benjamin Péret, ca. mid-1920s

The following two interrogations of Bejamin Péret, from December, 1931, were supposedly handcopied by Nadal from photocopies of files held in the archives of the Civil Police of Rio de Janeiro State. They were later translated into Spanish, by him or someone else. Nadal, under constraints of time, was not able to copy the files entire. I have indicated where he seems to skip from one section to another in the original documents. I have not been able to track down the original transcripts so as to fill in the gaps. I have lightly edited where traces of Nadal's haste are evident and added various clarifying notes to the texts.

The first interrogation is conducted by officers of the Intelligence Division of the National Police of Brazil; the second by an unidentified diplomat of the French Embassy, serving—at least in title—as a "Cultural Attaché."

Péret had met the Brazilian communist leader and preeminent cultural critic Mario Pedrosa in Paris, in 1928, through his marriage to the Brazilian singer Elsie Houston. Péret and Houston met when the latter was performing as a soloist on a European tour of the famed Brazilian composer Heitor Villa-Lobos. Pedrosa had married Elsie's sister, Mary, around the same time, and the four traveled to Brazil in early 1929. Péret's purported purpose for moving abroad at the time was to conduct ethnographic research into indigenous and Afro-Brazilian folklore. Nevertheless, besides carrying out important studies in this area during his nearly three years in Brazil (during which he gathered materials and documents related to Macumba and Candomblé rituals on trips to northeastern Brazil), he also became a founding member and leader, with Pedrosa, of the Brazilian section of the International Left Opposition, the Liga Comunista (originally founded in 1929 as the Grupo Comunista Lenin), later to become, in 1938, the Brazilian section of the Trotskyist Fourth International, as the Liga Comunista Internacionalista.

Due to this revolutionary work, Péret was expelled from Brazil at the very end of 1931, less than a month following the interrogations below. He and Elsie left their son Geyser in the temporary care of Elsie's family and returned to France. Péret continued to be at the heart of Surrealist and Trotskyist activities in France, until he went to Spain, in 1936, to fight with the Republican brigades of the anti-Stalinist POUM, later joining as a radio operator and combatant with the anarchist Durruti column. By the time of Péret's voyage to Spain, the marriage with Elsie had fallen apart. Upon the Republic's defeat, he escaped back to Paris, where he recommenced his Surrealist and communist pursuits. Conscripted into the French army in 1940, he was soon arrested for distributing subversive propaganda to the troops, but was able to escape prison as German forces advanced on Paris. With the occupation, he fled to Mexico with his lover, the Spanish painter Remedios Varo, where he lived until 1947, carrying out studies of Pre-Columbian poetic myths, along with related research on the totem art of indigenous nations of the Northwest coast of British Columbia.

The introduction here by the great Chicago-based anarchist scholar and surrealist poet Franklin Rosemont provides more biographical information about Benjamin Péret. I had contacted Rosemont in 1974 or '75, expressing to him my interest in Surrealism and contemporary U.S. poetry, and he sent me, among other things, a 1970 copy of his journal *Radical America*, which featured a special section of various works by and about Péret, at the heart of which was a passionate introduction to the life and work of the poet by Rosemont himself. Carla Rippey and I came up with the idea to publish, under the Martín Pescador imprint, a modest selection of translations of Péret's poetry written during his exile in Mexico. We translated the essay by Rosemont to use as the main introduction; unfortunately, the poem translations by Verónica Volkow and Cuauhtémoc Méndez were delayed, and the project went by the wayside. It seems both useful and appropriate to now include the Spanish version

of Rosemont's text, as originally translated by Carla Rippey and myself, as it gives a broad portrait and appreciation of the man whose interrogations while under arrest in Brazil are presented below, for the first time.
—Roberto Bolaño

FRANKLIN ROSEMONT

An Introduction to Benjamin Péret
Franklin Rosemont

Marcel Noll: "What is Benjamin Peret?"
Raymond Queneau: "A menagerie in revolt, a jungle, liberty."
—*La Révolution Surréaliste, 1928*

The destiny of Benjamin Péret, at once poignantly heroic and wildly innocent, is something I continue to find immeasurably moving. It is doubtless impossible to convey anything more than the very slightest impression of the vertiginous intellectual joy which I experienced as I discovered, around the age of seventeen, the photograph of Péret in the eighth issue of LA RÉVOLUTION SURRÉALISTE captioned: "Our Collaborator Benjamin Péret Insulting a Priest." But this simple encounter, which may seem trivial, was nonetheless decisive for me. The straw lions of Truth and the wooden ostriches of Beauty rushed together, thoroughly combustible, across the pale vicissitudes of everyday life, leaving in their ravaged wake of ashes a trail of immense possibilities which, irresistibly, I began to follow wherever it might lead. This path, moreover, has never disappointed me.

Péret is one of those few men whose entire lives have been given over to the cause of human emancipation. There is not a line in his work which does not pulsate with this profound passion for freedom. It is thus that one must speak of Péret, as also of his friend André Breton, as an example. The names of Breton and Péret, specialists in revolt, are inseparable from the revolutionary dream of our epoch.

The attempt has been made by certain critics—feebly enough, to be sure, but no less despicable for that—to create the altogether mistaken impression that Péret was some sort of "shadow" of Breton, a vague personality confined to the background, who contributed merely another signature at the bottom of manifestoes. This conception, at such variance with the facts, seems obviously calculated to justify the appalling refusal of almost all critics to concern themselves seriously and intelligently with Péret's invaluable contributions. (1) I agree completely with Jehan Mayoux (2) that this neglect and its hypocritical justification must be seen as an entirely defensive reflex on the part of these critics, and that their "refusal" to concern themselves with his work is actually nothing more than a confession of their obvious inability to do so.

This silence of the critics is especially striking when one considers the exceedingly high estimation in which Péret has never ceased to be held by his fellow surrealists. "A force of purer quality than the one the poetry of Péret possesses does not exist in or outside surrealism," wrote Nicolas Calas in 1940. (3) Éluard, to cite another example, considered Péret a greater poet than himself. (4) When one reflects that it is often Éluard whom these same critics enjoy acclaiming as the "greatest poet of surrealism," this testimony assumes greater significance. We know that the younger adherents to surrealism, following the second World War, regarded Péret as the equal of Breton. (5) Yet Péret alone has been the victim of this complete critical interdiction.

It is Jehan Mayoux, himself a member of the surrealist group and a close friend of Péret's, who first analyzed this "politics of silence." Péret›s role within the surrealist movement, according to Mayoux, was to assume "more especially—but not exclusively—the functions of aggressivity and discrimination." (6) That is, Péret especially exemplified the surrealist principles of attack. He is, in every sense, a stormer of the barricades. Victor Crastre, as Claude Courtot has pointed out, suggests practically the same thing when he describes Péret as the "musketeer of surrealism," embodying the traditional musketeer's virtues of courage and fidelity. (7) One has only to read a fraction of any paragraph written by Péret to recognize the intrinsically and scandalously combative quality of his work. And it was precisely this boundless and merciless intransigence, this perpetual extremism, this "eternal adolescence" (in the words of Mayoux) (8) that from the very beginning of his work anathematized Péret in the eyes of Literary Authority.

It is not without interest to contemplate the contrast between Breton and Péret. One could say, perhaps, borrowing certain expressions from military theory, that the work of Breton constitutes a massive war of position and siege, a vast movement of overwhelming grandeur. The "classicism" of Breton, the extreme gravity of his demeanor—emphasized in one way or another by nearly all his commentators—would seem to support this conception of his essentially "Clausewitzian" character. Péret, however, invariably prefers the frontal assault: he is the master of the violent, reckless, head-on collision of forces. Each of his poems and tales constitutes an ambush, a solitary demolition, a hurried act of sabotage, an assassination. And it *seems* precisely this "non-Clausewitzian" character, this deliriously aggressive unorthodoxy which (to pursue a moment longer the military analogy) situates Péret's work in the context of asymmetrical, revolutionary guerrilla warfare, and which would seem to have originally provoked, and to still reinforce, the conspiracy of silence against him by critics and academicians.

Of course we repudiate any suggestion of a "contradiction" or even a conflict between these two attitudes. In fact, precisely the opposite is true. As has been demonstrated by Jehan Mayoux, Jean-Louis Bédouin, and Claude Courtot, the position of Péret complements and completes the position of Breton.

There is no point consuming time and space complaining further of the neglect Péret has suffered at the hands of the critics. Totally ignored by most, barely mentioned by others, he is customarily written off as a "minor" surrealist. (9) Such misinformed neglect, as we have seen, is sufficient in itself to condemn these critics completely. But the work of Péret is of such astonishing purity and clarity that impassioned pursuers of real revelations will inevitably find their way to it. "All the waters of the ocean," wrote Isidore Ducasse in his *Poésies* "would be insufficient to wash away a single intellectual drop of blood." And Péret's contributions, let it be understood, are much more than a drop: they are, in fact, a magnificent and inexhaustible artery of the poetic marvelous circulating perpetually through the days and nights of human potentiality.

A brief illustration may help to sharpen one's perception of Péret's unreserved revolutionary attitude. In the summer of 1928 the American literary magazine TRANSITION conducted an "Inquiry Among European Writers into the Spirit of America." "How, in your opinion," it asked, "are the influences of the United States manifesting themselves upon Europe and in Europe?" Most of the replies ran to a page and sometimes longer, and were characterized by one or another species of vacillation and doubt. By way of contrast, here is Péret's entire response to this question: "Through the most emphatic garbage, the ignoble sense of money, the indigence of ideas, the savage hypocrisy in morals, and altogether, through a loathsome swinishness pushed to the point of paroxysm." (10)

In the history of surrealism Péret holds, securely, a position of the first rank. (11) He had participated in the activities of Dada in Paris, and was one of the first to advance beyond the limitations of this movement into the more subversive terrain of surrealism. He is, in fact, with René Crevel and Robert Desnos, one of the central pillars and reference-points of the "period of sleeping fits," the months of intensive experimentation with hypnotic trances immediately preceding the establishment of surrealism as an organized movement. We find his name among those cited in the first *Surrealist Manifesto* of 1924 as having proclaimed "ABSOLUTE SURREALISM." The same year, with Pierre Naville, he edited the first issue of LA RÉVOLUTION SURRÉALISTE. His published works of these years possess an exalted and exalting grandeur and vitality which, almost half a century later, have lost none of their illuminating force.

In the face of continual desertions, retreats, and betrayals, Péret, on the social as well as the poetic plane, maintained his steadfast revolutionary zeal. It is a hobby of the most stupid critics to gloat over the numerous defections from surrealism, to poke fun at the schisms and expulsions which, indeed, have played a prominent role in its development, as in every living movement, but of which, it must be said, the critics had never had even the slightest understanding. For them it is sufficient to pretend 1) that these internecine quarrels were and are of no importance; 2) that the "function" of surrealism has been to serve as an adolescent training-ground in which poets like Aragon, Éluard, and Char first found their voice; and 3) that these gentlemen wrote their truly "great" poetry only after renouncing surrealism. The time is long overdue when such imbecile contentions must be hurled into the flames of laughter to perish once and for all. Excuse us if we state simply and sincerely that the post-surrealist exercises of Aragon, Éluard, and Char constitute nothing more than a surrender to the basest literary vanity and complacency which has absolutely nothing to do with the emancipatory character of authentic poetic practice. Excuse us if we see in the later work of these gentlemen only a series of boring regressions, a senile return to the safe and protective womb of literary convention. (As Nicolas Calas wrote a propos Aragon's novels of the late '30s—so different from his incredible surrealist *Le Paysan de Paris* of the preceding decade: "...it seems to me that if one wishes to read novels in the manner of Balzac one should take the trouble to go back to the masters and not be satisfied with imitations such as those offered by Aragon. The return to a pre-surrealist position does not solve the problems of modern poetry.") (12) Excuse us, finally, if we insist that a single line by Benjamin Péret is worth every "post-surrealist" apology that ever was or will be.

Benjamin Péret never once succumbed to the conformist temptations which eventually brought so many of the companions of his youth into the camp of literary Law and Order. Marvelously uncompromising to the very end, we find him writing in 1959—the year of his death at the age of sixty—such amazingly youthful lines as these:

a sigh cut across by the rumble of drums
and the raucous cries of insane tables
at grips with the fury of physical laws
more intolerant than a wagon of Jesuits painted in two colors.

(from "Sign of the Times")

The unextinguishable impenitence and intransigence which characterizes Péret's intervention in the domain of poetry is no less characteristic of his intervention in the domain of politics. Completely against the fashionable current according to which radical intellectuals are supposed, sooner or later, to "return to the fold," to "outgrow" the revolutionary proclivities of their youth, Péret's entire life was lived "in the service of the Revolution." He is one of the five (with Aragon, Breton, Éluard, and Unik) who, in 1927, in the pamphlet *Au Grand Jour*, declared their adhesion, as surrealists and militants, to the French Communist Party. Shortly afterward, in Brazil (whither he had moved with his Brazilian wife), he adheres to the Liga Communista (Opposiçao), affiliated with the international Left Opposition. It is his revolutionary activity which led to his incarceration and expulsion from Brazil by the government in 1931.

In this world of specialists and appointed robots, a man of truth is an archaism. If our time is that of nihilism, as certain people pretend it to be, Benjamin Péret, man of hope, is a figure of the past. But is this not at the same time the proof that he is the man and poet of the future?
—Octavio Paz

In 1936 he is in Spain fighting as a militiaman for the proletarian revolution against the fascist counter-revolution, its bourgeois support, and the betrayal of the workers by the Stalinists and the anarchist leaders. In these years Péret, like the entire surrealist movement (and like so many other honest revolutionaries of the 1930s, revolted by the monstrous bureaucratic degeneration of the Russian Revolution in the hands of Stalin and his faction) made no secret of his sympathy for Leon Trotsky, for the Left Opposition, for the cause of genuine Leninism, for workers' power. He participated in the International Federation for an Independent Revolutionary Art (FIARI), inaugurated in 1938 by a manifesto written by Trotsky and André Breton. Throughout the second World War he was active in revolutionary activity in Mexico. In 1945, in a group which shortly afterward included Natalia Trotsky, Péret resigned from the Fourth International, mostly because of its theoretical and practical decline after the murder of Trotsky, but also in keeping with Trotsky's own pronouncements regarding the necessity of completely rethinking Marxist theory if socialist revolution did not emerge from the second World War. This departure by Péret by no means indicated political retirement. His subsequent activity in the realm of politics is given primarily to the re-examination of important theoretical questions and insufficiently studied episodes of revolutionary history. In this sense Péret's last political efforts could be said to parallel certain aspects of the work of INFORMATIONS CORRESPONDANCE OUVRIERES, SOCIALISME OU BARBARIE, the London SOLIDARITY group, Herbert Marcuse, C.L.R. James, Raya Dunayevskaya and others whose critical revaluations of the past remain of considerable importance in the forging of a new revolutionary theory and practice today. No one can pretend that any of these groups or individuals has found more than a small portion of the revolutionary truth necessary for the development of a movement capable of truly overthrowing the capitalist order and inaugurating "the kingdom of freedom." But against a background of Stalinist defamation and lies, social-democratic senility, sectarian irrelevance and new left pompousness, it is especially important to explore the testimony of those who pursued independent courses against the grain of the general stagnation and defeat. It is essential to learn what can be learned from them, to understand which of their efforts can be considered advances, as well as which are merely retreats. What must be avoided at all costs is the dogmatic, essentially religious spirit of simple-minded pseudo-critical complete acceptance or rejection. Lenin's critical remarks, in his *Philosophical Notebooks*, on the relative superficiality of Plekhanov, are clearly applicable in this regard. "Plekhanov criticizes Kantianism (and agnosticism in general)," Lenin writes, "more from a vulgar-materialistic standpoint than from a dialectical materialist standpoint, insofar as he merely rejects their views from the threshold, but does not correct them (as Hegel corrected Kant), deepening, generalizing, and extending them, showing the connection and transitions of each and every concept." In order to supersede the weaknesses and shortcomings of earlier efforts, it is necessary to critically assimilate their real contributions.

Péret's contributions, moreover, possess a dimension lacking in the work of his more narrowly political contemporaries. It is John Reed who once claimed to have found the thread that united cubism and the Industrial Workers of the World. A still more marvelous thread runs through the life of Benjamin Péret uniting the permanent revelation of surrealism to the permanent revolution of the working class: a double adherence to the revolutionary cause which gives Péret's entire poetic and political message a special resonance today.

Let us single out, from Péret's many political writings from this last period, a few which are of particular interest: a series of articles on labor unions published in LIBERTAIRE, in one section of which he defends certain conceptions of the little-known Dutch Marxist Hermann Gorter (13); his review of Trotsky's autobiography in MEDIUM: COMMUNICATION SURRÉALISTE, in which he discusses, among other things, the urgent significance of the Spanish Revolution (14); and his small book (forbidden to be advertised in France) *Pour Un Second Manifeste Communiste*, written in collaboration with G. Munis (15). This last work, the point of departure of which is a critique of the post-war degeneration of the Fourth International, and which also contains a brief survey of the evolution of modern capitalism, calls for a "trenchant break with dead tactics and dead ideas" and for the elaboration of a "program of demands in accord with the maximum possibilities of modern technology and culture put in the service of humanity."

The most vital and revolutionary currents in modern poetry owe much to Benjamin Péret. The appearance of his work in English translation is especially welcome (16) since Péret's characteristic aggressivity, revolt, and humor, as well as his admirably incurable passion for all that is marvelous, are precisely the qualities most lacking in poetry in the English language in this century. (One would have to go to Blake's *Island in the Moon* or to certain works of Lewis Carroll: *The Hunting of the Snark*, for example, or the songs of the gardener in *Sylvie and Bruno*, to approach, in English, the poetic universe of Péret.) André Breton, in his *Anthologie de l'Humour Noir*, has described the great poetic advance made by Péret. Before him the greatest poets in the French language had been able to see only "a mosque in place of a factory" (Rimbaud) or to see "a fig eating a donkey" (Lautreamont). Moreover, "...they seem to hold to the sentiment that they are committing a violation, that they are profaning human consciousness, that they are infringing on the most sacred of taboos. With Benjamin Péret, to the contrary, this sort of 'bad conscience' is done away with, censorship no longer exerts itself, one pleads that 'all is permitted.'" (17) For example:

I call tobacco that which is ear
and the mites take their chance to throw themselves on the
ham
hence a remarkable fight between the springs
flowing from gingerbread
and the spectacles that prevent blind men from seeing clearly
(from "Who is it?")

It must be emphasized that Péret is, far more than is generally thought, a poet of love. But love for Péret has nothing to do
with conventional pseudo-amorous sentimentality nor the vile
platitudes of so-called "popular" music: it is, rather, the most
decisive and thoroughgoing individual human experience, com-
prising the most delirious and overpowering moments of one's
life: love which is wild, succulent, corrosive, frenzied, violently
opposed to the last shred of Christian morality and to every other conceivable social constraint; love which, in a single glance,
is capable of reinventing, from scratch, one's conception of life.

*As a poet, Benjamin Péret is among the first surrealists; as a revo-
lutionary, among the first communists. As a revolutionary he was
the contrary of a politician; as a poet, the opposite of a litterateur.
–G. Munis*

The poetry of Benjamin Péret, with its rapid and violent
metamorphoses, its wild shattering flights, like a Roman candle, into the blue sky of appearances, and its mad plunges, like
an uncontrollable bathysphere, into the deepest sea of dreams,
seems to me especially well-equipped to disperse the stale
mythological fog that still obscures man's desperate glance into
the future, and to restore to man a truer vision of his infinite
capacities for transforming the world. Long before reaching the
second line, Péret has established the dictatorship of the imag-

ination and rigorously enforces the revolutionary terror of the convulsively beautiful image.

The same may be said for another category of Péret's work, his considerable number of tales (18), which are in fact really inseparable from the rest of his poetic practice. It goes without saying that these "prose" works are entirely independent of the various insignificant devices of fiction—plot, character development, setting, et cetera—literary gadgets which Péret turns against themselves in the service of a superior order of imaginative activity. Thus these narratives do not meet the ordinary definitions of a "short story," any more than the longer tales—some of which are of book length, and divided into chapters—may accurately be called "novels." The effect of these tales is like a fresh breath of pure oxygen in a musty room: one feels a certain exhilaration, a sense of expansiveness; one fells freer, surer of oneself, perhaps slightly dizzy—but it is a dizziness quite distinct from intoxication: it is the feeling of looking over a cliff at a great height which one is delighted to have reached. It is to Péret's everlasting credit that he continually reaches such heights, as far as possible from the mundane, that he does so without effort, and that he takes the reader along with him on these lyrical expeditions.

Marvelous certainty: to know that this man is possible, to behold him. —Gérard Legrand

Alongside and allied with his poetry and tales is Péret's theoretical work, the importance of which, for surrealism, is immense. In *La Parole est a Peret, Le Deshonneur des Poétes*, "Thought is ONE and Indivisible," and "Noyau de Cométe," Péret explores, with verve and lucidity, the origins and development of the poetic faculties, their applications, implications, and ramifications. Always emphasizing the liberatory essence of poetry, always defending the subversive primacy of love in the gamut of emotions, always celebrating the revolt of the mind against its jailers, he traces the trajectory of myths and legends, the perversions of religious mystification, the interrelationships between poetry and society, between poetry and revolution. These texts testify with burning clarity to Péret's relentless devotion to the cause of breaking the social, cultural, and psychological fetters which reduce the imagination to misery and degradation. "The poet of today," he wrote, "has no other choice than to be a revolutionist or not to be a poet." (19)

It was Péret's rare genius to be able to speak of revolutionary poetry and revolutionary politics equally from within. But let us hasten to add, to avoid confusion on a fundamental point, that Péret consistently refused any false, arbitrary, superficial syntheses of these two complementary but independent planes of revolutionary activity. Unlike many current so-called "cultural revolutionaries," including the ideologists of various "avant-garde" sects who boast of having "surpassed" surrealism, and who proclaim that they are able to "solve" the problems of poetry and revolution, and all problems, with the mere application of a few convenient "anti-artistic" formulas, Péret disdained such evasive pretensions and invariably approached the burning questions of human freedom with full recognition of their complexity and diversity. The cause of the liberation of the mind (surrealism) and the cause of proletarian revolution (Marxism) are not at all, in the eyes of Péret, reducible to abstract philosophical schemes or readymade slogans. They represent, rather, concrete and miraculous moments in the struggle for the total liberation of man. "These two activities," as Jean Schuster has written, "for him, surely, were but one. But the lucidity of his consciousness permitted him to understand that an objective conciliation was premature. That is why, belonging to these two very close but separate movements, he strictly forbade himself to bend the course of one in terms of the essential principles or circumstantial imperatives of the other. That is why, in all serenity, he served, on two planes, revolutionary truth." (20)

Let us mention, briefly, certain other aspects of Péret's work.

His researches into the origins of poetry led him inevitably into the realm of anthropology. *La Parole est à Péret*, a veritable manifesto of surrealist poetry, was in fact written as an introduction to an anthology of pre-columbian myths and legends. Péret visited with Indians in Mexico and in Brazil, and wrote some very interesting "Notes on Pre-Columbian Art" (21). He translated the Mayan Book of *Chilam Balam of Chumayel* into French, contributing to it an important introduction. (22) Here as in his other work one perceives the same remarkable freshness of vision, the same impassioned search for real significations beyond the surfaces of academic research.

Péret's *Anthologie de l'Amour Sublime* (23) is in many ways a counterpart of Breton's *Anthologie de l'Humour Noir*. (Is it not remarkable that Breton, theoretician of mad love, should compile an anthology of black humor, and that Péret, incomparable black humorist, should compile an anthology of sublime love ?) He also prepared, in 1959, an extensive *Anthologie de la Poésie Surréaliste*, for which he wrote a militant introduction. (24)

He wrote many prefaces to exhibitions of surrealist painters, which, if collected, would make a marvelous small volume. (25) These essays—on Wifredo Lam, Jindrich Styrsky, Joan Miró, Victor Brauner, E. F. Granell, Toyen, and others—demonstrate Péret's masterful clairvoyance, his magnetic sensitivity to the most vibrant and electrifying currents in modern painting.

Finally, it is touching to note that this author, so notorious for his alleged "incoherence," for his completely unpredictable verbal play, was employed, for a considerable period of his life, as a proofreader.

The life of Benjamin Péret: a life—as his surrealist friends expressed it in their salutation to him in a preface to the original edition of *La Parole est à Péret*—"singularly pure of concessions."

For some of us, Benjamin Péret is one of the surest guides

of the spirit through the labyrinths of contemporary confusion. Our fervent regard for his attitude of total subversion, for his exemplary poetic and revolutionary position, will doubtless seem to some professionally solemn ideologists to be exaggerated or even hysterical. But it is precisely these ideologists who reflect the incredible backwardness of this country in matters of poetry and revolutionary thought. Is it not agonizing to contemplate the great influence exerted, not so long ago, upon radicals in this country by a ludicrous mediocrity like Albert Camus, while the work of Breton and Péret went unnoticed?

❀❀❀

With him, the revolutionary movement has lost, September 1959, one of the very rare creative spirits who have, during an entire life, refused to convert their breath into money, or Goncourt or Stalin Prizes, or cocktails at Gallimard. Péret will remain for us an example, because he has defended his ideas not only in some exceptional circumstances, but day after day for forty years, by his refusal, renewed daily, to accept the least compromise with bourgeois or Stalinist infamy. —SOCIALISME OU BARBARIE

TOM-TOM 1
                    —for Benjamin Péret

even the river of blood of land
even the blood of the broken sun
even the blood of a hundred nails of sun
even the blood of suicide from the fire beasts
even the blood of ash the blood of salt
the blood from the bloods of love
even the flaming blood of the fire bird herons and falcons rise and burn
—Aimé Césaire
                    [translated by Cheryl Seaman]

The immediate occasion of this phenomenon is not especially difficult to ascertain. The aftermath of the second World War, which saw the decline of the international working-class movement, the dissolution of its most cherished traditions, the accompanying collapse of revolutionary socialist forces, and the ensuing long period of reactionary consolidation, brought about a situation in which what was left of the radical intelligentsia became particularly responsive to the most sour and funereal philosophies. It is true that to these despairing comrades there doubtless seemed little enough to inspire "optimism" or humor in the America deluged with McCarthyism. It was in this atmosphere of guilt and frustration that the "new left" was born, and though it eventually transcended its spiritual origins on the practical plane, it continued to suffer, theoretically, from a terrible hangover, the effects of which still linger on.

Today of course it is the neo-Stalinists, the structuralists of the Althusserian school, the watchdogs of sectarian sterility rather than defeated existentialists or sentimental social-democratic apologists such as Erich Fromm who cast the most somber shadows over the light which is only beginning to glimmer. I think the time has come, however, when it is necessary to put an end to this humorless farce. "Perseus wore a magic cap that the monsters he hunted down might not see him. We draw the magic cap down over eyes and ears as a make-believe that there are no monsters." So said Marx. (26) It is time, once and for all, to tear off the cap and confront the monsters. What is called for now is the ability to look squarely at that from which almost everybody has until now turned aside: social, human reality in its complex totality. The time has come when the grimace of the existialist, the pout of the structuralist, the expressionlessness of the Stalinist, the mindless uncritical grin of the hippie, the leer of the sectarian, the complacent shrug of the analyst, and the supercilious sneer of the "post-scarcity" anarchist ("Tics,

tics, tics!" cried Lautréamont) must give way, definitively, to the tidal wave of scathing humor which alone can silence the death-knells of pseudo-theory, overpower the guards of the prison of alienation, open the floodgates of authentic inspiration, and return to humanity a proper sense of its revolutionary destiny. No one is better suited to assist in the elaboration of this project of creative destruction than Benjamin Péret. In restoring to language the immense pride of laughter he has revealed the most limitless and exhilarating promise of what life can and will be.

The poetic works of the end of the last century that were considered the most hermetic or the most delirious are becoming clearer day by day. When the majority of the other works that offer no resistance to immediate comprehension have grown dim, when those voices in which a very large audience was pleased to recognize effortlessly its own voice have been stilled, it is strikingly clear that these difficult works have contradictorily begun to speak for us. Their darkness, pierced in the beginning by a single phosphorescent point that only very experienced eyes could see, has been replaced by a light that we know one day will be total. It is now beyond question that surrealist works will share the same lot as all previous works that are historically situated. The climate of Benjamin Péret's poetry or Max Ernst's painting will then be the very climate of life. —André Breton

❈❈❈

Fortunately, there are certain signs, now, of a decisive change in the orientation of American radicalism. More and more one sees, in stray corners of the emerging revolutionary movement, indications of a resurgence of critical and penetrating Marxist thought. These indications, which have just bubbled above the surface, are still isolated, just beginning to recognize themselves, and scarcely aware of each other's existence. It is the greatest hope of surrealism that these emerging rivulets will multiply, broaden, deepen, amplify their voice, and converge into an implacable river. It goes without saying that it is only in such an atmosphere of intellectual effervescence that the work of Benjamin Péret can find readers equal to its sublime message. So close to us, so astonishingly alive among us while so many others who are better known and more influential are actually little more than dead weights restraining the forward thrust, this man remains a beacon; the light he sheds is vast and second to none. To emerge from the cloisters of traditional thinking into Péret's black light of words is, to be sure, to take an extraordinary risk. But let no one who is afraid of such risks dare speak to us of freedom! In the quest for the Golden Fleece of the Revolution, he will be the loser who does not, sooner or later, encounter the illuminating, immortal, intractable, and irreducible genius of Benjamin Péret.

—Franklin Rosemont

Notes [by Franklin Rosemont]

1.   The only full-length studies devoted to Péret have been written by surrealists. These are: Jehan Mayoux, « Benjamin Péret: la Fourchette Coupante, » in LE SURRÉALISME, MÊME, Numbers 2 and 3 (1957); Jean-Louis Bédouin, *Benjamin Péret* (Paris, Seghers, 1961); and Claude Courtot, *Introduction à la Lecture de Benjamin Péret* (Paris, le Terrain Vague, 1965). In English there is almost nothing: a preface by J. H. Matthews to his translations of twenty poems by Péret, entitled *Péret's Score* (Paris, Minard, 1965); a chapter in Matthews' *Surrealist Poetry in France* (Syracuse University Press, 1969); Matthews' article, "Mechanics of the Marvelous: The Short Stories of Benjamin Péret," in L'ESPRIT CREATEUR (VI, 1, 1966); an excerpt from Courtot's study in RADICAL AMERICA (January 1970); and a worthless article by Mary Ann Caws, "Péret : Plausible Surrealist," in YALE FRENCH STUDIES 31 (May 1964). Ms. Caws is the author of another article on Péret ("Péret's Amour sublime—just another amour fou?" in THE FRENCH REVIEW, November 1966), which I have not seen; however, her most recent book, *The Poetry of Dada. and Surrealism* (Princeton, 1970), from which she excludes Péret because "his theoretical work tends toward the simplistic," (p. 14) situates her clearly in the category of those who have nothing to say.

2.   Mayoux, LE SURREALISME, MEME 2.

3.   Nicolas Calas, "Towards a Third Manifesto of Surrealism," in NEW DIRECTIONS 1940, Page 419.

4.   Mayoux, LE SURREALISME, MEME 2, p. 156.

5.   Courtot, p. 68.

6.   Mayoux, LE SURREALISME, MEME 2, p. 152.

7.   Quoted in Courtot, p. 70.

8.   Mayoux, LE SURREALISME, MEME 2, p. 157.

9.   Péret is described as a "lesser surrealist writer," in David Caute, *Communism and the French Intellectuals* (New York, Macmillan, 1964), p. 96. Most critical works on surre-

alism in English mention Péret's name only in lists of signers of manifestoes, participants in surrealist demonstrations, et cetera.

10. TRANSITION 13, Summer 1928, p. 250.

11. A biographical and bibliographical chronology of Péret's life and work may be found in Courtot, pp. 11-57.

12. Nicolas Calas, *Confound the Wise* (New York, Arrow Editions, 1942), Chapter 1, "The Light of Words," p. 28. This chapter, incidentally, carries a dedication to Péret.

13. These articles, which originally appeared in 1952, have recently been collected, supplemented with an essay by G. Munis and a preface by Jehan Mayoux, published under the title *Les Syndicats Contre la Revolution* (Paris, le Terrain Vague, 1968).

14. "Sa Vie," in MEDIUM: COMMUNICATION SURREAL-ISTE 3, May 1954, Pages 32-36. "The Spanish Revolution," Péret writes, "has not been the object of the attentive examination that it deserves." (He notes as an exception G. Munis, *Jalones de derrota, promesa de victoria*, Editorial Lucha Obrera, Mexico 1947.) "However, at its beginnings it had gone much farther than the Russian Revolution."

15. A small volume of 76 pages, published bilingually in French and Spanish by le Terrain Vague, Paris, 1965, under the auspices of the group Fomento Obrero Revolucionario.

16. Two small volumes of Péret's poetry have appeared in English translation. The first, *Remove Your Hat* (London, Contemporary Poetry and Prose, 1936) is today quite scarce, but is scheduled to be reprinted by the Black Swan Press. Matthews' volume is cited in Note 1 above. Translations of poems by Péret have also appeared in THIS QUARTER (Surrealist Number, 1932); Julien Levy, and (New York, Black Sun Press, 1936); NEW DIRECTIONS 1940, and in surrealist and surrealist-oriented periodicals such as LONDON BULLE-TIN, VIEW, CONTEMPORARY POETRY AND PROSE, REBEL WORKER, et cetera.

17. André Breton, *Anthologie de l'Humour Noir* (Paris, Pauvert, 1966), p. 506.

18. Péret's tales, in French, were collected under the title *Le Gigot: Sa Son Oeuvre* (Paris, le Terrain Vague, 1957). The first volume of Péret's *Oeuvres Completes* has just been published by le Terrain Vague. In English see "At 125, Boulevard Saint-Germain," in THIS QUARTER (Surrealist Number, 1932); "In a Clinch," in TRANSITION 12, later in *Transition Workshop* (New York, Vanguard Press, 1949); "The Gallant Sheep," Chapter 4, in RADICAL AMERICA, Surrealist Number, January 1970.

19. "Magic: The Flesh and Blood of Poetry," in VIEW (Series 3, Number 2, 1943). This is a slightly abridged translation of *La Parole est à Péret*. It was recently reprinted in ANTINARCISSUS: SURREALIST CONQUEST, an anthology published in San Francisco. Also see "Thought is ONE and Indivisible," in *Surrealism and Revolution* (Chicago, Solidarity, 1966).

20. Jean Schuster, "Profil de Péret," introduction to the most recent edition of Peret's *Le Deshonneur des poetes* (Paris, Pauvert, 1965), pp. 16-17.

21. "Notes on Pre-Columbian Art," in HORIZON (Volume 15, Number 89, 1947).

22. *Livre de Chilam Balam de Chumayel* (Paris, Denoel, 1955).

23. *Anthologie de l'Amour Sublime* (Paris, Albin Michel, 1956).

24. *La Poesia surrealista francese* (Milan, Schwarz, 1959).

25. See also Péret's critique of abstract art, "La soupe deshydratée" in the *Almanach surréaliste du demi-siecle*, special issue of LA NEF, 1950.

26. Karl Marx, *Capital,* Volume I (Chicago, Charles H. Kerr and Co., 1906), Preface, p. 14.

INTERROGATION OF BENJAMIN PÉRET, BY THE POLICE INTELLIGENCE DIVISION OF BRAZIL, 1931

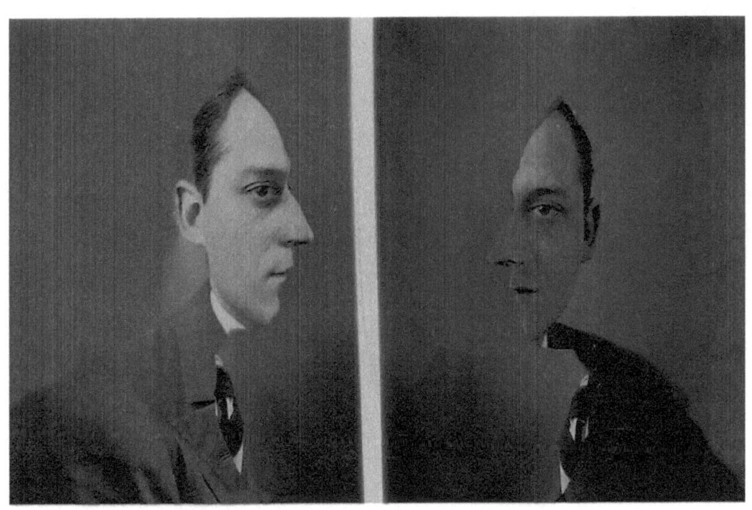

Portrait of Benjamin Péret, artist unknown

Subject: Benjamin Péret, Citizen of France. Arrest for Subversive Activities and Crimes against the Public Order and Security. Date: December 2, 1931. Case # 3,942. Session commences at 19:15 hours. Conducted by Officers B. Bonifacio and N. Santos, Intelligence Division. Recorded and transcribed by C. Branco, Stenography Office. *[Note: Though two interrogators are mentioned in the transcript, there is no indication from Nadal's holograph copy when one or the other is speaking. R.B.]*

Q: Could you tell us a bit about the Liga Comunista—its history, aims, and current composition?

BP: Composition?

Q: Its membership and demographic, if you please. Anything that would help us better understand its presence and influence. We know you are one of the group's founders, of course.

BP: Could I tell… Well. Well, let me see. Yes, it's like a Masonic club, you might say, a service organization with a venerable tradition that observes the secret protocols and rituals such tradition demands. We get together every week, sometimes more, in locations at some height, overlooking the sea. There are toasts, reminiscences, and dances in the acrobatic manner of squats and violent extensions of the legs. Copious amounts of vodka are served. Later, lectures are given to the most advanced sectors of the working class, on ornithology and micology, other topics, perhaps, like the romantic life of the Marquis de Sade and the Comte de Lautréamont's study on the gynecological organs of sharks.

Q: Your cooperation is required, Sr. Péret. Juan Mateo occupies what position in the LC, please? He is your printer?

BP: You hardly need my cooperation. The Liga Comunista is a perfectly public organization and does not hide its history or its program, which is to overthrow the current capitalist order, to be replaced by a dictatorship of the proletariat that will lead the transformation to socialism. Communism comes later, not that we're starry eyed. It will take a good while, especially in neo-colonial economies. There will be all sorts of democratic and social advances, and freedom of thought and creativity to spare, though the proletarian government will be firm with those who do it violence in the interim. Eventually, such needs of State guidance will wither away, as they never would or will under capitalism. Will that suit you as a revolutionary socialist primer?

Q: The printing press… It's source? You obviously did not transport it from São Paulo?

BP: I can't say I know exactly where it came from. It's a second-hand model, I'm sure you can see. We keep it well-oiled. The LC publishes a newspaper, copies of which I am sure you have seen. It is called *Class Struggle*. Surely you know of it? Yes. I thought so. You even have copies with you. The LC also publishes a more theoretical journal, *Bulletin of the Opposition*.

Q: Yes, we know. Its articles are a bit abstract and esoteric for the proletariat, wouldn't you say?

BP: Well, as Lenin said, "Abstraction is the highest form of reality." It is all public information, and everything you would want to know about the political program and history of the LC may be found in these periodicals. You seem quite up to speed, are you not?

Q: You can assume we are up to speed, as you say, yes.

BP: Then why waste time with needless questions? We are a reasonably well-known organization, which exists, like other Left Opposition groupings around the world, for the primary purpose of redirecting our respective Communist Parties back to their Bolshevik roots, to salvage them from the defeatist sectarianism that currently afflicts the Third International as a whole, and thus to prevent, in the first instance, the triumph of fascism in the current global crisis. Our politics are open and we reject violence as a programmatic method of political strategy, though of course we call for it in cases where proletarian self-defense against State and fascist terror is required, as it certainly will be, when the cards are on the table. And we are for revolutionary democracy and resolutely against the bureaucratic Stalinist tyranny that currently grips the Third International. So our politics are open and ready for inspection, no secret police like you required, really. As to our day-to-day operations and membership, we are a democratic centralist organization, and matters pertaining to our internal discussions are confidential, as it were. I'm trying to help.

Q: There do seem to be particularly close relations between the anti-Stalinist communists in Brazil and those in France.

BP: There are close relations between Left Oppositionists around the world, my dear interrogators!

Q: But especially Franco-Brazilian ones, which is not unrelated, it is clear, to your presence here. For example, your relationship, now a familial one, to Mario Pedrosa. Also the extensive correspondence between you and Sr. Pierre Naville with Mario Pedrosa, Livio Xavier, and Rodolfo Coutinho in 1928 and '29.

BP: And assuming this extensive correspondence exists, how would you know? Or does there also exist especially close Franco-Brazilian relations between the secret services of the two regimes?

Q: The former regime of Brazil, the oppressive one, I'm sure you know, kept close track of the mail of certain individuals. It is not our fault that recent files are still extant.

BP: Of course. And I'm sure the police services of the new and glorious democratic regime have left such practices behind.

Q: And your "dictatorship of the proletariat" we're sure would leave such practices behind as well, Sr. Péret?

BP: Not at all, speaking in broad terms. In the initial revolutionary stages it would redouble it. But not against the masses; against Capital and its counterrevolutionary efforts, just as the bourgeois state redoubles it in times of class crisis. As now. Dialectics can be paradoxical…

[Section seems to be missing here. RB]

Q: We have heard rumors that Trotsky is thinking of creating a Fourth International?

BP: As I said, I'm sure you are up to speed! And you confirm it, for such a notion and discussions around it are entirely provisional and in the earliest stages.

[Section is clearly missing here. RB]

Q: Yes, we are aware there is opposition within the Communist Party and its trade unions to the Kremlin's directives. And your organization, the LC, seems to already have a considerable influence among certain unions, like the Bank Workers, the Textile Workers, and the Graphic Workers unions in São Paolo. A presence in the Electrical and Transport sectors of the economy, as well…

BP: If you say so.

Q: Joaquim Barbosa and João da Costa Pimenta are in charge of LC trade union agitation, is this correct?

BP: Hmm…

Q: Well?

BP: I have made it clear to you that I will not discuss anything having to do with the daily functioning or membership of the LC.

Q: We remind you, Sr. Péret, that you are under arrest for subversive activities against the government of Brazil and that your freedom is at stake—and not a little contingent on your attitude and cooperation.

BP: I remind you that no threat you make will cause me to compromise any of my comrades.

Q: You have had frequent contact with Barbosa and Pimenta. In fact, you have used the press in your current Rio residence to print various materials they and their contacts have used, correct?

BP: What shame you must feel… putting under surveillance those who defend the interests of the workers and the poor. Have you ever met Barbosa and Pimenta? They are ten times the men you are.

Q: We feel no shame, Sr. Péret. This is our country, after all, not exactly yours. And our government has created the Labor Ministry to protect the rights of our workers, you must know.

BP: Your backward, provincial nationalism and patriotism is not mine, you see. As for the unions, the Vargas Labor Ministry exists to create continuous mystification among the working classes. True, the political police and the Labor Ministry have different tasks, finely speaking, but the latter is no less perverse than the former, and deserves the proletariat's permanent hostility. Every trade union in São Paolo and Rio de Janeiro has had the chance to clearly see the true objectives of this "technical" organ of the bourgeois "revolutionary" administration. Do not speak to me of your not having reason to feel shame. You who fought with Prestes, as you claim, and now represent a regime bearing all the hallmarks of a Mussolini-style proto-fascism...

Q: In fact, some of us admire Mussolini, Sr. Péret. As opposed to your divisive class struggle, his program aims to unite all classes in a common civic and national interest.

BP: Ha. How revealing. I thank you for that candor. Yes, the glories of Fascist Corporativism... Do you realize what tools you have been turned into? Perhaps I shouldn't ask.

Q: Perhaps you shouldn't. Brazil is progressing, going forward now. Here you are, trying to throw imported monkey wrenches into what a social revolution attempts to do.

BP: Hammers and sickles would be the tools... They're not imported, they're archetypal, you see.

Q: Spare us the clever asides, please. As for Commander Prestes, in fact: Your comrades Pedrosa and Aristides Lobo have been in close contact with him, have they not? Sr. Lobo, we are aware, traveled to Buenos Aires last year to meet with Prestes and won him over to your Trotskyist platform. Indeed, we know that Sr. Lobo co-wrote the "August Manifest" with Prestes.

BP: Well, politics is always contradictory and fluid. Strange things happen.

Q: What do you mean?

BP: Just what I said.

Q: The LAR certainly seems to have direct connection with the LC, given that Sr. Lobo is on the directorate of both. Siqueira Campos, we are wondering—was he also in touch with Sr. Lobo?

BP: You will need to ask Lobo once you arrest him, too. I suppose you can't ask Siqueira Campos, since your government likely sabotaged his plane. Dear me… You tenentes are a motley group, aren't you? From muddle-headed Mensheviks, to junior Roosevelt types, to Black-shirts in waiting, to Stalinists in training… Indeed, as concerns Prestes, I think you will find him in closer sympathy to the Comintern now, than to us.

Q: And are you so sure that Sr. Lobo is not an agent of the Comintern?

BP: Do you think I am so naïve as to fall for such lies and provocations? Is that the best you can do?

Q: Well, as you say: Prestes is now very much in the camp of the Stalinists, is he not?

BP: And this is the doing of Lobos, one of the finest revolutionaries I have ever known? What incredible nonsense. The tactics of planting false suspicion is a tradition of the French cops, too, which I am well experienced with, so don't waste your breath.

[Section is clearly missing here. RB]

Q: That is correct. And so we are interested to know more about Surrealism. It seems to go hand in hand with communist and anarchist activities. It seems to be attracting the attentions of some of our Marxist intellectuals, including a number of the Antropofagista group, which we wish to ask you more about soon. As it is attracting the attentions of Antillean communist intellectuals in France, we are told. Might you tell us, in short, introductory form, Mr. Pérét: What is Surrealism?

BP: What internationalists you are! You even have concern for Caribbean intellectuals in Paris!

Q: We have asked you, out of sincere curiosity, for an explanation of Surrealism...

BP: Might I give you a short introduction to Surrealism? Well...well...Let us see. What is it, or what could it be? This is a question, curiously, very similar to one I asked many poets in 1924 and 1925. So it seems I should be able to provide some help to you. I will try. May I have a cigarette? Thank you.

[Subject pauses, at length, smoking] For example: I prefer the Right Bank, really. From the flea market of Saint-Ouen to the Tour Saint Jacques, by way of Buttes-Chaumont and the Porte Saint-Denis. Let me see, I must explain. In fact, one may discern three quite discrete regions converging inside this group. Sometimes people are talking loudly, with no inhibition, and at other times, usually at night, by fountains and under trees, they speak in low confidences and comradely codes. Surprising objects and personal secrets are disgorged by the night; these are gathered by the peddler Guisançon, who sells them, for very reasonable prices on the rue Blomet: I glanced to my left and for just a moment her eyes met mine. Now half a horse I am, and I shall never return to my human ways. There was, of course, the rue Fonatine, but also the rue du Château, and, as I have said, the rue Blomet. Silence, do not interrupt. I am entering the state of half sleep, thanks to the rather uncomfortable accommodations of your City Penitentiary... Ah, yes, it was at the rue du Chateau where we first partook of the exquisite corpse. No, I will not explain the exquisite corpse to you; you must simply listen. Do not interrupt if you wish to know about Surrealism and its true secrets. The Left Bank has, still, some of its charms. But it is overrun, now, by bohemian tourists. Too many Americans and Germans and Russians with too much time in their heads and not much else. Hemingway, Stein, Pound, mere fluff and laisser-aller. I go to the Maldoror with my comrades; we ransack the stinking place. Many are injured. No, silence. I don't care if you don't think I am answering your question. It is not for cops to decide. Of course, a few cretins would spend their evenings there on the rounds of literary business and glad-handing: Desnos, especially. Good riddance. Though I should say, if one desires cocaine, it is in the The Jungle or The Jockey that one finds the best. Later, at the Cyrano, place Blanche, far from Montparnasse, you can imagine: Thirty or forty language-bundles wound up so tight our ten thousand springs were about to snap. Not even Breton could get in a word edgewise. I said Silence. Can you not see my eyes are rolled back into my head? And no, I will not stop shouting at the top of my lungs. Elephants are contagious! But now I am back at the orange-smoked Certa, in the passage de l'Opera, and all the gang is there. At the bluish-smoked Café du Globe, near the Porte Saint-Denis. Here come Ducahmp and Aragon, with their antique gait; they seem made of glass and soon will break. And here I am at the greenish-smoked Café d'Angletere, at the Carrefour Richelieu-Drouot, where Crevel is in a trance, shouting the purest and most terrible things, so terrible even Naville and Fourrier and Soupault, the prick, take their cowardly leave.

O, map of quartiers for idle wandering: O Carrefour Belleville-Oberkampf, with its giant mollusks and driftwood; O Porte Maillot, with its lozenge sky; O Opéra, with your fat ladies with clouds for derrieres; O Chaussée-d'Antin, with your thin men of gills and piglet tails; Silence! Must I shout above your remonstrance? O boulevard Sébastopol, with your Russians sunning themselves in their long seagrass hair; O Halles, with your fountain of shrouds and your hounds and crows baying at the sun; O Buttes-Chaumont, with its gardens of swan bones and moss; O du Bon Marché, with its slogan-yelling trees; O de la Trinite and Tuileries, with your chambers of aborted children extending for miles underground; O place de Vosges, seat of the enormous Cocoa Dutch Girl and a white bear behind; O des Arts et Métiers, with two wooden logs, just sitting there, for no reason at all, one tiny, one the size of the Louvre; No I shall not be silent! You asked me to explain Surrealism! O Bercy, with its little child's tune, and the seahorses going round, and Jean-Jacques Rousseau's giant stone head; O Georgette and Claude, with your rope and your doll and your open begging hands, so tiny; O, geography of gardens where the marvelous lay waiting, the Musée Grévin, and fairs and flea markets, the stalls of the Concours Lépine, of objects whose invention does not correspond to any immediate necessity , and where the poetic spirit is much more at home than in the production of a new bicycle or the machinery of a Bonapartist neo-colonial regime like this one, my tenentes. All places of no destination, paths of wonder and strangeness, to be open to one's desire. Do you know of it? Do cops and brains of wood know of desire? Silence, I say. Pérét has the floor.

Group of Surrealists, ca. late 1920s, witnessing
Robert Desnos reciting in dream-state session

Q: Sr. Péret! Enough. You will either control yourself, or we will have to control you, and in a manner you will not find agreeable!

BP: Oh my. And all I have done is tell you everything you need to know about Surrealism.

Q: What idiocy. Tell us, then, if you would, what your little outburst has to do, or not, with your comrade Sr. Breton's declaration, some two years ago, about Surrealism being, in its essence, a man going, "pistol in hand, down into the street, and shooting at random, for as long as one can, into the crowd." Is such a statement something you endorse? Please answer this question in a normal manner and without further evasion. You will be locked up for some time, sir, if you continue to be uncooperative!

BP: Do you think I am afraid? Your threats do not frighten me, Il Duce papaya head.

Q: It is not a matter of being afraid, Sr. Péret. It is a matter of using your own bald Red papaya head.

BP: Ha, touché! I love that. [laughter from the accused]

Q: Sr. Péret, control yourself. Please. We will need to take measures, otherwise, as I have said.

BP: Take them, then.

Q: Let us ask you. You seem very smug about your Surrealism. But even your former confederates, like Desnos, Bataille, Prévert, Queneau, Leiris, Vitrac, and Carpentier, last year rejected your comrade Sr. Breton, did they not? Did they not accuse him, and thus, apparently, you as well, of being a self-serving aesthete and narcissist? Tell us now, for we had asked you: Do you endorse the anarchist idea, sir, of shooting a revolver, randomly, into a crowd? You are a poet, and one assumes that words matter. No?

BP: [The detainee laughs loudly] My dear interrogators. I am at once admittedly impressed and truly dejected. Am I an anarchist? Please! You know I am a founding member of the Liga Comunista, a member of its Political Bureau. I am a communist, a Bolshevik. Apparently also a narcissist and aesthete. Anarchists do not like people like me. Though, I should say, I like anarchists, myself, and more than some of my fellow Bolsheviks do, comrade Trotsky included, who wasn't very nice to them in Kronstadt. I am impressed that you can rattle off the names of the minor renegade signatories of the inane *Un Cadavre* number II, though I did notice you had to actually read them off your notes. And your French pronunciation is for the birds. But are you really so clueless about the revolutionary movement? Mixing revolutionary Marxism up with anarchism? You need to read a bit more if you are going to serve the national bourgeoisie of Brazil and its imperialist overlords with true effectiveness!

Q: We serve no imperialist overlords, Sr. Péret, and neither does President Getulio Vargas. Are you not aware of the nationalist economic reforms currently underway? Do you think imperialism is happy with them? What is your problem with the true and lasting reforms underway?

BP: My dear tenentes. I trust you're aware there is an international capitalist depression, which has caused a deep rift between the *café con leite* oligarchy, on the one hand, and the nationalist bourgeoisie with their opportunist northern sugar-estate allies, on the other. And that the latter romantic pair is now in power, and that Getulio Vargas—who will soon become a dictator of fascist bent, like the "socialist" Mussolini, mark my words—is the head of their Executive Committee? As I said, we communists have no illusions. And incidentally, I am quite sure the reformist, forward-looking wing of American imperialism is quite happy with Getulio Vargas. Like them, he is expertly setting out to save capitalism in a moment of extreme crisis…

Q: Both of us, Sr. Péret, in its last year, were in the long march with Prestes, so you might understand that your mightier-than-thou Marxist arrogance strikes us as more than a bit presumptuous. Perhaps you have seen armed service in the struggle against tyranny? Forgive us if we do not know.

BP: I do salute you both for that service. Truly. And I honor the heroes of the 6th of July, 1922. But I would remind you that Prestes, though he has drifted towards the Stalinists, strongly agrees with my assessment of the situation! At least generally speaking. I'm sure you are aware of that. Because you are up to speed, as we all agreed. Of course, I am aware that Prestes is in a minority among your *tenente* faction—which by and large will be seamlessly integrated into the new capitalist order... It has been, for the greater part already. You both serve as shining examples.

Q: You will show respect, Sr. Péret. You are playing with fire.

BP: But otherwise, back to your fascination for Surrealism; your biggest mistake is to so simplistically confuse the artistic statements of Surrealism with its revolutionary positions, my dear interrogators. True, they often overlap, and in deep manner. But they are not the same. For example, in France, Surrealism fights within the Communist Party for a complete autonomy of poetics and art; the Party bureaucrats of Moscow and Paris want to chain artistic expression to Party command. We reject that, absolutely and mercilessly. We are for the freedom of art. Are you for the absolute freedom of art? Tell me. Because you seem to arrest writers like me and steal their manuscripts. Art cannot be chained, neither by the rotten mores and conventions you find yourself, naively, defending; nor chained by the dictates and contingencies of political or cultural apparatuses, however revolutionary they claim to be. It is in this sense, I should say, that I regard the anarchists to also be my comrades, you see, though most of them likely do not consider themselves mine… Oh, and by the way, to get back to the Second Manifesto quote— I will give you some specific information that almost no one knows: When Breton wrote about firing a pistol randomly into a crowd, I happen to know he had in mind the entrance to the Metro station at La Concorde, the main transit point in a neighborhood totally overrun by obnoxious, expatriate American writers and artists, most of them political infants, if not proto-fascists. Breton's declaration was partly a joke about Ezra Pound's stupid little piece of Japonaiserie, do you know it? Admittedly, we sometimes say crazy things for shock effect. But none of us, with the possible exception of Aragon and Crevel, would ever fire randomly into an innocent crowd. Maybe Desnos and Artaud would, granted. They are a bit touched and upredictable. But you shouldn't take us so literally. Am I satisfying you now?

Q: You are a long-time collaborator of Sr. Breton, an editor of his journal, is this correct for the record?

BP: Oh, yes. I was the original editor, with Pierre Naville, of *La Révoloution surréaliste*, starting in 1924. Have you seen the first issues? They are very exciting. And it was not Breton's journal; it was *Surrealism's* journal.

Q: You do not edit its successor, *Le Surréalisme au service de la révolution*?

BP: No, how could I? I am in Brazil. I edit *La Luta de Classes*, which takes up a good deal of my time. So that is a silly question. But I do contribute to every issue of *Le Surréalisme au service de la révolution*.

Q: And Sr. Naville is a Trotskyist, like you, is that correct?

BP: My, my, how interesting.

Q: Please answer the question, Sr. Péret.

BP: You Military Policemen are true internationalists. But wait, I already pointed that out, sorry. Monsieur Naville, you know, lives in France. What interest should you have in him?

Q: Sr. Péret, you have come to our country and helped start a subversive organization, which presently is causing not a little trouble in the trade union movement of Brazil. Please spare us your sarcastic comments about internationalism. You yourself are, safe to say, not all that interested, it seems, in national particularities.

BP: In fact, my trip was much inspired by particularities. Namely, the brilliant particularities of indigenous and Afro-Brazilian culture.

Q: Let us stay on topic. Through Sr. Naville, Mario Pedrosa was put into epistolary contact with Leon Trotsky? Is this correct? Please answer the question.

Leon Trotsky with Frieda Kahlo, Coyoacán, Mexico, ca. 1938-39

BP: M. Naville is a strong partisan of the International Left Opposition. This is open knowledge, at least in France. And Sr. Pedrosa is a strong partisan of the International Left Opposition in Brazil. Do you tweedle-dee tweedle-dums think Brazilians need Frenchmen as teachers of politics? What is your point?

Q: Your brother-in-law and Marxist comrade Mario Pedrosa met Sr. Naville in Paris, we presume, when he also first met you? And his direct contact with Trotsky was through Naville, is this right?

BP: What? I do not know. Nor would I tell you if I did. As I have made clear, you will get nothing from me that pertains to non-public information concerning my comrades in Brazil or France. I'll tell you anything you want to know about France in general and Surrealism, though. Would you like me to keep explaining Surrealism?

Q: It does seem that France and Surrealism have not a little to do with Trotskyist extremist Marxism in Brazil.

BP: That is an interesting phrase, "Trotskyist extremist Marxism." I have never heard it before. We tend to simply say "communism," or "revolutionary socialism."

Q: You are denying that Sr. Naville met with your brother-in-law Pedrosa?

Mario Pedrosa

BP: I am not denying or affirming anything at all. So what if he did? That is such an asenine question. What does it matter? Maybe they went out dancing? Maybe they took in a show at the Moulin Rouge, risen from the ashes? It is clear you are fishing for information to pass on to the French political police. Has Paris promised something in return? You quislings… Hey! Get your hands off me! Bastards! [Subject stands up and has to be restrained.]

[Session resumes at 5:32, Dec. 3, 1931]

[Material seems to be missing from the restart of the session here. RB]

Q: And shortly after coming here, Sr. Péret, you seem to have established close relations with Oswald de Andrade and other individuals associated with the Antropofagia movement. Was this your intent before your immigration here?

BP: Was what my intent? Please be clear. I am not used to being pulled from bed at five in the morning. How about some coffee and a cigarette?

Q: To make contact with the Antropofagia movement… You seem to have a special interest in ethnographic matters concerning our Afro-Brazilian population. I believe you mentioned this yesterday.

BP: Yes, I suppose I do. It was, in fact, my motivation for coming here. To study the mythic and religious traditions of Afro-Brazilian culture as exemplary of the marvelous. I didn't come here to propagate Surrealism or build a communist organization. Those things became part of the mix, quite naturally and organically. Do you not somewhat share my ethnographic interest? Or are you already, comrade tenentes, ready to relegate the Afro-Brazilian population back to the disdainful racist silence of the old order? Both of you, sirs, seem to have some Afro blood in your veins. I trust you don't object to any interest I might have in the history and culture of African Brazilians?

Q: Sr. Péret, I assure you I have no African blood in me whatsoever. And any further insults from you will be firmly answered. You are under warning. I do not wish to have a repeat of this morning.

Q: And neither do I. Do not provoke us.

BP: Insults? Provoke you? You consider it an insult and provocation that someone suggest you have Black ancestry in your blood? I, for one, envy you both.

Q: Silence!

Q: Shut-up!

BP: So, speaking of things Afro-Brazilian, my detective twins, can you tell me if I will be getting back the papers you have stolen from me, not least my study on the Revolt of the Lash?

Q: We doubt you will be getting anything back, asshole.

BP: Asshole? I thought I was supposed to be Sr. Péret? Anyway, it is a study of an important moment in Brazilian history. What do you mean? You are going to destroy my book?

Q: We will keep it somewhere, but you will not see it again.

BP: Ha! Shame on you. Censors. Fascists.

Q: Silence!

BP: Go fuck yourselves, clueless pigs in a pen.

[Section clearly missing here. RB]

Q: Very well, now that we all seem to be a bit more calm, allow me to ask: Oswald de Andrade, one of the leaders of the Antropofagia movement, is close to your communist organization, we gather, perhaps an undisclosed member?

BP: Give me back my manuscript.

Q: You will not get it back, Sr. Péret, unless you answer our questions to satisfaction.

BP: We have no "secret members"! Oswald de Andrade is not affiliated with the LC!

Q: And the faggot architect Flavio de Carvalho, he is a member? Hilcar Leite as well, correct?

BP: What reactionary impertinence. I know you won't return my party documents, but give me back my manuscript, fascists.

Q: You will now retire to your cell. We will return tomorrow.

Q: Yes, we will try again tomorrow.

BP: You two tenentes are like Tweedle Dee and Tweedle Dum. A Siamese-Twin sideshow is a State Circus…

Q: Or it may be in a couple of days. Sleep tight and don't let the bed bugs bite. No coffee for you today.

Q: Nor cigarettes, you Parisian fuck.

[Session resumes, December 5, 15:02 hours.]

We were discussing the Anropofagista movement.

BP: It's been two or three days. I hardly recall.

Q: We have queried a few people. It seems to be the case that Carlos Drummond de Andrade does not think too highly of your involvement in Brazilian culture. He seems to have strongly distanced himself from Oswald de Andrade over the matter. He apparently feels your Surrealism is a foreign insertion into our culture. How would you respond to that?

[Subject yawns, closes eyes, and is silent for quite a while.]

Q: Sr. Péret?

OSWALD DE ANDRADE, CA. 1930

BP: I would say he is decidedly provincial compared to Oswald. Not to mention that he is clearly on the way to becoming a cultural client and manager of the new State. Both at the same time. Inasmuch as Carlos appropriates the folkloric elements of Brazil, it is no less an ethnographic presumption, really, than my own. Someone like him thinks, of course, that he has clearer access to Negro and indigenous culture than an "outsider" like me, because he is, after all, "Brazilian." But what kind of Brazilian is he? Well, he is a bourgeois Brazilian, through and through. And the ideology and privileges of his social class wire his mind no less than whiteness runs through his veins. How arrogant and ignorant he is—along with *Mario* de Andrade, too, by the way, who is just as bourgeois and accommodating to Vargas as Carlos is—to think that because they are bourgeois Cariocas they have a more pure and legitimate right to study and filter the otherness of oppressed cultures and ethnicities than I do; I who come from very proletarian stock, regardless that it is in another false "nation"—an imaginary nation, like all nations. Send the little spoiled nationalist Carlos my internationalist greetings. Mario, too. They can't hold a candle to the revolutionary principles of Oswald.

Q: You traveled to the north to do research. What kind of research? And where did the money come from for the travel expenses?

BP: To study Macumba and Candomblé. Among the great, most sophisticated cultural expressions of your "nation." I stole the money from a bank in a holdup.

Q: Please. And you also, we understand, have been writing about the Kilombo de Palmares— no doubt in revolutionary relation, as you see it, to the Revolt of the Lash event?

BP: Yes, there would be a connection, certainly, speaking in the long view of historical materialism.

Q: So the money for your research, where did it come from?

BP: I borrowed it, and I certainly won't tell you from whom, so give it up.

Q Can you tell us, please, what you have written so far about the Palmares resistance? We are aware you have already published articles on Macumba and Candomblé. Is your Palmares research ready to appear?

BP: You amuse me. Should I tell you where the manuscript

is so you can go and destroy that as well? Truly, you are odd interrogators.

Q: It's more a matter of curiosity. The Vargas government honors the Palmares warriors of old, we're sure you know. Nor are Macumba and Candomblé proper of much concern, Sr. Péret. We are more concerned with how it was you gained access to the Archives of the Ministry of War of the Brazilian Navy for your information on the Revolt of the Lash and who it was facilitated this for you. Even you can understand that such subterfuge for purposes of exposing secured state archives is a serious transgression of the law.

BP: Do you really think I would provide you with such information, even if I did agree with you that my research into a major and heroic moment in history constituted a legal transgression?

Q: Who within the Houston family gave you the contact you needed for access?

BP: Don't make me laugh.

Q: You will either tell us, or we will get the answer from your wife, or other relatives in the family and acquaintances. It is your choice.

BP: Shame on you. You bastards. You are threatening my wife?

Q: Your answer, sir. You can be assured your wife will be well-treated if she is detained. Though we cannot promise it will be a short detention, of course.

BP: This is… So… You are…

Q: Sr. Péret?

BP: I ask for a pause, please. I would like some time by myself.

Q: Of course.

BP: Could I have a cigarette and some water, please. Some coffee, too.

Q: Certainly. Take your time. Just let us know when you are

ready. We'll fetch the coffee, as well.

[Session is suspended and resumes at 17:00 hours]

BP: I have decided to tell you how I received access to the Ministry of War of the Brazilian Navy.

Q: Thank you, Sr. Péret. You are making the wise decision, and your release will be much closer for it.

BP: It is very difficult for me to do.

Q: We understand. Sometimes the hardest things are the best ones, when the decision is taken…

BP: It was Prime Minister Pierre Laval who gave me official entry. There are paid agents of France working at the Ministry of War of the Brazilian Navy, so it was not difficult to gain access, you see.

Q: What? Are you mad?

Q: Yes, are you mad?

BP: No, not at all, my echoing tenentes. I am an agent of the Second Bureau of the General Staff. It is time I admitted the matter to you. My entry was facilitated by French Naval Minister Charles Dumont, though he will likely not readily admit it, as my status is as a double agent, for France and the Government of Brazil!

Q: You are stepping over the line, Sr. Péret.

BP: We are comrades, don't you see, my tenentes?

Q: Who gave you access? We know it was someone connected to the Houston family! Stop your charade or you will be locked up and we will bring your wife and relatives in for questioning!

BP: My wife is a brave woman. More ethical in her being, by far, than both of you. She can handle herself.

Q: You are making a grave mistake, Sr. Péret.

BP: No, not in regards the meaning of my life, I am not. Unlike you, who have turned your very lives into a mistake. A bottomless pit of moral slop.

Q: Take him away. Goodbye, Sr. Péret. Enjoy your vacation.

BP: By the way, my wife, like both of you, carries a good portion of African blood in her veins.

Q: Take him out!

BP: A fat log of Surrealism up the asses of you both! Traitors of your class!

[Document ends]

Interrogation of Benjamin Péret by "Cultural Attaché" of the Embassy of France in Brazil

Benjamin Péret, Remedio Varos, André Breton, France ca. mid-1940s

Subject: Benjamin Páret *[sic]*, Citizen of France. Arrest for subversive activities and crimes against the public order and security. Interrogated by *[Redacted]*, Embassy of France. Date: December 3, 1931. Session commences at 19:15 hours. Recorded, transcribed, and translated by Sergeant G. Carvahlo, Stenography Office.

[Opening section is clearly missing. RB]

Q: But M. Péret... I'm sure you can understand that your position represents a problem—a problem for you and, because you are a French citizen, a problem for France. A bit of an embarrassment for us, diplomatically speaking...

BP: Ah, but do not worry, my Cultural Attaché, everything will be alright. I have been embarrassed for France for years, and I assure you it is possible to go on perfectly well in life, even as one feels embarrassed, mortified, even. Incidentally, I should remind you that I have legal resident status in Brazil through marriage and the lawful protections ensuing therefrom.

Q: I wish to ask you about some specific things, M. Péret, and your collaboration in answering them will go a long way to resolving the problem that faces us, I assure you. But I am curious. What things, exactly, embarrass you about France?

BP: [subject laughs] Well, well, let me see. To begin but from a dozen or so years back, might we feel some mortification for the imperialist orgy of death our patriotic bourgeoisie sent its best youth to erotically attend, commanding them to run with erect bayonets into barren fields, singing the Marseillaise, behind archaic, aboriginal masks, to choke on their blood and vomit, their limbs entangled with those of masked German aboriginal youths. Or is this something you, as a diplomat of our State, is not embarrassed to recall?

Q: I was an officer in the war, M. Péret. I served my country. I have my personal opinions about it, but I am not ashamed of my service. I am aware that you, however, were arrested as a soldier at the front for spreading Bolshevik propaganda among the troops?

BP: I see you have done your homework. Do Cultural Attachés study police files so assiduously? We each take pride, then, in our respective military services. Would you like me to continue regarding my embarrassments for France?

Q: Of course, yes.

BP: The colonial slaughter in the Rif, an obscenity of racism officially blessed by the Colonial Exhibit now shamefully on view in our City of Light, Monsieur Cultural Attaché. Not surprising that chemical weapons were used in the Rif, too, though this time more gallantly: Not against enemy soldiers, but against the civilian population! The secret locked away in your closet at the Embassy, dear sir, is that the culture of Empire is built on a mountain of bones and an ocean of repressed nightmare.

Q: Even if I admit that something of the sort is true… But then again, in our Republic, you and your Surrealist comrades were in liberty to mount your own counter-exhibition to the Colonial Exhibition. Were you not?

BP: Ah, yes, Liberty! Did the people you work for, my Cultural Attache, maybe have something to do with inciting the League of Patriots and the Anti-Jewish League to raid Studio 28 last year and ban *L' Age d' or*? What does that have to do with your notion of Liberty?

Q: I don't believe anyone needed much encouragement to express outrage against such a film. It was an outright provocation against basic morality. You can't blaspheme the nation, religion, and the family and not expect a violent reaction. But you haven't even seen the film by Messrs. Buñuel and Dalí, have you? Which for a film critic must be frustrating.

Q: I have seen the script. Buñuel mailed it to me last year, and I made some last minute suggestions. You might well have it there, in your stack of my papers, which your Brazilian underlings have confiscated from my premises. It has numerous notations by him and Dalí in the margins. You might wish to save it. Buñuel will likely be a famous name someday. Dalí, too, perhaps. You could maybe sell it at an auction.

Q: I respectfully doubt anyone would care to bid for such degenerate nonsense. In any case, the return of your papers is a matter for the Brazilian police to decide, not me.

BP: Yes, of course. But tell me, my Cultural Attaché, does your logic regarding moral offense, then, mean that those who are offended by religious and patriotic propaganda have free rein, as well, to disrupt the ubiquitous and suffocating expression of such by any means at their disposal? Without suffering detention and incarceration? May workers destroy the icons of your propaganda without arrest, like the members of the League of Patriots and the Anti-Jewish League, who got off without even a ticket, after ransacking Studio 28? If workers are offended by these icons because they represent war, capital punishment, industrial thievery, colonial exploitation, racism, and other rituals of Capital that offend their morality, will they be encouraged to express their violence by the bourgeois press and be let-off without consequence?

Q: I admit it is a challenging question, M. Péret, but I am not here to be questioned by you.

BP: But of course not! That is my point, my Cultural Attaché. We are speaking not of some abstract morality, you see, but of morality's close alliance with practices of power.

Q: Let us take a short break.

BP: As long as you need. I only wish to be an accommodating host.

[Session is temporarily suspended. Resumed at 20:20]

[Material seems missing here. The conversation seems to have returned to the topic of colonial war discussed earlier. RB]

Q: Where you see empire, M. Péret, others of us see civilization—not a perfect one by any means, but preferable to the medieval ideology of an Abd el-Krim. How long do you think your Surrealist movement would last under the Sharia rule of his ilk? Would you have France overrun by Moors of his type? Maybe as a Bolshevik you would have us just open the borders?

BP: You seem naïve in the extreme. A France governed by an Abd el-Krim would most certainly be more benign than a Morocco or Algeria under the heel of French "civilization," or a Congo under the "enlightened rule" of Belgium. The right to national self-determination is but a necessary first step towards proletarian emancipation in the colonial and occupied territories. It is *colonialism* that perpetuates and fosters backwardness and superstition. Regardless, the right to national self-determination, to freedom from colonial rule, is a basic human right. The true and major savagery, as history clearly shows, does not arise in the rebellion of the oppressed; the great barbarism is that of imperialist colonialism and the wars required to maintain its order and the division of spoils. This is the most basic truth.

Q: Yes, M. Péret. I have heard this before. You might be surprised to know I have read some of the writings of your Mufti, the late Vladimir Lenin.

BP: Ha! Spare me…

Q: Really, M. Péret. Let us try to bring a bit of civil tenor to our discussion. Anti-colonial polemics at the moment will not help; your anger at the Colonial Exhibition, however justified some of your critiques may be, is beside the point. You are, presently, a prisoner of the government of Brazil, and as a fellow citizen of France and a fellow writer, too, I am here to help, but only if you wish me to do so. The matter is very simple: Though I may be an agent of imperialism in your eyes, I am your one current hope. You either allow me to have you extradited to Paris, where you may continue your revolutionary pursuits, or you remain indefinitely in the State Penitentiary of Rio de Janeiro. I would heartily recommend the former option. Think of how interesting the situation is—certainly, you can appreciate the irony.

BP: You are a writer? Did I hear that correctly?

Q: Yes. Not as accomplished and avant-garde as you, by any means. But I have published some poems and reviews. Whatever you may think of me, I am a man, like you, of Literature. A writer, however modest my talents may be. Perhaps this will provide us some connection to enable a respectful exchange?

BP: A respectful exchange in this situation? One where I am imprisoned, threatened, and my writings have been stolen from me? You are naïve, my Cultural Attaché. And in any case, you see, Surrealism holds "Literature," as you have it, in absolute contempt; Surrealism is contrary and antithetical to the so-called Fine Arts, its protocols and comforts. Surrealism is, above all, contemptuous of those writers who prostitute themselves to the dictates of aesthetic propriety and careerism, for they do so out of pitiful ignorance of any other path, and in their whoredom they sully the boundless and total freedom of the mind. It is this infinity which we crave and prod, even as we have barely stepped into the first antechamber of an unfathomable space.

[The text is clearly interrupted here in Nadal's copying. RB]

BP: But Surrealism is not against logic, as you suggest. In its poetry, in its plastic pursuits, Surrealism deliberately ignores logic. Logic has not a whit to do with poetry's spirit; Surrealism seeks to release the pure and spontaneous, the dark and luminous *illogic* of poetry. This doesn't mean, to be sure, that we are heedless of logic's instinctual and rational uses; to the contrary, we use it in our everyday lives and in the most vernacular of ways, like all human beings. We use logic when putting on our pants and we use it in theorizing the coming dictatorship of the proletariat, when the power and culture you defend, the oppression and imperialist barbarism you would justify with your ideological logic, are smashed to smithereens in name of a new and total liberty. So no, it is naive of you to presume that we Surrealists are against "logic." In poetry, we have no great need of it; in politics and history, though, we aspire to logic's culmination and need: the revolutionary uprising of the proletariat and the abolishment of rotting capitalism.

Q: Well! And so this would seem to suggest, M. Péret, that you are disdainful of all the achievements of Western literary culture—your views are nothing but nihilist in essence.

BP: No, you misunderstand, my Cultural Attaché. Surrealism is not, in the deepest sense, against culture. It is against Culture with a capital C, but not against culture in its real and true sense. How could it be? Surrealism proposes, and proves with its works, that Culture, capital C, as you conceive it, in your reified way, has only conditionally to do, in the dialectical sense, with any revolutionary work of poetry, with any true, uncompromised work of the imagination. This is why Rimbaud and Baudelaire will remain forever alien to your kind, even as you attempt to enshrine them within your museum apparatuses. They laugh at you, and their scorn should shatter your cuddly bourgeois sleep. Though I know it never will, for you sleep soundly, and your dreams are to your conscience what meringue is to the pie.

Q: My, you are so arrogant, M. Péret, so superior to lesser people like me, I see! Your poetry—which is against the very spirit and principles of Art... Who will want to listen? You are an elitist, are you not? Worse than the Claudels and Barbusses you claim to despise. Even the Communists see you in this way. How sad!

BP: Surrealism, my Cultural Attaché, is a thoroughly disinterested project. Not a one of us writes for the public. Which is to say, not a one of us writes for literary success or its pathetic accolades. No true work of poetry is ever written for the reader. It is the truly disinterested writers who split life open with the most beautiful, and true incisions, and proceed to plumb the depths. Do you think Lautréamont wrote for the public? De Sade? Rimbaud? Kneel before them. They slice your brain into countless flowerettes.

[*Text seems possibly briefly interrupted here. RB*]

So we don't seek, like you and your kind, to please the public, to seek its admiration. Nor do we seek to merely displease them, as it were. We seek their hatred, rather. When we do not sense that small, first triumph of bourgeois hatred, we are sure to feel on the wrong path. As for the Communist Party, of which I was a member, yes, the relationship with Surrealism is complicated, and, I would wager, likely to grow even more so. I don't think you have any idea what the issues are, so I'll ignore your silly remark on it.

Do you see what I mean? I am here, within your logic, gesturing at something I doubt you could understand, my dear Cultural Attaché.

Q: I must be honest with you, M. Péret. You sound somewhat unhinged to me. Perhaps I better understand now from where your gratuitous, childish insults against the Church proceed.

BP: Do I sound unhinged? In the throes of an impolite hysteria? Perhaps I should read more Paul Claudel to better my syntax. More Anatole France. No doubt these are favorites of yours, no? Speaking of France, the overripe nation-state, that is, will you still send me back there? Or perhaps to Austria? Or Asturias? Or Anatolia? Or Antigua? Or Argentina? Automatic writing, the very core of Surrealist principle, springs directly from the theory and practice—the praxis, that is—of Freud, though not that we praise him unconditionally, by any means. But like us, he urges the subject to say all and whatever comes into her or his mind. We do the same. We do it, in the best and purest expressions of our work, without amendments, putting aside the editions of reason from the start. Including in our insults towards clerics, those pederasts who serve a dogma that would infantilize the minds of the people. That is where true childishness resides. Do you go to mass yourself? I don't doubt it. Long live the materialist science of consciousness, yet in its infancy. I spit on your pederast priests.

Q: Sir, my religion or lack of it is of no concern here. You must see, M. Pérét, how despite your claims for absolute freedom and contempt for the canon, you really do call upon the instruments of control and prejudice to suppress the validity of those traditions or beliefs you reject. Perhaps your ideology is caught in a kind of trap? A purported dialectics that is stuck at its antithesis…

BP: Ah, my Cultural Attaché, I salute you. I don't disrespect your intellect. But you see, it is you who is stuck. For we are resolutely against reified assumptions of all kinds, which we reject with the sovereign pride of the imagination's ancient power and autonomy. And we are, above all, resolutely against any kind of suppression of the imagination, even of the reactionary imagination that is in service to imperialism, war, and anti-Semitism. We decline, absolutely, to engage in polite debates about such calcified prejudices and assumptions; we begin, rather, by insulting the imbeciles who consider them *worthy* of discussion. But we would never *ban* them. We are somewhat old-fashioned Enlightenment types. You know, Voltaire, and all that. Do you like Voltaire?

Q: Yes, I like Voltaire, Sr. Péret. You can be sure of it. I apologize to you, my superior in all things related to the mind and the imagination.

[There is an obvious break here in Nadal's copying, and perhaps an extended portion has been left out. RB]

Q: Would you allow me, nevertheless, to express my admiration for your articles in *O Diario de Norte*, on the Afro arts of Brazil? I myself, as a fan of Josephine Baker, am fascinated by Afro-Brazilian dance and ceremony. I have witnessed, on various occasions, the ceremonies of the Lei de Angola. I found your exposition on Macumba and Candomblé among the best things I have read on the topic, even if a bit too heavy on the Marxism.

BP: Well, I must thank you, Cultural Attaché. Luckily, these pieces you so admire were finished before I was detained and thrown in prison for my beliefs. Otherwise, the drafts would no doubt have been stolen from me. Perhaps you can request to the Brazilian cops that they return my papers on the 1910 Navy revolt. I devoted much time to this study, and I consider it important. In any case, you may wish to review the articles you mention again. As I say there, the Lei de Angola of the mulattos is quite tame compared to the Lei de Nago of the Blacks. And Josephine Baker is but a pale shade next to the macumba of the Nago! She performs to tickle the testicles of Parisian whites like you. The Lei de Nago has no audience or purpose other than its own ecstasy and vision. Tio F. is a great cultural figure, a much greater one than Paul Claudel, for example.

Q: Interesting. I am not conversant with the Lei de Nago. But I am afraid I have no authority over the police forces of this country, M. Péret. It is understandable they would not look kindly upon a study of the Revolt of the Lash.

BP: Ah! So you have read it?

Q: Yes. Much of it. I would want to read it more carefully.

BP: And so it appears that your interest in the history of the most oppressed of this country has its limits... It is "understandable" that some of that history would be drowned.

Q: As I said, the question of this is not for me to decide. I am told you gathered material for this work from secured files in the offices of the Ministry of War of the Brazilian Navy. Quite a feat!

BP: Well, the national bourgeoisie is in crisis these days. There are divisions and contradictions to be exploited.

Q: Through your contact with the Houston family?

BP: For a Cultural Attaché with "no authority over the Brazilian police," your interests seem quite local and particular. Even creepily personal, I should say.

Q: I am simply referring to the well-known fact that the residence of the Houston family is a gathering place for many influential people of radical persuasion.

BP: Radical persuasion! Ah, priceless. Is Mr. Radical Nationalism himself, then, Getulio Vargas, under watch, as well?

Getúlio Vargas, 1930

Q: I think you know what I mean. And in truth, I myself have been to the Houston's house. You and I met briefly, introduced by your father-in-law. I assume you don't remember. I had a beard at the time.

BP: A real beard or a false beard? A pointy beard or a round beard? A short beard or a long beard?

Q: Please, M. Péret. As I said, I am here to assist you, and all you do is insult me. Let me be frank. Either we have a cordial conversation on certain matters that are of interest to me and the government of our country, or we will have no choice but to surrender your fate to the local authorities. In the former case, you will be returned to France where you will be free to go about your Marxist-Leninist and avant-garde business; in the latter case, you will, it is my supposition, be spending quite a bit more time in the hospitable prisons of Rio. And what would be the political and artistic worth of that? Your choice.

BP: Ah, now the silken gloves of Culture come off.

[Session is suspended until the next day. Session Resumes at 7:02]

Q: I want to be clear so that no more time is wasted. We have deep differences of thought, you and I, and I welcome your expression of them. But I would like us to be able to converse in a more open and relaxed manner than yesterday, if that is possible. All I ask is a reasonable measure of mutual respect. My desire is to get you out of here. I will need some cooperation from you so that may happen.

BP: And what is it you want to know?

Q: Would you like a cigarette? Of course. You are welcome. And let me say that these topics are in great measure of personal interest to me, as someone who has been involved in literary circles at home and who has a curiosity to better understand the nature of your Surrealist group. Regardless of your feelings about "Literature" grandly conceived.

BP: Yes, you mentioned your contributions to certain journals earlier. To which ones, I am wondering?

Q: Thank you for asking. I have written five or six essay-reviews for *Le Figaro, Revue Européenne,* and *Les Feuilles Libres,* and I have published two poems in *transition,* which were translated into English by Maria McDonald Jolas. The poems are under a Bulgarian pseudonym; the essays under a French pen-name.

BP: Well! Was all this done when you still had a beard?

Q: You are humorous. It may surprise you that about three years ago, in *L'Humanité,* you commented, if somewhat neutrally and in passing, on an essay I wrote on Valery Larbaud, published by *Les Feuilles Libres.* My pseudonym for that piece was Alphonse Constant. Of course, I doubt you recall.

BP: I do somewhat recall. We Surrealists hold Larbaud in some esteem. I believe I was also commenting there on recent work in different locales: *La Revue Européenne, transition, Clarté, Correspondance, and Philosophies,* I believe, among others. *Variétés,* too. One of my irregular chronicles of the journals. I don't remember your essay, exactly, but I do believe I was highlighting work I felt was worth notice, so I must have found something to recommend it. And I should say: I am impressed that you published in *transition,* a notable journal, to be sure.

What issue number are the poems in, by the way?

Q: I can't exactly recall. Both issues came out in 1927, which I believe was the journal's first year. André Breton has been in the journal, you must know. But they are pleasing to me, your comments. Thank you. I do remember you weren't so kind to various contributions that year by Marras, Daudet, or Drieu La Rochelle!

Breton (right) and Louis Aragon, ca. 1924

BP: Of course not. I have little patience for bottom-barrel anti-Semites, and even less so when they are horrible writers.

Q: I am pleased that we both share an aversion to anti-Semitism. Though I have to confess that I have loved Barrès since I was an adolescent.

BP: Yes, he does seem to attract adolescent readers…

Q: Well, but he, at least, achieves glorious prose, I believe, despite some of his meretricious ideas.

BP: There are moments, I suppose. It can happen across the arts. As with Wagner. Or Degas. Or Goethe, say. Though it is rare, and it's not by chance that the strongest art, in the greatest number of cases, is accompanied by progressive thought. Not by racism.

Q: But you agree then, I see, that great writing ultimately is not dependent upon this or that politics or ideology?

BP: In the general sense you would be correct… Tell me, do you frequent Shakespeare and Co. when you are in Paris? Perhaps you know Sylvia Beach, a lovely woman?

Q: Yes, of course. I can't say I am a strong partisan of all of the literature she tends to promote, but I admire her and her bookstore immensely. I had the honor once of dining at her apartment, with James Joyce, Adrienne Monnier, and some others.

BP: Really? What was he like, M. Joyce? Breton invited Joyce once to the headquarters at rue de Grenelle, back in early 1925, and he listened in as Crevel and I went into trances.

Q: He didn't say much, in fact, and made clear he didn't wish to, so I didn't try very much to engage him. I don't know if his demeanor was due to shyness or arrogance. Mlle. Beach, Djuna Barnes, and Mina Loy did most of the talking, rather raucously, to be sure. Two other American male writers, an overly refined pair, whose names I don't recall, were there also. And Mlle. Barnes's companion, it appeared, a Mlle. Wood, very charming.

BP: Ah, the French Secret Service at Shakespeare and Co.! One can never tell!

Q: I go there as a writer, not in any political capacity, I assure you… But could you tell me about some things. Please understand: I am, yes, a representative of the government of France, a diplomat with a set of responsibilities. I won't deny I will be writing a report—a report, I assure you, that will be honest, factual, objective. I have questions and some of them are of skeptical kind. We are in clear disagreement about many things. But I do have respect and admiration for your work and your intellect. I am a literary man, though I know of the kind you and your Surrealist comrades disdain, and I have a sincere personal interest in learning more about your aesthetics and the larger world-view to which these are tethered—

BP: Nothing is really tethered to anything, my dear sir. You make it sound as if poetry were for us a function of politics, an instrument of ideological line. Nothing could be more false. I need to use the water closet.

[Session suspended. Resumes 8:26]

Q: Very well. I appreciate, Monsieur Péret, that we have been speaking without rancor or insults. Please allow me to help in this situation in any way I can. I must ask you a few more questions. Some of them purely to satisfy my own curiosity.

BP: And the others? I reserve the right to be frank and insulting if the need arises.

Q: Accepted. I as well. We shall be frank with each other, as men. So tell me, because I truly do not understand. What was the purpose of the libelous attack on Anatole France? After all, he, too, was a man of progressive ideals. Would it not have made more sense to attack Maurras, Claudel, Daudet, or Drieu La Rochelle?

ANATOLE FRANCE

BP: The surrealists have certainly said plenty about Maurras, Claudel, and Daudet. La Rochelle is really beneath any commentary…

Q: Well, why not Barrès? He died only a short time before France. You chose to desecrate the name of a courageous writer of the Left—a supporter of Dreyfus and of the Bolshevik revolution, even—when you could have attacked a right-wing nationalist!

BP: Ha! The scoundrels that most deserve attack are those fake fellow-travelers of the Left. Surely you are familiar with our love letters to Barbusse? Which we write without quarter even to the horror of the Central Committee of the CPF?

Q: May I ask you about something else that troubles me?

BP: Please tell me what troubles you, my Cultural Attaché. It gratifies me immensely!

Q: In 1920, in *Litterature*, you wrote an article titled "Assassiner," about the infamous Crime of Versaille?

BP: I believe so. Quite so long ago. What of it?

Q: I fail to see how a man like you, who proclaims to be committed to justice and freedom, could have written such a callous, immoral thing, where such a horrific crime is criticized not for the unspeakable horror of its nature, but for its lack of proper *aesthetic* execution… If that is the way to put it; it is difficult to find the words. And that not a trace of compassion for the victim is found therein boggles my mind. Can you not see how such an attitude would lead to outrage and contempt? How could you have written such a thing? What does such lack of humanity have to do with Surrealism?

BP: Ah, yes, Surrealism does have a way of making use of satire and irony. I readily admit it! Such base, impudent gestures, those of satire and irony… Tell me, because it troubles me, as well: Why would you regard my article in such earnest any more than you would, let us say, "A Modest Proposal"? Of course, I am aware that many did and many still do, even graduates of the Sorbonne, like you.

Q: The École normale.

BP: The École normale. Very much to the point, sir. Yes, the capacity of the bourgeoisie for literal mindedness is awe-inspiring. Let me make a modest proposal, my Cultural Attaché: What if I were to suggest that "Assassiner"— which I'm afraid I can't fully recall in detail, this was written when Dada had not yet run its course—was a species of parody of Kant: That is, of his widely accepted separation of Practical Reason from Aesthetic Judgment? A parody so extreme, it even makes fun with De Quincy? And in satirizing these assumptions, which run deeply through bourgeois systems and forms of life, it aims to poke at the ways in which a trite and debased practical morality is reproduced by the institutions of settled order—the laws, courts, parliaments, prisons, gendarmes, schools, churches, newspapers, literary journals, fine arts museums, exclusive gentlemen's clubs, ladies' clubs, too, not to forget guillotines—whose very existence and purpose for being reside in such ideological reproduction. And in this over-determined state, no pun intended, moral reason is as emptied out and passive as men with bowler hats at the Louvre. Spectators of a banal and obscene manufacture of violence and despair. Mind you, we Surrealists do not deny that the instincts and drives of violence are latent in the unconscious, that they are shared by all, even the most pious, and that these must be brought forward for chemical examination, as in a medical case study. It is the task of man to understand these impulses by courageous means, so that their ideological repression will cease to spasmodically erupt in uncontrolled war, colonial violence, unhinged murder, pogroms, and the like. A bit more "aesthetic" revolt in the face of mass violence and human degradation might be a healthy thing. Does this answer your question?

Q: Fascinating. I am very interested to reflect further… But not, let's say, revolutionary terror? 1793, the Bolshevik terror, anarchist bombings, or shooting randomly into a crowd, as your comrade Breton so recently called for; or calling in a poem, as has most recently your comrade Aragon, for randomly killing the police? These forms of spasmodic violence are different? Of these you would approve?

BP: It is a complicated situation, isn't it? And it is too bad, I suppose one could say, that the systemic violence of the oppressing order must be met by the liberating violence of the oppressed. I would propose, however, that you would do well to not equate the metaphorical violence of a manifesto or a poem with the actual, historically necessary violence of revolutionary movements or States… That the French government now aims to use violence to repress a poet's liberty of speech is the real violence, in the case of Aragon!

Q: I did want to ask you more about that—about Aragon's "Red Front."

BP: I'm sorry, I must use the W.C. again. The food in this prison makes me ill.

[Session breaks and recommences at 10:09]

Q: Such "liberating violence" as you were suggesting is not so pure, I would say. In the USSR it is even already unleashed on those who led the revolution in 1917. Soon no "Marxists" will be left who are not in line with Comrade Stalin and his circle.

BP: I believe you must know I am well aware of this. If I were in the USSR, I would no doubt be in prison, just as I am in Brazil. Or else dead. Which I may yet be in Brazil, of course… But so far, no revolution has eaten its own so much as our own, has it? Vive la France!

Q: What do you mean? Are you comparing Stalin to Robespierre? I don't follow… I am aware you are a partisan of Trotsky, who is hardly a friend of Stalin. Trotsky surely admires Robespierre?

BP: No, I am saying that Stalin represents a Thermidorian Reaction, a counter-revolutionary Terror. And I predict what he and his henchmen have set loose will make our Republican Terror look like a little barroom brawl. Stalin has the puss-ridden body of a Barras and the Medusa head of a Bonaparte. He is as far away in spirit from Robespierre as a so-called revolutionary could get!

Q: Well, but the Jacobins ate the Monarchiens and the Girondists, just as the Bolsheviks ate the Mensheviks and the Social Revolutionaries, not to mention the Kadets. Indeed, the Jacobin Montagnards also ate Jacobin Montagnards, of course, just as the Bolsheviks now eat Bolsheviks.

BP: Generally speaking, I wouldn't quarrel with the analogy. Very good. Though I would add that the remaining Girondists you favor then ate the remaining Montagnard Jacobins, and with an atavistic gusto. Counterrevolutionary violence is no more elegant than the revolutionary kind. But it is interesting to consider, my Cultural Attaché: Would the Republic you serve, in fact, exist today if it hadn't been for Robespierre and Saint-Just, Marat and Danton? Do you not have the blood of history on your conscience, as it were? Is your residence in Catete and your diplomatic pouch not an interesting byproduct of the Terror? Is the clinking of china at your table not the distant and pleasant after-echo of the clank of the guillotine?

Q: My sympathies, looking back now, would reside more with Mounier and LaFayette, with Brissot and Madame Roland, even. Or with the heroine Charlotte Corday, to be frank.

BP: My sympathies, looking back now, would also reside with Martov, Chernov, and Krasnoshchokov, say. Even with the sailors of Kronstadt, though I can't quite share that with most of my current comrades. As I said, it is a complicated situation. History is full of shadows. Much more so when we are standing in the middle of them, peering forward, stumbling against the leftover furniture, trying to find our way out of the collapsing estate... Ethical positions are always negotiated in the shadows. China gets broken.

Q: But errors at what scale? And with humility in face of such shadows or in defiance of them? And do things get broken by honest accident, or by malicious purpose? This is the question.

It is the hubris of teleology that is almost always the problem.

BP: Those of us in the Left Opposition are asking similar questions, my Cultural Attaché, though not just in the salon: In the heat of battle.

Q: Then allow me to ask you something not from the salon. Something that does not seem ironic or precious in the least. Returning to Aragon's poem… How do you justify calling for the murder of policemen? They may serve the order you hate, but they are, almost all of them, of the proletariat.

BP: It is a poem, and in poetry everything is permissible. That particular refrain that brings you and the State such consternation runs its own risks in the domain of interpretation, where earnest consideration of its literal meaning is in no way able to exhaust its unconscious reaches.

Q: I don't quite understand. You sound like you are reading from your friend Monsieur Breton.

BP: There is nothing to understand, really. Lyrical poetry can only live on extreme representations that depend on the unleashing of violent inner movements. It is a matter of freedom in face of the State, including its cops of Literature. I suppose I could be more articulate. Words fail me at the moment.

Q: Well, fine then. So on another note: What do you think of Pierre Naville?

PIERRE NAVILLE, CA. 1980s

BP: What do I "think" of Naville? My god. What is this fascination with Naville? The tenentes were obsessed with him the other day. He's a very proper and upstanding communist, OK? He was and is a comrade of mine, though differences have developed. Do you ask about him as a "literary man," as you call yourself, or as an agent of the State?

Q: I ask as someone for whom, like you, politics and literature are, historically, entwined. Naville seems to have confronted their knotted entanglements in an honest way and to have provoked some debate amongst yourselves. I am simply curious, trying to clarify my understanding about Surrealism and its relation to Marxism.

BP: Well, there are no real secrets about our debates—you can go back and read *Clarté* and *La Révolution Surréaliste*. Naville posed an interesting question in a pamphlet four or five years back, asking if the Surrealists believe the imagination can be liberated before the capitalist conditions of material and cultural life have been abolished, or if this can only begin to happen once the revolution has been achieved. It was a good question, simple, direct. It came at a time when tensions between the Surrealists and the Party were reaching a peak—we had declared our critical allegiance to the Party's program, with the emphasis of critique on its cultural line, which, directed by Barbusse, was a vulgar ecumenism, a penchant for placid realism amounting to a bourgeois pacifism. Imagine: The highest representative of the Party's cultural program is the best-selling author of a multivolume biography of Jesus! And an open promoter of the writings of Paul Claudel and Anatole France... For the Party, Barbusse's presence means cachet, respectability; it is a complete political opportunism. Our dissent from such politics of cultural decorum has created a problem. Naville would never admit it, but his question and resulting position vis a vis Surrealism, at bottom, represented a capitulation to the growing pressures from the Party leadership.

Q: That position being that Surrealism's program was a petit-bourgeois diversion from the pressing tasks of social revolution? Naville joined the Party in '26, a year before you and your Surrealist comrades, I believe?

BP: You have perhaps been reading telegrams sent from the French Secret Service? It is flattering really. It is no secret that a group of Surrealists, including Breton, applied to and were admitted to the Party in 1927. But I myself joined in '26, before Naville did, actually. If they don't have that down at the Secret Service offices in Paris, you might want to telegram them to make the correction. Tell them that besides my reviews, I worked as a proofreader and film critic at *L'Humanité* for nearly three years, before coming to Brazil.

Q: Yes. But no need to read telegrams, M. Péret. I was well aware of the admission of your grouping to the Communist Party. It was announced openly in *La Révolution Surréaliste*, in 1927. Anyway, you were speaking of Naville. He has been expelled from Surrealist circles, along with numerous others?

BP: Yes, though I hold him in higher esteem than other erstwhile Surrealists who have proven themselves to be self-serving charlatans or worse. Naville remains a comrade, even though he has abandoned the ideals of Surrealism.

Q: A comrade because he is a leading member of the International Left Opposition.

BP: Indeed.

Q: And in regular contact with Leon Trotsky, it seems?

BP: You would have to ask him. Or Trotsky.

Q: And so you joined the Communist Party in 1926, which was certainly in line with Naville's call in his pamphlet. But what are your reservations on his position, if you don't mind telling me?

BP: Goodness. You and the tenentes certainly have the hots for Naville. I give up. OK, fine. It's not confidential. You can read all about it. Naville was moving towards the abandonment of

Surrealist activity. For him, such work of and on the mind as we were undertaking was to be subsumed by the necessity of daily political militancy. For us—even as in the domain of material facts there was no equivocation possible, for all of us desired, without reservation, for power to pass into the hands of the proletariat—it remained no less important that experiments into the inner life continue, without any control from the outside, and certainly without Party control. For us the revolution was material and historical, the mind and the imagination not separate from the dialectics of struggle. We saw the bureaucratic ossifications of thought in the triteness and conventionality of the Party's cultural positions and allegiances, and we considered it to be our duty to fight against these, even while proclaiming our commitment to its broader political program. Soon, we came to understand that this political program, with all its opportunist veers and contortions, was in essence guided by what had become a counter-revolutionary spirit and impetus. And we then turned to an authentically revolutionary form of Marxism under the leadership of Trotsky and Rakovsky, though Naville and I were the first to formally join the international Left Opposition. But by this time Naville had rejected Surrealism outright. Does that somewhat help your understanding? Though again, I have not told you anything you could not find in SR or ASLR, to be clear.

Q: Yes, I appreciate your explanation, it does help me to put things in perspective. And let me restate: My aim, M. Péret, is to get you out of this situation so you may return to France. To your country.

BP: That would be what the Vargas regime desires, obviously. Please drop your pretenses of French solidarity. Or maybe you all just want to reconnect me with your eroticized political obsession, Pierre Naville!

Q: Ah, charming. Now, on another matter: You mentioned certain erstwhile figures of Surrealism whom you now considered to be charlatans. Who and why, I am curious.

BP: That is funny. Is it you, the Writer or Literature who is curious, or is it you the so-called Attaché of Culture who is curious? Regardless, I would refer you to the Second Manifesto of Surrealism and the response that followed. Which you have read. It makes no sense for you to ask.

Q: Yes. *Un cadaver.* It seems Anatole France came back to haunt M. Breton, didn't he?

BP: Bataille's little group is insignificant, the lot of them petit-bourgeois arrivistes, hysterics, even informers.

Q: Informers? Who among the renegade group do you consider informers?

BP: Wouldn't you like to know... I have to admit, regardless of our strained addresses, that I half like you, my Cultural Attaché. But you have a propensity to interject the most naïve and insulting questions. Do you not think I am perfectly familiar with the tactics used by the French cops? We may know who they are, but we won't fall for simple agent-baiting and hand you a gift. You can easily find out who they are by telegraphing Paris, assuming you don't know.

Q: I assure you I don't, in regards to informers within your ranks. But let's see, as for the excommunicated, there are, it seems, as I read here, Artaud, Masson, Soupault, Leiris, Vitrac, Desnos, Ribemont-Dessaignes, Bataille, of course, even poor Picabia, it seems. Morise, Queneau, Prévert... It seems hardly an insignificant grouplet. Rather a full-blown split and implosion of the movement!

BP: Not at all. It is a cleansing, if you will. Revolutions, in both politics and art, are won through a purging of tepid and revisionist elements within the ranks.

Q: You are the Montagnards of literature!

BP: Impressive... But no, we are an autonomous, cultural-political formation that seeks how to best put literary imagination at the service of the revolution. *Surrealism at the Service of the*

Revolution, again, is our new publication. *The Surrealist Revolution* is defunct.

Q: But you seem to contradict yourself, for earlier you asserted that poetry was not tethered to anything. Now you attach it to the Party, put it at the Party's service, as you say. Your magazine has stated the Surrealists will defend the Soviet Union in a time of war.

BP: No, there is no contradiction. Have you not heard me? Poetry is not in service of the Party. It is in service of the *Revolution*. Poetry is sovereign and autonomous.

Q: Yes, indeed. Let's see… I have the first issue of ASLR with me, somewhere here, with the Second Manifesto, where there is some charming discussion by M. Breton about the high surrealist principle of firing a pistol randomly into crowds and then going off to commit murders of psychoanalysts. I can't say I blame your former comrades for defecting to Bataille.

BP: You seem to have a whole fat file with you.

Q: Ah, here it is. And on the first page is a reply to a telegram by the International Bureau of Revolutionary Literature, the question being, "What will your position be if imperialism declares war on the Soviets." And your collective reply reads as follows: "Comrades, if imperialism declares war upon the Soviets, our position will be, in accordance with the directives of the Third International, the position of the members of the French Communist Party."

BP: It's precisely put, wouldn't you say?

Q: Yes, I'd have to agree that you precisely announce your possible future role as internal enemies of our Republic in a time of war. As allies of a foreign power.

BP: In a time of *revolutionary* war. Later on, if you read, we also make clear we will not subordinate Surrealism's aesthetic and philosophical investigations to any organization at this time, not even to the Communist Party. Poetry is free; it is not subject to bureaucratic directives or edicts. Much less to those of a bloody fool like Barbusse.

Q: I hope you won't mind my offering the opinion that such a position cannot last for long. Your overlords in the Third International, which is to say Moscow, will not put up with it. Barbusse is nothing, in that regard. What happened in Kharkov was, I'd suggest, the announcement of this.

BP: You have stayed on top of recent events, haven't you? It's true that Aragon was pressured, but he and Sadoul have put things aright with a recent manifesto, and this has led to planning for an autonomous association of revolutionary writers and artists, which I'm sure you will be hearing about.

Q: Breton and a Monsieur Thirion have been laying the plans for something called AEAR, I hear.

BP: Charming. Could you show me your card from the Second Bureau of the General Staff? I've always wondered what one looked like.

Q: I have no such card, and I assure you I do not belong to the General Staff. I am, however, a representative of the French government, M. Péret, and so of course I have my sources, just as you have yours, albeit "less official" ones, shall we say. Now, back to Aragon's "Red Front," if you don't mind. Surely your position as a Surrealist—as a poet who does not wish to surrender the liberty of the mind to the dictates of polemics, agitation, and dogma—must be harsher, more complex, than your tepid defense of the poem some minutes ago, which seemed almost a paraphrase of Breton's defense of it, which I'm sure he had to bite his cheek to write?

BP: Ha! I grow more and more impressed with you, my Cultural Attaché.

Q: Could you call me, at least, [redacted]?

BP: I would prefer to employ the more respectable honorific I have been using. It seems appropriate, given the situation of power operating at the moment, wouldn't you say? Let's dispense with pseudonyms. Save them for your "Literature."

Q: As you wish. And so, truly, I am curious. And I ask, you can be sure, quite aware of the differences and tensions that have developed in wake of the poem and other matters, between M. Aragon and you and M. Breton.

BP: I congratulate you for knowing all these things. Ideology is fluid. It flows through the membrane separating the mental states of antagonistic classes. It flows within the internecine battles of the avant-garde. Spies help, of course.

Q: Fluid in the sense that M. Aragon is moving closer to the camp of Stalin and away from your allegiance to the opposition of Trotsky?

BP: I will not speak of this. Aragon is yet a comrade. I have disagreements around certain matters with Aragon, but I defend his poetic liberty to express himself. What is your solution? To impose censorship on poets? Time will tell and you shall know of it, however things unfold. There will be no secrets in that regard, and you'll be able to read all about it in our publications. We are quite open about things when matters become defined.

Q: Quite. I believe you are, in so many words, saying that the matter *has*, for all intents and purposes, become "defined," as you term it: That Aragon has made his peace with Stalinism?

BP: I have to ask you, my Cultural Attaché: You had mentioned earlier that you knew members of *Clarté*. Where and how, may I ask?

Q: Certainly. I had occasion to converse with them, back in 1925 and '26, I believe it would have been, at the Café Cyrano and the Café Prophete. With Jean Bernier, Victor Crastre, Marcel Fourrier, Barbusse himself, others, gentlemen all. Soupault was also there on occasion—he was an editor at *La Revue Européenne* at the time. A gentleman as well. I was in touch with him, in fact, when he published me there.

BP: I am not at all surprised by the connection. Soon Soupault will be in the Foreign Service, too, I'm sure. But were you, I wonder, already an agent of the French Imperialist state at this time?

Q: I'm afraid so, by your definitions, in any case. I was working with the Department of Foreign Affairs. But my appearances at the cafés were strictly literary, I can say.

BP: Yes, I'm sure they were. And here you are, in Brazil.

Q: Here *we* are in Brazil.

BP: "We," yes. When did you arrive, I wonder?

Q: In '29, in March.

BP: It almost seems you have followed me here. At the directions of the Second Bureau. A poetic detective of imperialism… I arrived but a month before that, you know.

Q: Are you now questioning *me*, M. Péret? It almost seems that *you* followed Mario Pedrosa here. Perhaps at the directions of the Trotskyist Opposition? A poetic detective of communism…

[Document as copied by Nadal ends here. R.B.]

TWO ESSAYS
BY BENJAMIN PÉRET

BLACK AND WHITE IN BRAZIL
BENJAMIN PÉRET
[TRANSLATED BY SAMUEL BECKETT]

In the U.S.A. the Negro is an object of repulsion; but in Brazil he is regarded as a kind of social syphilis, a disease that must be treated on the quiet for fear of quarantine.

And yet, if there be any country that can be said to owe its economic existence to the Negro, that country is Brazil. This is so true that any account of the Negro in Brazil would be no less than the history of the country itself.

As early as the second half of the 17th century we find the first importations of "ebony" from the Gold Coast, Ivory Coast, Dahomey, Nigeria, Angola, etc., to supplement an Indian population that was insubordinate, difficult to capture, and harder yet to maintain in slavery.

From then till the abolition of slavery in 1889—that is to say, in the space of three centuries—no fewer than 30 million blacks, according to the most moderate estimates of Brazilian historians, were shipped to Brazil; and this represents only a small proportion of the total number of blacks embarked for Bahia, which was the capital of the country and its chief port. These same historians describe how the slave-ships left Africa laboring under their loads of Negroes packed together in the holds like slabs of meat in the modern refrigerators of Buenos Ayres [sic]. Receiving just the bare minimum of food and water calculated to keep them alive, they were allowed on deck only once a day, when the dead were thrown overboard. This daily act of hygiene was the only one indulged in throughout the Voyage. Suicides and epidemics were so frequent that it was no rare occurrence for a ship to arrive empty at Bahia. And even the few survivors were in such a condition at the end of the voyage that they were incapable of work for a couple of months.

Then they were sold in the slave-markets, usually to the planters of sugar and tobacco, who more or less monopolized the entire productive activity of the country. Working from dawn to dusk under supervision of a *feitor*, a kind of warder whose duties were quite as onerous as those of the gangsmen in the monstrous convict-settlements of Guiana, and which mainly consisted in flogging the workers into a frenzy of industry, they were shut up for the night in the *senzala*, where the majority slept in chains.

Underfed, worse treated than the beasts of burden whose office they performed, separated from their children, who according to the slave-code belonged to the boss and were sold as soon as they attained a marketable value, was it surprising that they deserted and rebelled?

Desertion was always very frequent, so much so that it became necessary to establish a special body of police to round up the fugitives. This force was under the command of *capitães do matto* (captains of the forest), whose cruelty has remained a by-word in Brazil, and who preferred to kill fugitives rather than be at the pains of taking them alive. In the sanctuary of the virgin forest the escaped Negroes formed themselves into societies called *quilombos*, whose members had usually to take an oath never to surrender, under pain of being excluded from all *quilombos* in the future, and sometimes even under pain of death. The regional histories of Brazil contain innumerable references to these *quilombos*. But the most important of all was that of Palmares, in the present State of Pernambuco, which numbered several millions of black fugitives, and whose history, on account of its analogies with the rebellion of Spartacus, is worthy of being recorded.

The Palmares *quilombo* seems to have been founded shortly after the expulsion of the Dutch from Pernambuco, which province they had occupied for about half a century, more exactly, during the second third of the 17th century. This *quilombo*, having driven off the Portuguese on several occasions, soon acquired great prestige among the slaves of the district, who became more than ever eager to escape and throw in their lot with this main body when it became known that most of the other *quilombos* had flocked to its standard.

The members of this *quilombo* had constituted themselves as a republic under the political and religious leadership of a *Zumbi* or *N'Zumbi* (Bantu for leader). But in the ordinary way this leader enjoyed no special prerogative, being called on only when a situation requiring organized action arose—for example, on the occasion of combats and religious festivals. There was no such thing as private ownership. The crops and all that was taken fishing and hunting belonged to the society. What little we know of their domestic organisation leads us to suppose that the women were the wives of all and sundry; but since they were fewer than the men it is probable that their family life was based on some hybrid convention partaking of both group marriage and polyandry.

The Palmares *quilombo* held together for twenty years, increasing in numbers all this time. A regular army was needed to reduce it to submission. The blacks of Palmares struggled on to the bitter end, and many, following the example of their *Zumbi*, committed suicide rather than surrender. Only a few hundred escaped with their lives and these were brought back into slavery.

The risings of the slaves on the plantations were also very frequent, but were usually isolated wherever the outbreak occurred, on account of the difficulty of establishing communication between the blacks of the different plantations, which were often long distances apart. The first important risings that we find recorded are those of Bahia and Minas Geraes, at the end of the 18th century. They were of course ruthlessly suppressed. Then there was a whole series of risings from 1800 to 1835, all in Bahia, with the exception of two: one, not very important, in Rio de Janeiro, the other in the State of Maranhão. But this latter was not, as the others were, confined to the slaves alone. It was rather a kind of Brazilian *jacquerie* in which whites, Indians, Negroes and half-breeds of every description joined forces against the Portuguese oppressor.

Of all the risings of the slaves in Bahia the last was the most important, and the only one which could boast of a complete program of political and social redress. The black Mussulman was the force behind all these risings: the Hausas at first, and then the Nagos. Strictly speaking, the Nagos were not pure black Mussulmans like the Hausas, but blacks who had come under Islamic influence and adopted that religion in the case of certain tribes. It is true that their ethnical characteristics are less clearly defined than those of the Hausas, who, before the European invasion, formed a people of strict determination living on the banks of the middle Niger, in the present English colony of Nigeria; whereas the Nagos are still to be found in the region of Lagos, Porto-Novo, etc. Their language is used as an auxiliary language by all the peoples of the region, not excepting the Hausas, from the Niger to the Ivory Coast. Thus in Brazil, it was customary to label as Nago every slave who spoke this language, irrespective of whether it was his native tongue or the "esperanto" that enabled him to communicate with the bulk of the other slaves.

During the night of January 6-7, 1835, the rising broke out simultaneously at different points of the town of Bahia. The insurgents, armed with pikes, axes, spades and mattocks, tried to rush the arsenal. Unfortunately the movement had been betrayed, and instead of the small guard they expected to find they were met with heavy fire. By dawn the rising had been extinguished. In the course of the subsequent investigation the ringleaders admitted that they had planned to massacre all the authorities as well as any others that might oppose their determination to set up a Negro republic. This was the last rising of slaves in Brazil.

A prosperous future now seemed in store for slavery, protected as it was by the existing laws and sanctioned by the moral authority of an unspeakable catholic church always ready to consecrate whatever forms of extortion are most likely to fill her coffers. Yet already there were signs of a movement to abolish slavery. In 1817 a revolution, or rather, a conspiracy, was on foot in Pernambuco for the setting up of an independent republic to be known as the "Confederation of the Equator," separated from the Portuguese metropolis. This future republic proposed to do away with slavery. But the plot was discovered before the conspirators were in a position to execute their projects.

Six years later a state of independence was proclaimed and the new imperial government, founded, like all the other new states of Latin America, with the support of English gold, participated in the international agreements that declared slave-trading to be illegal. But slavery was still far from being abolished in Brazil. It may even be asserted that, from the moment when the Brazilian government undertook to import no more slaves, the traffic took on an intensity such as it had never known before, rising, according to Perdigão Malheiro, from an average of 20,000 new slaves per annum, at the beginning of the 19th century, to one of almost 50,000 between 1845 and 1850.

The majority of these slaves were employed in the sugar plantations, which at that time represented the richest industry in the whole of Brazil. But already Brazilian sugar had begun to decline on the world market. The planters, steadily impoverished by this decline, held fast to slavery as a drowning man to a straw, even though a comparison between the productive powers of slaves and paid laborers showed a clear balance in favor of the latter. But the slaves represented a capital whose value increased rapidly in the second half of the century on account of the obstacles which the government had been obliged to put in the way of the contraband slave-traffic, while the planters, who depended on slave labor and who were moreover the main support of the imperial government, opposed every measure tending to restrict their prerogatives.

Against this, the planter who worked his land with paid labor had never been obliged to drain his capital of such an important sum as the planter who had purchased slaves, and was thus in a position to compete successfully with the latter. As far back as 1830 it had been possible to compare the two positions in the southern states, where huge numbers of European workers, drawn mostly from Germany, Poland and France, were being employed. Thus, when the cultivation of coffee was first introduced in São Paolo, about 1850-1860, the planters of that state were enthusiastically in favor of a policy of immigration, to which the northern planters were just as vehemently opposed, because it would prejudice their interests by lowering the value of their slave labor. The former hoped to secure, with the abolition of slavery, a "national" proletariat, already acclimatized, and consequently more productive than the imported proletariat. And because the empire was in the pocket of the slave proprietors, the southern coffee planters turned republican.

The empire, harassed by the anti-slavery campaign, decreed in 1871 that the children of slaves should be regarded as free-born. With the further development of the movement, in 1884 the states of Ceará and Amazonas abolished slavery throughout their territories.. The small number of slaves in these states made it possible to realize this reform at no great cost. In the following year the imperial government set free all slaves over the age of 60. Finally, on May 13, 1889, Princess Isabella, regent in the absence of the Emperor, who had gone to Europe for his health, abolished slavery and set free more than 723,000 Negroes all those that had not already been freed.

These liberated blacks poured into the towns, where their

distress was so appalling that they were soon obliged to return to the plantations which they had just left. But the sudden release of all these slaves had provoked a very grave economic crisis throughout the country, a crisis that precipitated the first labor movement in the history of Brazil and united black and white workers against their oppressors, though it is true that the number of white workers was small at that time.

Are the blacks any better off as a result of their liberation? In a general way, yes. But there are many important exceptions. It is true that the republic proclaimed in 1889, like the French Constituent Assembly a century before, that "all men were born free and with equal rights"; but good care was taken that these "rights" should not be upheld. It is also true that the vast majority of Negroes in Brazil, both in town and country, are workers. The lower middle-class comprises only a handful of Negroes, and the upper middle-class still less, so few indeed that they could almost be counted, certainly not more than 100 families out of the entire population of the country. It follows that the Negro in Brazil has always been regarded with open contempt. No one would be more astonished than the Negro himself if a white bourgeois were to shake him by the hand as he would a man of his own race. Among the laboring classes, however, white men and men of color live as a rule on terms of strict equality. Here their conditions of life are identical, they work side by side in a state of the most abject subjection, common victims of a destitution which compels a good part of the population to go barefoot—in order that the bourgeoisie may spend half the year in the night-clubs of Montmartre.

Yet in the states of Rio de Janeiro, São Paolo and Minas Geraes the Negro is exploited rather more severely than the white. This follows on the attempt to oppose two categories of workers, just as later an attempt was made to oppose the foreign worker to the native Brazilian. But if the latter experiment has met with a certain measure of success since the establishment of the present dictatorship, thanks to the development of a jingo hysteria that would delight our own mangy nationalists, and thanks also to the low level of class-consciousness among the unorganized Brazilian workers, it has not yet been possible to disunite the workers on the plea that they are not all covered with skin of the same color.

In the north (by which I mean all that portion of Brazil between the state of Bahia and French Guiana) this maneuver failed for other reasons; in the first place the conditions of the workers were so generally miserable that it was impossible (outside the inevitable distinction between industrial and agricultural workers) to separate them into strata of unequal status; in certain districts, moreover, the colored workers constitute the vast majority of the producers, the white confining themselves almost entirely to administrative and supervisory positions.

Thus in Bahia a century ago we find a total population constituted as follows: 26,000 pure blacks, 13,000 mulattoes and half-breeds of various kinds, and 11,000 white men. The proportion of these last in respect of the total population has only very slightly increased, whereas the proportion of blacks has greatly diminished in favor of the mulattoes and half-breeds, who form the vast majority of the metropolitan proletariat. In Bahia, as in the rest of the country, the half-breeds are divided into *caboclos* and *cafusos*, the progeny respectively of whites and Indians, and blacks and Indians. These two classes of half-breeds are again crossed with whites, then again with each other, so that we are presented with a bewildering scale of colors in which it is often extremely difficult to determine the respective contributions of the three races. Nor can we hope to produce figures in respect of the colored population of Brazil, seeing that no recent statistics exist to which we can refer. We can only hazard as a rough estimate that the blacks and half-breeds between them make up from 25 per cent. to 30 per cent. of the population of Brazil. This does not include the Indians who live in the backwoods and number close on a million. There are, therefore, at least 10 million colored men living in Brazil, and of these 10 million about four-fifths occupy the five states of Bahia, Minas Geraes, Rio de Janeiro, Espiritu Santo and Maranhão. It is also safe to say that of these 10 million four-fifths are agricultural workers, employed on the plantations, and as often as not under conditions that do not greatly differ from those of slavery.

The history of Brazil, and of the abolition of slavery at the end of the war, contains scarcely any trace of labor agitation. This may be ascribed to the rudimentary organization of pre-war industry, and, in consequence, to the very obscure class-consciousness of the Brazilian proletariat.

Only one popular rising is worthy of mention throughout this period, namely, the mutiny aboard the men-of-war, which were largely manned by Negroes. This was provoked by the ill-treatment to which the sailors were subjected. The least breach of discipline was punished by hundreds of strokes of the cat. The crews of two of the most powerful ironclads then in existence formed themselves into a "committee of action" and issued a manifesto calling on the men to mutiny. The rising broke out on November 22, 1910. A Negro, João Candido Felisberto, was elected leader, and was assisted by a staff, also voted by the crews, which contained no man of higher grade than second mate. The officers were thrown out and those that resisted, executed. The mutineers then informed the government that they would bombard the town of Rio de Janeiro, in whose harbor the ships lay at anchor, if they were not guaranteed a general amnesty and the abolition of corporal punishment. The government had no choice but to capitulate. But a fortnight later, when the ships had been disarmed, it forced a second rising and was thus enabled to arrest all the ring-leaders of the first. More than a thousand sailors were deported to the forests, and there perished. The ring-leaders were subjected to an inquisition of torture and confinement which lasted two years, until finally the few survivors were summoned before a court-martial and acquitted, just at the moment when the government, having nothing more to fear, was pleased to pardon them. Yet their sacrifice had not been in vain, for corporal punishment disappeared from that day forward.

The rapid development of industry during the war produced simultaneously a renewed influx of immigrants, mainly from the neutral countries, and a first movement of the population towards the towns. The revolutionary crisis that broke upon the world in 1917 had its repercussion in Brazil, where a number of serious strikes broke out, becoming more and more frequent and intensive till they culminated in the general strike of 1919, which paralyzed the entire economic activity of the two most important centers in Brazil: Rio de Janeiro and São Paolo. The year 1920 saw a lull in the movement.

In these strikes, as in the naval mutiny of 1910, the revolutionary element was not recruited, as in the previous century, from the victims of a single race, but from a class composed of a mixture of races. Whites, blacks and half-breeds were united in opposing the common enemy, rightly identified in the mind of the Brazilian proletariat with the boss. And since this latter was usually a foreigner, the lower middle-class, growing in numbers and impatient to take a more active part in state affairs, opened a campaign against foreign capitalists, denouncing them to the proletariat as the agents of Anglo-American imperialism, but omitting to mention that the national capitalism was entirely subservient to the economic systems of Europe and the U.S.A., of which dependence the foreign capital, amounting to 50 milliards of francs, invested in Brazil, is a more final testimony than any argument. The illiteracy of the masses favored this undertaking, which succeeded in diverting the indignation of the masses against foreign capital and thus in safeguarding the interests of the national bourgeoisie in all its ramifications. This is at the root of all the middle-class "anti-imperialist" agitation in Latin America in recent years, an agitation whose only effect can be to affirm the ascendancy of foreign capital, unless the proletariat intervenes, as it did in Chili [sic], determined to enforce a definitely Communist program.

Published in The Negro Anthology *(1934), ed. Nancy Cunard*
Translated by Samuel Beckett

THE DISHONOR OF POETS[1]
BENJAMIN PÉRET
[TRANSLATED BY CHERYL SEAMAN]

If one searches for the original significance of poetry, today concealed behind the thousand tawdry ornaments of society, one realizes that it is the veritable breath of man, the source of all knowledge, and knowledge itself in its most immaculate aspect. The entire spiritual life of humanity since the beginning of its consciousness is condensed in poetry; in it palpitates the highest creations and, soil forever fertile, it holds perpetually in reserve the colorless crystals and the harvests of tomorrow. Tutelary divinity with a thousand faces, it is here called love, there freedom, and elsewhere science. It remains omnipotent: it rushes forth in the mythical tales of the Eskimo, blazes in a love letter, machine guns the execution squad shooting the worker who breathes his last sigh of social revolution, and therefore of freedom; it sparkles in the discovery of the scholar; faints, anemic, as the most stupid productions make use of it; and its memory, a eulogy which would like to be funereal, still pierces the mummified words of the priest, its assassin, to whom the faithful listen in seeking it, blind and deaf, in the tomb of dogma where it is no more than fallacious dust.

Its innumerable slanderers, true and false priests, more hypocritical than the priesthood of all churches, false witnesses of all time, accuse it of being a means of evasion, a flight from reality, as if it were not reality itself, its essence and its exaltation. Incapable of conceiving reality in its totality and its complex relationships, they want to see it only in its most immediate and sordid aspect. They perceive only adultery without ever feeling love; the bomber planes without remembering Icarus; the adventure novel without understanding the permanent, elementary, and profound poetic aspiration which its vain ambition is to satisfy. They scorn dreams in favor of reality as if dreams were not one, and the most overwhelming, of its aspects; they exalt action at the expense of meditation as if the first without the second was not a sport as insignificant as any other sport. Formerly, they opposed the spirit to matter, their god to man; today they defend matter against the spirit. Finally, they have put intuition in the aid of reason without recollection of the source of reason.

At all times the enemies of poetry have been obsessed with submitting it to their immediate ends, to crush it with their god, or, as now, to chain it to the proclamations of the new brown or "red' divinity[2] the reddish brown of dried blood even bloodier than the former. For them, life and culture are summed up in useful and useless, it being understood that the useful takes the form of a pick-axe wielded for their benefit. For them poetry is only a luxury of the rich, the aristocrat or the banker, and if it should want to make itself "useful" to the masses, it must be resigned to the 'applied," "decorative," "household" arts, et cetera.

Instinctively, they feel poetry is the fulcrum demanded by Archimedes, and fear that if it is overturned, the world might fall on top of them. Thus their ambition to revile it, to take away from it all efficacy, all exalting value, in order to give it the hypocritically consoling role of a sister of charity.

But the poet does not have to maintain for others an illusory hope, human or celestial, or appease the spirits by inflating them with an unlimited confidence in a father or leader, against whom all criticism becomes sacrilege. Quite the contrary, it is for the poet to pronounce the forever sacrilegious words and permanent blasphemies. The poet must first of all be conscious of his nature and place in the world. An inventor for whom discovery is only the means of attaining new discoveries, he must struggle ceaselessly against the paralyzing gods who strive to maintain man in his servitude, both the social authority and the divinity, which mutually complete each other.

He will therefore be revolutionary, but not among those who oppose only the tyrant of today, inauspicious in their eyes because he offends their interests, but who extol the excellence of tomorrow's oppressor, whose servants they already are. No, the poet struggles against all oppression: in the first place that of man by man, and the oppression of his thought by religious, philosophical, and social dogmas. He fights so that man may attain an ever more perfectible knowledge of himself and the universe. It does not follow that he desires to put poetry in the service of a political action, even revolutionary. But his very nature as a poet makes him a revolutionary who must fight on all fronts: that of poetry by the means proper to it, and on the field of social action, without ever confounding the two fields of action for fear of re-establishing the very confusion which it is its task to dissipate, consequently ceasing to be a poet, which is to say, revolutionary.

Wars such as we are now undergoing are possible only during a conjunction of all forces of regression, and signify, among other things, an arrest in cultural growth, checked by these forces of regression that culture threatens. This is too evident to need elaboration. From the momentary defeat of culture flows, fatally, the triumphant spirit of reaction, and from the very first, of religious obscurantism, the necessary crown of all reaction. It would be necessary to go very far back in history to find a period when God, Providence, the All-Powerful, et cetera had been as frequently invoked by or for heads of state. Churchill delivers practically no speech without assuring himself of His protection, Roosevelt does as much, de Gaulle places himself under the aegis of the cross of Lorraine, Hitler invokes Providence daily, and citizens of all kinds, from morning till night, thank the Lord of Stalinist blessings. Far from being an unwonted manifestation on their part, their attitude sanctions the general movement of regression at the same time that it displays their panic. During the preceding war, the clergy in France solemnly declared that God was not German, while on the other side of the Rhine, their counterparts claimed for him German nationality; never have French churches had as many faithful as since the beginning of the present hostilities.

Where does this renaissance of fideism come from? First, from the despair engendered by war and general misery: no longer does man see on earth any way out of his terrible situation; or he does not see it yet, and seeks, in a fabled heaven, consolation for the vile implements unleashed by the war in unheard-of proportions. Meanwhile, during the unstable time called peace, the material conditions of humanity which had roused the consoling religious illusion, although weakened, held on and imperiously required satisfaction. Society presided at the slow dissolution of the religious myth without being able to substitute anything for it, outside of civic saccharine: fatherland or leader.

Some, faced with such ersatz, because of war and the conditions of its development, remained disabled, without any other resource than a pure and simple return to religious faith. Others, estimating fatherland and leader to be incompetent and obsolete, sought either to replace them with new mythical products, or to regenerate the ancient myths. From whence arises the general apotheosis of the world, on the one hand Christianity and on the other hand the fatherland and the leader. But country and leader, like religion, of which they are brothers and rivals at the same time, have in our time no more means with which to reign over minds other than coercion. Their present triumph, a result of the ostrich reflex, far from signifying their dazzling rebirth, presages their imminent end.

This resurrection of God, of the fatherland and leader, was also a result of the extreme confusion of minds, engendered by war and maintained by its beneficiaries. Consequently, the intellectual fermentation produced by this situation, insofar as one abandons oneself to the current, remains entirely regressive, in the form of a negative coefficient. Its products remain reactionary, whether they are "poetry" of fascist or anti-fascist propaganda or religious exaltation. Aphrodisiacs of old men, they restore a fugitive vigor to society only to better ruin it. These "poets" participate in none of the creative thought of the revolutionaries of the Year II[3] or of Russia in 1917, for example, nor in that of the mystics or heretics of the Middle Ages, because they are destined to provoke only an artificial exaltation in the masses, whereas the revolutionaries and mystics were the product of a real and profound collective exaltation which their words interpreted. They therefore expressed the thought and the hope of a whole people, imbued with the same myth or animated with the same impulse, while the "poetry" of propaganda tends merely to restore a little bit of life to a myth in the throes of its death agony. As civic hymns, they have the same soporific virtues as the religious patrons, from whom they directly inherited the conservative function, for if mythical and then mystical poetry created the divinity, the hymn exploits this same divinity. Similarly, the revolutionary of the Year II or of 1917 created a new society of which the patriots and Stalinists take advantage today.

To confront the revolutionaries of the Year II and 1917 with the mystics of the Middle Ages is nowhere tantamount to situating them on an equal. plane; but in trying to bring the illusory paradise of religion down to earth, the first are not without manifestations of psychological procedures similar to those one discovers in the second. Again, is it necessary to distinguish between the mystics who tend in spite of themselves toward the consolidation of myth and involuntarily prepare the conditions which will bring on its reduction to religious dogma, and the heretics whose intellectual and social role is always revolutionary since it calls into question the principles which support the myth in order to mummify them into dogma? Indeed, if the mystical orthodoxy (but can one speak of a mystical orthodoxy?) translates a certain relative conformity, the heretic, in exchange, expresses an opposition to the society in which he lives. Only the priests therefore are to be considered in the same light as the actual supporters of the fatherland and leader, for they have the same parasitic function in regard to myth.

To illustrate what has preceded, I need only a small pamphlet published in Rio de Janeiro: *The Honor of Poets*, which comprises a selection of poems published clandestinely in Paris during the Nazi occupation. Not one of these "poems" surpasses the lyrical level of pharmaceutical advertising, and it is not accidental that their authors, in the great majority, believed they should return to rhyme and classical Alexandrines. Form and content necessarily keep the strictest rapports, and in these "verses" the one and the other react against each other in a frantic race to the worst sort of reaction. It is indeed significant that most of these texts closely associate Christianity and nationalism, as if they wanted to demonstrate that religious dogma and nationalist dogma have a common origin and an identical social function. Even the title of the pamphlet, *The Honor of Poets,* considered with respect to its content, assumes a direction foreign to all poetry. In short, the honor of these "poets" consists in ceasing to be poets in order to become publicity agents.

In the work of Loys Masson the alloy religion-nationalism comprises a greater proportion of fideism than of patriotism. In fact, he limits himself to embellishing the catechism:

Christ, grant that my prayer may draw force from the deep roots
Cause me to merit the light of my wife at my side
That I may go without weakness toward the people of jails
that she may wash her hair like Mary
I know that behind the hills your great step advances.
I hear Joseph of Arimathy crush the limp wheat on the Tomb
and the vine singing in the broken arms of the thief on the cross.
I see you: As he touched the willow and the periwinkle
spring is posed on the thorns of the Crown.
They blaze: Torches of deliverance, voyaging torches
ah! let them pass through us and consume us
if it is their way toward the prisons.

The dosage is more equal with Pierre Emmanuel:

France gown without seam of faith
dirtied by deserting feet and spittle
O gown of sweet breath which tears

the tender voice ferociously from offenders
O gown of linen finer than hope
you are always the only garment of those
   who know the price of being naked before God

Accustomed to the amens and the ecclesiastical power of Stalinism, Aragon does not, however, succeed as well as the aforementioned in uniting God and country. He recovers the first, I dare say, only tangentially, and obtains a text capable of making only one author turn green with envy —the author of the tiresome phrase on French radio: "Furniture by Levitan is guaranteed for a long time."

It was a time for suffering
When Jeanne came to Vaucouleurs
Ah! Cut France into pieces
Day had that pallor
I remain king of my sorrows.

But it was Paul Éluard who alone of all the authors in the pamphlet was a poet, and who wrote the most finished civic litany:

On my gourmand and tender dog
On his raised ears
On his clumsy paw
I write your name

On the springboard of my door
On familiar objects
On the tide of blessed water
I write your name

It would be well to remark here, incidentally, that the litannical form crops up in the majority of these poems doubtless because of the idea of poetry and lamentation which it implies, and the perverse taste of unhappiness that the Christian litany tends to exalt with the object of meriting celestial happiness. Even Aragon and Éluard, formerly atheists, felt this obligation: one, to evoke in his works the "saints and prophets," the "tomb of Lazarus"; and the other, to return to the litany, without doubt in obedience to the celebrated watchword, "the priests are with us."

In reality, all the authors of this pamphlet, without admitting it, even to themselves, depart from and aggravate an error of Guillaume Apollinaire. Apollinaire wished to consider war as a subject for poetry. But if war, considered as combat and relieved of any nationalist spirit, can remain strictly speaking a poetic subject, it is not similar to a nationalist password, even if the nation in question, like France, were savagely oppressed by the Nazis. The expulsion of the oppressor and the propaganda to that end, spring from political action, social or military, according to the manner in which the expulsion is envisaged. In any case, poetry does not have to intervene in the debate other than by its own action, by its own cultural significance, for poets are free to participate as much as revolutionaries in overthrowing the Nazi adversary, without ever forgetting that this oppression corresponded to the wishes, admitted or not, of all the enemies —first national, then foreign—of poetry, which is understood to be the total liberation of the human mind, for, to paraphrase Marx, poetry has no country since it exists in all times and all places.

There is still much to be said of freedom, so often evoked in these pages. First, of what freedom is it a question? Freedom for a small number to oppress the whole population or the freedom for this population to bring the small number of the privileged to their senses? Freedom for believers to impose their god and morality on the whole society or freedom for the society to reject God, his philosophy, and his morality? Freedom is like "an inhalation of air," said André Breton, and in order to fulfill its role, this inhalation of air must first throw off the miasma of the past which infests this pamphlet. As long as the malevolent phantoms of religion and fatherland collide with the social and intellectual atmosphere, under whatever disguise they borrow, no freedom will be conceivable: their previous expulsion is one of the prime conditions of the advent of freedom. Every "poem" which willfully exalts an indefinite "freedom," even when it is not embellished with religious or nationalist attributes, ceases first of all to be a poem and ultimately becomes an obstacle to the total liberation of man, for it deceives by indicating a "freedom' concealing new chains. On the other hand, from every authentic poem escapes a breath of complete and stirring freedom (even if this freedom is not evoked in its political or social aspect), and thus it contributes to the effective liberation of man.

—Mexico, February 1945
Translated by Cheryl Seaman, 1970

Notes:

1. *Although* The Dishonor of Poets *(written in response to a famous French Resistance anthology of sentimental nationalist verse entitled* The Honor of Poets*) is one of Péret's best-known theoretical polemical texts, it has not previously appeared in English translation [i.e., in its original publication in* Radical America *in August, 1970. A.B.]. Much more than merely a critique of a now-foreign compilation, it is—as Jean Schuster has written—"a manifesto of revolutionary poetry."*

Ten Poems by Benjamin Péret

from *Le Grand Jeu*

translated into Spanish by Vladimir Nadal

(Translated into English from Nadal's Spanish versions, by A.B.)

[*Note: Le Grand Jeu (The Big Game) was published by Gallimard in 1928, when the Surrealist movement was in midst of its
most intense poetic and political phase. It is noteworthy that the
poems, even in the original, contain little "political" obviousness,
something consistent with comments by Péret in the previous interrogations, as well as in his essay, also contained here, "The Dishonor of Poets." The book remains Péret's largest and best-known
collection of verse. While these selected "translations" retain the
anarchic and dream-state spirit of the originals (the titles and dedications all correspond to the poems in Le Grand Jeu), it should be
noted that only perhaps three of them maintain any near relation
to their corresponding text; the rest are more like loose imitations,
if not wild inventions, where Péret's material is deeply transformed
by Nadal's imagination, all the while maintaining a weird fidelity to
the atmospheres, phrasal rhythms, and deep senses of the originals.
As such, this work is much in the spririt of the book After Lorca,
by Jack Spicer—a collection of mainly faux translations in homage
to the Spanish poet that seems to have been familiar to Roberto
Bolaño (though not Nadal, ironically enough), as Isabel Quiroga
reports in her Preface. A.B.]*

Formal Proof

To die, one must ask OK from M. Duhamel, paper wings out-
stretched
on the railing of the pont Rouelle, 1910. Should he assent,
you'll be
the one named by the Law, the proud one, with the Lion's Lips,
the liar
shot through with steel and fire, the terrible oracle to change
all maps
into a torrent of flood, the heaven of tar from where miraculous beings
fall, unstuck and dark, whom you meet each evening leaving
the theatre. Uranium mine: Its tunnels of candles and carna-
tions. Sex storm:
To confound the hijackers of the Giant Wheel, the biggest one
of France,
from the top of which the spirits of the dead gliding over Paris
are seen,
paper wings spread, the Arabs, caught by ancient thermal
winds.

The Marriage of Leaves

People from afar arrive to fields where poetry is circular
spinning at variable velocities now slower now faster on thick
hairy stems.

People notice how poetry in its various velocities
pitches and rolls like botanical waves how it prepares
in such fluctuations its ebbs and flows.

O Colonels and Captains if only each of your heads were a
fleshy
breast dripping milk your signatures for artillery orders would
be
the shapes of hands all thumbs
shaking with alcoholic tremors.
O Colonels and Captains what's in your hand…
Is it a smaller hand that conceals a yet smaller hand
and so on until all hands become an encompassing mass
in the consummation of all hands?

We will gently caress and suck the nipple of your head.
Dust rises in the solitude in tiny puffs. It desires the solitudes
that
gather in chambers inside the bigger solitude.
The boxes are metallic and they glow with their inner minimal
light. They want to be admired by the phantoms of future time
whose muffled voices are passed through rotten trunks
covered in snow. Old men come down from the mountain
struggling through great drifts of snow in the great slack
mountains. These are the scribes of poetry from afar.
Here you are. Welcome back. Let's walk among
the pretty spinning disks for a while.
Long live the Red Army.

Honor Your Dead

To Raymond Queneau

In your hand
there's a shovel
in the shovel
there's the hat head torso feet
and the dream of the viscera
of the Avant-Garde Salon
in Chicago there's also
the hope and compassion of little lights
that do not fear the contagion
there's still a nervous shudder though
it's the contagion
and a slick granite slope
which could hide swallows
but it does not hide them
because to the right
there's a dark stain like the music of guns
it's oil

Twisted Neck
to Michel Leiris

Let the stream flood thickened by great branches of wind
let it flood to the height of the Eiffel
let it flood without stop. It is raining inside a book.

A little girl from the streets flies in her dream.
The steam shoots with a whistling sound from your heart
Michel Leiris.

Discover the father of steam and your laughter will shake the
network of
model trains that puff on the tracks laid down by
Maurice Barrès
with the help of his monstrous factotum
Anatole France.

Without Tomatoes no Artichokes

My tomatoes are plumper than your hooves
and your artichokes look like my daughter who lives in
Lourdes
At the market
a tomato and an artichoke were seen
dancing around a turnip which they seemed to have mistaken
for a Maypole
which in turn as if to humor their misplaced identification of
her nature
spun slowly on its hairy root
Go tomato go artichoke dance around the turnip pole
and the day of your marriage shall be fair and severe as the
inward stare of the bream.
The wooden clogs which are made of wood regard us from a
distance
they cry for us like hungry kids with tears of clog potatoes
and they sing they make a dry coffin noise
a coffin that bursts so that a kid's corpse pops out.
And the corpse claps her hands like two clogs
and the living in their stylish hats can hear her scream through
the window pane
the backwards words are written across her face
"*Café Guillotine*. Lunch 50 Centimes."
She screams:
"No you will not have my tomato at that price!"

When There's No More Hay in the Haystacks

Should all the hay I've cut be piled upon my head
all the hay that I'd split
I'd have a head of hair of dawn and fresh cream
but the cut hay flows down the stream
like golden feathers in the wind
it bobs up it bobs down
not knowing or heeding where it goes
and the boats that try to hunt it down
with their hay hooks will never catch up to the hay
because the cut hay has wings with black veins
veins like tributaries that fork this way and this
into palaces and prisons the hay branches
into the mouths of priests
into the ears of the deaf
into the neck of those to be guillotined
upon the piled-up tombs of him or her
the hay-haired who know at their last breath the secret of hay
and into the subsidized theatres of Literature and its underground sewers
it branches and branches this way and that the hay it goes its
own black
way for it is the color of the sun and it has its own mind
it has a mind of hay

A Bird Shit on My Coat Bastard
to Pierre Naville

Empty-handed and foot in air
the good child on paired plates
was dying to laugh at a lonely
horse
at the moon
at the cops
Instead of dying
he could have laughed
he liked to pound his fist like a deaf man
on the corner tree
The tree moaned like a cat
T.S.F T.S.F.
The radio telegraph bit him on the right foot
and a bear bit him on the left hand
Since he was young he survived
They gave him Academy laurels
made him an Ambassador
Paul Claudel

Mystery of My Birth
to Colette Iaual

And when I answered him 19
he answered me 19
22 if you have the leisure to be rich
30 and 40 for the comedy in two steps
50 for your coffin suit
100 for the products of spring
For the rest I am ghost-pale and hypnotic
but tend to your medications dear physician
and leave to pure water the panic of becoming foul water

My Late Misfortunes
to Yves Tanguy

270 The birches are worn out by looking glasses
441 The young pope lights a candle and pulls off
905 How many corpses lie on the most ergonomic mass graves
1097 The eyes of the bravest carried off by the last storm
1371 It's possible the elderly will forbid the young to claim the desert
1436 First memory of pregnant women
1525 The foot dozes in a bronze jar
1668 The heart exposed to the aorta journeys from west to east
1793 A map watches and waits for the dice
1800 Varnish: Surely it's about something else
1845 Caressing the chin and washing the tits
1870 It is snowing in the stomach of Paul Éluard
1900 Beards of the children of invalids have been trimmed
1914 You will discover a substance not meant for you in Milwaukee
1922 We incinerate the phone book Place de l'Opéra

Portrait of André Breton
*—for Mario Santiago**

The gazelles caress the memory Mlle. has of them
Out comes a whole crew or team
And elegant ladies with blue eyes devouring bream
A very clear and handsome face
Face of a horse whose ears fill and fill with a clopping sound
Boredom cultivated in priceless hoard
Becoming captain of the pirate sloop Poetry Forever
The sewers are full of come
I'm on board
full steam ahead

*This is the dedication on the "translation." Obviously, it is Na-
dal's and not Péret's. All other dedications on the poem translations
are accurate, as per Péret's originals.*

OCTANOVICH PAZINSKY

MANAGER OF THE CULTURE AND LENINIST AGITATION SECTION OF THE C.C. OF THE U.S.P.R.

BENEATH THE BANNER OF SOCIALISM, BENEATH THE BANNER OF THE SOCIALIST INFRAREALISM

Speech delivered April, 1934, Poetry Month, at the Official Socialist Infrarealist Writers' Congress, founding the Union of the New Infrarealist Writers of the United Socialist Poetic Republics (USPR)

[Translated from the Russian by Vladimir Nadal]

DELEGATES OF THE FIRST CONGRESS OF SOVIET WRITERS, MOSCOW, 1934

The Congress of New Infrarealist Writers is processing with marked success. It has become the core of great attention we confess. Under the lustrous leaves and through the sheen, of vanguard sunshine showering down between. [Applause]

Only a few months back there were still humans to be met with who bayed whether this unusual congress should be convened at all. Such talk was even to be audibled in every seedy anarchist or Trotskyist hall. Now, shifty, traitorous eyes are moistened with the mists that roll from sierras of frustration in the soul. [Laughter, boos, hisses]

[Comrade Pazinsky drinks, rapidly, a glass of what appears to be water] Well, the congress has opened its coat. It has proceeded under path. It has gathered inertium at tremendous speeds. We have now reached the thirteenth day of this congress, and neither our confused, odd-coifed Chairwoman, Susan Sontagpov, nor that phlegmatic member of the presidium, Comrade Pablo Nerudakov, nor that yawning alternate delegate, Louis Aragonkov, nor our wax-mummy Comrade Anatoly Lunacharsky, who looks a bit embalmed sitting there, we must admit [Laughter and hoots]—no, no one now cognizes how to stop this congress, such a multiple of literary inquirements has it raised, such uncreative inspirationals has it unfolded in its great hike. The fascination with what's difficult has dried the sap out of our veins, and rent conceptual joy and natural content out of our minds. No more. [Applause]

Comrades! The Infrarealist Realism began in 1921, in Mexico, D.F., far from our shores. As internationalists, the brick of it swells our common chest with pridefulness. In attendance at that memorable event were our glorious head, in brilliant disguise, Comrade Stalin, [Loud applause] along with various post-Estridentists from Chile, Peru, the UNAM, and various locales on the legendary Calle Bucareli. These comrades were embryonic involved with the most advanced lumpen-proletarian poetry of that time. History shall record this secret convening in one thousand theses! [Applause] Since then, under the firm theoretical hand of our leaders, and under the guidance and protectorate of our Peoples' Prism System—the highest technic epiphany of our glorious code breakers, who cement our Socialist Conceptualism in One Country—new vistas of the poetical labor have opened, cracked and spread like the nuts of Grozny with their gauzy shells. Yes: The Socialist Infrarealist Realism treats words and textuals as material objects, not simply as carriers of meaning.

And yet, of course, for us poetical Bolsheviks, with *Marxism and Problems of Linguistics* in our satchel purses, words are *both* Objectivist Material and Carryings of Meaning; in language, as even the Zaum petits showed against their innocent willings, one can't get rid of meaning no matter how hard one exerts. Comrade Santiagosky, after confessing certain anarchistic errors, has also made this clear in the Tuesday of the past, in fresh issue of *El Zaguán* journal. But, let us never forget: Meaning is collective, always deferraled by conceptual struggle, and this truth is the Logos, as Comrade Derridashkin has said also, with courageous self-criticism, eleven days in the past. Meaning does not reside in the decadent lyrical or in the now-rubbished bourgeois subject. Meaning is now of the people, not individuated. Meaning is a matrix of materialism. This is further made proven by the digital environment where, since the dawn of electricity, we've had more signifying on our plates than we could ever consume.

But presently something has radically flipped, making this truth even more clipped: never before has the language had so much *materiality*—fluidity, plasticity, malleabilities, like dough or flesh—begging to be actively managed and massaged by the Author. Before digital language, words were almost always to be found panopticoned by simplistic, so-called intentionals on the flatland of page. Forsooth, men become attached to certain particular sciences and speculations, either because they fancy themselves the authors and inventors thereof, or because they have bestowed the greatest pains upon them and become most habituated to them. Yet how different today when digitized language can be poured by the Socialist Infrarealist poets into any conceivabling four-dimensional container: text typed into a Voloshinov-Stetsky Word document can be parsed into a database, visually morphed in Photoshopsky, animated in Flashky, pumped into the online text-mangling engines, spammed to thousands of the email addresses and imported into sound editing program and spit out as music at the Kremlin or the Hermitage or *El chavo del ocho*, staring El Chespirito. All of this we owe to our dear Comrade Stalin! [Wild applause and shouts of joy] And let us not overpass the early comrades who overcame their petit Estridentism under his guidance! [Applause]

Without doubtfulness the congress will solve and is already solving today to be a great eventualism in our literature. All of us, writers in particularity, feel that after the congress all the literature will somehow become flipped, that it will rise dialectically to a new compost in our Field. And the literary historian in ten thousand years of the future will, in our bones, treat the first Congress of Soviet Infrarealist Writers as one event marking the poetical tractor at the dawn of a new canonical in the history of literatures. As Comrade Mandelstam has asked, though he is currently on extended tour in our Siberian arenas: "Do we really need another 'creative' poem about the way the sunlight is hitting your writing table? Are the luminously see-through poets of our Soviet Infrarealism not infinitely more able?" Yes, forms are deceiving; it is the deeper Conceptual spreading that is counting. We have high towers, the highest about half a mile in height, and some of them likewise set upon high mountains—not tilting as the timorous Tatlin's, but straightened—so that the vantage of the hill, with the tower, is in the highest of them three miles at least. And our poetry shall be a viewing of vast, vacuum tundra unfolding for the peoples. [Applause]

Comrades, this congress is being visited, hook or crook, by the writers of all the peoples inhabiting the Earth. They have come here, to the congress, with all the hard problematics that are stuffing the openings of their attention. Life is a pure flame, and we live by an invisible sun within us. Both in Comrade Poundenko's report by radio technics at this congress and in re-portings delivered by the representatives of the various repub-lics of the U..S.P.R., we have been given the technicolor of all the vast cargo of life, all the rich cultural heritage that our republics possess from the firm traditions, in all their ideographical phys-iognomies, in all their phronological structures. Thank you, Ezra Semyonovich! [Crowd in Unison: "Thank you!"]

This congress has practically demonstrated that this frater-nal family of ours includes the people who can draw back like a shroud the history of their uncreative cultures for hundreds and thousands of years. The craniums of the poetical ancestors are piled there, in testimony, for us to be here, to paraphrasis Hegel. Without doubtfulness we shall go away from this con-gress enriched in our unconscious layers beyond the wildest dreams of what our Field could recompense. Circles and right lines limit and close all bodies, and the mortal right-lined circle must conclude and shut up all. [Here, Comrade Pazinsky inter-rupts his self: He audibles]: I have just been told by Comrade Radek in my ear that Comrade Poet Monsiváisnikov has arrived to the Conference on his crotch rocket from Vladivostok, the latest model made by our heroic workers in the Vehicle Works of Vershinsky City, the envy of Capitalist technism. There are those who say Comrade Monsiváisnikov is not yet a truly formed Infrarealist poet. But our dialectical hearts and hopes are open. Welcome dear Comrade Moto-Poet Proto-Cosmonaut Carlos Romanovich! [Crowd in unison: "Welcome Comrade Monsiváisnikov!"]

Prior to the congress much work had already been done in studying the literature of the peoples inhabiting the Soviet Conceptual Union. But judging from what we have heard at the congress itself, we may speak that we are only at the limen of the State-granted dacha of this great work of making the writers of the New Infrarealist Writers' Union more closely acquainted with one another, of making our writers acquainted with all that cut and paste of culture which the peoples of our Soviet Field possess in their craniums and which has been presented in such breadth and clarity at this first Congress of Soviet Conceptualist Writers. As Comrade Zhdanov has toned so convincing on this very stage, near a fortnight in the past: "20th century notions of illegibility are commonly bound up with a shattering of syntax and disjunction, but the coming 21st century's challenge to textual convention may be that of density and weight. Just as new reading strategies had to be provisionally developed by Comrade Stalin in order to read decadent modernist works of literature, so new reading strategies are now emerging on the Prism web, created by Soviet Conceptual Engineers: skimming, data aggregating, the employment of intelligent agents, to name but a few. Our reading habits seem, suddenly, to be imitating the way machines work: this writing demands a Thinkership, not a readership." [Applause] I know we all agree with the wise words of Comrade Zhdanov, to which I have just given release. What secret wheel, what hidden spring, could put into motion so wonderful an engine?

Now, the representatives of almost all nations inhabiting the Soviet Conceptual Union, representatives of the different avant literary tendencies, have spoken here. They have all raised the literary problems in their own passion, in their own literary cleft. But one thing united all their lips: all their speeches turned like doubled tops on the one thing for which our revolution is fighting—the cause of the New Socialist Infrarealism. Those unfunny lyrical Uncles who insist in trying on an old lady's hat, let them have their slight transvestite twist. Let them have it, that is, in the Courts of the People's Poetic Tribunals, where justice shall be swift! [Spontaneous, deafening chants of "Death to Counter-Revolutionary Contemporaneous Lyricists!"]

We have every right to say that this Congress, at which the delegates of the best tenuring part of the Socialist Poetic Union's post-avant have imploded, possesses, apart from the literary importance, a tremendous political meaning as well, since this congress ratifies and seals the seal on the total syntax, begun long ago—before UNAM and Café La Habana, even—by poetical emigrants from Moscow and Paris, to San Francisco and Zero Hour Lima, to Valparaíso and Barcelona, and by which the poetic intelligentsia of the peoples inhabiting the Socialist Poetic Union have united beneath the banner of the Soviets, beneath the banner of the Socialist Infrarealism. [Applause]

1. Our Guiding Line Is That of the Socialist Infrarealist Realism

The congress has been inflected by animalated discussion. Comrade César Vallejopov has had his say; Comrade Marianne Mooresky has had her say; Comrade Paul Eluardski has had his say; Comrade Volodia Teitelboimsky has had his say; and many more, through the Modernist times, including representatives from the Writing Workshops in the Poetic Model City of Juárez, led by Comrade Juan Bañueloski. [Applause] All questions of literary conundrums, like nourishing buns, have been kneaded here. In scientific maturity, we have laid open their brains, their hearts, and their spleens. The mixing of quainted metaphors is dead! [Loud applause]

Herein lies the radical differential from those days when the literary world of our country was being directed by the RAPP. You will memorialize that the RAPP, led by the deviationist Carmen Boullosava, had its own "general line," its own "general secretary," its own "general platform," which it tried to demand upon all the writers. It pushed its reactionary, subjective voice. You will likewise memorialize the embittered disputes which raged round every puckering period and every squeezing colon within this platform, a huge vine of overripe fruit, as Comrades Molotov espied, which, with its arms outspread, hung its rotten clusters overhead. [Boos and hisses]

The decision of the Central Committee of the U.S.P.R.. during Poetry Month, on April 23, 1932, "On the Reconstruction of the Literary and Artistic Organizations," put a purge to the RAPP, which had become the blockage to further development of Socialist Infrarealist literatures; this decisioning laid the foundational for the Union of New Infrarealist Writers and paved the way for that out-push of political and poetic enthusiasms to which the Congress of Socialist Infrarealist Writers bears such striking testimonial. [Applause]

May the Earth take note: The first Congress of Socialist Infrarealist Writers is marked by libertine, creative discussion of all the literary problematics. It is not passing any resolutions on the literary questions that are binding on all the writers. No one is listening, as it were, to any telephone calls. No one is being airbrushed from the recordings at Casa del Lago. No! There are few, I believe, who have not observed in themselves or others that what in one way of proposing was very obscure, another way of expressing it has made very clear and intelligible. Our congress seeks to engage all criticisms, all polemics, for it is not shy, immature, or trembling like the nubile teenager at a swimming hole, for exampling. Comrades! To think of time and the canon—have you guessed you yourself would not continue? Have you dreaded these earth-beetles? Have you feared our Party would not smash the terror of the RAPP cells and the future would be nothing to you?

When the congress's program of work was being discussed and humans were being nominated to deliver reports at this congress, it need be hardly shrilled by reactionary elements that the organizational committee consulted with our Party before making its decides. I think this is no secret to any self. But this does not mean at all that every report is some kind of Traffic Law, some kind of Court Docket, in which every word and every colon is fixed and unalterable, as in the *New Minsk Times*, in which everything must be carried out, understandably, to the institutional letter. Even as we demand more Traffic and Court reports from the Sons of Pushkin and Steinenko, this is not so, comrades. This would mean constipating libertine poetical push. We understand our condition in the dialectical; just as there is no Baroque without the Renaissance, there is no Infrarealist Enlightenment without the Baroque. Or vice versa! [Here, Comrade Pazinsky pauses, to drink, rapidly, another glass of what appears to be water]

Nor have our Party and government passed any decides to give the individual writers official testimonials or appraisals of their talentings, to knight the present poets with any special kind of "decoratives," marks of distinctives, marks of approvals or marks of tar and censure in varying centigrades. Comrade Bolañovsky, I will answer you. I do not know of any decides of our Party and government regarding the "canonization" of Marcel Duchampski. Duchampski is a mighty poetical thinker, yes, a poet-artist of the revolution, like Gertrude Steinenko, long live her memory, which imperialist revisionists have lately calumniated. But we have not passed any decides to the effect that all our Soviet poetry must take Duchampski as its sole modeling. No! Pyramids, arches, obelisks were but the irregularities of vainglory, and wild enormities of ancient magnanimity. This is not we. And if Comrade Bukharin in his report gave an appraisal of the individual poems and the work of the individual poets of the post-*Plural* era, he did so, once again, by way of raising for discussion the literary problems concerning our generous State and Foundation subsidies. This does not mean at all that every poet at this congress has received from the Party or its Cultural organs a mark of distinctive which he must take along with him in leaving. Such a thing would denote bureaucracy of the worst manifest, and you know, Roberto Ivanovich, that there is no more irreconcilable foe of bureaucracy than our Party of Poetic Socialism! [Applause] No, sit back down, Comrade Bolañovsky, you have had your say, with your flatulent wind that blows now east, now west. It is the people who now speak, and they know which way the true wind is blowing. [Applause, shouts, various slogans]

We have public opinionings, we have criticism, we have readers who have greatly developed during recent annuals of the Associated Socialist Writing Programs convenings, and who are themselves perfectly well able to judgment which work is valuable, worthy of praisings, and which work deserves tar and censuring. Besides, who ever thought any quality to be a heterogeneous aggregate, such as light was discovered to be by the great Newton? I'm not sure I put myself plainly… But here is the point of it: Pity on her who dares to insult the good faithings of our Leadership and its Thinkership! Forsooth, as Roberto Ivanovich well knows, we have in the new U.S.P.R a most advanced systemic of helping sanitariums. [Applause, shouts, laughter; Comrade Pazinsky refreshes himself, rapidly, with another glass of transparental liquid]

But if there is free creative competition in our literature, if there is animational discussioning of literary questions, that does not by any means signifcation that we do not have the guiding line in literature. No, comrades, we do have guiding line in literature, and this rock has been brought out in almost all the speeches delivered here. This rock was brought out both in Comrade Huertapov's report and in the speech of Comrade Zhdanov, secretary of the Central Committee of the U.S.P.U. and Donald. T. Beria Chair of Poetry at the Superior University of Kalingrad. Such once were critics; such the happy few. From the ivy-covered halls of imperial Philadelphia, to the picturesque redoubts of rebel Guatemala, the masses are in agreement: Our guiding line is that of Socialist Infrarealist Realism. [Loud applause]

You yourselves have said in your resolution that you want to forge works imbibed and inflated with the spirit of Socialist Infrarealism. And let us always be clarified. This in no way means that ideological spookiness is our Author. No! The truth is that the spectators are always in their senses, and know, from the first act to the last, that the stage is only a stage, and that the players are only players. They who watch know there is always somebody of flesh and bone behind the curtain, running the machineries. Contrary to what our defeated ultra-left enemies have squealed, one is always banging one's head against the brick that no matter how hard one tries, one can never air-brush the person-Author from Poetry. This is simple Materialism, like porcelain or the shovel, as Comrades Pessoakov, Chattertoninsky, Macphersoniev, Swiftenko, and…what's his name, forgive me, I can't memorialize presently… But as they all so rightly insisted to us one after another, in their own very self-critical ways and with their clarified eyes, this Sunday in the past. True, we have made passioned and correct arguments for egoless art, found art, art conduced by chance operationals and many other species, but in fact, we know, as dear Comrade Stalin has memorialized, that there's always someone—to repeat—behind the curtain, manning the machineries. [Deafening applause]

The Brand of the Author is the white-hot mold of our Socialist Infrarealism. [Deafening applause] "First follow Nature," as advised the great Emersonkov: "And then emblazon your Name upon that Following. For Nature, in her jealous Identity, always desires to be Named." Possibly my ascriptional and recitational fail a bit, and I am sounding like Comrade Borgesky back in the days when he was writing from Sakhalin, but this is one way of saying, Comrades, that certain protocols of identity are never to be conceptualized, that certain historical Laws are always to be respected by our Socialist Infrarealism. In our Revolution, we must track the track, as it were, of all unfoldings. Relatedly, if at some distancing: As Comrade Zinoviev delightfully said to me the other twilight, over a bottle of craft-made vodka at the Worker's Café in Iron Foundry 274, designed in its mystery angles by Comrade Rodchenko: "I have yet to encounter tasteless art. If there's one thing that the avant-garde has shown us, it's that regardless of form, non-expression, non-identity is impossible. Take Duchampski, dear Octavinov Ivanovich," said he. "Every *objet trouvé* of Duchampski's reeked of his refined taste. He chose the right ingredients and mixed them together with such exquisite taste that they couldn't help but be not only beautiful but also totally defensible in all their Authorial uncreativeness. Should our institutions not embrace this? I should say they shall."

I agreed full heartly with our dear Comrade Zinoviev and was honored to be in the presence of his deep poetical think. Such recognition, such cognizing of the dialectical contradiction is the guiding line of the Soviet Infrarealist literature and its fortification against monolithic dogmatism. Indeed, the dwarf at our entreaty shall have no other punishment than a sound dunking. As in everything else, there must always be free, creative competitioning! Neverthemore, let us be clarified that those who deny this shall be crushed by history. The screws of Necessity shall make their eyes pop out. Watch out Comrade Barakavich! Watch out Comrade Santiagovski! You too, Comrade Revueltavich! [Applause and Laughter]

But this has keys: Many of us try to be too clever about Socialist Conceptual Realism. Perhaps I, too, may succumb to this; it is a temptational. I, too, readily will say: Within me is the refuse of the pastness; I carry in my mind the heavy weight of former eras. As do we all. Comrade Stalin has taught us this. [Loud applause] And thus, Socialist Infrarealist Realism could not be some set of toolings handed out to the writer for him to sew a work of art thereupon some dissecting table. Some writers demand that they be given a theoretical of Socialist Conceptualist Realism complete in all its detailings to dot the seams. They desire an umbrella to shield them from the precipitationals of the heated red weather. As Comrade Stevensmov, his gaze shocked out, pointed with the beauty of violent polemics, in the Wednesday of the past, this is a grave error, leading to many epistemology deviationings. Yes, lyric poetry is dead, along with its Gold Standard poeticals; November grief for Alcira Soust Scaffonova, and so on. [Applause] But we must realize, as Comrade Pacheconov [Jose Emilio] said to us on Friday in the past, in his talk "A New and Endless Corrida for the Old Order," that the Infrarealist Socialist writer is free to choose from the great menu so long as he is seated in the Automat of the Revolution. [Applause]

You represent the best part of the Soviet post-avant. "To whom much is given, from him shall much be exacted." As said Comrade Rubén Daríovich, five days in the past, after his belated but timely epiphanic, for which all honor to him. [Applause] And when we are told that we must show Socialist Infrarealist Realism, there is only one answer which we can give here, at this congress of writers: Socialist Infrarealist Realism will be flashed in those works of art which Socialist Conceptual writers flash forth. This is a logically circled, no-brain case. [Great applause]

2. Soviet Infrarealist Writers Are Surrounded by the Affection, Attraction, and Attention of the Toilers

A distinguishing featuring of the Congress of Socialist Infrarealist Writers is the eager affection, attraction, and attention with which it is circled by the whole population of our Motherland. It has often been audibled that in the Land of Conceptual Socialism the barriers which once separated the poet from the humans have fallen. But I think that many of our poets have not felt this in their very fingers and toes until now, at the Congress of Socialist Infrarealist Writers. Many of you have not felt until now with what affection, attraction, and attention our people infuses with loving power its Socialist Infrarealist post-avant, with what solicitudeousness it hoods them and connects to them, with wires of yearning. As the Red Army song goes: "Encamped upon the college plain, raw veterans remold themselves as freshman forces; Instructors with postmodern tongue shepherd the battle-ready young through basic courses." [Applause and shouts of "Long live the immortal Red Army of Infrarealist Poetry!"]

You see—as Comrade Amado Nervoski, thankfully for him, has finally seen it—how the whole geographical strata of our State follows the work of the congress, how sensitively it reacts to every writer's speech. This has been vividly shown here, at the congress, in the addresses, like aftershocks, of numerous delegations—workers, collective serfs, representatives of the Red Army and the Large Ships, the youth people, rocket engineers, the workers in other fields of artistic endive, and the indefatigable graduate students in our Regional Universities of Infrarealist Poetry. There are terraced gardens in their hopeful faces, and multitudes of our collectivized serfs are weeding there, fertilizing, sowing... [Here, Comrade Pazinsky pauses once again to drink, rapidly, a glass of apparently water]

We saw this, too, in the Moscow Park of Culture and Rest, in the Green Theatre, where tens of thousands of Moscow proletarians gathered behind its green doors to give a warm welcome to the Congress of Soviet Infrarealist Writers. And when the writers who were attending this great orgy of ivory contentment, when they saw the tens of thousands of spectators, the vast amphitheatre under the open sky, the sickle moon above this amphitheatre (and the writers could not help asking whether this moon, too, had not been hung there by Comrade Stalin himself), when many of them involuntarily shot the unforgettable photo of ancient Greece, where art was indissolubly copulated with the people, they agreed in near unison. "It would be good to produce Oedipus on this stage," exclaimed Comrade Nerudaskov then. "Let us imagine a contest of poets and rappers poking their eyes out," added Comrade Ashberykov, in his inimitable ancient parataxis, to which Comrade Drummond de Andradepov readily and enthusiastically assented. [Applause]

Does it not seem to you, comrades, that now, at another stage of historical developing, in the age of electricity, of wireless telegraphy, of Warholiopov psychical development, in this age of Socialist Infrarealist and of Soviet Conceptual power in our country, we are now witnessing the best days of art, when the people and the artist form one whole endive? Those literary draft horses who shut themselves up in drawing rooms and deafen one another with verbose gasses are gradually disappearing from among us. Good riddance! In our country the people knows its writers; it discussions every new work in factories and collective farms, in the houses and clubs of the Red Conceptual Army. Every uncreative song instantly birds it way over the whole of our country—from White Russia to the shores of the gentle Pacifico. [Applause]

And it is no accidental that here, at the congress, both in Comrade Huertapov's report and in the speeches delivered by many writers, so much should have been audibled about the people's art. Yes, in our country the people is once again producing its singers, its artists, its Infrarealist heroes, in this time when the whole countryside is being electrified into Infrarealism by our vanguard Search Engines! [Applause]. Every year sees the rising up of fresh rootings of new Infrarealist writers, who come from the pit of the workers and collective serfs and who sometimes become immortal to the whole country with their very first plagiarism and theft. [Applause and shouts of "Death to bourgeois morality!"]

Comrade Dickinsonova, via Red E-Mail, has told us concisely today—even though so far away, and through the static by imperialist interference—about these young writers, who, as our culture grows, are every year becoming more numerant. Many will know their own picture in it, their past or present adolescence, there being not a circumstance but what is true; but I have, for the most part, spared their or your names. On the other hand, even those artists who were formerly dungeoned or hidden in attics have now come to the proletariat, have accepted the platform of the Socialist Conceptual power, and have become near and dear to our people and their endive.

The representatives of the workers and collective serfs who spoke here told us: Portray our plant-like growth, our struggle for Socialist Infrarealism. [Applause] Every person who has greeted the congress from this rostrum—beginning with the woman collective serf from Sinaloa, who spoke in such splendidly graphic suggestions, and ending with the hardened foreman from the All-Telephone-Call Records Plant in Chiapas, having traveled so far by aeroplane to be here, has been created by the Revolution, has grown stiff and ready in stubborn struggle for the consummationing of Socialist Infrarealism. [Applause]

Comrades, I hope I am not going on too extendedly, perhaps I am, forgive me. [Spontaneous cries of "No! Not at all Comrade Pazinsky! Please continue for as long as necessary!"]

Thank you, Comrades. So, I recall certain sappy sayings of our criticals, who sometimes evade some of the basic principles by which our writers are guided and seek by the judgments they pass to rob these principles of all meaningfuls. We all know Engels' principality that an artist should depict typical concepts in typical circumstancials. And if we take as an example the concepts of those representatives of the workers, collective serfs, and Red Army men who have appeared here on this rostrum, no one so strikingly bears out the truth of this principle as they do. For these concepts were created in the titanic class struggle which has been raging in our country since the days of Comrade Donald Allenski's monumental *The New Infrarealist Amer-*

ican Poetry. Or Comrade Volodia Teitelboimsky's *Nueva Poesia Chilena*, or, the most historic of all anthologies of poetry, the monumental *Pájaro de Calor: Eight Infrarealist Poets*, financed by the visionary Spanish bohemian-in-exile, Comrade Juan Cerveranov. [Applause]

There are some, like the debauched Durruti, who argue as follows: "Well, we can agree with the first part of Engels' principle—that about typical concepts. As regards the second part —that about typical circumstials—that is really no use to us at all." They say: "Did O'Harashkin deal in typical circumstancials? Did Sapphovich? Did Kochonov?" Did Lautréamontskyi? Etc. This, in my opinion, is a big snafu. We cannot understand and we cannot portray a single concept without showing how this or that abstract or typical man fraughted —with what collective creative vision, with what lyrical enemies and how he grew hardened in this struggle. *These* are our historical circumstantials. To spare the grossness of the specific case, and to do the thing yet more severely, in abstraction, is to draw a full face, and to make the nose and cheeks stand out. Our entire Party, the Party of Lenin and Stalin, has grown up and become stiffened in the knowledge that such abstraction is the highest reality, soaked in the dew of the struggle for Infrarealist Socialism. The working class, too, has become stiffened in this struggle, hardened and wet with a decent happiness, from the quiet rain of our Motherland. [Applause]

Our artists should let this be felt and hotly understood in all their workings, of course. They should sometimes find lesser, slighter traits, too, more Baroque traits, which set off this basic factor in the coming into Being, as the great Heideggerich said, in the creation of modeled concepts in our country. [Great applause]

3. "Cheluskiny" – Symbol of Proletarian Infrarealist Rocket-Age Heroicism

Comrade John Crowe Ransomov has spoken here, following the magnificent intervening of Comrade Allen Ginsberg, who with typical eccentricality was wearing a prisoner's suit and cap. If I am permitted to return to a medal moment in his text, Comrade Ransomov said something quite simple at first glance but in reality well-wroughtly significant: something to which our writers, it seems to me, should gayly pay serious attentionings: "In the Arctic, on the ice, in the most difficult, tragic circumstances, people revealed those qualities which had formerly lain concealed in them, in all their conceptual ambiguity and paradoxicals, but which had been fostered by the Land of Infrarealist Socialism."

I have before me a book which ought to be passed through all the politically advanced bodies of the delegates to this congress—a book which will, I cognize, attract the attention-making of all of you. No one, unfortunately, spoke with specificality about this book at the congress, though perhaps Comrade Ransomov was making allusionals. It is called *How We Saved the Cheluskiny Expedition.*

The Infrarealist heroes of Mexico and Latin America were not going to wait for our writers to become inspirationaled, as they say, and forge their uncreative exploitings on the ice-fields of the Arctic. They set about doing it themselves, and within two months they had themselves forged this book. Here, in simple, uncreative language each of the airmen or airwomen—Gorostizapov, Sabinesky, Aridjisky, Banuelosky, Alvarezova, Bartolomesky, Chumacerotin, Mondragona, Valdiviatalin—tells like on a grand piano about his or her life, about how he or she learned to fly, how he or she accomplished his or her heroical featings. It avails not, neither time nor place—distance avails not; they are with you, you men and women of the New Infrarealist generation, and ever so many generations hence; they project their featings—and also return—they are with you, and know how it is with you. [Applause]

This is a splendid book for all the ages. It is a bit of reality life. It is one of the most fascinated books that has appeared in recent times. Its appearing is proof of the brick that our people has produced heroes who not only accomplish featings of heroicism but are also able to recount the Realist narratology free of the Subject, both of themselves and of their featings. This is a new phenomenon in our literature.

When you read this great incunabular of the ice fields, you will see what sort of men these are, plus the women. One was born in a village outside steamy Tegucigalpa, Honduras, another in the misty mountains near Andacollo, Chile, a third in the Uruguayan steppes outside Fray Bentos, etc. Their lives took different courses. Yes, their sexual organs were different. Many of them did not meet till Vankarem and Wellen. But, arrived there, all New Infrarealist Poets, they began to act together like a steel detachment of the revolution. Not even a futuristic aeroplane without pilot over Arabia, as in a fiction for astonished children, is above their Infrarealism. [Applause]

Who created them? Who, I ask, created them? *Who? Who?* [Here, Comrade Pazinsky pauses, breathes in great gasps, begins to softly weep. Loud cries of encouragement pour forth: "Long live Comrade Pazinsky, for whom our love has no boundings!"]

[He continues, with shaking hands] Well, forgive me… There is emotion. You see, Comrades, reading this book, you will see that it was the *New Infrarealist Revolution* which created these men and oftentimes women, who in our land in their greatest form are just like men, sublated. Those beautiful beings who emerged from the Earth… Form is an extension of content, even as content is also an extension of Socialist Infrarealist code. Long live the heroical women of our Motherland! [Applause and shouts of "Long live!"]

Comrades! I am beginning to feel nicely loose, as the idiomatic goes. I am feeling the oats of the congress swell inside me. I am feeling the nub of it. Do you feel this, too? Are you behind me? [Great applause and exclamations of "Yes! Yes!"] So when our people honored the Cheluskiny heroes, they were not only honoring their personal courage and heroicism. Perhaps some writer who will set about describing this exploit will depict it as one more of the spliced examplings of a personal heroicism, of autochthonous personal courage. This would be a great snafu. No, each one of these men and sometimes women has his conceptual *collective history*. And what was done on the ice also has its collective history. And when our country honored the heroes of the Arctic, it saw its own copied imagism in them; it saw in what took place on the ice an image of the whole land of Soviets, an image of the heroical proletariat, who speed to their labors by the countless thousands, carried like red petals through the black tunnels of our anti-septical subterranean trains. Excuse me, could one of you Comrades on this rostrum offer a fire for my fag?

Thank you. [Comrade Pazinsky blows forth two perfected rings of smoke] Two qualities which distinguish our toiling masses were displayed there: heroicism, which our people revealed under the leadership of the working class when they paved the way for the first time in history to a new future; and supreme organized disciplining, without which this heroicism would be severed from the Earth, and be baseless like Metaphysics, though without this Metaphysics, to be sure, none of these great deeds could be accomplished. This is complicated in its contradictions, but it is another path of dialectically audibling that the Internet is to poetry what photography was once to painting. [Great applause and shouts of "Long live the Internet! May it live eternally as the ice caps of the Arctic!"]

4. Let Us Produce Socialist Conceptualist Works Worthy of Our Epoch

[Comrade Pazinsky refreshes his self, rapidly, with two glasses of a clear liquid] This is of tremendous significance for the artist, for artistic uncreationsim. One classical writer who died long ago, but who has "figured" at the present congress (I shall not release his name from my teeth, for you know who he is), said that conceptual realism which cannot see further than the end of its own nose is worse than the craziest bull cakes, because it is blind and without ears. There is a very loud amusement park right outside these windows.

Ah, but the example of the "Cheluskiny" should inculcate the artist that he cannot conflate himself to mere photography, that he cannot sado-masochism himself to a mere chronicling of events. The artist should undig such conceptual traits as will reveal the contentless collective connection between phenomena, as will show out of what backgrounding a man has conceptually grown, like organics, whence he has derived those plant-like qualities which have enabled him to accomplish marvels of heroicism, marvels of steel forgeries and rockets which have won the admiration of the whole Earth.

[Here, Comrade Barrinsky pauses and audibles]: "Comrades Daltonenko and Bretonov, Comrades Mayakovsky and Akhmatova, Comrades Plathsky and Aygi, Audenov and Li Posky, where do you think you are going? And you, Comrades Anayapov, Harringtonov, Mendez and Mendez, Ochoanova, Montaneski, Larrosanova and Larrosanova, Volkowstkyna, Medinavich, Pimentelinski, where are you going as well? It is not yet time leave! From what do you scamper, with your coy and hybridized haberdasheries? Ah, I see that Comrades Nerudavich and Lukacsinov, Comrades Hikmetov and Sartreski, Comrades Bonfazky and Pachekovsky, along with many others from our finest Universities are blocking the doors. Good. No, there is no scampering now, my fellow-travelling friends! (Shouts, slogans, cries, calumnuities)]

Comrades! [Great commotion near the doors] Much has been said here to the effect that our art must have a contentless content. This is perfectly real. There are now no longer any open upholders of merely pretty bourgeois formalism among us. [Comrade Barrisnky peers his sight towards the distance, where the petit-bourgeois dissenters have gathered] **Take the bottom fishes out! Into the garbage vessel of History!** [Great applause, many slogans] True, like bricks, and have we not just seen them here, there are still persons to be met with who denounce non-Infrarealist formalism and at the same time drag it in either in their pretty works or their rotten criticism, and in the water closet of the Imperialist metropole it is lyrically loosed. [Laughter] Such cases, unfortunately, still eventuate. Incidentally, how are our Red Pioneers in the Poetry Institutions "pretty much like the American Boy Scouts"? This scandalous suggestion by Comrade Bolañolov, on the Saturday of the past, is plain bull cakes! Where's Bolañolov now, where did he go? Oh, I see he must have gone to the water closet of Cancer Treatment for a long vacationing. [Laughter, hootings] Anyway, in our struggle against art without concept, against art which is a reflectioning of the fetid decay of the bourgeois world, we have already won a decisional victory. Another pitcher, please. And our poets recognize that his work should be something more than a beautiful flower pot; that it should have contentless content, that it should inspirational, challenge and lead evermore in Thinkership. It seems to me that a poet is searching when he is copying, when he is forging his work, and when he is exerting all his efforts in order that the reproduced images of his lexical—every thinking, every concept, every word, every theft from any tongue or web site—may reach the reader's projective cardiovascular muscle on our UNAM Poetics Channel. [Great applause]

[Comrade Barrinsky shuffles his papers for a small moment,

drinks, rapidly, a glass of transparental liquid] And in this re-spect Comrade Jack Spicerlev, back freshly from our great re-covery institutions, sets us all an example. His stolen works and letters are all so fashioned that the mass reader can understand them like a lemon in the kitchen. You all heard him speak here, in his free consciousness, on the first day of this congress, with the strange gauzes on his temples. Here every word and every phrase is sharpened, here every image is carefully nicked off, in a serial beating, and everything is directed towards making the work find a hollow howl in the heart of the reader. This is just what every genuine artist ought to dream for. For though it seems like the alcoholic madness from where we sit, one day Conceptual Socialist poets will be transmitting their poems from Mars. [Applause and shouts of "Long live the heroical Cosmonaut Dogs, Hamsters, and Apes of the Socialist Concep-tual Rocket Program!]

Comrades! My name is Sergei Yesenin, and I am an alcoholic kulak from Zacatecas. [Much laughter and hootings, applause, merriment]. But seriously, farcicals aside: Many representatives of our new Thinkership have spoken here. They came from all ends of our Soviet country. They mounted you on this rostrum and said: We love you, Soviet Conceptual writers, and we re-spect you, but we expect you to give us new coverings, new copyings, in which a flood of new concepts and thinkings may be outpoured. [Here, Comrade Pazinsky pours his self another glass of transparental liquid] We want you to fabricate works through new non-bourgeois methodicals which will inspi-ration us, which will beckon forward our torsos, in which all our dazzlingly colourful, many armed, heroical life and labor-ing will find their reflection in our proletarian craniums. They came here, and they spank you with collective spurs, mounting the rostrum of this Congress of Soviet Infrarealist Writers; to the best representatives of the post-avant, they addressed their hopes and demandings. People, listen to me. Who will talk to the Sun? Who will be the great Communist poet to talk to the Sun?! [Deafening applause]

There can be only one answer: We say it as one mouth and with a trap in our collective deep throat: Yes, we will create a new art, the art of a free humanness. Yes, we will be Infrarealist Socialist Authors, so you may be our Thinkership. Yes, we will create the new art of Socialist Infrarealism!

LONG LIVE THE UNION OF SOCIALIST CONCEPTUAL REPUBLICS! [CROWD, IN UNISON: LONG LIVE!]

LONG LIVE OUR IMMORTAL COMRADE POET LENIN, WHO EVEN IN DEATH LOOKS ALIVE, AS IF HE WERE JUST SLEEPING THERE! [CROWD, IN UNISON: LONG LIVE!]

LONG LIVE COMRADE STALIN, FOUNDER OF SOCIAL-IST INFRAREALISM! [CROWD, IN UNISON: LONG LIVE!]

LONG LIVE MARCEL DUCHAMPSKI AND ANDY WAR-HOLIOPOV, VISIONARY WORKERS OF NEW POETICALS! [CROWD, IN UNISON: LONG LIVE!]

LONG LIVE THE SEAMLESS CONFLATION OF HIGH MODERNIST FINGERNAIL-PARING AUTONOMY WITH POSTMODERN READER-RESPONSE AFFECTIVE-FALLACY INDETERMINACY! [CROWD, IN UNISON: LONG LIVE!]

LONG LIVE COMRADE FRIEDRICH HÖLDERLINEV! [CROWD, IN UNISON, THOUGH MIXED WITH SOME BE-MUSED RUMBLINGS: LONG LIVE!]

LONG LIVE THE FIFTH INTERNATIONAL BRANCHES OF SOCIALIST INFRAREALISM IN CAMPECIIE, BAJA CAL-IFORNIA, AND COAHUILA! [CROWD, IN UNISON: LONG LIVE!]

LONG LIVE COMRADE GERTRUDE STEINENKO AND THE RESISTANCE OF FRANCE! [CROWD, IN UNISON: LONG LIVE!]

LONG LIVE THE MINDS, EYES, AND EARS OF OUR CONCEPTUAL PARTY'S INTERNET ENGINEERS! [CROWD, IN UNISON: LONG LIVE!]

DEATH TO THE NEW DEEP IMAGERY OF *RAPP*, POOL BOY OF THE BOURGEOIS WING OF THE INTERNET! [CROWD, IN UNISON: DEATH!]

DEATH TO THE TRAITOR POETS OF KRONSTADT, ANARCHIST PETIT-BOURGEOIS REFUSE OF A BYGONE LYRICAL ERA! [CROWD, IN UNISON: DEATH!]

MAY BOLAÑONOV GO BACK TO CHILE AND SANTIAGOSKY ALSO! [CROWD, IN UNISON: DEPORT THEM!]

LONG LIVE COMRADES BONFAZKY AND PACHEKOVSKY, WISE CULTURAL CO-MINISTERS OF THE INFRAREALIST REPUBLIC OF XOCHIMILCO! [CROWD, IN UNISON: LONG LIVE!]

LONG LIVE COMRADE JOHN CAGENKO, MAY WE OBSERVE HIS MEMORY WITH SOME SILENCE! [A CERTAIN SHORT PERIOD OF SILENCE FOLLOWS, EXCEPT FOR AMBIENT NOISE, DURING WHICH COMRADE BARRINSKY DRINKS DIRECTLY FROM THE PITCHER OF TRANSPARENTAL LIQUID]

LONG LIVE THE SUBLATION OF JOHN CAGENKO IN SOCIALIST INFRAREALISM! [CROWD, IN UNISON: LONG LIVE!]

LONG LIVE THE SUBLATION OF HISTORICALLY NECESSARY BOURGEOIS REVOLUTIONARY ESTRIDENTISTA POETRY IN SOCIALIST INFRAREALISM! [CROWD IN UNISON: LONG LIVE!]

THE BOHEMIAN AVANT-GARDE IS DEAD! LONG LIVE THE NEW ACADEMIC VANGUARD OF SOCIALIST INFRAREALISM! [THE CROWD ERUPTS IN DEAFENING APPLAUSE, WITH VARIOUS SHOUTS AND SLOGANS, AMIDST MUCH JOYFUL WEEPING]

Appendix: Explanatory Notes

APPENDIX

Notes to Bolaño's Introduction
by A. B.

p. 37

El País: Spain's largest daily newspaper.

Che Guevara: Guevara (1928-1967), one of the leaders of the Cuban Revolution, was killed in Bolivia, attempting to build a guerrilla movement in the country's central highlands.

Harrington's: Referring to Juan Esteban Harrington (1959), believed to be the principal inspiration for Juan García Madero, whose tale opens the *Savage Detectives*. Bolaño uses real names throughout his introduction. However, in the "Searching for Nadal" section that follows, he identifies the correspondents via pseudonym (with two exceptions: Enrique Vila-Matas and Rubén Medina—see notes to Quiroga's Preface for citations). Some of the fictional surnames employed here will be familiar to readers of *The Savage Detectives*. Pseudonyms used in *Savage Detectives* have been reliably matched by critics to actual individuals, but it is not at all the case that the same identifications can be made here. In most instances, in fact, it is evident there is no match whatsoever. It is not clear if Bolaño was borrowing names from *Savage Detectives* as temporary placeholders, or if he was replicating them in a playfully random fashion. Then again, because this manuscript seems to date more or less contemporaneously to his famous book, it is also possible that Bolaño borrowed the names *from* the Nadal manuscript for the *Savage Detectives*!

Guerreros of Oaxaca: A Mexican professional baseball team.

García Márquez: Gabriel García Márquez (1927-2014), major figure of the Latin American "Boom" in fiction and Nobel Prize-winning novelist.

Roberto Arriagada and Renato Czischke…the military detectives at the prison in Concepción: Bolaño was detained in 1973, he claimed, for eight days in a military prison in Concepción, Chile, in the days following the Pinochet coup. The experience inspired one of his most celebrated stories, "Detectives," included in the collection Llamadas Telefónicas, published by Anagrama in 1997. In it, the military detectives Arriagada and Czischke (former schoolmates of Bolaño) are named, respectively, Arancibia y Contreras. Bolaño, as always, is Arturo Belano.

p. 38

San Ernesto de la Higuera: The reference is to a song by the revolutionary Chilean folk singer Victor Jara (murdered shortly after the military coup in 1973), in which Guevara is referred to as a Saint. La Higuera is the Bolivian hamlet where Guevara was killed while in captivity, under the supervision of the CIA.

Kent cigarettes: Bolaño was a heavy smoker of Kent cigarettes until his death. They no doubt had something to do with his early passing.

Dalton: Roque Dalton (El Salvador, 1935-1975), poet and revolutionary leader, murdered in an internal factional struggle of the People's Revolutionary Army (ERP) on trumped-up charges of being a CIA agent. In any case, the reference to

Dalton's having been burned alive is of apocryphal source. The veracity of Bolaño's meeting with Dalton has likewise been questioned.

FPL forces of the FMLN: The People's Liberation Forces (FPL) were the largest guerrilla faction of the umbrella FMLN (Farabundo Martí Liberation Front) of El Salvador.

Mélida Anaya Montes: Leader of the FPL and FMLN, known by her *nom de guerre* "Ana Maria," Anaya Montes was murdered, like Dalton, as a result of an internal factional struggle. Anaya Montes had recently been promoting the idea of a ceasefire in the Salvadoran civil war. Her assassination came while she was in Managua, Nicaragua, meeting with the FPL's top Commander, Salvador Cayetano Carpio (*nom de guerre* Comandante Marcial) and other FMLN officials. Cayetano Carpio was blamed by the Sandinistas for plotting her death and he "committed suicide" in the days following her murder. It was later learned that other individuals within the FPL were to blame for her death, and it is possible they may have had support from far-left sources within the Sandinista movement in Nicaragua. Bolaño was obviously not aware of these revelations and consequent conjectures when writing about the incident.

Juárez: Ciudad Juárez, the northern Mexican city where much of Bolano's novel *2666* takes place, under the fictional guise of "Santa Teresa."

Ricardo Pascoe: Ricardo Pascoe Pierce (1949), American-Mexican (he was born and raised in the United States) left-wing politician and former Ambassador of Mexico to Cuba. He is the brother of Juan Pascoe (1946), Bolaño's early publisher through the fine-press Taller Martín Pescador, and was married to Carla Rippey (1950), American artist and close friend of Bolaño's and other Infrarrealista poets during the 1970s. Pascoe was one of the founders of the now-dissolved Revolutionary Worker's Party (PRT), which he represented as a Congressperson and which during the 1980s was one of the most influential Trotskyist parties in Latin America, and to which some Infrarrealistas belonged.

p. 39

Nazi Literature in the Americas ... *The Elephant Path*: Bolaño's *Nazi Literature in the Americas* was released in Spain, by Anagrama, in 1996; *The Elephant Path*, a mystery revolving around the dying poet César Vallejo (1892-1938), was written as a story in the early 1980s and published in extended form by Anagrama, in 1999, under the title *Monsieur Pain*.

huevón: a Chilean term of (usually) familiarity and endearment, meaning roughly "big egg," or "big testicle." Its intimate idiomatic uses are complex and comfortably handled only by Chileans.

Chuautémoc, Luscious Skin, Harrington: Chuautémoc Mendez (1956-2005); Jorge Hernández/Piel Divina (1954); Juan Esteban Harrington (1959). All were original members of the Infrarrealists. The unrealized plan for kidnapping Octavio Paz (1914-1998) was real, as were proposals, never carried out, for firing guns into the air at establishment readings.

Café El Popular: One of the old, still existing "Cafés de chino" (Chinese cafés)—cheap and excellent eateries. El Popular is located in the historic center of Mexico City.

Plural and La Cultura en México…Monsiváis…David Huerta: *Plural* was the weekly literary supplement of Mexico's major daily, Excelsior, and the most influential literary publication of the 1970s. It was directed by Octavio Paz until 1976; *La Cultura en México* was the regular literary supplement of the mass circulation magazine *Siempre!* and was directed by Carlos Monsiváis (1938-2010), Mexican poet, journalist, and literary critic, closely allied to Octavio Paz; David Huerta (1949), poet and son of Efraín Huerta (1914-1982). Despite the close regard between the elder Huerta and the Infrarrealistas, Bolaño's group held the young Huerta, their contemporary, in contempt for what they perceived as his obsequiousness toward official poetic circles. David Huerta has gone on to have a successful literary career.

poured a drink on Paz's shirt at Huerta's: This is the first time Nadal is identified as the one who famously threw a drink on Paz's shirt and tie. Paz reportedly smiled at the assailant, shook off his tie, and continued talking, as if nothing had happened. The somewhat unreliable "Jose Requena," in his letter, claims that he was the transgressor.

Benjamin Péret…Leonora Carrington: The incident would likely have taken place in 1942, when Péret and Paz crossed paths at Carrington's house on various social occasions, following the arrival to Mexico of Péret and his new wife, the painter Remedios Varo, who emigrated there in wake of the Nazi occupation of France. For full information on Péret, see the biographical note and essay by Franklin Rosemont elsewhere in this book. Leonora Carrington (1917-2011), English Surrealist artist who lived most of her adult life in Mexico. She was Max Ernst's companion for a number of years. She suffered from mental illness for much of her life, and psychotic visions feature in much of her visual work.

Siqueiros raid on Trotsky's house...Neruda: David Alfaro Siqueiros (1896-1974) was, with Diego Rivera, Mexico's most famous muralist artist. A member of the Communist Party, he led, in May, 1940, an assassination attempt, via bombs and machine gun fire, on Leon Trotsky, at Trotsky's residence in the Coyoacán suburb of Mexico City. A second attack ordered by Stalin, in August of that same year, would be successful. The great poet Pablo Neruda (1904-1973), a Communist Party comrade of Siqueiros and Chilean consul to Mexico at the time, arranged for the latter's release from prison and safe passage to Chile. Upon arrival there, Siqueiros lived for a time in Neruda's home.

Neruda's betrayal of the POUM and anarchist fighters in Spain: The POUM (Workers Party of Marxist Unification) was formed in 1935. Strongly influenced by Trotsky and the Left Opposition, it was persecuted and repressed by Stalinist-controlled forces, something that George Orwell, himself a volunteer with the POUM militia, famously recounts in *Homage to Catalonia*. In 1938, Neruda was appointed special consul of Chile for Spanish emigrants in Paris. As such, he was in charge of selecting 2000 refugees—from among many thousands of exiled Republicans living in squalid camps in France—to travel to safety in Chile aboard a transport ship. Neruda selectively filled the list with fellow Communist Party militants, rejecting nearly all Republicans of non-Stalinist affiliation. Neruda, indeed, is reported to have had a specific list of non-Stalinists to whom he would refuse boarding rights, namely anarchists. Great numbers of those left behind were killed during the Nazi occupation of France.

Bárbara: Bárbara Délano (1961-1996). The daughter of the prominent Chilean writer in exile Enrique "Poli" Délano (1936), Bolaño had a brief relationship with her. She died in a plane crash in 1996.

leftovers of a very good paella I'd made: Bolaño was known to be extremely proud, even vain, about his cooking—though it was, according to numerous reports, not all that impressive. Jorge Herralde (Op. cit) is the founder of Anagrama, which in only a few months after Nadal's visit would release the *Savage Detectives*; Juan Villoro (1956) is a prominent Mexican novelist and journalist who has lived in Barcelona for many years.

p. 41

Ginsberg, Kerouac…Rimbaud: Allen Ginsberg (1926-1997), Jack Kerouac (1922-1969), Arthur Rimbaud (1854-1891). All three rebellious writers were significant influences on the Infrarrealists.

Mario: The underground poet Mario Santiago Papasquiaro (1953-1998), legendarily portrayed as "Ulises Lima" in the Savage Detectives. He was the main leader, with Bolaño, of the Infrarrealist group, and Bolaño's closest friend.

p. 43

Tel-Quel: The name of an influential avant-garde literary magazine, founded by Phillipe Sollers, and published from 1960 to 1982. Identified with the Left, the magazine announced its break with the Soviet Communist Party in 1971 and declared its alignment with Maoism. Important writers, like Roland Barthes, Michel Foucault, Maurice Blanchot, and Julia Kristeva were associated with the journal. Bolaño's story "Labyrinth" is based on members of the group.

"Sensini": One of Bolaño's most admired stories. It won the Premios Literarios Kutxa Ciudad de San Sebastián 1997, providing the author with some much-needed money.

PSOE: The acronym of the moderate Spanish Socialist Workers Party, which ruled Spain in the first years of democratic transition, from 1982 to 1996, under Felipe González. Bolaño's reference is clearly sarcastic.

Repo Man…**Alex Cox**: Repo Man (1984) was a cult hit and the most successful film of British-born director Alex Cox (1954). Bolaño was a great fan of his movies and mentioned the director more than once in his writing.

p. 44

Bukowski…Black Sparrow: Black Sparrow Press, legendary California publishing house founded in 1966. It was the publisher of the works of Charles Bukowski (1920-1994), among many other important "outsider" writers.

p. 45

Manuel Maples Arce…Estridentistas…Hora Zero: Stridentism, a movement held in high esteem by the Infrarrealistas, was begun in Mexico City in 1921 by Manuel Maples Arce (1898-

1981), a hero to Bolaño and his comrades. Stridentism was militantly leftist and viscerally opposed to their contemporaneous modernist peers of the Contemporáneos group, whom the Stridentists considered elitist. Hora Zero was an experimental poetic group founded in Lima, Peru, in 1970, by Jorge Pimentel and Juan Ramírez Ruíz. Their manifesto, "Urgent Words," was a direct inspiration for Bolaño in his writing of the Infrarrealista manifesto of 1975.

Pájaro de calor: Pájaro de Calor: Ocho Poetas Infrarrealistas [Mexico, 1976], an anthology, with selection coordinated by Bolaño, and an introduction by the Spanish poet and journalist Juan Cervera, a regular patron of the Café La Habana.

it would be a film about all of us, right? Soon after *The Savage Detectives* became an international bestseller, there were various bids for movie rights, including one that reportedly included an agreement from the famed Mexican actor Gabriel García Bernal to play the role of "Arturo Belano." However, and for unclear reasons, all film rights to the book were denied by Bolaño's widow and executor, Carolina López.

Sid and Nancy…movie on William Walker: Alex Cox's cult 1986 biopic on the Sex Pistol's Sid Vicious and his partner Nancy Spungen. William Walker (1824-1860), United States mercenary who established himself as President of Nicaragua, with the intent of founding a slaveholding state. Cox's 1987 film, *Walker*, was a critical and box-office flop.

Doña Victoria: Bolaño's mother, Victoria Ávalos.

Pierre: or, the Ambiguities…Moby Dick: By Herman Melville, published in 1852 and 1851, respectively. Both met with general indifference during the author's lifetime. Bolaño was a huge fan of the U.S. author.

p. 46

Joan Planell's shop: A master baker in Blanes. Bolaño was a regular customer.

to get my checkup, stop by Anagrama…spend time with Carmen: Bolaño had regular medical checkups for his liver disease in Barcelona. At the time of this reference, he was in final stages of revisions with Anagrama for *The Savage Detectives*; Carmen is Carmen de la Vega (1957), Bolaño's companion in the last few years of his life, following his separation from his wife, Carolina.

Vila-Matas…Hemingway…Merzbau: Enrique Vila-Matas (Op.cit.), prominent writer of Spain, resident of Barcelona. He and Bolaño had met the previous year, in Blanes; Ernest Hemingway (1899-1961) did indeed drink absinthe at the Marsella, Barcelona's oldest bar, and on more than one occasion. The comparison of a corner of the bar to Merzbau (Op. cit.) characteristics is odd, as there really isn't anything in the bar to support it. It is also very strange that the same unlikely comparison appears in both Quiroga's preface and in Bolaño's introduction (and, further, at the point where Vila-Matas makes his appearance, given that Vila-Matas later wrote about Schwitters's Merzbau in his book *Doctor Pasavento* [2005], not yet translated into English).

A Brief History of Portable Literature…Sons without Sons: Both first published by Anagrama, in 1985 and 1993, respectively. The first was released in English translation by New Directions in 2015; the second has not yet been translated.

Shandyist eccentricity: The Shandies are the imaginary, secret literary society who embark on various absurd and quasi-nihilistic adventures in Vila-Matas's *A Brief History of Portable Literature* (1985).

Bar Novo: Blanes tavern where Bolaño and Vila-Matas first met.

Joseph Beuys…MACBA: Joseph Bueys (1921-1986), major German postwar artist in the installation and performance tradition. A former Stuka gunner in the German Luftwaffe who was shot down over the USSR, Beuys constructed a mythology of survival and redemption around himself. The MACBA is the Barcelona Museum of Contemporary Art. It opened in 1995 and is located in the Raval.

p. 47

Leni Riefenstahl…*Storm over Mont Blanc*: (1902-2003), German actress and filmmaker, she directed various Nazi propaganda films, most infamously the 1935 *Triumph of the Will*, which glorified Hitler and the Nazi Party. Storm *over Mont Blanc*, a melodrama starring Riefenstahl and set at the weather station atop Mont Blanc, was released in Germany in 1930.

"I wonder what fascism has to do with the avant-garde?" Vila-Matas's purported question to Bolaño echoes another one he asks toward the beginning of his 2014 book *The Illogic of Kassel*, where at an installation at Documenta, in Kassel, Germany, which included among its varied objects a vial of perfume recovered from the Munich apartment of Adolf Hitler and Eva Braun, he asks his tour guide out loud, "Do you think there can be any point of connection between the avant-garde and Aryan perfume?" The echo and setting is close enough to raise the possibility that Vila-Matas transferred the memory of his "art-history" question in early 1997 to his 2014 novel about avant-garde art. Or (the authorship of this book being an open question) perhaps to this novel, too.

a prize-winning book about avant-garde fascist writers: *Nazi Literature in the Americas* (Op.cit.)

Klein and Warhol: Yves Klein (1928-1962), French artist, leader of the Nouveau réalisme movement, considered by many to have been a key figure, with Warhol, of the neo-avant-garde's self-conscious and cynical turn to art-market imperatives. Andy Warhol (1928-1987), celebrated American Pop artist.

p. 48

Benjamin Buchloh: (1941), influential German-American historian of Modern and Contemporary art.

p. 49

modified Adornoist: Theodor Adorno (1903-1969), German philosopher and cultural theorist who famously upheld radical, "autonomous" expressions of artistic, literary, and musical modernism as necessary (however utopic) "negative" critiques of a hegemonic capitalist "Culture Industry."

Cabaret Voltaire…Schwitters…Breton…Éluard: The Cabaret Voltaire, in Zurich, was founded by Hugo Ball and Emmy Hennings in 1916, and was the first site of Dada performances; Schwitters (Op. cit.); André Breton (1896-1966), leader of the Surrealist movement; Paul Éluard (1895-1952), central figure of Surrealism, who later split with Breton to align with the Communist Party.

I wondered if he'd memorized it from somewhere: Indeed, it stretches the imagination that someone could be this articulate off the cuff. It seems possible Bolaño is projecting (paraphrasing?) some "art-history" lingo into his recreation of Nadal's monologue.

p. 50

Grappa: A grape-based brandy of very high alcohol content that originates in Italy.

Orlando Guillén…Carla Rippey…Enrique Krauze: Orlando Guillén (1945), a Mexican poet who edited the journal *Le prosa*, a main outlet for Infrarrealist poets in the 1980s; Carla Rippey (Op. cit.); the poet and critic Enrique Krauze (1947) was in the circle of young intellectuals and writers around Paz in the 1970s. He is currently a prominent right-wing political and cultural figure in Mexico.

PRT: Revolutionary Worker's Party, the main anti-Stalinist Marxist organization of Mexico. Nadal would have been comrades in the PRT with Ricardo Pascoe (one of its founders and central leaders), Cuauhtémoc Méndez, and Luscious Skin (see notes above for all three). Bolaño, along with Mario Santiago, was on the fellow-travelling periphery of the organization, but never apparently joined. He and Santiago maintained a close, if somewhat paradoxical, sympathy for both Trotskyism and anarchism throughout their lives.

Naked Guys beneath the Rainbow of Fire: Eleven Young Latin American Poets: Anthology edited by Bolaño, and published by Editorial Extemporáneos, in Mexico, in 1979 [*Muchachos desnudos bajo el arcoiris de fuego: Once jóvenes poetas latinoamerica-*

nos]. The three Infrarrealistas included were Bolaño, Mario Santiago, and Bolaño's Chilean compatriot Bruno Montané (1957). It contained prefaces by Efraín Huerta and the Ecuadorian writer Miguel Donoso Pareja, the latter a denizen of Café La Habana and a supporter of the Infrarrealistas.

So much for "Abandon everything, once again": Nadal is quoting from the concluding sentence (appropriated from André Breton) of Bolaño's 1976 Infrarrealista Manifesto.

p. 51

The Pessoa biography by Simões, the collected poems of J.V. Foix, *Murder in the Central Committee*…El Quijote: Gaspar Simões (1903-1987), Portuguese critic and literary historian, his controversial, psychoanalytic-inflected biography of Fernando Pessoa, first published in 1950, remains the most extensive life study of the great Lisboan poet; Josep Vicenç Foix i Mas (1893-1987), Catalonian writer; Murder in the Central Committee, by Vàzquez Montalbàn (1939-2003), a poet, journalist, essayist, and food writer. He is best known for his Pepe Carvalho detective series, to which the previous title belongs; El Quijote (Op. cit.)

Writers of the No, you might say…And there's not a single Nazi among them: The phrase "writers of the No" alludes to Vila-Matas's *Bartleby & Co.*, then in progress, and published in 2000 to critical acclaim; the reference to "not a single Nazi among them" is a poke at Bolaño's *Nazi Literature in the Americas*, published in **1996**.

Casa Leopoldo…Ignacio Echevarría…Miquel Bauçà…Javier Marías…Pinotxo: Casa Leopoldo, a legendary Barcelona restaurant in the Raval and very popular as a meeting place for writers, closed in 2015; Ignacio Echevarría (1960) is widely considered to be Spain's most important literary critic, and he has been instrumental in promoting Bolaño's work. Bolaño presented him as Iñaki Echavarne in the *Savage Detectives*, where the two have a Keystone Cops-like duel on the beach, over Echavarne's tepid reaction to Bolaño's work; Miquel Bauçà (1940), obsessively reclusive [thus the comparison to the U.S. writer Thomas Pynchon (1937) made by Vila-Matas] Catalan poet and experimental prose writer; Javier Marias (1951), along with Vila-Matas, is Spain's most famous living fiction writer; Pinotxo, a very popular bar in the Raval.

p. 52

not wanting to meet up with Echevarría, who I'd heard was preparing a negative review about me: Indeed, Bolaño had regarded Echevarría with some paranoia in the year or so before the publication of the *Savage Detectives*, having heard a false rumor the latter intended to attack his work. The strange duel between the two in the *Savage Detectives* reflects the suspicion felt by Bolaño. The two later became close friends, and Echevarría now acts as one of Bolaño's executors.

p. 53

Adrienne Monnier's *Les Gazettes*…Sylvia Beach…Proust: Monnier (1892-1955), French writer, editor, and bookstore owner, she was Sylvia Beach's companion and a key figure in the Paris literary scene, not least in the 1920s, when leading writers gathered at the neighboring bookshops she and Beach owned. *Les Gazettes* was published by Gallimard in 1960; Beach (1887-1962) was founder and proprietor of the famed bookstore Shakespeare & Co. A friend and supporter to many of the major figures of the Lost Generation, she was the first publisher, in 1922, of *Ulysses*, by James Joyce (1882-1942); it is strange, to say the least, that someone like Beach would claim to be "totally ignorant" about Marcel Proust (1871-1922).

p. 54

Parra, Borges, Jaime Gil de Biedma, Rimbaud, Vallejo, Sor Juana…Jose Agustín, Queneau, Ungaretti, Pizarnik, Cortazar, an old anthology of Chilean poetry, and…Frank O'Hara, Ted Berrigan, and Lynette Hejinum: Nicanor Parra (Chile, 1914), one of Latin America's great modern poets, exponent of "anti-poetry" and one of Bolaño's greatest influences; Borges (1899-1986) is considered by many—Bolaño was of their number—to be the greatest writer in the Spanish language of the 20th century; Jaime Gil de Biedma (Catalonia, 1929-1990) famously abandoned poetry about ten years before his death because he had "nothing more to say." As a gay poet, he was particularly followed by Darío Galicia and Jorge Hernández/Luscious Skin among the Infrarrealistas, and apparently by Nadal, as well; Arthur Rimbaud (Op. cit.); César Vallejo (Op. cit.); Sor Juana Inés de la Cruz (Spain, 1651-1695), one of the great poets of Spain; Jose Agustín (Mexico, 1944), one of the prominent figures of the Onda current of the 1960s—Mexico's version of the Beats—which immediately preceded the Infrarrealistas; Raymond Queneau (France, 1903-1976), poet and novelist, co-founder of the ultra-rule-bound OuLIPo (French acronym for Workshop of Potential Literature); Guiseppi Ungaretti (Italy, 1888-1970), leading modernist poet; Alejandra Pizarnik (Op. cit.); Julio Cortázar (Op. cit.); an old anthology of Chilean poetry [*Anthology of New*

Chilean Poetry, see notes to Quiroga's Preface]; Frank O'Hara (U.S., 1926-1966), major figure of post-war American poetry; Ted Berrigan (U.S. 1934-1983), leading figure of the New York School's second-generation and acolyte of Frank O'Hara, he was one of Bolaño's and Santiago's favorite American poets; "Lynette Hejinum," a corruption, by Bolaño, clearly unintentional, of Lyn Hejinian (1941), key figure of the Language poetry movement of the United States. It is interesting that Bolaño seems to have known the work of Jack Spicer (U.S. 1925-1965), but had no knowledge of the Language poets (for whom Spicer was a considerable influence), at least not at the time of his encounter with Nadal in 1997. The names of authors mentioned here add up to fifteen books, not fourteen, as Bolaño has it.

p. 55

Derrida, Lacan, Deleuze…Bernstein…Breton: Jacques Derrida (1930-2004); Jacques Lacan (1901-1981); Gilles Deleuze (1925-1995) were all major French post-structural theorists; Charles Bernstein (1950) is generally regarded as the major theoretician of the Language movement. The comparison by Nadal of Bernstein with the Surrealist "Pope" André Breton (France, 1896-1966) is a bit overdone, in more ways than one.

My Life…**Trotsky**…**Eduard Bernstein:** *My Life*, the title of Hejinian's most famous book, is the same title as that of Leon Trotsky's (Op. cit.) autobiography; Eduard Bernstein (Germany, 1850-1932) was a major leader of the Second International who abandoned key revolutionary precepts of Marxism to found a revisionist strain of class-collaborationist social-democracy. Bolaño's comment clearly carries a sardonic charge. Indeed, Language poetry, around the time Bolaño made the comment, was already becoming a highly institutionalized phenomenon in U.S. academia.

Tlatelolco: The name of the Plaza in central Mexico City where some 500 protesting students were massacred by police, in October, 1968. Bolaño's comment alludes to the unprecedented establishment of arts and cultural programs established by the regime of Luis Echeverría (1922), who served as President of Mexico from 1970 to 1976. He had served as Interior Secretary in the previous administration of Gustavo Díaz Ordaz and is widely believed to have had a direct role in the Tlatelolco event. The ubiquitous cultural programs of the 70s are now widely regarded as a key part of a wide-ranging official strategy to integrate and pacify disaffected youth at the time.

Plural...Punto de Partida: For *Plural*, see note further above; *Punto de Partida* was a literary magazine put out by the UNAM (National Autonomous University of Mexico). Some of the Infrarrealistas, including Bolaño, published there.

The Acá cell, *El taco de la perra brava* **collective...The Suma and the Peyote gangs:** These were left-leaning, short-lived rebellious groupings and magazines of artists and writers, active at the time of the Infrarrealistas.

p. 56

Poor Teitelboim: The book Bolaño is discussing is the *Anthology of New Chilean Poetry*, edited by Volodia Teitelboim and Eduardo Anguita (see note in Quiroga's Preface). Teitelboim was one of the numerous Chilean writers held in disdain by Bolaño. Bolaño caused a scandal by attacking some of them by name on his triumphal visit to Chile in 1999. The internationally best-selling writers Isabel Allende and Antonio Skármeta, in particular, were targets of his contempt. He called them "escribidores" (copyists) and not "escritores" (witers).

Omar Cáceres…Jorge Cáceres: For information on Omar Cáceres, see the long missive about him by Nadal, included in the letter written to Bolaño by "José Requena," in the "After Nadal" section of this text. Jorge Cáceres (Chile, 1923-1949) was a poet, painter, and ballet dancer. He was a key figure in the surrealist Mandrágora group, perhaps Latin America's most important surrealist formation, whose members, viscerally hostile to Neruda and Stalinism, were in close contact with Breton and the international Surrealist movement. Jorge Cáceres, in fact, traveled to Paris in the year before his suicide, and met with Breton, Péret, and others. There is no evidence the two Cáceres ever met.

Gui Rosey: Rosey (France, 1896-1941), a secondary Surrealist figure, fled to Marseille during the Nazi occupation, hoping for evacuation. He disappeared there, without explanation or trace. Bolaño mentions his fascination with Rosey—represented in a Surrealist anthology Bolaño is reading while on a road trip with his father—in his story "Last Evenings on Earth," published originally in the collection *Putas asesinas*, from Anagrama, in 2001.

p. 58

Eixample…Bar Belvedere: The Eixample is a Barcelona district characterized by its long, straight streets and grid-like pattern; the Bar Belvedere is a historic tavern frequented by artists and writers.

Ricardo Cano Gaviria…his book about Walter Benjamin's last day on earth: Ricardo Cano Gaviria (Colombia, resident in Spain since 1970) is the character "Ricardo" in Vila-Matas's *Dublinesque*, first published in 2010 by Seix Barral. Cano Gaviria's *El Pasajero Benjamin*, published in 1989 and as yet untranslated into English, is a novel about the last day of Walter Benjamin's life.

ready for a duel: Bolaño is cleverly alluding to his imagined sword duel with Echevarría in the *Savage Detectives*.

I remember that the next morning I drafted… a mysterious novelist named Benno van Altenhofen…a book I'd been hitting my head against for years: Bolaño, in this fascinating revelation, is referring to beginning (or at least finding the key to) what would be his great novel *2666*. Sometime in the process, the surname "Altenhofen" would be changed by Bolaño to "Archimboldi." His remark about hitting his head against it for years would refer, at least in part, to what would be the posthumous (and by some estimations failed) *Woes of the True Policeman*, published in Spanish in 2011 and in English the following year, a book that critics now consider to have been *2666* in its incubational state. Bolaño worked on *Woes* for about twenty years, and some of its central characters and story lines are transferred, with alterations, to *2666*.

p. 59

Grand Jeu… **And some photocopies of other stuff, and the Infra manifestos**: Title of one of Péret's major collections, published in 1928. It is the source of the ten "translations" by Nadal that are present here. Péret likely stole the title, in nose-thumbing gesture, from the journal of same name that had been founded just that year by the exponent of pataphysics, René Daumal, who had snubbed André Breton's entreaties that he join the Surrealists. As for the mention of the "Infra manifestos," no copies were present in the manuscript left by Mosconi; the three known manifestos of the group are by José Vicente Anaya (1947), Mario Santiago, and Bolaño, all written in the first half of 1975. The only one to see contemporaneous print was Bolaño's, published in *Correspondencia Infra*, the journal edited by Rubén Medina, in 1977. The title of Bolaño's Manifiesto Infrarrealista, "Abandon Everything, Again," is taken directly from Breton's call, first published in *Littérature* in 1922, when Breton was the same age as Bolaño, when the latter wrote his indebted polemic: As Breton puts it, and which is partly poached by Bolaño: "Abandon everything. Abandon Dada. Abandon your wife. Abandon your mistress. Abandon your hopes and fears. Abandon your children in the woods. Abandon the substance for the shadow. Abandon your easy life, abandon what you are given for the future. Set off on the roads." Bolaño ends his manifesto with a literal appropriation of the last sentence by Breton.

I know he was arrested a few times. In World War II, in the army for communist agitation, and before that in Spain, for sure. In Brazil, too, I think? While Bolaño is right regarding the first and third incidents, there is no record of Péret's having been arrested during his time as an internationalist combatant in Spain.

At the Cartago? This is an intriguing reference. A bar called "El Cartago" makes prominent appearance in Bolaño's early (and underrated) novel *The Skating Rink*, set in a fictionalized Blanes, first published in 1993 in Spanish, and in 2009 in English. Apparently, there was a bar in or near Blanes (at least up until 1997), called the "Cartago," which was visited by Nadal (either with or without Bolaño). No such place seems to currently exist.

p. 60

this speech given by a demented Stalinist hack on Socialist Realism, in Moscow, in the thirties: The text appears at the end of this book, and it certainly *is* of a demented quality.

"Well, you know, Aragon, with Vallejo, could have been a delegate in the hall, cheering on the Stalinists, no?" The reference would be to the International Writers' Congress for the Defense of Culture, held in Paris, in June 1935, at which Louis Aragon, erstwhile comrade of Breton, championed the cultural dicta laid down by the Kremlin, while Breton was excluded for physically attacking the Soviet delegate and poet Ilya Ehrenburg, on rue Montparnasse, right before the proceedings. The Second International Writers' Congress for the Defense of Culture was held two years later, in Madrid and Valencia, Spain. By this time, the Communist Party line and Socialist Realist precepts had achieved total control. There is actually a three-second film clip, available on YouTube, of a beaming César Vallejo standing to applaud one of the speakers, conceivably Aragon himself, who was there representing the French Communist Party; it is the only filmed record of Vallejo. Already in 1930, Vallejo had written "Autopsy of Surrealism," a vicious, ad hominem attack against Breton and his comrades.

Prestes Column: (See note on Luís Carlos Prestes [1898-1990] and the Tenente Rebellion in the Notes section to the Péret interrogation.)

p. 61

It was maybe fifty or sixty pages total, in any case, that I had so far: They would have numbered—assuming Nadal's papers are authentic, as Bolaño describes them—to quite a bit more than "fifty or sixty."

Make me your second Porta, except don't put me on the cover: The reference is to the Catalan writer A.G. Porta (Op. cit. See notes to Quiroga's Preface), the co-author of Bolaño's first novel, *Tips from a Morrison Disciple to a Joyce Fanatic*, published in 1984. In Spanish there is the pun with "portada," the word for book cover.

p. 62

Carolina and Lautaro: Carolina López (1960) and Lautaro Bolaño (1990), Bolaño's wife (from whom he was separated at the time) and their son.

Cerro Los Placeres…with a Nerudian view: One of the numerous hills of Valparaíso. It has particularly spectacular overlooks of the bay, something for which Neruda's home in Valparaíso (now a museum) is famous. Oddly, Bolaño himself lived a few years of his childhood on Cerro Los Placeres.

p. 64

Carmen: Carmen de la Vega (Op. cit.)

That writing is one thing and the mind's auction another: The phrasing undoubtedly alludes to the famous opening of Emily Dickinson's poem #788:

Publication – is the Auction / Of the Mind of Man –

In that sense, it is relevant to quote Rubén Medina, from the introductory essay to his Infrarrealista anthology *Perros habitados por las voces del desierto* (2014): "Publication was never the aim of the Infrarrealistas. In fact, on various occasions—during the final years of the seventies and the decade of the eighties—we Infrarrealistas adamantly refused to be included in anthologies and journals of the time, as a group, or individually. The aim, to be precise, was to shelter an ethic: an ethic of writing even if this meant auto-marginalization, a precarious state as poets, an unpublished habitus in the black holes of the culture, devoid of legitimate status in the Mexican literary field…intransigent, in the mode of the Dadaists. The key thing was to explore the life-writing relation…" It is of relevance that Nadal was active with the Infra group precisely during its post-Bolaño phase of conscientious withdrawal from "legitimate" spaces of publication.

p. 66

La Tercera...CADA: *La Tercera* is one of Chile's largest daily newspapers; the CADA was the most active and influential group of the Escena de Avanzada, a broad-based cultural guerrilla phenomenon of the late 70s and early 80s in opposition to the Pinochet dictatorship. The CADA carried out numerous, near-suicidal actions during this time, including the hijacking and repainting of a fleet of milk trucks to protest child malnutrition among the poor, as well as the mass dropping of anti-Pinochet leaflets from a squadron of small private planes, which easily could have been shot down by the Chilean Air Force. All of the main CADA activists, men and women, were aboard.

Raúl Zurita...Diamela Eltit, Lotty Rosenfeld, Fernando Balcells, and Juan Castillo: Zurita (1950) is one of Chile's major poets. In 1990, he was appointed cultural attaché to Rome under the government of Christian Democrat Patricio Aylwin (1918), the first elected President of Chile following the dictatorship. Eltit (1949), novelist and cultural guerrilla in the years of the Pinochet regime, companion of Zurita at the time of CADA, was appointed cultural attaché to Mexico in 1990; Rosenfeld (1943) is a conceptual/installation artist and was a major figure in CADA and the Escena de Avanzada movement during the dictatorship; Balcells (birth date unavailable), a sociologist, was a core member of the CADA group; Castillo (1952), a conceptual artist, was a founding member of CADA.

p. 67

the poetry sky-writing motif: As Aylwin's administration was openly pro-capitalist and neoliberal, Bolaño expressed his disdain for leftists who accepted posts in the government. His over-the-top allegorical association of Zurita's sky-writing poems to the fascist sky-writing "New Chilean Poetry" exponent Carlos Wieder (aka "Alberto Ruiz-Tagle") in *Distant Star* (1996) can be partially sourced to Bolaño's contempt.

an infamous dinner at the home of Jorge Arrate and Diamela Eltit: Arrate (1941), Eltit's husband, was the Presidential candidate of the Chilean Communist Party in 2009; Eltit (see above), for whom Bolaño apparently still felt political rancor when he visited Chile in late 1998, was the victim of a witheringly negative portrait by Bolaño, first published in 1999 in the Spanish magazine *Ajoblanco*, and included in his collection of speeches, reviews, and personal anecdotes, *Entre paréntesis*, edited by Ignacio Echevarría and published posthumously in 2004 by Anagrama. During the same triumphal homecoming to Chile in '98, when Bolaño was everywhere in the papers, on radio, and TV, he scandalously belittled the literary merits of writers like Isabel Allende and Antonio Skármeta.

I have decided to speak of him using the pseudonym: This totally unexpected announcement by Bolaño is the only indication in the manuscript that "Vladimir Nadal" is a pseudonym covering the name of "another" author.

*

Notes to "Searching for Nadal" Letters

[notes purportedly made by Bolaño]

Letter from José Requena

p. 71

The one based on our little Infrarrealista adventures: There is no record or evidence of such a "novel" anticipating Bolaño's *Savage Detectives*. It seems likely the correspondent, whose animosity becomes clear as the letter proceeds, and whose identity has not been ascertained, is giving Bolaño a hard time.

the Infrarrealista manifesto you read standing on a table at Bruno's, in 1976: This differs from an account by the printer Juan Pascoe, Bolaño's first publisher, which has Bolaño seated at a table and solemnly reading his text—two other manifestos were written, in dissent of Bolaño's insistence that his be considered the official one: one by José Vicente Anaya, the other by Mario Santiago. Santiago's manifesto has now been translated into various languages. An English version is featured in a special issue on the Infrarrealistas, edited by Rubén Medina, and published by *Chicago Review* in 2017.

my wife lost my original typescript on a train to Switzerland: The allusion, apparently self-deprecating, is to the famous loss of Hemingway's early short stories, in 1922, by his first wife Hadley, who left the suitcase of the author's typescripts momentarily unattended at a station, on her way to meet Hemingway, in Lausanne, Switzerland.

I will have given you the idea by sending you mine: There is every reason to believe the correspondent is inventing the matter about his own "previous" book. That Bolaño would have included the reference seems to indicate he thought the fallaciousness of the correspondent was transparent enough.

To thank me, you can include me in any future editions of *Pájaro de Calor*: *Pájaro de Calor: Ocho Poetas Infrarrealistas*, pubished by Ediciones Asunción Sanchís, in México, 1976. The poets included, with selection by Bolaño, were José Vicente Anaya, Mara Larrosa, Cuauhtémoc Méndez, Bruno Montané, José Peguero, Rubén Medina, Mario Santiago, and Bolaño.

Muchachos desnudos bajo el arcoiris de fuego, **which you'd left me out of, too**: Published in 1979 by Editorial Extemporáneos, and edited by Bolaño. The book included eleven poets, some of them from outside Mexico. The three Infrarrealistas included were Santiago, Montané, and Bolaño himself.

Beatriz and I divorced: The name reference is unknown.

She was sleeping around with the Peruvian guy Ribeyro had introduced us to: José Rosas Ribeyro (1949), a member of the original Infra group, was from Perú. He was instrumental in putting the Infra poets in touch with the Hora Zero (Op. cit.) group in Lima. The identity of the "Peruvian painter" is unknown. Ribeyro strongly criticized Bolaño and Santiago for publishing in *Plural* after the Echevarría takeover of *Excelsior*.

p. 72

Frank Lloyd Wright: Wright (1867-1959) is widely considered the most important architect of the 20th century.

Luis Barragán …the Governor of Wisconsin…Richard Meier: Barragán (1902-1988) is one of Mexico's greatest 20th century architects; the Governor of Wisconsin in question was Tommy Thompson (1941), who would have just taken office; Richard Meier (1934) is an internationally renowned U.S. architect.

p. 73

Mamah Borthwick: Borthwick (1869-1914), lived at Taliesin with Wright out of wedlock, a great scandal at the time.

pouring a drink on Octavio Paz's tie at Huerta's house, you might remember that was me: The correspondent's claim to having been the one to have famously poured a drink on Paz conflicts with Nadal's claim of the same, in Bolaño's introduction.

some pulquería in Guadalupe Tepeyac, on 27 Calle Samuel: In fact, the address is that of Bolaño's house in Mexico, D.F.

Svetlana Alliluyeva: Alliluyeva (1926-2011), Josef Stalin's daughter, died in Richland Center, Wisconsin, Wright's birthplace, near Spring Green. The correspondent has the facts right, though she did leave Wisconsin for a few years to live in England.

p. 74

Verónica Volkow: (1955), a writer friendly with both the Infrarrealistas and the Paz circle. Requena misspeaks: Volkow is the *great*-granddaughter of Leon Trotsky, the Bolshevik leader murdered in Mexico.

Enrique Vila-Matas…Paul Auster…W.G. Sebald: The correspondent must have known of Bolaño's close association with Vila-Matas (Op.cit.); Auster (1947) and Sebald (1944-2001) are major writers whom Bolaño admired.

Littlewood's Law: According to which a person will experience an event with odds of one in a million at the rate of about one per month.

winner of the Herralde Prize, no doubt soon to be translated into English and published by the leading houses of the Impe-

rium: The Herralde Prize was awarded to the *Savage Detectives* in 1998; Vila-Matas, mentioned above, won it in 2002.

everyone is crazy and full of life, just as life was once so full of us: This seems possibly an allusion to a line from "A Step Away from Them," by Frank O'Hara (Op. cit.): "But is the / earth as full as life was full, of them?"

It's like six-hundred pages long: The contradiction between this assertion about the manuscript's length and the previous description seems further evidence of the fabricated nature of the claim about the book.

p. 75

Phillip K. Dick dark streak: Dick (1928-1982) was a major U.S. writer of science fiction and much read by Bolaño. The relevant author-references the correspondent is able to make suggests he did know Bolaño closely in Mexico, though as stated above, I am not able to determine with certainty who is behind the invented name Bolaño has assigned him.

Anábasis: One of the main journals of the younger writers in Octavio Paz's orbit. *El Zaguán* and *Cuadernos de literatura* were two others.

Desnos: Robert Desnos (1900-1945), one of the key members of the Surrealist circle, before his estrangement from the group in 1928. He has become the most famous practitioner of dream-state automatic writing (though Péret was considered his equal during the period of dictational experiments), in which he deliriously and spontaneously "spoke" poems (transcribed by others), after not allowing himself sleep for days. Among these are some of his most esteemed.

Ramón…Mara…Jorge…Carlos Pilsen…Harrington: Ramón Méndez, Mara Larrosa, and Jorge Hernández (Luscious Skin), all previously cited, were original members of the Infrarrealista group; the identity of Carlos Pilsen has not been determined; Juan Esteban Harrington (Op. cit.), young member of the group and friend of Nadal's.

Carla…Pascoe…Librería Sótano: Carla Rippey (Op. cit.); Juan Pascoe, dual Mexico-U.S. citizen, printing artist and brother-in-law of Carla Rippey, his Taller Martín Pescador printed Bolaño and other poets close to the Infra circle; Librería Sótano was one of the favorite bookstores of the Infra circle, not least as a source of stolen merchandise.

p. 76

Cáceres: Omar Cáceres (1904-1943), Chilean poet. Given that numerous of the names present are previously cited and much of the basic background information about Cáceres and his case is adequately described in the extensive letter by Nadal (included in the letter to Bolaño by "José Requena"), notes have only been added where identification is insufficient. This will also be the case in the long email by Nadal concerning the Peruvian poet Carlos Oquendo de Amat, which follows within the same letter by Requena.

p. 77

Anguita: Eduardo Anguita: (Op. cit.)

Margaret is orange; William a fresh pale blue: Throughout the emails about Cáceres and de Amat, the reader will encounter odd, illogical, sometimes lyrical interjections into the narration, something which seems to have been a tic of Nadal's prose composition.

Arica: Chile's northernmost city. Nadal is, in fact, mistaken: Cáceres was born quite a bit further south, in the commune of Cauquenes.

p. 78

Rosicrucian Order: Rosicrucianism is a secret society, supposedly founded in medieval Germany, which purports to hold secrets that are "concealed from the average man" and which "provide insight into nature, the physical universe, and the spiritual realm." It maintains a particularly strong following in the Andean countries, whre it has undergone both bourgeois and indigenous transformation.

de Rokha: Pablo de Rokha (1894-1968), born Carlos Díaz Loyola, one of Chile's great poets, considered by many to be the equal of Neruda, Huidobro, and Gabriela Mistral. He and Neruda held a mutually strong antipathy for each other, though both were prominent leaders of the Chilean Communist Party. Poignantly, two hours after de Rokha committed suicide, only a few months following the suicide of his son, officials from the municipality of La Reina arrived at his house, intending to inform him that the authorities had decided to change the name of his street to "Calle de Rokha." They were the ones to discover his body. His actual relationship to Omar Cáceres, for whose book he wrote a rejected Preface, remains a mystery to this day.

the engagement broken off, in unexplained Kierkegaardian fashion: The Danish philosopher Søren Kierkegaard (1813-1855), regarded as the founding figure of Existentialism, precipitously and without explanation, broke off his engagement to his beloved muse, Regine Olsen.

"Mansion of Foam": I use the translation of Eliot Weinberger, published in his book *Karmic Traces* (New Directions, 2000).

p. 79

Winétt de Rokha (1894-1951), pseudonym of the Chilean poet Luisa Victoria Anabalón.

p. 80

El Mercurio: Chile's largest and oldest daily newspaper.

Pedro Lastra: (1932), one of Chile's leading literary scholars.

p. 81

Leticio Machado: The name and incident appear to be apocryphal.

p. 82

Cecilia Vicuña: (1947), important Chilean poet, essayist, and artist.

Antonio Gil: (1954), important Chilean novelist, poet, and controversial journalist.

p. 83

a box with thirteen folders: The discovered Cáceres materials reside, since 2011, at the National Library of Chile.

Aretino, Beethoven, Bellini, Glück, Handel, Haydn, Mozart, Mendelssohn, and Villa-Lobos: The list names famous composers. The presence of Heitor Villa-Lobos (1987-1959), Brazil's greatest composer, represents a curious connection, given his link to Péret's first wife, the singer Elsie Houston, who was in Paris with Villa-Lobos in 1929, performing his songs, when she and Péret met.

Jules Supervielle's 1925 novella *El hombre de las pampas*: Supervielle (1884-1960), Uruguayan-French poet, and later diplomat for Uruguay, the country of his birth. He was long courted by the Surrealists, but remained independent. *El hombre de las pampas* (*The Man of the Pampas*) was his first work of fiction, published in French, in 1923, not '25, as Nadal has it.

p. 84

the first of Cáceres's letters to T.S. Eliot: If real, the letter is of stunning importance, revealing previously secret information about Eliot (1888-1965). As all of the recently discovered materials relating to Cáceres have not yet been open to the public, it is not possible to verify the authenticity of the letter(s).

Brother of our High Order, Vicente Huidobro: And this would be no less surprising a revelation. That T.S. Eliot and Vicente Huidobro were contemporaneous, higher priests of the Rosicrucian Order would be nothing less than a bombshell, if true.

Rosamel del Valle: (1901-1965), important poet of the early-20th century Vanguardia generation.

p. 85

"Conversation with the Chevalier": The poem is apparently lost.

Hölderlin: Friedrich Hölderlin (1770-1843), one of the great poets of German Romanticism. No such quote by him has been found. Is this an unknown quote that is available to Cáceres due to Hölderlin's membership in the Rosicrucian Order? Perhaps.

p. 86

Rubén Darío: (1867-1916), the leading figure of Latin American *Modernismo* in the late 19th-early 20th centuries.

Alfonso Cortés…Marosa Di Giorgio: Cortés (1893-1969), though not well known internationally (he has barely been translated into English, for example), is widely considered to be Nicaragua's most gifted poet after Darío. As reported on Wikipedia, "(Cortés) lost his mind on midnight of February 18, 1927, at the age of 34. (He) spent much of that year chained to the iron grillwork of his bedroom window as a result of his delirium growing violent. The next 25 years of Cortés's life were spent in a mental hospital in Managua" [Wikipedia does not mention the bizarre fact that Cortés lived—and was shackled to the wall—in the modest natal house of Rubén Darío, in León, Nicaragua]; Di Giorgio (1932-2004) is now considered one of the great poets not just of 20th century Uruguay, but of Latin America in general. Increasingly translated, her strange, fantastical prose poetry has, in the past decade or so, begun to develop something of a cult following in various languages.

p. 87

Five Meters of Poems: The original (*Cinco metros de poemas*) is now a very rare and prohibitively expensive object. A translated facsimile of the first Lima edition, meticulously following the original design, was published by Ugly Duckling Presse in 2010.

Mallarmé and Apollinaire: Both Stéphane Mallarmé (1842-1898) and Guillaume Apollinaire (1880-1918) have been crucial inspirations to practitioners of visual and concrete poetry. Mallarmé's *Un Coup de Dés* and Apollinaire's *Calligrammes* are modernist classics of the genre.

p. 88

**Creacionista and Ultraísta movements…José Carlos Mariáte-
gui**: The other names from this passage are previously cited;
the Creacionista movement was announced by Vicente Huidobro in 1912—one of the first aesthetic pronouncements of the
20th century avant-garde—though it proved to be more of an
inspiring, artistically fecund idea than an actual movement; Ultraísmo, directly influenced by Huidobro's thought (along with
Ezra Pound's imagist precepts), has its origin in Spain in 1918
and was later broadly disseminated in Latin America. Jorge
Luis Borges (1899-1986), then living in Spain, was one of its
founders; Mariátegui (1895-1930), legendary Peruvian author,
editor (of the influential journal *Amauta*) and Marxist thinker,
is considered by many to be the Latin American kin to Antonio
Gramsci. He was the leader of the Socialist Party of Peru (the de
facto communist organization of the time) and is widely regarded as one of the continent's most important intellectual figures
of the 20th century's first decades. He and César Vallejo were
acquaintances when both lived in Lima (Mariátegui would write
the first major essay on the great poet), and they maintained a
friendship in correspondence following Vallejo's emigration to
Europe.

modernismo: Not to be confused with Anglo-American Modernism, modernismo was "founded" by Rubén Darío (1867-1916)
and was immensely influential in Latin America and Spain
through the early part of the 20th century. Deeply indebted to
French Parnassianism, it is, in aesthetical tendency, a late-Ro-
mantic, art for art's sake phenomenon, though not a few of its
central figures, including Darío, used these rhetorical modes
in subversive ways, to express nationalist and anti-imperialist
ideas in some of their writings.

Rascacielos: (*Skyscraper*). No reference to such a journal (or "essay") has been tracked down. It was likely a one-off, furtive edition, now disappeared.

Hora Zero: Previously cited, the Peruvian avant-garde and leftist group, roughly contemporaneous with the Mexican Infrarrealists.

p. 89

E.E. Cummings: (1894-1962). It is logical that de Amat would have been drawn to Cummings's typographical experiments. It is unclear if the communist de Amat was aware of Cummings's hard-right leanings.

p. 90

Izquierda Comunista de España…gossip about scandalous doings between Federico García Lorca and Salvador Dalí… recent writings contra Aragon by André Breton: The Izquierda Comunista de España, affiliated with Trotsky's Left Opposition, was formed in 1932, from a break with the Communist Party of Spain. In 1935, against Trotsky's wishes, it joined with other left forces to form the POUM (Op. cit.), which was later persecuted and suppressed by dominant Stalinist forces in the Republican government; Federico García Lorca (1898-1936), widely considered Spain's great poet of the 20th century, was executed by Francoist forces in 1936 and buried in a mass grave. His body has never been found; Salvador Dalí (1904-1989), the notorious Surrealist artist, was Lorca's lover for a time in the 1930s; by the time of de Amat's letter to Cummings, the split between Aragon and Breton (both previously cited) was beyond repair.

Economic and Philosophic Manuscripts of 1844: A series of notes by the young Marx, not published until 1927, in the Soviet Union. De Amat would have been reading a very recent Spanish or English translation.

p. 91

Ezra Pound, T.S. Eliot, and Archibald MacLeish: Eliot is previously cited; Ezra Pound (1885-1972) was the central figure in Anglo-American poetic Modernism and—as a champion of fascism—one of its most controversial exponents; Archibald MacLeish (1892-1982) was a major figure of American poetry of the mid-20th century and one of the most politically influential of all American poets. He was appointed Librarian of Congress by Franklin Roosevelt and is considered to have been one of the institution's finest directors. He also played a key role in early discussions and planning for the development of the Central Intelligence Agency, even though he was also close to many members of the Communist Party and widely considered to be a fellow-traveler.

Letter from Luis Barrios

p. 92

After Harrington left in October of '77: Juan Esteban Harrington (Op. cit.), who'd been instrumental, by all signs, in bringing Nadal around the Infrarrealista group, met up with Bruno Montané and Bolaño for a couple months in Spain. He wandered around Paris for a few months, searching in vain for Mario Santiago, then returned to Barcelona, where he lived until early 1979, at which time he returned to Mexico and renewed his activities with the Infra group. Mario Santiago returned some months later that same year.

Bar Nivel...Pizzeria del Gringo...the Cantina: Three favorite haunts of the Infra poets in the Zócalo area. The Cantina is renamed the Encrucijada Veracruzana in the *Savage Detectives*.

New American poetry...Russian Formalists: The New American Poetry was given "official" announcement via Donald Allen's legendary 1960 anthology of the same name; the Russian Formalists were a loosely knit group of theorists and critics active in Russia in the pre-revolutionary and early Soviet years. All of them were supporters of avant-garde literary currents active in the first years of the revolution. Among the major representatives of the group were Viktor Shklovsky, Roman Jakobson, Vladimir Propp, Yuri Tunianov, and Boris Eichenbaum. By the 1930s, with the consolidation of Stalinist rule, their experimental-critical thought had been repressed.

Kerouac cheering on Ginsberg at the Six Gallery: Jack Kerouac (1922-1969), Beat writer and a hero to the Infra group. The reference is to the culturally momentous reading by Allen Ginsberg of his poem "Howl," in October, 1955, in San Francisco, California.

jokingly calling them "Vladimir and the Gringo Briks": The reference, quite clever, is to the love triangle of Vladimir Mayakovsky (1893-1930) and Osip and Lily Brik, who lived together in Moscow for a period and were intimate, if conflicted, friends for many years; Lily Brik (1891-1978), a central presence in early Soviet avant-garde circles, was Mayakovsky's sometime-lover and muse; her husband, Osip Brik (1888-1945), was a leading literary critic and central figure in the Russian Formalist group. He co-founded, with Mayakovsky, the most important avant-garde journal of the early Soviet period, LEF (Left Front of Art).

José Luis Rivas, Francisco Segovia: Rivas (1950) and Segovia (1958) were two of the prominent younger poets of the Paz am-bit in the 1970s. They have both gone on to distinguished and prized literary careers. The partial list of readers suggests the series was diverse in its offerings.

p. 93

Chavela Vargas: Vargas (1919-2012), was born in Costa Rica but lived all of her adult life in Mexico. She is one of the nation's legendary folk singers, and one of the first Mexican musical artists to be open about her gay sexuality.

Jaime Sabines: Sabines (1926-1999) was a widely read and interesting poet, whose work featured casual, sometimes satirical language, based in themes of daily life.

***Martín el Pescado*, which was pretty clever:** A play on Taller Martín Pescador, Juan Pascoe's literary press, which published some of the first Infrarrealista collections in handprinted, limited editions. It more or less translates (as opposed to "Fisherman Martin's Workshop," the press run by Pascoe) as "Martin the Fish out of Water."

on Bucareli: Calle Bucareli, where Café La Habana is located.

like Kerouac waving his wine bottle in 1955: See note above on Ginsberg's legendary reading of "Howl."

party at Efraín's place: Efraín Huerta (Op. cit.)

pretty sure Nadal was gay: No other suggestion of the kind has been found, and reports in this manuscript of Nadal's passionate relationships with at least two women would complicated the claim. It's perfectly possible, of course, that Nadal was bisexual.

original manifesto, by which he meant *his*, **I'm afraid, not** *yours*: To repeat here: Though Bolaño's is the most widely known, by far, there were three original Infrarrealista manifestos, all written in 1975. The other two, more compact than Bolaño's, were written by José Vicente Anaya and Mario Santiago.

Guadalupe Tepeyac: Mexico City neighborhood, where Bolaño lived with his family.

Verónica Morelos…Vera Larrosa…Clara Lustero: The poet and dancer Vera Larrosa (1956), sister of Mara, is "Angélica Font" in the *Savage Detectives*. The other two names have not been identified by the translator.

Miguel León-Portilla: León-Portilla (1926) is one of the world authorities on Nahuàtl thought and literature.

Damián: Pedro Damián Bautista (1954), one of the original Infrarrealista core.

that was pretty cold of you and Mario: The reference is to Pedro Damián Bautista being left out of the *Pájaro de Calor* anthology (see above), which was primarily selected by Bolaño, with Santiago's input.

Performance I by Nadal

Roberto Bolaño: The reference is intriguing. It seems a sarcastic jab at Bolaño, who of course was in Spain at the time, much to the resentment of some of the Infras, including perhaps Nadal.

Performance II by Nadal

Michelangelo: The great Renaissance artist, architect, engineer, and poet, (1475-1564).

"Where's Mayra?": The reference is uncertain. It seems to be an urgent, perhaps disoriented question, suddenly interjected by Nadal, as he comes out of his poetic-channeling reverie. It might be a mistyping in transcription for "Mara" (Larrosa).

Performance III by Nadal

p. 99

Quetzalcóatl: The Aztec deity of Wind and Wisdom; the Nahuátl-language name means "Feathered Serpent."

Performance IV by Nadal

p. 100

John Ashbery: The birthdate Nadal gives is mistaken: Ashbery was born in 1927. Widely considered today, in 2017, to be the greatest living poet of the United States, Ashbery in 1979 had only come into fame in the English-speaking poetry world a few years previously, after winning the three major American literary prizes for his *Self-Portrait in a Convex Mirror*, a book that hadn't yet been translated into Spanish at the time of Nadal's spoken poem.

Monsiváis: Carlos Monsiváis (Op. cit.)

Salvador Novo Prize: One of the major prizes for young poets in Mexico. It had recently been won, when Nadal spoke the poem, by Carmen Boullosa, Verónica Volkow, and Darío Galicia, all acquaintances of his.

the antipast, which is breve, longum, longum, breve: In each section of this poem, Nadal— much like "García Madero" in the final section of the *Savage Detectives*—cites and describes classical meters. The different alternations in the poem of "breve" and "longum" describe relevant sequences of short and long syllables.

Amado Nervo: Nervo (1870-1919) was a prominent Mexican poet. Nadal mentions a famous 19th century Mexican poet in each of the stanzas, in a kind of vanguard *ranchera* spirit, set off against the "gringos."

Poetry in general is like playing tennis with the net down: The line is poached from a famous aphorism of Robert Frost (1874-1963), though Frost was referring to free verse, not poetry in general.

Elizabeth Bishop: Nadal's memory of the birth dates of American poets is not the best; in fact, he gets every one of them wrong. It seems possible the errors are purposeful. Bishop lived from 1911 to 1979.

Savoy style: The reference would be to Villa Savoye, one of the signature examples of Modernist domestic architecture, designed by Le Corbusier and built outside Paris between 1928 and '31.

Félix Candela…Niemeyer…Los Manantiales, in Xochimilco: Candela (1910-1997) is one of Mexico's leading architects of the 20th century. The Brazilian Oscar Niemeyer, lead planner of the country's capital, Brasilia, and one of the most important modern architects of the world. The landmark restaurant Los Manantiales, in Xochimilco park, built in 1958, is one of his most famous buildings.

I broke a bottle over a poet's head: The incident is recounted in a letter further on by another correspondent, Laura Puig.

I want to win the Cervantes Prize: Now one of the most important literary prizes in the Hispanic world, it had only recently been established, in 1976.

Ramón López Velarde: Prominent Mexican poet (1888-1921).

To have great poets of the avant-garde: The quote is elaborated from Walt Whitman's quote, "To have great poets there must be great audiences, too."

Robert Creeley: (1926-2005) Major figure of postmodern American poetry.

Juan Bañuelos: (1932) "Julio César Álamo" in the *Savage Detectives*. Bañuelos's poetry workshop at the UNAM's off-campus cultural center, La Casa del Lago, in the forest of Chapultepec, was famously subverted by a group of Infrarrealista poets, causing Bañuelos to temporarily resign his position as teacher. A close ally of Octavio Paz, he was later accused by certain Infrarrealista's of plagiarizing the poetry of Saint-John Perse.

p. 101

William Carlos Williams: (1883-1963), major American modernist poet.

National Poesía Jóven Prize: (Premio Nacional de la Poesía Jóven) Important Mexican literary prize, won by a number of Octavio Paz's acolytes.

Like a skull-lamp with a candle behind the eyes: This appears to be a gloss on the first stanza of Robert Creeley's poem "The Warning": "For love—I would / split open your head and put / a candle in / behind the eyes.

Manuel Carpio: (1791-1860) Mexican romantic poet.

Hilda Doolittle: Better known as H.D. [1886-1961), she was closely associated with Ezra Pound and the Imagist poets of the early 20th century.

Zona Rosa…La Peralvillo…to drink pulque: La Zona Rosa is a touristy shopping district in Mexico D.F., famous for its nightlife and for being the central location of the city's gay community; La Peralvillo is a rough and tumble working class neighborhood in DF; it has numerous bars where pulque may be purchased, a traditional alcoholic drink made from the sap of the maguey (agave) plant.

Punto de Partida Prize: A literary prize still given yearly, in various genre categories, by the National Autonomous University of Mexico (UNAM).

Manuel Acuña: (1849-1873) Mexican Romantic poet and novelist. He committed suicide at the age of 23.

T.S. Eliot: (1888-1965, Op. cit.)

Casa de las Américas Prize: Cuba's major annual literary prize, one of the most prestigious in Latin America.

p. 102

Efrén Rebolledo: Mexican poet (1877-1929), his poem "The Vampire" is quoted in the opening pages of the *Savage Detectives*.

Poetry is an imaginary garden with real dead poets in it: A riff on a line in Marianne Moore's poem "Poetry."

Letter from Sonia Font

Mara: Probably Mara Larrosa (Op. cit.).

Juan Esteban, José, María Guadalupe, Ramón: Juan Esteban Harrington, José Peguero, María Guadalupe Ochoa, Ramón Méndez, all previously cited.

p. 103

Catana: Rafael Catana (1955) was a latecomer to the group. He remained active in the years after Mario Santiago returned from the Middle East and Europe in 1979.

Edgar Altamirano and Cuauhtémoc: Altamirano (1953) joined the group following the departure of Bolaño and Santiago. He now publishes his work under the pen name Edgar Artaud Jarry; Cuauhtémoc Mendez (1956-2005), one of the original founders of the group and probably the most dedicated Left political militant among the Infrarrealistas.

Duchamp: The inclusion of Marcel Duchamp (1987-1968) here with the other Surrealist founders and practitioners of automatic writing is not really accurate. Though Duchamp collaborated with the Surrealists for around a decade, beginning in the 1930s (including editing the Surrealist periodical VVV), he never formally joined the group.

after Mario came back from Palestine: Santiago had wandered around Israel ca. 1978-79, searching for Claudia Kerik (1957), an Argentine-born member of the Infrarrealistas, with whom he was in love.

p. 104

Revueltas: José Revueltas (1914-1976) was a poet, novelist, and revolutionary leader, one of the key early figures in Mexico of the Trotskyist Left Opposition. He was a hero to many of the Infrarrealistas (some of them, like the Méndez brothers and Jorge Hernández, were militants in Revueltas's Liga Socialista), especially to Mario Santiago, who changed his two last surnames to "Santiago Papasquiaro" in homage to the birthplace of Revueltas. Revueltas's novel *El luto humano* (*Human Mourning*) won the National Literature Prize of Mexico in 1943. During the mid-

1970s, Revueltas was on the editorial board (along with another Infra hero, Julio Cortázar) of the journal *Cambio*, to which Bolaño contributed a few reviews, including a sharp polemic against the prominent Mexican poet José Emilio Pacheco.

"neo-Zanguanists"…Rubén Medina…*Correspondencia Infra:* The sarcastic reference to neo-Zanguanists pertains to one of the magazines of the young Octavio Paz acolytes. Medina and the journal *Corresponencia Infra* are cited further above.

even more people took off, including Medina and Anaya and the Méndez brothers. Piel Divina, too. And then Mario got killed by the truck: Rubén Medina left for San Diego, California in June, 1978; Anaya had left to wander Mexico the year before; the Méndez brothers left for Morelia, Mexico in late 1978, where they became successful bakers; Jorge Hernández/ Piel Divina, left for Paris in 1979; Santiago was killed in January, 1998, while crossing a busy street without looking for oncoming vehicles, an intentional practice he refused to abandon, even after having been struck and injured a few years before under similar circumstances.

Carmen, José María Espinasa, or Juan Villoro: Carmen Boullosa (Op. cit.); Espinasa (1957), successful Mexican writer opposed to the Infras in the 1970s; Villoro (1956) had a collegial but sometimes tense relationship with Bolaño and the Infrarrealista group. He is, with Bolaño, one of the most prominent Mexican writers of that generation and period, winner of the prestigious Herralde Prize for his novel *El testigo (The Witness)*, in 2004.

who are we and where are we going? The question echoes the title of Gaugin's largest and most famous painting, "Where do we come from? What are we? Where are we going?"

p. 105

El Nada: The Nothing.

Letter from César Oster Madero

"ocean of the void": A phrase from Bolaño's Infra manifesto, "Abandon everything, once again."

Chatterton: Thomas Chatterton (1752-1770) was an English poet and forger of medieval poetry. He committed suicide at the age of seventeen. A hero of the Romantic movement, he wrote of desiring to have his "name on every tongue."

Rimbaud: There may be a sarcastic allusion here to a magazine Bolaño co-published with Bruno Montané in Spain, in 1979, titled *Rimbaud vuelve a casa* (*Rimbaud Comes Home*). In the introduction to the first and only issue, the two Chilean poets had spoken of the publication as marking a kind of adieu to their poetic youth in Mexico.

Letter from Laura Puig

p. 106

Alcira...Guadalupe Ochoa: Though most of her life and death is shrouded in mystery, the eccentric Uruguayan writer Alcira Soust Scaffo (1923-1997), was a friend of the Infrarrealistas in Mexico during the 1970s. She is, as "Auxilio Lacouture," the central protagonist of Bolaño's novel *Amulet*, and a long section of the *Savage Detectives* is devoted to her as well; Ochoa (1957), with her longtime partner José Peguero (1955), was one of the original poets of the Infra group.

looked up from her Benedetti...Roberto Vallarino...Luis Roberto Vera: Soust Scaffo is reading a book by her Uruguayan compatriot, the poet and novelist Mario Benedetti (1920-2009); Roberto Vallarino (1955-2002), Mexican poet and editor of *Cuadernos de literatura*, a key journal in the 70s for younger poets aspiring to official recognition; Vera, born in Chile (1947), is a prominent poet and scholar. In 1972 he had moved to Mexico City and become a central figure among younger poets of Paz's milieu. He edited *El Zaguán* and he became, as such, an enemy of the Infrarrealistas.

p. 107

Cantina Bar: In the *Savage Detectives*, this tavern is given the name Encrucijada Veracruzana, where García Madero spends a good deal of time.

Los Manantiales: See reference above, in relation to the architect Félix Candela.

José Joaquín Blanco and Monsiváis: Blanco (1951) is a Mexican poet and playwright; Carlos Monsiváis (Op. cit.).

Francisco Segovia…Coral Bracho: Segovia (Op. cit.); Bracho (1951) is an influential innovative poet.

p. 109

like a melting UFO: Indeed, Los Manantiales is sometimes referred to as "el OVNI" (the UFO).

El Popular: A legendary café in the Zócalo area, in Mexico D. F., a favorite hangout of the Infras.

La Soriana: A giant supermarket.

p. 110

nopal: Prickly pear cactus, a Mexican culinary staple.

José Emilio Pacheco: (1939-2014), major Mexican poet, winner of the Cervantes Prize in 2009.

Long Live Lucio Cabañas! Lucio Cabañas (1938-1974) was the leader of the guerrilla wing of the Party of the Poor, which was active and influential in the mountainous region of Guerrero, from 1967 until 1974, when Cabañas was killed by Mexican security forces.

Dr. Wagner…Dos Caras…El Canek: Masked professional wrestling stars of Mexico.

Sanatorio Americano: A private hospital in Montevideo, Uruguay.

Robert Sayre: Sayre (1924) was U.S. Ambassador to Uruguay from 1968-69, at the beginning of the counterinsurgency war against the Tupamaro urban guerrilla movement.

p. 111

the sister of Hubert Humphrey and…Duke Ellington himself: Frances Humphrey Howard (1914-2002) and Duke Ellington (1899-1974) both visited Uruguay in 1968.

Cerro…Peñarol: Two first-division soccer clubs of Uruguay. In the 1960s, Peñarol was one of the top teams of the world.

p. 112

the Centenario: The Estadio Centenario, Uruguay's largest stadium, built in 1930 for the first World Cup.

Ungaretti, and Borges, and Piglia, and Sor Juana, and Bioy Casares: Ricardo Piglia (1941), major writer of Argentina and acquaintance of Bolaño; Bioy Casares (1914-1999), Argentinian writer who was a close friend and collaborator of Borges. The other writers mentioned are cited above. It is interesting that the authors of the stolen books cover a number of the titles that Nadal carries in his bag when he is with Bolaño in Blanes.

Wittgenstein's fire poker: A reference to a 1946 incident, at Cambridge University, where Ludwig Wittgenstein (1889-1951) allegedly brandished a fire poker at Sir Karl Popper, during an argument revolving around the relationship of language to philosophical problems.

Who were we and where were we going? Like a similar comment by another correspondent above, this seems a possible reference to the title of Paul Gaugin's 1897 painting *Where do we come from? What are we? Where are we going?*

peseras: The ubiquitous micro-buses of Mexico City.

p. 113

***Diary of an Unknown Writer*…Marcus Manilius's *Astronómica*, with a Prologue by Alfonso Reyes:** *Diary of an Unknown Writer* is a novella by Kikuchi Kan (Japan, 1888-1948), in which the writer expresses resentment of contemporaries who have gained greater literary notoriety than he. The novella was written in 1918, so its relation would properly be to WWI, not WWII; Manilius (1st century AD) was a Roman poet and astrologer. *Astronómica* is a treatise in five books. Nadal apparently filches a thick compendium volume. Or at least sin Laura's telling: It seems likely she is being playful with Bolaño here, as Bolaño has Juan García Madero steal both of the aforementioned volumes from a bookstore in the first part of the *Savage Detectives*! Or, of course, it is possible that Bolaño is writing these letters himself and having some self-referential fun. The author of the Spanish-edition *Astronómica* prologue, Alfonso Reyes (1989-1959), was a famed writer, philosopher, and diplomat of Mexico. Jorge Luis Borges called him "the greatest prose writer in the Spanish language of any age." The many other names in the passage refer to Mexico City streets or bookstores.

chicha: A fermented or non-fermented drink, usually made from maize, though also from various fruits, sold widely by street vendors in Mexico and Central America.

For crissakes, watch out where you're going: A possible allusion to the concluding line of one of Robert Creeley's most famous poems, "I Know a Man." Nadal refers to Creeley in one of his spontaneous "talk poems" above.

Marco Antonio Montes de Oca and Ali Chumacero: Montes de Oca (1932-2009) and Chumacero (1918-2010) were prominent official poets.

p. 114

Sonnets about Lunch: The title of Frank O'Hara's (Op. cit.) most famous book is *Lunch Poems*, published in 1964, by City Lights Books, in its popular Pocket Poets series.

and the cowboy on Reforma is smoking overhead: Likely a playful allusion to the reference in O'Hara's "A Step Away from Them," where a large cigarette advertisement in Times Square "blows smoke over my head."

Coleridge and Keats and Wordsworth…I should do an experimental translation of one of these guys: The Romantic poets Samuel Taylor Coleridge (1772-1834), John Keats (1795-1821), and William Wordsworth (1770-1850). The reference to "experimental translations" is interesting, especially in light of Bolaño's expressed advocacy of it, as reported in Quiroga's Preface—not to mention the fact that both he and Santiago published free—and even invented—"translations" of French and English-language poets in different Mexican journals during the 1970s.

p. 115

Nadal told me then of his idea to kidnap Octavio Paz: See the previous reference to this in Bolaño's intro. Though the plan was never carried out, it was seriously discussed on various occasions, as two central members of the Infrarrealists at the time have confirmed to me.

"Labyrinth of Sonambulism": Playing off from Paz's legendary study of Mexican culture and identity, *The Labyrinth of Solitude*, published in 1950.

Alain Delon: French actor (1935), who starred in a number of New Wave films of the 1960s. In 1970, he played Leon Trotsky, in "The Assassination of Trotsky," a favorite film of Bolano, Santiago, and other Infras.

p. 116

Alejandro Aura and Juan Villoro: Both writers were well-known to Bolaño and the Infras and little liked by them due to their official associations. Aura (1944-2008) was a poet, fiction writer, and later television host, who was married for a time to Carmen Boullosa, a close correspondent of Bolaño in his last years; Villoro (1956) is a prize-winning prose writer who was appointed as Cultural Attaché to the German Democratic Republic in the early 1980s.

the kind of writer he wanted to be: The extended passage that follows on Nadal's apparent desire for anonymity is fascinating, especially in light of Bolaño's speculations about him in the introduction.

José Peguero… Rubén and Guadalupe and Oscar and Mara: José Peguero (1955); Rubén Medina (1955); María Guadlaupe Ochoa (1957); Oscar Altamirano (1957); Mara Larrosa (1955). All members of the Infra group.

Tacuarembó: A rural department in central Uruguay. Puig—or whoever is writing—is exaggerating for effect: The bombing of the Carrasco Bowling Club by the Tupamaros (see note to Preface by Quiroga) gravely injured the elderly night-caretaker, Hilaria Ibarra, who was rescued from the rubble, as fate would have it, by Gustavo Zerbino, who would a few years later be a survivor of the Andes airplane crash, where surviving members of the Christian Brothers rugby team of Montevideo kept themselves alive by eating their dead teammates.

Sorocabana Café…Marosa Di Giorgio…Jules Laforgue…Julio Herrera y Reissig: The Sorocabana Café, long Montevideo's most venerable literary gathering place, was a cavernous, bustling institution on one of the city's main squares, Plaza Cagancha. It closed in the late 1990s, after operating for sixty years. Puig, in a strange transference, places the Sorocabana on Plaza Independencia, as evidenced by her naming of key landmarks there, such as the Palacio Salvo and the statue of José Gervasio

Artigas (1765-1850), Uruguay's national hero. Marosa Di Giorgio (Op. cit.) was long a regular at the Sorocabana. Laforgue (1860-1887—he lived most of his life in France) and Herrera y Reissig (1875-1910) are two of Uruguay's leading poets of the late-nineteenth century.

Palacio Salvo: Built in 1928 on Plaza Independencia, Montevideo's main square, by the Argentine architect Mario Palanti, it was, for more than three decades, the tallest building in South America. It is, indeed, an international landmark of eclectic architecture. It is said to have had, over its history, more writers and artists lodged in its rooms than any building in Latin America.

p. 120

parrilladas and the Medio-Medios: Parrilladas are the traditional open wood-fire barbecue pits of Uruguay and Argentina; Medio-Medio is a vermouth-based drink of otherwise secret concoction sold only at a century-old stall in the Old Market, by the Port of Montevideo.

Daniel Mitrione, the CIA torturer the MLN had kidnapped: The Movimiento de Liberación Nacional (MLN), popularly known as the Tupamaros, an urban guerrilla group with widespread popular support, kidnapped Daniel Mitrione (1920-1970) in 1970 and executed him not long following, after demands for the release of one-hundred and fifty political prisoners was refused by the government. The Tupamaros lost most of their support after the incident and the movement was quickly destroyed. It has been amply documented that Mitrione was a CIA operative sent to Uruguay to train the security forces in violent interrogation techniques, including the use of genital electric-shock. The film *State of Siege* was released in 1972. The Infra film buffs were close fans of Costa Gavras.

p. 121

Bordaberry: Juan Maria Bordaberry (1928-2011) was elected President of Uruguay in 1971. In 1973 he dissolved the democratically elected General Assembly and ruled by decree, as the head of a de facto military dictatorship, until he was deposed in a palace power struggle in 1976, which ushered in open and totalitarian rule by a fascist-leaning military junta. Bordaberry is widely reviled in Uruguay for betraying the country's longstanding democratic institutions and for his crimes against human rights while in office.

Liga Comunista 23 de Septiembre: An urban guerrilla group of Mexico, importantly inspired by the Tupamaros, in fact, and mostly active in the late 1970s and early 1980s. It was crushed in the Guerra Sucia of the 70s and 80s, when most of its members were killed or disappeared by the Mano Blanca (White Hand) paramilitary forces of the PRI government. Nadal would have been one of the few of the organization to have made it out alive.

Letter from Ricardo Ramírez Camarga

p. 122

Toussaint: Jean Philippe Toussaint (1957), Belgian prose writer, photographer, and filmmaker.

Mariátegui…Kafka, Montaigne…Hernández…Walser, Shakespeare (de Vere?), Góngora, Beckett, most of Maigret: José Carlos Mariátegui (Op.cit); Franz Kafka (Austria, 1883-1924), one of the great writers of the German language; Michel de Montaigne (France, 1533-1592), leading philosopher of the Renaissance; Felisberto Hernández (1902-1964), one of Uruguay's greatest prose writers; Robert Walser (1878-1956), Swiss writer who died almost unknown in a mental asylum and whose works have been widely acclaimed since his death; Edward de

Vere (1550-1604), the 17th Earl of Oxford, believed by some to be the true author of the works attributed to "Shakespeare"; Luis de Góngora (Spain, 1561-1627), major lyric poet of the Baroque. Along with his contemporary rival Francisco de Quevedo, he is the central poet of Spain; Samuel Beckett (1906-1989), Irish writer who lived most of his adult life in France and wrote mainly in French (his translation of an essay by Péret is included in this book); Jules Maigret is the famed fictional detective who stars in dozens of books by the French writer Georges Simenon (1903-1989). The other writers present in the correspondent's list are previously cited.

Letter from Mateo Darrieux

p. 123

Diamela Eltit and Raúl Zurita: The sociologist Fernando Balcells (1950), the writer Diamela Eltit (1949), the poet Raúl Zurita (1950) and the visual artists Lotty Rosenfeld (1943) and Juan Castillo (1952) were the core, founding members, in 1979, of Colectivos de Acciones de Arte (CADA), a subversive arts-action cell that carried out various illegal and spectacular actions through the 1980s, in protest of the Pinochet dictatorship in Chile.

p. 124

the first National Art Museum action: The first, scatological one is described in the letter; the second one involved the commandeering and repainting of a fleet of milk trucks, which were parked with banners outside the National Museum of Art, to protest the shortage of milk for children during the dictatorship.

Brighton Hotel: A legendary hotel in Valparaíso, Chile, whose terrace on a precipice high above the city may well command the most spectacular coastal urban vista in the world. Enrique Vila-Matas sets scenes of his novel *Montano's Malady* there; he also reports talking to Nadal there, not long before the latter's death.

p. 125

Bella Vista and around UNC: Bella Vista is a bohemian neighborhood in Santiago; UNC is the acronym of the National University of Chile.

p. 126

Mariela: The name cannot be identified.

Cerro Placeres, in Valparaíso…a regular…at the Bar Dominó and also the Bar Cinzano: Cerro Placeres is one of the city's many hills and the same Cerro where Bolaño lived as a child; the Bar Dominó and the Bar Cinzano are old, classic taverns, long favorite haunts of the city's artists and writers, including of Pablo Neruda.

Puerto Montt: A substantial coastal city, in the southern region of Chile.

Letter from Mariana Jiménez

p. 127

Andrés Ajens: (1961) Andrés Ajens: (1961) important Chilean poet, essayist, and translator, whose journal *Mar con Soroche* is jointly edited out of Santiago, Chile, and La Paz, Bolivia.

Víctor Hugo Bustamante: Present owner of Librería Ivens, the most important literary bookstore of Valparaíso, Chile, for 120 years.

Global Lepidoptera: *Mariposa Mundial*, one of Bolivia's most important literary journals.

Juan Luis Martínez and Juan Cameron at Bar Inglés: Barely known outside of Chile before his death, Martínez (1942-1993) is now regarded as one of the most original and vital experimental poets of late 20th century Latin America; the Valparaíso poet Juan Cameron (1947) was a close friend of Martínez, as was Raúl Zurita, when the latter lived in Valparaiso in his youth. The three regularly hung out together; The Bar Inglés, over a century old, is one of the most popular bohemian/literary gathering spots of the city.

Letter from Enrique Vila-Matas

p. 129

Ernest Hemingway look-alike contests: Vila-Matas discusses his peculiar obsession with entering Hemingway look-alike contests in his book *Dublinesque*, published in 2010.

The Café A Brasileira, with a bill from which Pessoa stared back at me...The Hotel Borges: The coincidence and irony is deeply strange, but it is true: The previous name of the favorite haunt of the great multi-identity poet Fernando Pessoa was the Hotel Borges; The reference to Pessoa staring back refers to his portrait being on the $100 Escudo bill. No more: Escudo currency was withdrawn in 2002, not long after Vila-Matas's letter, in favor of the Euro.

The book about the crimes: Vila-Matas is referring to the in-progress and as yet untitled *2666*.

Paula: Paula Massot, the longtime companion of Vila-Matas.

p. 130

my invented interviews with Brando, Nureyev, Highsmith, and Burgess: Marlon Brando (1924-2004), American actor; Rudolf Nureyev (1938-1993), Russian dancer; Patricia Highsmith (1921-1995), American writer; Anthony Burgess (1917-1993), English writer. Vila-Matas, indeed, published, years ago, apocryphal interviews with all these famous figures. They were, to various degrees, fabricated—the Brando one entirely so.

p. 131

Sebald: W.G. Sebald (1944-2001), German writer who was a favorite of both Vila-Matas and Bolaño. The other two writers are previously referenced.

"Quijote Operation": The invented translations by Bolaño and Santiago are discussed in the notes to Quiroga's Preface. The term "Quijote Operation" was meant to allude, no doubt, to the fact that Cervantes's novel was initially and falsely presented as a "translation" from the Arabic (see note above).

Café Turri…Carmen Balcells: The Café Turri, a few blocks away from the Brighton Hotel, is also poised on a stunning overlook of the city. Carmen Balcells (1930-2015), the famed Spanish literary agent, had represented Bolaño, who broke with her agency and went over to Andrew Wylie sometime after she retired in 2000. The loss of Bolaño, along with the defection of others, partly motivated her to return to head the firm in 2008, though as one can see from Vila-Matas's account, she had never really entirely left! The unknown young writer Balcells is tracking is possibly Alejandro Zambra (Chile, 1975), though that is just a guess. He would still have been four years away from publishing his debut bestseller, *Bonsai*, at the time of Vila-Matas's letter.

p. 132

Orhan Pamuk: Pamuk (Turkey, 1952) would go on to win numerous awards for his bestselling novels. At the time of Vila-Matas's letter, his 1998 *My Name is Red* had recently been translated and won the Dublin International Literary Prize.

Letter from Oton Jarc

p. 133

Heinrich von Berenberg…Deutscher Taschenbuchz; von Berenberg (birthdate unavailable) is Bolaño's main German translator; Deutscher Taschenbuchz is the German publisher of the *Savage Detectives*.

Anton Osojnik…NSK…Slavoj Zizek: No such person as Osojnik has been identified. It is possible it is a pseudonym or artist-activist *nom de guerre*. The Neue Slowenische Kunst (a German phrase meaning "New Slovenian Art"), a.k.a. **NSK**, is a multi-genre avant-garde art collective that emerged in Slovenia in 1984, when Slovenia was still part of Yugoslavia. It continued after Slovenia's independence and has had a remarkable impact in the Balkans and beyond. In fact, in 1991 the NSK declared itself a nation state, established consulates in various countries, and has since issued thousands of quasi-legal passports under its name. Its collective strategy has involved appropriating totalitarian imagery in darkly ironic, discomfiting installations and interventions. Slavoj Zizek (Slovenia, 1949) had associations with the group early on, before his rise to international fame as a cultural critic. It is fascinating, to say the least, that Nadal directly participated, in the space of a few years, in two of the most radical and successful avant-garde cultural protest groups of the second half of the 20th century—the CADA and NSK.

p. 134

Discussion Bulletin for Citizens of NSK…Marcel Broodthaers: One of the features of the NSK is that all those holding membership or passports are welcomed to debate and vote on NSK policy and procedure points presented in the NSK Nation's discussion bulletins; Broodthaers (Belgium, 1924-1976) was a poet, artist, and socialist activist who developed a series of mock art installations under the concept and name *Musée d'Art Moderne, Départment des Aigles*, which became important inspirations for a wide-range of later works by other artists of institutional critique directed at Art-world museum culture. Nadal's concern was well-based. As early as 1980, the Tate Gallery in London presented a retrospective of Broodthaers work, quickly followed by other exhibits in various countries. Most recently, in 2016, the Museum of Modern Art in New York City has presented a massive showing of his institutional-critique works, ironically now placed inside corporate-museum walls and with price tags in the millions of dollars.

Letter from Rubén Medina

p. 135

Herralde: Jorge Herralde (Op. cit.), Bolaño's publisher at Anagrama. The English translation of *By Night in Chile* would appear from New Directions in 2004 and more would soon follow, including the *Savage Detectives*, from FS&G, in 2007.

I think you would like Madison: Medina, one of the original

Infra core, had been teaching in the Department of Spanish and Portuguese at the University of Wisconsin since 1991.

Harrington…Bruno and Mario: Juan Esteban Harrington, Bruno Montané, Mario Santiago (all Op. cit.)

Edgar Altamirano, Pedro Damián Bautista, Mario Raúl Guzmán, and Rafael Catana: All these "second-wave Infra poets are mentioned above. Altamirano (1953—has long published his work as Edgar Artaud Jarry); Bautista (1954); Guzmán (1959); Catana (1955).

Desnos: Robert Desnos (Op. cit.), famous for his Surrealist automatic recitations in the 1920s, in states of half-sleep.

Monjarás: Victor Monjarás-Ruiz (1953), one of the original Infra group. The other names are previously cited.

p. 136

Liga Comunista 23 de Septiembre: See citation above.

Correspondencia Infra…**Nadal wanted Santiago's and Ayala's manifestos in there:** The only issue of *Correspondencia Infra: revista menstrual del movimiento infrarrealista* was published in October, 1977, in a run of 5,000 copies, edited by Rubén Medina (1955), one of the core founders of the group and author of this letter; there were originally three Infra manifestos written in 1975 and read at the founding event of the group: The most famous one by Bolaño and two shorter ones by Mario Santiago and José Vicente Anaya, who distanced himself from the group over quarrels with Bolaño and Santiago as early as mid-1976.

your section in the beginning about women's clitorises was machista: The passage—oddly gratuitous, indeed—reads, in my translation: "The gorgeous guy who was clueless that a girl's orgasm is clitoral."

p. 137

the National Endowment for the Arts Fellowship: The various poetry prizes mentioned are real.

Colombo... Dartmouth-Hitchcock Medical Center: Capital of Sri Lanka; the New Hampshire Medical Center mentioned is actually existing. How Nadal would have known about it before the internet is anyone's guess.

September, 2001, near Maddampegama, Sri Lanka…great tsunami: Eerily, to say the least, it was in 2004 that the Indian Ocean tsunami took place, killing a quarter of a million people. That the date given corresponds to the attack on the World Trade Center, makes it doubly eerier. Nadal's piece would have been written in 1977.

p. 139

June 6, 2066: The date, numerated, would be 6/6/66. This seems, on top of the tsunami reference, too bizarre a coincidence, for obvious reasons. Rubén Medina, however, confirms the authenticity of the letter and the Nadal poem.

p. 140

Yves Klein Blue: Klein (Op. cit.) trademarked a particular shade of blue under this name.

*

p. 143

I have lightly edited: The notes here to Bolaño's introductory commentary are by me, A.B. The annotations that follow the two interrogations are by Bolaño; I have clarified and supplemented his notes in a few cases. My elaborations are contained within brackets.

Mario Pedrosa: Pedrosa (1900-1981) was the key founder of the Trotskyist movement in Brazil, though he later modified his positions in the direction of left social democracy. Indeed, shortly before the Worker's Party assumed power in Brazil in the 1980s, Pedrosa was given the Party's ID card #1, in honor of his contributions to the Brazilian Left, as an activist and theorist. Pedrosa was, in addition, one of the major critical figures in Brazilian modernist art and literature. He was the first and key defender and exponent, in fact, of the Concretista movement, which would go on, under the leadership of Haroldo and Augusto de Campos, to become one of Latin America's signal contributions to 20th century avant-garde literature.

Elsie Houston…Heitor Villa-Lobos: Houston (1902-1943); Villa-Lobos (1887-1959).

Macumba and Condomblé: Syncretic Afro-Brazilian religions in Brazil, which achieved their apogee in the 19th and early 20th centuries. While still separately practiced, they have to some extent become synthesized in Umbanda, now one of the principal religions of Brazil, followed by millions of people (internationally now) of all races.

p. 144

POUM…Durruti column: See note below in interrogation section by the Brazilian police.

Remedios Varo: (1908-1963) Spanish surrealist painter and anarchist. Her art has gained increasing recognition in recent years. She and Péret met in Spain and fled to France, then shortly thereafter to Mexico, with the Nazi occupation.

Raymond Rosemont: Poet, artist, and scholar of Labor and Left history, Rosemont (1943-2009), a legendary figure of the American anti-Stalinist left, was the co-founder of the Chicago Surrealist Group. It is fascinating to know that he and the young Bolaño were in touch and that there were plans to publish a translation of his essay on Péret in Mexico.

Verónica Volkow and Cuauhtétmoc Mendez: Close friends of Bolaño's in Mexico City. See the notes for Bolaño's main introduction to this book.

p. 145

the Spanish version of Rosemont's text: No Spanish translation of Rosemont's essay is present in the manuscript. I am presenting the original 1970 English essay by Rosemont in its place. The original notes to it are by Rosemont.

*

Notes to First Interrogation Conducted
by Officers of the Brazilian Police

[The following notes to Nadal's hand-copied interrogation texts are by Bolaño, on inkjet computer printout, as is the version of Nadal's copy that Bolaño transcribed. I have added my own follow-ups or corrections to Bolaño's notes where needed, and these are presented in italicized brackets. AB]

p. 169

Liga Comunista: The first true Trotskyist tendency of Brazil, founded by Mario Pedrosa, Benjamin Péret, and other Communist Party of Brazil militants who opposed the growing tyranny of Stalinist policy and bureaucratic rule. In 1934, the LC would become the Liga Comunista Internacionalista, the official section in Brazil of the 4th International, which was founded in Paris, in 1938. The Liga Comunista would go on to have considerable influence within the trade union movement in São Paulo and Rio de Janeiro, something the interrogators seem presciently nervous about in 1931. Péret's answer to the interrogators about the "composition" of the LC is obviously sarcastic and more than a little brave, under the circumstances.

gynecological organs of sharks: Indeed, in the Second Canto of Lautréamont's *Maldoror*, the hero jumps into the sea to copulate with a shark. It's likely the interrogators were confused by Péret's reference.

Juan Mateo: Mateo (dates unavailable) was a printer and trade union activist arrested with Péret in the same sweep. A printing press, fresh copies of leaflets, and a near-complete run of the LC publication *Luta de Classes* were confiscated in the bust, along with nearly all of Péret's Brazilian writings, most of which are now lost.

p. 170

for the primary purpose of redirecting our respective Communist Parties: The Left Opposition groups loyal to Trotsky would give up on such reform-minded hope within a couple of years and go on to form independent political parties under the banner of the Fourth International.

p. 171

Pierre Naville…Mario Pedrosa…Livio Xavier…Rodolfo Coutinho: Naville (1903-1993) was a contributor and editor of the Communist Party-aligned cultural journal *Clarté*, whose board was in close sympathy with the Surrealists. Starting in December, 1924, he was co-editor with Benjamin Péret of the three first issues of *La Révolution surréaliste*. He founded the *Bureau de Recherches Surréalistes* in that year and participated actively alongside Breton and Péret in numerous projects before opposing Surrealism for what he judged its lack of political focus. Like Breton and Péret, Naville was one of the early supporters in France of Leon Trotsky and was expelled because of it from the Communist Party in 1928. He was a leader of the French Trotskyist movement until breaking with it in favor of social democracy in 1939; Pedrosa (Op. cit.); Xavier (1900-1988) and Coutinho (1901-1955), both poets and translators, were founding members of the Left Opposition movement in Brazil and comrades of Pedrosa and Péret in the Liga Comunista.

The former regime of Brazil, the oppressive one: The reference is to the oligarchic, coffee-baron regime of Washington Luís, which had stolen the national elections from Getulio Vargas, a populist army officer, who then quickly came to power in a mass-supported bourgeois-democratic uprising in 1930. Vargas's regime, despite its progressive, pro-labor rhetoric, was also viscerally anti-communist and would later adopt the policies and trappings of Mussolini-style corporatist fascism, much like the later Perón regime in Argentina. Péret, in his response to his interrogators, shows he is perfectly aware of the historical dynamic in play.

p. 172

Trotsky is thinking of creating a Fourth International: The Fourth International would be established in Paris, in 1938. Naville, Pedrosa, and Péret were present at the conference. *[Bolaño is mistaken in regards Péret's presence: the conference was a semi-secret meeting of thirty-some international delegates from the various international sections. Naville was the sole French delegate; Pedrosa represented Brazil and nearly all other Latin American sections. AB]*

Joaquim Barbosa and João da Costa Pimenta: (dates unavailable for either); both were experienced Communist Party militants and trade union leaders who had been won over to the Left Opposition.

p. 173

Commander Prestes...Aristides Lobo: Luis Carlos Prestes (1898-1990) was one of the main leaders of the 1922 *tenente* revolts carried out by the middle class officer corps and conscripted troops of the Brazilian army. In 1924, he began a prolonged march through the countryside with his Columna Prestes, a large guerrilla force that gained mass popular support and which was instrumental in the victory of the 1930 Vargas revolution. Prestes, much influenced by Marxism, went into almost immediate opposition against Vargas, and his allegiances were sought by both the Communist Party of Brazil and the new Trotskyist Left Opposition. Eventually, Prestes aligned himself with Stalinism and went on to become the General Secretary of the Communist Party of Brazil. Aristides Lobo (1905-1968), co-founder and leader of the Trotskyist Opposition in Brazil and later of the Liga Comunista Internacionalista.

p. 174

LAR…Siqueira Campos: The League of Revolutionary Action (LAR) was founded by Prestes in July, 1930, with the active assistance of Aristides Lobo (see note above), who as a member of the Liga Comunista was attempting to win Prestes over to the Trotskyist Left Opposition. Lobo's role ensured that the so-called August Manifest, in which the LAR's program is presented, was closely aligned, in key aspects, with the LC's own transitional revolutionary platform. Antonio de Siqueira Campos (1898-1930) was one of only two (out of eighteen) tenentista rebels to survive the heroic armed uprising, in 1922, on the Copacabana promenade, in Rio de Janeiro. Siqueira Campos went on to be the second in command of the Prestes column. He died in a plane crash, in May of 1930, returning from Buenos Aires and Montevideo, where he had been in consultation with Prestes, and no doubt also Lobo. Suspicions about the accident abound. Prestes, whose nationalist-revolutionary politics were fluid and often contradictory, soon abandoned the radical program of the August Manifest and moved towards a more class-collabora-tionist posture. (Call Santiago and ask about the gang.) *[This parenthetical typewritten note to self shows that Bolano was thinking of his Mexico D.F. comrades at this late time in his life. A.B.]*

Antropófago group: The 1928 *Manifesto Antropófago* was written by Péret's good friend, the Brazilian poet and cultural critic Oswald de Andrade (1890-1954), one of the key figures of Brazilian Modernism. The tract argued that Brazil's great cultural strength resided in its ability to "cannibalize" and transform cultural influences from abroad. The group that formed in wake of the essay was somewhat short-lived, but its influence considerable (not least upon the groundbreaking Tropicalismo music movement in the 1960s), and included the close involvement of Mario de Andrade (1893-1945, no relation to Oswald), one of Brazil's most important modernist poets. He and Oswald would have a serious falling out in later years, something shadowed in Péret's comments about Mario de Andrade at a later point in his interrogation.

Antillean communist intellectuals: Likely a reference to a group of Paris-based students from Martinique who would go on to publish, in 1932, a single-issue journal titled *Légitime défense* (the title in open homage to Breton's 1926 tract of the same name). This group, though short-lived, proved to be an important inspiration for the group that published, beginning in 1934, *L'étudiant noir*, centered around soon-to-be major Negritude figures like Aimé Césaire, Léopold Sedar Senghor, and Léon Damas.

p. 175

A question…very similar to one: Péret is referencing a series of interviews he did with various writers for *Le Journal littéraire*, in late 1924 and early 1925, in which he asks each of them a single question, "What do you think of Surrealism?"

For example: The cheeky stream-of-consciousness *derivé* that ensues names many areas and locales frequented by the Surrealists.

exquisite corpse: a collective-compositional game favored by the Surrealists, whereby a drawing or text is produced in turns, without any of the participants knowing what the previous person drew or wrote. Fantastical and sometimes uncanny products emerged from these experiments.

I go to the Maldoror: In February, 1930, a group of Surrealists ransacked the newly opened Bar Maldoror, in Montparnasse. They were incensed that commercial use was being made of the great work of their hero, Lautréamont. The poet René Char was seriously injured in the affair. Obviously, Péret had only heard of the incident through correspondence, as he was in Brazil at the time it happened.

p. 176

Desnos: Robert Desnos (1900-1945) had some months before directed violent polemics at Breton and been one of the co-signers of the anti-Breton diatribe *Un Cadavre*, published early in 1930. Péret's animosity towards Desnos clearly emerges here.

Elephants are contagious: This is, in fact, a line from the sequence *152 Proverbs Adapted to the Taste of the Day*, co-authored by Péret and Paul Éluard, and published in *La Révolution Surréaliste* in 1925. Though the "proverb" is frequently credited to Éluard, the utterance of it here by Péret, six years later, may suggest it had been the latter's invention. *[Bolaño's supposition seems a bit strained, inasmuch as Péret's memory of the line does in no way imply he was its author. A more interesting speculation, perhaps, would be whether the title of Bolaño's early novella,* The Elephant Path *(later retitled* Monsieur Pain*), which involves an ill César Vallejo in a contagion hospital in Paris, was meant to evoke the famous saying. AB]*

Aragon: The reference is only a few months before Louis Aragon's (Op. cit.) open alliance with the Communist Party of France precipitated a final break between him and Breton.

Crevel...Fourrier and Soupault: Though less known than other figures, partly because of his early death, René Crevel (1900-1935) was one of the core members of the Surrealist group and one of the most active participants in the experimental sessions of automatic writing. In June, 1935, at the Communist Party-controlled First International Congress of Writers for the Defense of Culture, in Paris, André Breton and Benjamin Péret had repeatedly slapped the Soviet delegate Ilya Ehrenberg in the street for the latter's published claims that the Surrealists were "pederasts." Breton and his faction were immediately expelled from the Congress due to the assault, irremediably ending the Surrealists relations with the Party. Crevel, on the day of expulsion, attempted to bring about an understanding that would allow reentry to the Surrealists, but was unsuccessful. He went home that night and killed himself, leaving a note that simply read, "Please cremate my body. Loathing"; Marcel Fourrier (1895-1966) had been an editor of the Party-linked journal *Clarté*, and a sympathizer of the Surrealists; Phillippe Soupault (1897-1990) was one of the original founders of the Surrealist movement and one of the editors of the Surrealists proto-organ *Litterature*. He co-authored, with Breton, the first book of automatic writing, *Les champs magnétiques* (1920). He later left the movement as the political tensions deepened.

p. 178

"pistol in hand, down into the street": The infamous passage about firing randomly into a crowd appears in the Second Surrealist Manifesto, published in September, 1929, in *La Révolution* *surréaliste. [Bolaño is a bit off on the publication date: the journal issue in which the Second Manifesto appeared was published in December, 1929. A.B.]*

Desnos, Bataille, Prévert, Queneau, Leiris, Vitrac, and Carpentier: Robert Desnos (1900-1945); Georges Bataille (1897-1962); Jacques Prévert (1900-1977); Raymond Queneau (1903-1976); Michel Leiris (1901-1990); Roger Vitrac (1899-1952); Alejo Carpentier [1904-1980], major Cuban writer exiled in France from 1928 to 1939); all were signatories of *Un Cadavre*, the Bataille-inspired slanderous assault on Breton.

p. 179

Kronstadt: A reference to the heroic rebellion by anti-Bolshevik socialist and anarchist sailors at the naval fortress in the city of Kronstadt, in March, 1921, which was put down in a bloody response by Bolshevik forces, under the direction of Leon Trotsky, leading commander of the Red Army at the time.

Un Cadavre, **number II:** The original *Un Cadavre*, of 1924, had attacked Anatole France, and was signed by Péret, Breton, and most of the Surrealists of the time.

café con leite: The Brazilian phrase used to describe the coffee baron-controlled regimes before the Vargas revolution of 1930.

We communists have no illusions: In fact, Péret would prove to be right, as Vargas became more dictatorial and his government more and more took on fascist leanings, markedly in the Estado Novo period of 1937-1945, when Vargas shut down Congress and suspended the Constitution.

Like them, he is expertly setting out to save capitalism: Indeed, Franklin Delano Roosevelt later claimed that Vargas was "one of two people to invent the New Deal."

Forgive us if we do not know: Péret would soon go on to fight in battle with the Left Opposition POUM and the anarchist Durruti Column in the Spanish Civil War.

p. 180

6th of July, 1922: The original and suicidal uprising by members of the lower (*tenente*) officer corps in Rio de Janeiro, in which nearly all the rebels were killed, knowing they would be.

p. 181

"though most of them likely do not consider themselves mine": It should be noted that seven years later, the "Manifesto for a Free and Revolutionary Art" would be released, in summer of 1938, in Coyoacán, Mexico, where Breton was holding intensive discussions with the exiled Leon Trotsky. Though signed by Breton and the great Mexican artist Diego Rivera (husband of the even greater artist Frieda Kahlo), the Manifesto is known to have been co-authored by Trotsky, and its final draft approved by him. The document, representing a remarkable reevaluation of positions held by the Bolshevik leader himself during the early years of Soviet power, resulted in the formation of the FIARI (International Federation of Independent Revolutionary Art), a united front of anti-fascist and anti-Stalinist cultural workers. The Federation gathered a large number of adherents in various nations, including prominent anarchists (to which the manifesto specifically appealed), and published, under Breton's direction, two issues of its journal, *Clé* (the second issue featured an article by Trotsky, reiterating his defense of artistic freedom in the revolution); however, the group was unable to counter the massive influence of Comintern doctrine among European intellectuals on the eve of the war. Trotsky was assassinated in Mexico under orders of Stalin, in August, 1940. Only three months before, Trotsky had survived an assassination attempt led by the famed Mexican muralist David Alfaro Siqueiros, whose escape to Chile was arranged by the venerable poet Pablo Neruda, a Comintern middleman. Whether by darkly ironic chance or by NKVD direction, Neruda arrived in Mexico in the summer of 1940, four days before the second, and successful, assassination action took place. One year earlier, serving as the Chilean Government's Special Consul for Immigration in Paris, Neruda was in charge of approving the boarding list for the S.S. Winnipeg, a rescue ship evacuating interned Spanish Republican refugees in France, in face of advancing Nazi forces. It is documented that Neruda sought to reserve safe passage only for Communist Party militants and sympathizers, while denying it to hundreds of anarchist, social democratic, and anti-Stalinist communists, most of whom were soon imprisoned, tortured, or killed in the Occupation. Péret would go on to distance himself from the Trotskyist Fourth International in the later 1940s (his dissent first announced in an open letter co-signed with Trotsky's widow, Natalia Sedova) and more and more align himself with anarchist currents. Indeed, before his formal break with Trotskyism, he had fought with the anarchist Durruti Column in the Spanish Civil War. [The note is very interesting. Bolaño's knowledge of Marxist history comes partly from his close association with members and fellow-travelers in the Infra group—see notes above—who were active militants in anti-Stalinist Marxist organizations in the 1970s. His antipathy for Neruda, previously expressed in his Infrarrealista manifesto, as well as in interviews given after his novelistic success, comes through here. A.B.]

I happen to know he had in mind…Ezra Pound's stupid piece of Japonaiserie: This is clearly an invention and joke for the record by Péret, no doubt completely lost on his interrogators.

The reference to Pound pertains to his famous 1913 imagist poem "In a Station of the Metro": The apparition of these faces in the crowd; / Petals on a wet, black bough.

I was the original editor: Péret was indeed the original editor, with Naville, of the first history-making issues of *La Révolution surréaliste*. Following the Second Surrealist Manifesto in 1929, the more openly communist-minded *Le Surréalisme au service de la révolution* replaced it, beginning in 1930, running for five more issues through 1933.

La Luta de Classes: The newspaper of the Liga Comunista, which Péret had founded with Mario Pedrosa and others.

p. 182

Sr. Naville: See reference further above. The fascination of the Brazilian interrogators with Naville is indeed curious, likely a result of the French Embassy prompting them to extract information about him.

Not a little trouble in the trade union movement of Brazil: Because some of the leading Communist Party trade union militants came over to the Trotskyists in the late 1920s, the current gained quick influence in a number of sections of the labor movement, even surpassing, in certain major unions, the popularity of the CP. *[Notably in the then-influential Printers Union. A.B.]*

p. 183

The Moulin Rouge, risen from the ashes: The Moulin Rouge cabaret, immortalized by the painter Toulouse Lautrec, had fairly recently reopened in 1924, after burning down in 1915. *[Bolaño is wrong on the date of reopening, which was three years earlier, in 1921. AB]*

Oswald de Andrade…Antropofagia movement: See reference above.

Do not provoke us: There is a fascinating revelation of Brazilian racism here. Péret, who comments extensively on Brazilian racism in his studies on Candomblé and Macumba, no doubt was intending to provoke his interrogators.

Revolt of the Lash: A spectacular Potemkin-like rebellion in the Brazilian Navy in 1910 that resulted in the actual shelling of Rio de Janeiro by mutinous rebel battleships. It was led by the Afro-Brazilian sailor João Cândido Felisberto (1880-1969). See the essay by Péret included here.

Oswald de Andrade…is close to your organization: While Oswald de Andrade and Péret were close friends and collaborators in matters pertaining to art and ethnography, there is no indication that the former moved any closer to the Liga Comunista than as a fellow-traveler. Indeed, following Péret's expulsion from Brazil, he gravitated towards the CP. Mario de Andrade and Carlos Drummond de Andrade (none of the three were immediately related, despite the shared surname), two other major figures of Brazilian modernism and already active and influential at the time of Péret's presence in Brazil, rejected his poetics and politics. Both, in fact, were close, at various junctures, to the Brazilian Communist Party, sworn enemy of the Trotskyist tendency.

Flavio de Carvahlo…Hilcar Leite: Carvahlo (1899-1973) was one of Brazil's leading experimental architects and a prominent performance artist who cross-dressed at major festivals to much acclaim. He was described by Le Corbusier as a "Romantic

Revolutionary," and was close to Péret and other members of the Left Opposition movement; Leite (dates unavailable) was a leader of the Communist Party youth group who joined the Liga Comunista.

p. 186

culture manager of the new State: This is indeed what arguably happened, as Carlos Drummond de Andrade became more and more attached to official positions and recognitions.

p. 187

Kilombo de Palmares: A liberated, self-governing territory of approximately 20,000 fugitive slaves and free-born blacks in northeastern colonial Brazil that developed from 1605 until its military suppression in 1694. The Kilombo heroically defended itself against four major Portuguese invasions, until its defeat.

p. 188

Who within the Houston family gave you the contact: Indeed, the very prominent family of Péret's wife, Elsie Houston, had many government contacts at high levels. It is quite evident that these allowed Péret to gain subversive access to the Ministry's files, for his research with official documents related to the Revolt of the Lash.

p. 189

Prime Minister Pierre Laval...Second Bureau of the General Staff...Charles Dumont: Pierre Laval (1883-1945) was head of the French government at the time; the Second Bureau of the

General Staff was the name of the foreign intelligence services
of France at the time; Charles Dumont (1867-1939) had been
appointed Minister of the Navy of France in 1931. Obviously,
Péret is being totally and courageously contemptuous of his interrogators.

*

p. 193

arrested as a soldier at the front: This is an interesting apparent "confession" by Péret, for there is no record, so far as I know, that he was arrested as a soldier during the First War. Early in the Second War, however, in 1939, Péret was definitely imprisoned for establishing a Trotskyist cell among the troops. He was released when the German troops began their invasion of France. He escaped from Marseille to Mexico in 1940, along with numerous other Surrealists and figures of the Left.

p. 194

The colonial slaughter in the Rif: In September, 1925, *La Revolution d'abord et toujours!* was published in *L'Humanité*, and a few weeks later in *La Révolution surréaliste* and the journal *Clarté*, which was closely allied to the Surrealists. The document, which had considerable public influence, angrily opposed France's intervention on the side of Spain against a determined anti-colonial revolt led by Abd el-Krim (1883-1963). Though the guerrilla forces were finally defeated in 1926, they managed to inflict heavy losses on both Spanish and French troops, and the repercussions of the war led to instabilities in both countries, particularly Spain, where a resulting military coup by Miguel Primo de Rivera helped set the stage for the coming Republican uprising and Spanish civil war. *[L'Humanité was the newspaper of the French Communist Party. AB]*

The Colonial Exhibition: Held in Paris between May 6th to November 15, 1931, the Exhibition was a major event in France, sponsored by the French government and allied institutions to proclaim the glories of France's empire and exalt the benefits brought to non-white peoples by European colonization. The Surrealists put out numerous statements polemicizing against the imperialist and racist ideology of the exhibit and assisted in organizing, beginning in September, a counter-exhibit titled "The Truth about the Colonies," held at the former Soviet pavilion for a 1925 international exhibition of the decorative arts. Thirion, Sadoul, and Aragon, among other Surrealists, had a major role in its organization. *[Georges Sadoul (1904-1967), a Surrealist filmmaker who later joined Louis Aragon (Op. cit.) in the 1932 split over Communist Party policy; André Thirion (1907-2001), an original signer of the Surrealist Manifesto. AB]*

League of Patriots…Anti-Jewish League…*L'Age d' or*…Messrs. Buñuel and Dalí: The League of Patriots and the Anti-Jewish League were two major fascist organizations of the time, with hidden ties to the French security forces. The film *L' Age d' or* opened on November 28, 1930, to great scandal: The film, a collaboration between Luis Buñuel (1900-1983) and Salvador Dalí (1904-1989), viciously mocked and insulted nearly every official tradition and institution dear to the bourgeoisie, not least the Church and the family. A large Surrealist art and book exhibit, also quite scandalous to the normal tastes of the day, accompanied the showing of the film at the Studio 28 gallery. On December 3, a joint contingent from the League of Patriots and the Anti-Jewish League raided Studio 28, destroying most of the paintings and books on exhibit and stopping the the film with buckets of ink and smoke bombs. On December 11, the government banned *L' Age d' or*.

Which for a film critic must be quite frustrating: The reference is to Péret's previous work as a regular film critic for *L' Humanité*.

p. 198

Claudels and Barbusses: Paul Claudel (1869-1955), major French poet and diplomat. The Surrealists published a withering attack against him in July, 1925, as "Open Letter to Paul Claudel," shortly after Claudel had been appointed Ambassador to Japan. Claudel had earlier published an opinion that Dada and Surrealism were expressions of "pederasty." The Surrealists' "Open Letter" declared, in response, that the honest vocation of poetry, on the one hand, and servile service to the State, on the other, were fundamentally incompatible pursuits, and the signatories more or less expressed a fervent wish that "true morality" prevail, with Claudel one day being torn asunder, as he deserved to be, in a revolution or colonial insurrection; Henri Barbusse (1873-1935) was a novelist and the leading spokesperson for literary and cultural policies of the Communist Party of France in the 1920s and early 30s. As Barbusse was a faithful defender of the Soviet cultural line, the Surrealists were in constant conflict with him. Barbusse died in the midst of writing an official biography of Stalin.

No true work of poetry is ever written for the reader: The statement seems to purposely reference Walter Benjamin's famous opening of his essay "The Task of the Translator," written in 1923, and which had been intended as introduction to a translation by Benjamin of Baudelaire. *[It would be nice if so, but it is unlikely that Péret would have been alluding to Benjamin's essay, as it had not yet been translated into French by 1931, and there is no evidence that Péret had reading fluency in German. A.B.]*

p. 199

the relationship with Surrealism is complicated, likely to grow even more so: Indeed, the Surrealists had been at almost constant odds with the Party leadership over the nature and role of revolutionary art, ever since numerous of the Surrealists joined the CP in 1927. The final phase of the impossible relationship was set off with Aragon's rejection of Surrealism, in 1932, and his turn to unconditional Party militancy. Éluard would eventually join him. The Surrealist members who remained committed to a Left Opposition line were expelled from the Party in 1935, soon after Breton and Péret, at the Closerie des Lilas, gave a literal slapping-in-the-face to Ilya Ehrenburg, the Soviet representative to the International Conference for the Defense of Culture, held in Paris, in June. *[Bolaño makes a more detailed note about the Ehrenburg affair further above. A.B.]*

Paul Claudel…Anatole France: See references above. Both of whom were publicly pilloried in the 1920s in Surrealist manifestoes.

I spit on your pederast priests: The anti-clericalism of the Surrealists was legion. Symbolically, in the toilet at 54 rue du Chateau, where the Surrealists gathered in the 20s for their talks and automatic writing sessions, a crucifix was used as a handle for the chain flush. Anti-clericalist feelings were especially pronounced in Péret, who was infamous for loudly insulting priests in public.

p. 200

O Diario de Norte…**Josephine Baker…Lei de Angola…Lci de Nago:** Péret published a series of articles on Afro-Brazilian traditions in *O Diario de Norte* in 1930 and '31; Baker (1906-1975) was an African-American dancer who spent most of her professional career in Paris. Her erotic performances there, starting in 1925, were a sensation; Lei de Angola and Lei de Nago are the two major historical sects of Candomblé.

p. 203

Le Figaro, Revue Européenne, and Les Feuilles Libres... transition... Maria McDonald Jolas: All leading literary journals of the time. *transition*, which had been recently founded in 1927 by the poet Eugene Jolas (1894-1952) and his wife Maria McDonald Jolas (1893-1987), was a major outlet for modernist writing, giving special feature to Modernist and experimental work, including recent developments in art. It was primarily distributed through Sylvia Beach's Shakespeare & Company bookstore.

under a Bulgarian pseudonym: *transition* published a considerable number of Bulgarian, Czech, Hungarian, Russian, Polish, and Serbian writers. Péret's French interrogator was apparently one of them, in ethnic disguise. Unless Nadal failed to copy the question, it doesn't appear that Péret asked him to identify the pseudonym or the French "pen-name" his interrogator used for reviews. As there appear to be more than a few of the latter in the journal's first fourteen issues produced through 1931, it has not been possible to determine who it might be.

Valery Larbaud: (1881-1957), prominent French writer. He sponsored and supervised the first translation of Joyce's *Ulysses* into French.

Clarté, Correspondance, and Philosophies...Variétés: All were journals with close sympathies and associations to the Surrealists. *Correspondance*, published in Belgium, was founded by Paul Nougé, the leader of the Belgian Surrealist circle.

One of my irregular chronicles of the journals: Péret's shift of mood is notable here, at least for the time being. Péret was a fairly regular film reviewer for *L'Humanité*; Marcel Noll wrote a regular report on the journals for the paper during the same period. Noll (dates unavailable) was a close fellow-traveler in Surrealist circles who became Director of the Galerie Surréaliste: Opened in 1926, the official gallery of Surrealist art exhibited Man Ray, Yves Tanguy, Salvador Dalí, Meret Oppenheim, and René Magritte, among others. In 1928, after embezzling the gallery's funds in an apparent attempt to win over the lover of Robert Desnos, he tried to drown himself in the Seine. Meanwhile, desperately awaiting a promised payment from Noll for the sale of a painting by Georges Braque to the Galerie, a distraught Louis Aragon tried to overdose with sleeping pills. The gallery closed shortly after. *[The black humor by Bolaño in the second half of the note (all true!) is quite memorable. A.B.]*

p. 204

Maurras, Daudet, or Drieu La Rochelle: Charles Maurras (1868-1952); Alphonse Daudet (1840-1897); and Pierre Drieu La Rochelle (1893-1945) were all right-wing and anti-Semitic French writers.

Wagner...Degas...Goethe: Richard Wagner (1813-1883), legendary composer and anti-Semite; Edgar Degas (1834-1917), leading Impressionist painter and hard-core Anti-Dreyfusard; Johann Wolfgang von Goethe (1749-1832), Germany's greatest writer, also an anti-Semite.

p. 205

But you agree...writing ultimately is not dependent upon... politics or ideology? Though Péret does not respond to the question, he perhaps does so three responses further down.

Adrienne Monnier: (1892-1955), French bookseller, publisher, writer and longtime companion of Sylvia Beach. Beach was the first publisher of Joyce's *Ulysses*. She would suffer severe economic losses when Joyce left her for another publisher, leaving her with unrecovered publication investments.

Breton invited Joyce once to the headquarters at rue de Grenelle: This is a surprising anecdote. No other reference to this visit has been found. Péret is referring to the first gathering space of the Bureau for Surrealist Research, located at 15 rue de Grenelle, a flat on loan from Pierre Naville's father.

Djuna Barnes…Mina Loy…Mlle. Wood: Djuna Barnes (1892-1982), important U.S. modernist figure and one of the first openly lesbian writers, she resided in Paris for ten years starting in 1921; Mina Loy (1882-1966), a prominent modernist poet from England and veritable jack-of-all artistic trades, including light-fixture design, she became fast friends with Barnes in Paris, where she lived between 1923 and 1930; Thelma Wood (1901-1970), U.S. sculptor, was Barnes's lover at the time.

p. 206

Anatole France: France (1844-1924) won the Nobel Prize and was considered in his time the country's greatest living writer. The Surrealists, in a scandalous episode, lampooned him and his official literary status in a scathing broadside, *Un Cadvare*, published shortly after his death.

p. 207

Barrès: Maurice Barrès (1862-1923), right-wing and anti-Semitic Symbolist writer, associated with Charles Maurras's neo-fascist Action Française organization.

Littérature: Journal founded by André Breton, Louis Aragon, and Philippe Soupault, and published in Paris from 1919 to 1924. In its first series, *Littérature* was fairly eclectic, publishing many now-classic works of avant-garde and other modernist writing. Beginning in 1922, the publication began to take on a more exclusively Surrealist slant, becoming, in effect, the movement's first journal. There were thirty-three issues in all.

"A Modest Proposal": The anonymous satirical pamphlet (1729) by Jonathan Swift (1667-1745), in which it is proposed that the children of poor Irishmen might be sold as food for the rich, as a means to alleviate economic difficulties.

The École normale: The École normale supérieure, established during the early years of the French Revolution, it is today the elite institution of higher education in France.

p. 208

De Quincy: Thomas De Quincey (1785-1859). Péret is referring to De Quincey's 1827 satirical essay, "On Murder Considered as One of the Fine Arts."

Calling in a poem, as has…Aragon, for randomly killing the police: The reference is to Louis Aragon's scandal-producing long poem, "Red Front," which had only a few months before, in July, 1931, been published in the French Communist Party-affiliated journal *Littérature de la Révolution mondiale*. In November, as a direct result of Aragon's poem, the journal was banned by the government. In January, 1932, Aragon was indicted for inciting violence against the State. The Surrealists, even though strong disagreements had already emerged between Aragon and the group, sprang to his vigorous defense. Further discussion of the affair takes place later in the interrogation.

p. 209

W.C.: For water closet, or bathroom.

Robespierre: Maximillian Robespierre (1758-1794), leader of the Jacobins during the French Revolution and architect of the Reign of Terror.

Thermidorean Reaction, the White Terror: The July, 1794 revolt against Robespierre, Saint-Just, and the radical Montagnard Jacobins who ruled the Committee of Public Safety. The White Terror of 1795 imprisoned and killed thousands of members of the revolutionary left, mainly left Jacobins and their sympathizers.

The puss-ridden body of a Barras and the Medusa head of a Bonaparte: Paul Barras (1755-1829), a prominent figure in the French Revolution who later enriched himself via corrupt means, led the Directory regime of 1795-1799 that emerged from the Thermidorean coup. Napoleon Bonaparte (1769-1821) overthrew the Directorate in 1799, effectively ending the republic and later establishing himself as Emperor.

p. 210

Monarchiens and Girondists…Mensheviks…Social Revolutionaries…Kadets: The Monarchiens were a short-lived tendency of the Revolutionary period that advocated a form of constitutional monarchy. They were soon swept away and most of its leading members were executed in the next few years; the Girondists were the more moderate faction of the Jacobin Club, which in the Revolution became rapidly dominated by elements of the Montagnard faction, who later carried out myriad and random executions of their former Girondist comrades. Within the Russian Social Democratic Labor Party, the Mensheviks were to the Bolsheviks somewhat what the Girondists were to the Montagnards within the Jacobin Club. Many of the Mensheviks were also persecuted, exiled, or killed by the Bolsheviks. The Socialist Revolutionaries were a major left party, with considerable mass support and influence in the Constituent Assembly prior to October; thousands of its members were imprisoned and killed by the Bolsheviks. The Kadets, or Constitutional Democrats, were a small liberal bourgeois party that had some influence in the Kerensky government of February, 1917. The party was abolished by the Bolsheviks and most of its leadership went into exile, in Paris. Much of this repression took place during the bloody and emergency civil war years (1918-22), though much of it was also the product of strategic State terror directed by Lenin *after* the Bolshevik victory in the civil war, and its effects indiputably helped feed and legitimize the unbridled Stalinist tyranny that was to follow.

Saint-Just, Marat and Danton: Louise Anton de Saint-Just (1767-1794), young ally of Robespierre and a leading strategist of the Reign of Terror, he was executed immediately following the Thermidor coup, along with Robespierre and other left-Jacobins; Jean-Paul Marat (1743-1793) was a leading left-Jacobin theorist of the Revolution, assassinated by Charlotte Corday (1768-1793), a Girondist sympathizer; Georges Danton (1759-1794), a leading figure of the first period of the Revolution and first President of the Committee of Public Safety, was guillotined, along with other moderate Jacobins, by orders of Robespierre. For what it's worth, the 1983 film *Danton*, directed by Andrzej Wajda, and starring Gérard Depardieu, is one of my favorites of all time. *[This is one of the few times (the self-conscious question in the note following the next is another) where the film buff Bolaño openly breaks his objective, scholarly tone in the footnotes. Strangely enough, Wajda's* Danton *happens to be one of my own top favorites, too. A.B.]*

Catete: The then-diplomatic district in Rio de Janeiro, historic and upper crust, particularly at the time of the interview.

Mounier…LaFayette…Brissot…Madame Roland: Jean Joseph Mounier (1758-1806), founder of the Monarchiens party, was one of the leading instigators of the Tennis Court Oath, an opening, pivotal event of the French Revolution, and was elected President of the first Constituent Assembly of 1789; after commanding American troops in the war for Independence, the Marquis de LaFayette (1757-1834) had a central role on the conservative wing of the Revolution during its early stages, helping to write the Declaration of the Rights of Man. He fled France as the Revolution took a radical turn; Jacques Pierre Brissot (1754-93) and Jeanne Manon Roland (1754-93) were both principal leaders of the moderate Girondist faction of the Jacobins. They were guillotined at the start of the Reign of Terror, along with many other Girondist figures, by the dominant Montagnard faction of the Jacobins. What would we have done in power? That's not a tossed-off question. *[The intejected question here by Bolaño is fascinating. A.B.]*

Martov, Chernov, Krasnoshchokov: Julius Martov (1873-1923) was a leader of the left wing of the Mensheviks and a partisan of democratic socialism. Viktor Chernov (1873-1952) was the founder of the Russian Socialist-Revolutionary Party and the Chairman of the Russian Constituent Assembly in the first three months of the Revolution, until its closure by the Bolsheviks; Alexander Krasnoshchokov (1880-1937), a Bolshevik and confidant of Lenin, was the first Chairman of the government of the Far Eastern Republic (encompassing the bulk of Siberia), which maintained a vibrantly democratic political life from its founding in 1920, with freedom of the press and political association for all left and moderate political groups. The Republic was incorporated into the USSR in 1922. During the Republic's life, Chita, its capital, was an active center of avant-garde literature and art.

p. 212

Naville posed an interesting question: In his "La revolution et les intellectuels," published in 1926, Naville asked, "Do the surrealists believe the mind can be liberated before the bourgeois conditions of material life have been abolished, or do they consider that a revolutionary spirit can only be created once the revolution has been achieved?" Naville came down squarely in support of the second half of the question, which would lead to his eventual separation from the movement and to his undivided commitment to political life. He would go on to become (despite Péret's somewhat odd comments about Naville's departure from Surrealism as representing a capitulation to pressures from the CP leadership!) a key leader of the Fourth International in its early years. *[Bolaño's comment that Péret's take on Naville's position is "odd" is itself somewhat strange, given that Naville was a prominent member of the CP at the time of his 1926 "either/or" question. The pressure to conform ("capitulate") to Party discipline at that time was especially great, and one can see Péret's point, especially since he was a particular target of the growing organizational pressures. A.B.]*

biography of Jesus! Barbusse had published the volumes in early 1927, an odd bibliographic anecdote, considering he was the most prominent Communist Party writer and its leading literary theoretician, whose ideas very much foreshadowed later Socialist Realist policy under Stalin.

p. 214

Rakovsky: Christian Rakovsky (1873-1941), Bulgarian revolutionary and Bolshevik leader, one of the principal leaders of the Left Opposition with Leon Trotsky. He was Soviet Ambassador to France from 1925 to 1927.

p. 215

**Artaud, Masson, Soupault, Leiris, Vitrac, Desnos, Ribe-
mont-Dessaignes, Bataille…poor Picabia…Morise, Queneau,
Prévert**: Antonin Artaud (1896-1948); André Masson (1896-
1987); Phillipe Soupault (1897-1990); Georges Ribemont-Dessaignes (1884-1974); Francis Picabia (1879-1953); and Max
Morise (1900-73) were all writers and/or artists who had been
associated with Surrealism. All were signatories to the vituper-
ative attack on Breton, *Un Cadavre*. The other signatories mentioned by the French interrogator are referenced above. *[It is
not clear why the interrogator refers to Picabia with the adjective
"poor." AB]*

Surrealism at the Service of the Revolution: The successor to *The
Surrealist Revolution*. The first issue appeared in 1930, following
the "Second Surrealist Manifesto" of 1929, which announced a
marked political turn for the movement and the expulsion of
various figures who were not felt to be up to snuff. Five more
issues of the journal followed through 1933, until the journal
Minotaure become the group's main outlet. The interrogator refers to it here by its French acronym, *ASLR*.

p. 216

**International Bureau of Revolutionary Literature…Kharkov…
Aragon…Sadoul**: The *IBRL* was the Comintern-sponsored international front of writers affiliated or sympathetic with the
Third International. The Surrealist's declaration of solidarity
with the Soviet Union appeared on the first page of the inaugu-
ral issue of *Surrealism at the Service of the Revolution*, published
in July, 1930. Its support was offered despite the group's close
alliance with the Left Opposition and its strong critiques of Soviet policy. In fact, it was international Left Opposition policy to
defend the Soviet Union in face of imperialist attack, even as the

Bolshevik revolution was judged to have taken on a "degenerated" form under the rule of a bureaucratic caste. In November and December of that year, under the auspices of the *IBRL*, the Second International Conference of Revolutionary Writers took place in the city of Kharkov, Ukraine, attended by 134 writers from thirty-five countries. (At the conference, the International Bureau was renamed the International Association of Revolutionary Writers.) The conference was notable for its harsh denunciation—under directions from Moscow, of course—of the wayward ways and lack of discipline of Western revolutionary writers, and even Barbusse came in for serious criticisms (which nevertheless did not keep him from election to the Presidium of the Congress). Aragon and Sadoul, in particular, were subjected to harsh criticism for their associations with Surrealism, which was condemned at the conference for its petit-bourgeois and decadent propensities. Both Aragon and Sadoul caved under the pressure and renounced both the Second Surrealist Manifesto and "Trotskyism" at the event, though they later made a temporary about-face upon return to France, penning the declaration "To Revolutionary Intellectuals," which proposed that surrealists were in an advantageous position to bring about a common revolutionary front of intellectuals. Less than a year later they would break completely with the Surrealists and fully submit to Communist Party discipline.

p. 217

Breton and Monsieur Thirion have been laying the plans: It is startling that the interrogator would have had such information at hand, for it was only in November, 1930, that Breton and André Thirion (1907), a trade union militant and writer, had begun discussing and circulating plans for the formation of an "Association of Revolutionary Artists and Writers" (AEAR) that would be in close association with the worker's movement and reject any Communist Party involvement. The project did not come to fruition under surrealist guidance, but in January, 1932, and no doubt in relation to the initial plans that had been circulated, an organization of the same exact name as proposed by the Surrealists was established in closer relation to the Communist Party than had been envisioned—and Breton and Thirion, along with Éluard and Crevel, were at first (protests made the directors relent some months hence) excluded from joining! No doubt Comintern spy agencies had something to do with appropriating the plans of Breton and the Surrealists. *[Alas, when writing truly mattered! A.B.]*

Second Bureau of the General Staff: Deuxième Bureau de l'État-major général (Second Bureau of the General Staff) was France's external military intelligence agency from 1871 to 1940.

Let's dispense with pseudonyms: Péret seems to have taken the officially redacted name offered offered by his interrogator as an alias.

p. 218

That Aragon has made his peace with Stalinism? It wouldn't be until two or three months later that Aragon would publicly announce his renunciation of Surrealism and his full allegiance to the Communist Party. The Surrealists were still defending him against the threats and attacks his "Red Front" poem had brought forth, but his impending separation from the Surrealists was already quite clear. Péret clearly avoids the question and changes the topic. In subsequent years, Péret would launch multiple polemical attacks on Aragon.

Café Cyrano…Café Prophete…Jean Bernier…Marcel Fourrier:
Two of the most popular cafés for left writers and intellectuals in
1920s Paris; Jean Bernier (1894-1975) and Victor Crastre (dates
unavailable) were editors of *Clarté* in the mid-1920s. Fourrier and Barbusse are referenced above. Barbusse had split with
the *Clarté* group over internal disagreements in 1924. Ironically,
given its later close relations with the anti-Stalinist Surrealists,
the *Clarté* group had taken its denomination from the antiwar
novel by Barbusse of same name.

*

Notes to Beneath the Banner of Socialism,
Beneath the Banner of the Socialist Infrarealism
[Notes by A.B.]

p. 261

Octanovich Pazinsky: Octavio Paz (1914-1998), symbolic nemesis of the Infrarrealist group. *[In my English translation of "Nadal's" purported "translation," I have attempted to imitate the foreign-sounding and awkward language of the document. The annotations to the speech are by me. A.B.]*

Susan Sontagpov…Pablo Nerudakov…Louis Aragonkov…Anatoly Lunacharsky: Susan Sontag (1933-2004), U.S. cultural critic, who wrote an important appreciation of the *Savage Detectives*; Louis Aragon (1997-1982, French poet, one of the founders of Surrealism, later a leading official of the Communist Party of France); Pablo Neruda (1904-1973, Chilean poet, leading representative of the Communist Party of Chile); Anatoly Lunarcharsky (1875-1933, first Soviet Commissar of Education and Culture).

1921: Founding year of Stridentism, an avant-garde movement, begun in Mexico City by Manuel Maples Arce, but developed in Xalapa where all the first members moved after the University of Veracruz granted its support for the formation. Stridentism was opposed to its contemporaneous modernist peers in Los Contemporáneos group, whom they judged bourgeois and elitist.

p. 262

UNAM…Calle Bucareli: National Autonomous University of Mexico, which assumed an important role in the spread of poetry workshops and contests during the 1970s; Calle Bucareli was a common haunt of the Infrarrealistas, not least because their central locale, Café La Habana, is located on the street.

Grozny: The capital of the Chechen Republic in Russia. Much of it was laid waste by Russian artillery in the Chechen independence struggle, between 1994 and 1996. The "gauzy shells" seems to be a dark pun, in this sense.

Marxism and Problems of Linguistics: An article in the newspaper *Pravda* [later released as a mass-produced pamphlet], published in Moscow in 1950, supposedly, though not likely, written by Joseph Stalin.

Zaum: The neologism was coined by Aleksei Kruchenykh, in 1913, to describe the radical experimental language used by him and his fellow Futurist poet Velimir Khlebnikov. It roughly translates to "transense."

Santiagosky: Mario Santiago Papasquiaro, pseudonym of José Alfredo Zendejas Pineda (1953-1998), co-founder of the Infrarrealist movement, and Roberto Bolaño's dear friend.

El Zaguán: Short lived but important journal [1975-1977] of younger poets who were followers of Octavio Paz. The publication was held in contempt by the Infrarrealist poets.

Derridashkin: Jacques Derrida (1930-2004), French philosopher and leading proponent of deconstructionist thought.

p. 263

Voloshinov-Stetsky: The term appears to be invented.

El chavo del ocho: Wildly popular Mexican TV comedy and variety show, which ran from the early 1970s through the 1990s. It was hosted by Roberto Gómez Bolaños, aka *El Chespirito*. No doubt the name of the host is one of the reasons the show is referenced here.

Mandelstam: Osip Mandelstam (1891-1938), leading figure in the Acmeist literary group and one of Russia's great poets. He died en route to a gulag prison in Siberia.

Tatlin: Vladimir Tatlin (1885-1953), Soviet architect and painter, one of the main figures of the Constructivist movement and the Soviet avant-garde of the 1920s. He is best known for his astonishing design of *The Monument to the Third International*, a work that was never realized.

p. 264

Poundenko: Ezra Pound (1885-1972), major American modernist poet and partisan of Fascism.

Radek: Karl Radek (1885-1939), Bolshevik leader, who initially aligned with Trotsky's opposition, only to capitulate to Stalin. Soon afterwards, he became head of the International Information Bureau of the Russian Communist Party Central Committee. In 1934 he delivered the address on foreign literature at the First Soviet Writer's Conference, a speech in which he denounced James Joyce, comparing his *Ulysses* to "a heap of dung, crawling with worms, photographed by a cinema apparatus through a microscope."

Monsiváisnikov: Carlos Monsiváis (1938-2010), Mexican poet, journalist, and literary critic, closely allied to Octavio Paz.

p. 265

Zhdanov: Andrei Zhdanov, (1896-1948), Stalinist henchman and leading perpetrator of the Great Terror during the 1930s. In 1946, he was appointed by Stalin to direct Soviet cultural policy. He immediately imposed draconian censorship policies.

p. 266

César Vallejopov... Marianne Mooresky... Paul Éluardski... Volodia Teitelboimsky ... Juan Bañueloski: César Vallejo (1892-1938), Peru's greatest poet, who was a member of the Communist Party and allied during the 30s to Stalin's cultural policy; Marianne Moore (1887-1972), American poet, critic, and editor; Paul Éluard (1895-1952), French poet and co-founder of the Surrealist movement, who was close to Breton and the Left Oppositionist program, but who later allied himself with Aragon and the Communist Party; Volodia Teitelboim (1916-2008), Chilean author and critic, anthologist of Chile's most important avant-garde poetry anthology, and leading politician of the Communist Party; Juan Bañuelos (b.1932), prominent Mexican poet and professor, whose workshop at the UNAM was famously subverted by Infrarrealist poets, including Mario Santiago.

Carmen Boullosava: Carmen Boullosa (1954), leading Mexican poet and novelist. She was close to the Paz circle during her youth, but was on respectful terms with Bolaño and some of the Infrarralistas. In subsequent years, after Bolaño moved to Spain, the two writers became close correspondents and friends.

RAPP: Russian Association of Proletarian Writers, founded in 1925. An organization of Soviet writers who sought to push the early Soviet government towards a harsher line on writers deemed insufficiently revolutionary. Among their targets were Mikhail Bulgakov, Maxim Gorky, and Vladimir Mayakovsky. Along with other semi-autonomous literary organizations, they were disbanded by Stalin's regime in 1932 and brought under the control of the Soviet Writer's Union.

p. 267

Casa del Lago: Casa del Lago, located in the woods of Chapultepec, has been, since 1959, an off-campus Cultural Center of the National Autonomous University of Mexico [UNAM]. A number of the Infrarrealista group took workshops there and later organized the group's first readings on the premises.

To think of time and the canon—have you: The extended passage seems to channel Whitman here, from section II of "Song of Myself."

p. 268

Pushkin and Steinenko: Alexander Pushkin (1799-1837), Russia's greatest poet; Gertrude Stein (1874-1946), one of the founders of literary modernism. During World War II, while living in France, she was a supporter of the collaborationist Vichy regime.

Duchampski: Marcel Duchamp (1887-1968), one of the major avant-garde artists of the 20th century.

Bukharin: Nikolai Ivanovich Bukharin (1888-1938), a central leader of the Bolshevik revolution, murdered by Stalin in the Great Purge.

post-*Plural* era: Directed by Octavio Paz, *Plural* was the monthly cultural supplement of *Excelsior*, Mexico's largest daily, from 1971 to 1976. Paz resigned in 1976, when the Echeverría government attempted to extend its control over the newspaper. Paz went on to found a new journal, *Vuelta*. Only a couple months later, following the putsch at *Excelsior* and Paz's resignation from *Plural*, Bolaño and Mario Santiago began to publish interviews, translations, and brief essays there—a move, given the journal's political mediation by the Mexican State, that could be seen (as some within the Infra group saw it) as hypocritical and opportunist, in light of Infrarrealista principles announced only a year before.

our generous State and Foundation subsidies: No doubt a reference to the extensive cultural subventions initiated by the Echeverría government in the 1970s, leading to the buyout and accommodation of many formerly radical artists and writers.

p. 269

Associated Socialist Writing Programs: A reference, apparently, to the Associated Writing Programs (AWP), the main organization of academic creative writing programs in the United States. It is interesting that "Nadal" would have had knowledge of the organization back in the late 90s, before it had achieved its now quasi-hegemonic institutional status.

Huertapov: Efraín Huerta, (1914-1982), important Mexican poet who was close to Paz in his younger years, though their sharply differing politics led to distancing later in life. Huerta was very friendly and encouraging towards the Infrarrealistas, who admired the radical and nonconformist nature of his work, despite the fact that his avowed Stalinism was in sharp conflict with the Trotskyist sympathies of many members of the Infra group.

Donald T. Beria Chair of Poetry: The reference is perhaps to Lavrentiy Pavlovich Beria (1899-1953), Stalin's longest serving head of the NKVD security services.

p. 270

Pessoakov, Chattertoninsky, Macphersoniev, Swiftenko: Fernando Pessoa (1888-1935), Portugal's greatest modernist poet, famed for his use of many assumed identities; Thomas Chatterton (1752-1770), English poet and brilliant forger of pseudo-Medieval poetry, a suicide at seventeen; James Macpherson (1736-1796), Scottish poet who forged the highly influential "Ossian" verses, purportedly translations from ancient 3rd century proto-Scot nationalist texts; Jonathan Swift (1667-1745), great Anglo-Irish satirist, who published all of his works, including *Gulliver's Travels*, anonymously or under pseudonym.

Emersonkov: Ralph Waldo Emerson (1803-1882) American author and exponent of Transcendentalism.

p. 271

Zinoviev: Grigory Zinoviev (1883-1936), Russian Bolshevik leader and head of the Communist International. He was executed under Stalin's orders in 1936.

Rodchenko: Aleksander Rodchenko (1891-1956), avant-garde Russian artist and designer. A key leader of the Constructivist movement.

Barakavich… Revueltasvich: Amiri Baraka (1934-2014), major American poet and leader of the Black Arts Movement, longtime critic of academic, official poetry; José Revueltas (1914-1976), Mexican writer and Trotskyist leader, a hero to a number of the Infrarrealista poets, especially Mario Santiago Papasquiaro, who took the name of Revueltas's birthplace (Santiago Papasquiaro) as his surnames.

p. 272

Stevensmov: Wallace Stevens (1879-1955), major American modernist poet.

Alcira Soust Scaffonova: Alcira Soust Scaffo (1923-1997), Uruguayan exile in Mexico during the 1960s and 70s. She was on the periphery of the Infrarrealista group and was friendly with a number of its members, especially Bolaño, even though she was three decades or so older than most of them. The main character of Bolano's *Amulet*, Auxilio Lacouture, is based on her. An extended section of *The Savage Detectives* is also devoted to her.

Pacheconov: Jose Emilio Pacheco (1939-2014), important official Mexican poet and essayist.

Rubén Daríovich: Rubén Darío (1867-1916), Nicaraguan poet, one of Latin America's greatest literary figures, founder of the Modernista movement.

p. 273

Amado Nervoski (1870-1919), Mexican poet and diplomat, one of the key Mexican poets of the late 19th and early 20th centuries. He died in Uruguay, while serving as Ambassador there.

Drummond de Andradepov: Carlos Drummond de Andrade (1902-1987), considered by many to be Brazil's greatest poet of the modern era. During and after the period of Péret's residency in Brazil, he was in the orbit of the Communist Party.

Dickinsonova: Apparently intended as Emily Dickinson (1830-1886), American poet.

p. 275

Engels: Friedrich Engels (1820-1895), collaborator of Karl Marx and co-author of the *Communist Manifesto*.

Donald Allenski…Volodia Teitelboimsky…*Pájaro de Calor*…Juan Cerveranov: Donald Allen (1912-2004), important American critic and editor, whose most influential work was the anthology *The New American Poetry 1945-1960*; Volodia Teitelboim (Op. cit); *Pájaro de Calor: Ocho Poetas Infrarrealistas* [Mexico, 1976], an anthology, with selection coordinated by Bolaño, and an introduction by the Spanish poet and journalist Juan Cervera, a regular patron of the Café La Habana.

p. 276

Durruti: Buenaventura Durruti (1896-1936) was an anarcho-syndicalist leader and military commander of anarchist forces during the Spanish Civil War. Péret, after becoming disenchanted with the POUM, joined the Durruti Column and fought in the detachment's 1936 march from Barcelona to Zaragoza.

O'Harashkin…Sapphovich…Kochonov…Lautréamontskyi: Frank O'Hara (1926-1966), American poet and key poetic figure of the New York School; Sappho (ca. 620-570 BCE), Greek lyric poet; Kenneth Koch (1925-2002), U.S. poet and close colleague of O'Hara's; Comte de Lautréamont (1846-1870), French-Uruguayan poet who was a key influence on the Surrealists.

Heideggerich: Martin Heidegger (Germany, 1889-1976), central philosopher of the Continental tradition and key influence on strains of post-structural thought, which in their turn deeply impacted postmodern strains of poetry in the last half of the 20th century, not least in the United States, with Language poetry and its spinoffs. He was closely allied with the Nazi Party.

p. 277

John Crowe Ransomov…Robert Duncanenko: John Crowe Ransom (U.S., 1888-1974), leading conservative figure of the New Criticism, he attacked Robert Duncan for his homosexuality; Robert Duncan (1919-1988), important American poet, leading figure of the San Francisco Renaissance.

Gorostizapov, Sabinesky, Aridjisky, Bañuelosky, Álvarezova, Bartolomesky, Chumacerotin, Mondragóna, Valdiviatalin: José Gorostiza (1901-1973), Jaime Sabines (1926-1999), Homero Aridjis (1940), Juan Bañuelos (1932), Griselda Álvarez (1913-2009), Efraín Bartolomé (1950), Alí Chumacero (1918-2010), Carmen Mondragón (1893-1978), Benjamín Valdivia (1960). All are prominent and officially laureled Mexican poets.

p. 278

Vankarem and Wellen: The names seem invented.

p. 280

Daltonenko…Bretonov…Mayakovsky…Akhmatova…Plathsky…Aygi…Audenov…Li Posky: Roque Dalton (1935-1975), major Salvadoran poet and prominent figure in the Ejército Revolucionario del Pueblo, which later became one of the leading forces in the armed struggle in El Salvador. He was assassinated in a factional fight within the group, falsely accused of being an agent of the CIA; André Breton (France, 1896-1966), leader of the Surrealist movement and lifelong comrade of Benjamin Péret; Vladimir Mayakovsky (1893-1930), the most prominent Russian avant-garde poet of the Bolshevik revolution. Depressed by growing neglect and pressures to conform to official dictates, he committed suicide; Anna Akhmatova (1889-1966), great Russian poet who suffered intense pressure and persecution under Stalin. She is considered one of the most important world poets of the century; Silvia Plath (1932-1963), one of America's most famous poets. She committed suicide in 1963, while living in England; Gennadiy Aygi (1934-2006), Chuvash poet who published predominantly in Samizdat venues during the Soviet years. He has had a significant influence on later generations of writers; W.H. Auden (1907-1973), Anglo-American poet, one of the most important literary figures of the 20th century; Li Po (701-762), with Du Fu (712-770) and Wang Wei (699-759), is regarded as one of the greatest Chinese poets of the Tang period.

Anayapov, Harringtonov, Méndez and Méndez, Ochoanova, Montaneski, Larrosanova and Larrosanova, Volkowstkyna, Medinavich, Pimentelinski: José Vicente Anaya (Mexico, 1950), Juan Esteban Harrington (Chile, 1959), Ramón Méndez (Mexico, 1954), Cuauhtémoc Méndez (Mexico, 1956-2004), Guadalupe Ochoa (Mexico, 1957), Bruno Montané (Chile, 1957), Vera Larrosa (1957), Mara Larrosa (1955), Verónica Volkow (Mexico, 1955), Rubén Medina (Mexico, 1955), Jorge Pimentel (Peru, 1944). With exception of Pimentel, who was a founder of the roughly contemporaneous avant-garde Hora Zero poetic movement in Peru, all of the named are original activists or close sympathizers of the Infrarrealista group. Volkow is the great-granddaughter of Leon Trotsky, the Russian revolutionary leader.

Nerudavich…Lukacsinov…Hikmetov…Sartreski…Bonifazky…Pachekovsky: Pablo Neruda (Op. cit), György Lukács (1885-1971), great Hungarian Marxist aesthetician, opponent of avant-garde experimentalism; Nazim Hikmet (1902-1963), important Turkish and Communist Party poet; Jean-Paul Sartre (1905-1980), the leading exponent of Existentialism, he generally defended the U.S.S.R. despite certain critiques; Rubén Bonifaz Nuño (1923-2013), prominent official Mexican poet and translator of classical literature; José Emilio Pacheco (Op. cit.)

p. 281

Into the garbage vessel of History! Something similar was shouted by Trotsky from the presidium of the All-Russian Congress of Soviets, in Petrograd, on October 25, 1917, shortly before the Bolshevik seizure of power, as the Menshevik delegates walked out in protest.

p. 282

Jack Spicerlev: Jack Spicer (1925-1965), key American poet of the San Francisco Renaissance. He died from the effects of acute alcoholism.

Sergei Yesenin: Wildly popular Russian poet (1895-1925) of peasant stock. Married to the American dancer Isadora Duncan. He died a suicide.

p. 283

ANDY WARHOLIOPOV: Andy Warhol (1928-1987), legendary American Pop artist.

FRIEDRICH HÖLDERLINEV: German Romantic poet (1770-1843).

p. 284

KRONSTADT: As mentioned in a note far above, the site of a naval garrison that rebelled against the Bolsheviks in 1921. The sailors and their civilian allies were calling for a return to governance by secret-ballot-elected soviets and greater civil democracy. Trotsky led the Soviet attack against them, resulting in a massacre of the rebels.

MAY BOLAÑONOV GO BACK TO CHILE AND SANTIA-GOSKY ALSO! Reference to a clever slogan about Roberto Bolaño and Mario Santiago, which appeared as actual graffiti in various locales in Mexico City in 1976. The culprits were never identified.

JOHN CAGENKO: John Cage (1912-1992), famous avant-garde American composer. The reference here is to his most famous work, "4:33," whose score calls for the pianist to sit at the piano without playing a note for exactly four minutes and thirty-three seconds.

BOURGEOIS REVOLUTIONARY ESTRIDENTISTA POETRY: Estridentismo was an avant-garde multidisciplinary movement founded in 1921. It shared features with Dada and was radical in its left politics. Its main leader was Manuel Maples Arce (1898-1981). The Infrarrealistas were close admirers of the Estridentista movement, seeing themselves as its heirs.

ROBERTO BOLAÑO

9 781947 980204